Looking Backward from the Tricentennial

A Timely Tale of Nonviolent Revolution

as told by Dante J. Unitas

First edition - February 2024
Second printing - June 2024

Looking Backward from the Tricentennial © 2024 as told by Dante J. Unitas is licensed under Creative Commons Attribution-NonCommercial-ShareAlike 4.0 International. This license requires that reusers give credit to the creator. It allows reusers to distribute, remix, adapt, and build upon the material in any medium or format, for noncommercial purposes only. If others modify or adapt the material, they must license the modified material under identical terms. To view a copy of this license, visit http://creativecommons.org/licenses/by-nc-sa/4.0

Listen to an audio version of this novel at: audio.com/dantejay

ISBN: 979-8-8691-0675-9

This book was professionally typeset on Reedsy.
(Special thanks to junior writing partners ChatGPT and Sudowrite)

Our nettlesome task is to discover how to organize our strength into compelling power so that the government cannot elude our demands. We must develop, from strength, a situation in which the government finds it wise and prudent to collaborate with us.

- Martin Luther King Jr.

Table of Contents

Introduction to the 2099 Edition	iii
Where have I been? (March 18, 2026)	1
Where am I? (March 10–17, 2076)	17
What do I want? (March 18–22, 2076)	113
What have I done? (March 28–April 3, 2076)	203
Why am I here? (April 14–17, 2076)	305
Where do we go from here? (May 1, 2076)	379
Epilogue	399
Afterword	408
Appendix I	411
Appendix II	415
Appendix III	427
Notes/Bibliography	438
Index	439

Introduction to the 2099 Edition

Written seventy-five years ago during the previous iteration of the Phoenix Cycle, *Looking Backward from the Tricentennial* was a pastiche of Edward Bellamy's 1888 novel *Looking Backward: 2000–1887* and Mack Reynolds' *Looking Backward from the Year 2000* (1973) and contained several lines from the earlier books.

Julian West, the protagonist of all the novels, appeared as a wealthy white man in the nineteenth- and twentieth-century versions. In the post-pandemic retelling, Julian West was a black man arriving in 2076, astonished by the social, cultural, electoral, legislative, economic, and criminal justice reforms that had taken place. In these novels, his education generally took the form of conversations with his host, Dr. Leete. *Looking Backward from the Tricentennial* was no different, but it provided a broader cast of educators, often juxtaposing the troubles of Julian's own time with solutions of the modern era.

All three novels painted vivid pictures of utopian futures, but in the first two, the strategy for delivering the envisioned change was left as an exercise for the reader. *Looking Backward from the Tricentennial* differed by offering a specific plan of action. (For readers interested in the elections of the time, the original supplemental material is included in the Appendices.) By doing so, it established a new but short-lived genre: beta-historian fiction. Near-future events were served up as an invitation for readers to take real-world action in order to influence—for the better—the history that would determine the storylines of sequels, such as *Looking Forward to the Tricentennial* (2026).

Part I

Where have I been?
March 18, 2026

The problems of racial injustice and economic injustice can not be solved without a radical redistribution of political and economic power.

- Martin Luther King Jr.

I would not hesitate to let the minorities govern the country. This is no academic belief. The solution is attended with no risk. For under a free government the real power will be held by the people.

- M.K. Gandhi

Chapter One

Sixty-eight minutes before he was shot, Julian West averted his eyes from the sidewalk-sleeping man in favor of the Washington Monument. Many in the crowd forming near its base, like him, carried signs. He wondered how many, like him, hefted lead pipes carefully concealed within innocent-looking cardboard tubes, held in place with generous amounts of hot-melt glue as the internet had instructed him. Julian squeezed the pole, simultaneously thrilled, reassured, and scared by the rigid core.

His stroll through the city had left him unable to estimate the number of homeless with any great precision. Some sprawled on benches, occasionally sheltered under blue tarps. Tents were strewn around McPherson Square like colorful candies. There had been a half-dozen ambitious panhandlers, whose handwritten signs all hit the same three points: announcing their status as a veteran by use of military rank; offering a few details of the circumstances or injustices resulting in their current plight and need for money; and concluding with a variation on the phrase "God bless." The closings often invoked America's name, punctuated by one or more exclamation points.

In the capital of the richest and most powerful nation on the planet, the glimpses of abject poverty through the veil of prosperity offered a little local flavor to tourists from around the world.

Movement from the sidewalk man caught Julian's attention, and the reason for the fellow's choice of sleeping location became apparent. It wasn't a random patch of concrete, but rectangular metal latticework and the source of the dull roar he heard. The dozing man shifted, the features of his white face tranquil, and rolled on his side. Air jetting from the grate tugged his tangled beard upward. As Julian walked by, he found the air warm and moist, triggering a childhood memory of holding his own hands under dryer vents at an apartment complex.

The morning sun was bright, waking the hangover slumbering in his skull; at thirty-four, the novelty had long worn thin. Joining the other pedestrians waiting to cross Constitution Avenue, Julian retrieved two aspirin from a jacket pocket and dry swallowed them. The pills went to work thinning his blood, which would be decidedly unhelpful in sixty-seven minutes.

A black woman approached from across 15th Street, illuminated by the morning sun as she stepped nimbly over the barriers of the bike lane, a rectangle of white poster board tucked under one arm. Julian appraised her discreetly. She was around thirty and sharply dressed, her skin as equally dark as his, and radiated confidence as she queued up for the walk signal. Julian took two steps backward and flashed a smile, tilting his head to make it obvious he was trying to read her sign.

She smiled back and pulled it from under her arm, effortlessly shifting her bag as she stretched it taut. The neatly hand-lettered words read, *Power concedes nothing without a demand*. Her grin widened as she studied him studying her sign. Racking his brain rapidly, trying to place the quote, knowing the light would change any moment, Julian made an educated guess. "Malcolm X?" he asked.

A flicker of disappointment prefaced her reply. "About a century earlier: Frederick Douglass." She glanced at the white foamboard stapled to his pole. "No justice, no peace," she read. "Classic."

Julian's nod offered acknowledgment and indicated her sign. "My mother read me his autobiography when I was a kid. She said it was important to understand our history." Ahead, the walk signal began to chirp. "I remember thinking it had some exciting parts."

A radiant smile emerged as she tucked the sign back under her arm. Her right hand reached out, fist clenched, which Julian bumped gently with his own. "Good to hear your mother started you off right," she said. "She must be a smart lady."

As they moved forward with the crowd, Julian hid his expression by looking down Constitution Avenue. "She was," he replied flatly, remembering her frightened expression as the paramedics took her. The disinterested looks from the drivers and the sunlight's glare off the windshield of a box truck brought him back to reality. No one cared.

"Sorry," the woman replied. They stepped up onto the sidewalk, and she gestured straight ahead to indicate her path while hooking him into continued conversation: "'Power concedes nothing without a demand; it never did and it never will. Find out just what any people will quietly submit to and you have found the exact measure of injustice and wrong which will be imposed upon them, and these will continue till they are resisted with either words or blows, or both.'"

"Good quote," Julian agreed. He glanced ahead to the monument, the obelisk's left face brightly lit by the morning sun while the right remained in shadow. "Does resisting with words actually work, though?"

"It can," she insisted, "under the right circumstances. Words are ideas; ideas have to percolate. Today we're applying a little heat." He nodded, and she introduced herself. "I'm Edith Bartlett."

"Julian West," he replied. "Reparations have been percolating for a long time. Forty acres and a mule, right? At some point we might have to turn up the heat, you feel me?"

"Like they did at the Capitol five years ago? I think there's a better way to work things out," Edith answered. "But it showed people will resist injustice, even if it's only perceived. Peace is more than just a lack of fighting."

"But fighting can bring people to the negotiating table, so peace deals can be worked out," Julian countered. "The status quo has inertia. Sometimes a little violence can mix it up. A riot is the language of the unheard, right?"

"Well, today is for speeches, not riots, Julian," Edith said, then peered suddenly to one side. "Is he robbing him?"

He twisted to look, but there was nothing out of the ordinary. "What?"

"Never mind," said Edith carefully. "Looks like it's going to be a nice

CHAPTER ONE

day, too. Glad I took off work." The last part felt like a discrete delivery of information, not simple conversational filler.

A growing current of excitement filled the air as they approached the monument. Beats blared from giant speakers around the stage where the Reverend Alvin Shaver would be speaking. The gathering multitude was mostly black, with a sprinkling of white faces, and Julian read a few of the signs they held: *Reparations! Not for the past, but the present and the future*; *Bridge the Wealth Gap*; and *Cash, Check, or Venmo?*

Edith continued to talk as they meandered through the thickening crowd, ending up close enough to the stage to see clearly without being totally deafened by the music. Julian learned she worked at Washington Memorial Hospital, and explained he was visiting from Philadelphia. She didn't press him on his own job, which saved him from any evasive answers. One and a half years after his release from prison, weekend shifts at the local Gas-N-Go were the best he could manage.

The conversation was going well, and her ring finger was bare. There'd been a woman at the bar last night that Julian had invited to text him at the rally, but this might be better, and he decided to test it. He retrieved two nips from a pocket, holding them discreetly for her to see. "Buy you a drink?"

Edith's reaction was perplexed and amused. "You want to have a drink with me?" she replied. "Now?"

"Well," he admitted ruefully, "it's medicinal, really. Hair of the dog, you know?" She laughed a short series of nonjudgmental musical notes. "Yesterday was Saint Patrick's Day; I guarantee you a lot of people here are feeling it this morning." Edith seemed interested but not sold, so he waggled the tiny plastic bottles at her and made a closing pitch. "Anyway, I prefer not to drink alone. Lady's choice?"

She took both bottles without looking, scrutinizing his face. "Are you married?" she asked suspiciously.

Julian swiveled his sign, angling unadorned knuckles toward her. "Not for a couple years now," he replied. The fact some woman wanted, at one point, to spend the rest of her life with him, and he'd been willing to make that commitment, ought to figure in his favor. Edith bit her lip, considering, and he flashed her a winning smile.

"Peppermint schnapps is more my speed," she decided, placing the other nip back in his hand. Edith transferred her sign under her arm and cracked open her bottle.

Julian tried gripping his own with the fingers of his left hand, but the thickness of the cardboard tube hindered him. When he spun the metal cap, the nip twisted free and fell to the grass. Balancing the sign pole, he crouched to retrieve it, very aware Edith was watching. "Want me to hold that?" she offered.

"No," Julian answered firmly, nestling the pole into his elbow, gripping the nip tightly, unscrewing the cap, meeting her gaze, "I don't need help." He absorbed the details of her face, mirthful brown eyes radiating questions from behind silver glasses. "Do you want to make a toast?"

"To reparations now!" Edith said, and tapped her drink against his.

"Reparations now!" he echoed, and they emptied the small bottles in a single pull, recommitting themselves to their common cause. Edith shuddered, and Julian held out his hand for the empty. Her touch was warm as she gently folded his fingers around it.

"Your sign is too bland," Edith announced, and began to search in her handbag. "It needs something." She held up a black marker. "Can I?" Wary of revealing the cardboard tube's weight, he acquiesced by leaning the sign toward her, waiting to see what she would produce. With deft strokes, she added four letters to his text. "There. That's profound."

Julian rotated the sign to see the revision: *know justice, know peace.* He nodded approval. "You're amazing, you know that?" he declared, falling silent, letting the compliment ferment.

Appreciation bubbled up as Edith replied, "Thanks!"

Julian leaned closer, delivering the second half of the combination with great sincerity: "Do you have someone who tells you that, every day, just how amazing you are?"

Edith laughed, just as he expected. The initial burst was at him and his naked flattery, but it softened on reflection, on recognition of her own

CHAPTER ONE

helplessness before the self-evident ploy, at the beauty of the maneuver in which her unspoken desires were recognized and justified as a basis for teasing information out of her, sandwiched around the implication he could be a partner in such validation. Women didn't always give him a direct answer, and Julian delighted at Edith's cleverness in flipping his own words back at him: "Not for a couple of years now."

"That's a shame," he replied, and waited. The crowd was thickening around them, buzzing with excitement, the program only minutes away from beginning.

Edith changed the subject, handing over her phone and asking him to take a picture of her. Julian snapped a few in quick succession, capturing her beaming smile. "I told my friend I'd send her some pics. She didn't feel comfortable coming out today," Edith explained. Her head jerked as though an idea had spontaneously occurred to her. "Hey, we should get one together," she declared, eyes sparkling as she motioned him close.

Julian took her side, holding his modified sign. Edith stretched her phone out in front of her, encapsulating as much of the monument's elevation as possible. "Get in closer," she directed. He inhaled the scent of jasmine as he moved just behind her, and then maneuvered his sign around in the margin of the picture until Edith was satisfied. The smiles displayed to the camera were genuine.

"Can you send that to me?" Julian asked.

A few taps on her phone called up a blank text message. "Throw down your digits," Edith directed, offering him the device. Julian entered ten numbers, still smelling the bouquet of jasmine, and when he looked up, her eyes beckoned him.

Just as he decided to kiss her, the music fell silent, and cheers went up around them as the rally organizer stepped up to the podium. The moment was broken, but when Edith took the phone back, her touch lingered, kindling a warmth inside him, a light that illuminated feelings of hope, of connection, of possibility for a future that lasted longer than forty-six minutes.

Chapter Two

Once again, Julian found himself unable to estimate the number of people around him with any great precision. Looking backward, he saw more than a thousand black faces peering up at the podium, filling the area with a comfortable density and not an oppressive one. The atmosphere felt like history in the making, the multitudes standing together with a shared intention, waiting to hear Reverend Shaver's call to action. Along the perimeter, vans from local television stations balanced cameras above them, recording the crowd as the program began.

After an opening prayer, a social media influencer stepped up to the podium and delivered an impassioned speech in the style that had earned him millions of followers. They were fighting against an unjust system that had existed since before they were born, he told them, a system that inertia would carry onward into eternity unless they worked together to shift its direction. The crowd roared approval.

An economist offered a vision of the financial power that would be unleashed by putting billions of dollars into black communities. "As Dr. King said," he reminded the audience, "'The poor, transformed into purchasers, will do a good deal on their own.'"

Next, a mayor from the Midwest spoke of the success of a pilot program in her city. She urged the crowd to pressure their local representatives for equitable economic policies and social programs to reduce poverty.

Excitement built as a member of Congress gave a rousing speech, first urging them to ask their own representatives to support HR 40, a bill to study reparations, and then challenging them to turn out and vote that fall. "Turn out and vote," Julian echoed disdainfully. "Like that'll make a difference."

"It could," Edith insisted. "We have power, Julian."

"Doesn't matter, not with the choices they give us." He gripped the cardboard tube, comforted by the unyielding center. "It's pay to play. We wouldn't all be here today if we were in the game."

Her eyes twinkled. "I'm all for changing the game."

The audience erupted with cheers as the Reverend Alvin Shaver was introduced. Bounding up the stairs with surprising agility for a man sculpted from generations of Southern cooking, the preacher boomed out a greeting through his headset microphone. In his late forties, his hair was still jet black, but his short beard was undergoing follicle gentrification. Around them, people pulled out their phones to snap pictures for social media. Edith held her own up, recording video of Shaver.

The reverend stood basking in the morning light, arms spread in a vaguely crucifixion-like pose as he began. "Dear Lord," he intoned, "we thank you for the bounty of your sunshine this morning. We're grateful for its warmth, which you have created in your wisdom, that every one of your children can benefit from. It is freely available to all of your creatures, it feeds the cycle of life, it brings order to our day.

"The sun, however, is a master of illusion." His hand pointed upward with an accusing finger. "We may think we see it, rising above the nation's capital, but we are really looking backward in time at the light let loose eight and a half minutes ago. Now, it's always good to look forward, but sometimes we benefit from looking backward as well, to examine how we arrived where we are.

"This year, we will observe the two hundred fiftieth anniversary of America's founding. Millions will celebrate—I will commemorate, I will remember, I will cast a critical eye backward over those two and a half centuries. Whatever you might call it—the semiquincentennial, the quarter millennial, or the sestercentennial—I call it a failure to live up to the plain words of that Declaration: all people have unalienable rights, and among them are life, liberty and the pursuit of happiness.

"Like many of you," Shaver said, his arms open to embrace the crowd, "I am a descendant of enslaved people. We stand here in the shadow of the Washington Monument, in the shadow of a man whose legacy is both figuratively and literally built on the backs of our ancestors. If we were to climb up and look out upon the district, we'd see a city where the average household income exceeds one hundred thousand dollars yet one in four children lives in poverty. We'd see a city where white households have eighty-one times the wealth of black households. We'd see a city which for centuries has directed a deliberate and determined diminishment of rights for people of color."

His voice quickened. "That legacy is indefensible. We are here today in pursuit of reparations for crimes against our humanity, committed by Washington and his spiritual successors. We hold this truth to be self-evident: we have a right to be made whole."

From the stage, the reverend pointed a finger at Edith. "There's a sister over here, with a sign calling up the words of Frederick Douglass, 'Power concedes nothing without a demand.'" Edith looked starstruck at the recognition. "We are here today to make our demand; to serve notice that justice is past due."

"You're famous," Julian whispered loudly to Edith.

She looked sideways at him, her eyes inviting his attention. "Hush."

"He even knew whose quote it was," Julian prodded.

"Hush up," Edith said again, a mischievous smile dancing across her lips. She bumped her hip against his to punctuate the statement, but as her gaze turned back to the stage, the contact persisted. Julian said nothing else, but pressed back firmly.

Shaver continued, "We can look backward across America's history—we can look backward to 2023, as the members of the Supreme Court, whose honorific I find ironic, struck down affirmative action. Close enough, they said; let's call it even.

"We can look backward to 2009, and the reduction of the sentencing disparity between crack cocaine and powdered cocaine from 100:1 to 18:1. Close enough, said Congress, a representative body for those with money and power.

"We can look backward to 1995, and the punitive policies adopted by Congress. Even as the tide of mass incarceration has begun to recede, the formerly incarcerated are still marked with the scarlet letters that empower the new Jim Crow today." Julian roared his frustration.

"We can look backward to 1971, and the launching of the racist war on drugs used as an excuse to restrict our rights.

"We can look backward to the 1950s, and the Federal Housing Administration's support of redlining, denying generations of blacks the opportunity to build wealth through homeownership.

"We can look backward to 1938, and the passage of the Fair Labor Standards Act. How a nation defines the word 'fair' gives great insight into its character. To systematically exclude a majority of black workers for decades was unjust; reparations are past due.

"We can look backward to 1913, and a president who reintroduced segregation to the Civil Service, requiring applicants to include a photograph so candidates of color could be weeded out.

"We can look backward to *Plessy v. Ferguson* in 1896, establishing the fanciful legal doctrine of separate but equal.

"We can look backward to America's centennial, and the deal struck to decide the presidential election. As Southern blacks watched federal troops march away, did they know that their 'brief moment in the sun' had come to an end, and that a long, violent night stretched out before them?

"We can look backward to 1862 and the passage of the Homestead Act, offering up hundreds of millions of acres of public land for Americans and immigrants alike—as long as they weren't black.[1]

"We can look backward to 1857, and the Dred Scott decision proclaiming blacks could never be citizens; they had no rights whites were bound to respect.

---

[1] Although tens of thousands of Blacks utilized the Homestead Act after the Fourteenth Amendment was ratified in 1868, the Act's authors had intentionally limited land claims to citizens and future citizens, which the *Dred Scott* decision proclaimed Blacks were ineligible to be.

"We can look backward to 1835, and see the first race riot in this city; not by the free blacks upset by the open trading of brothers and sisters being sold south, or the taxes they paid to support the district's schools whose doors were closed to their children. No, it was hundreds of whites who directed destruction against the black district, riled up by fraudulent accusations against a black teenager by a white woman.

"We can look backward to the Naturalization Act of 1790—the work of the very first Congress—which codified that the only immigrants permitted to become citizens were 'free white persons.'

"We can look backward to 1787, and the drafting of the Constitution. Dozens of rich white men gathered in the city of brotherly love, and very earnestly agreed the importation of slaves for the next twenty years was fine, as long as their government got a cut of the profits with a head tax.

"We can even look all the way back to Thomas Jefferson's draft of America's birth certificate, complaining that King George had interfered with 'our negroes.'

"Two hundred fifty years ago, the foundation of this nation was built on false promises. Blacks have been held back; in chains and incarcerated, by decisions and declarations. While we cannot change the past, we can correct the future, so that when we look backward from America's tricentennial, we no longer find ourselves living, as Dr. King said, on an 'island of poverty in the midst of a vast ocean of material prosperity.'

"When we look backward from the tricentennial, we will find that power conceded to our demand." Again, Shaver gestured to Edith and her sign, which waved up and down in response. "For this, we fight—reparations are our right!"

"I think he likes you," Julian stage whispered to Edith. She said nothing, but fixed him with an appraising glance. Her impish smirk left him contemplating the many hours left in the day and all the possibilities that might unfold. For good measure, he waggled his eyebrows suggestively before deliberately looking away.

"When we look backward from the tricentennial," Shaver continued, leaning into his subject, "we will see that America struggled with the truth

CHAPTER TWO

of what it owed the descendants of enslaved people, and reconciled itself to justice. For this, we fight," he called, and the crowd roared back the response, drowning out his words, "reparations are our right!"

"When we look backward from the tricentennial, we'll see that King's dream has been achieved; our children will be judged by the content of their character and not the color of their skin. For this, we fight."

"Reparations are our right!" Edith hollered enthusiastically, beating one hand against her thigh as she held her phone and sign with her other.

"When we look backward from the tricentennial," Shaver repeated, whipping the crowd into a frenzy of anticipation for the next pronouncement, "we'll see that our nation has been spiritually reborn, and at long last addressed his triple evils of poverty, racism, and militarism. For this, we fight."

"Reparations are our right!" Julian yelled.

"When we look backward from the tricentennial," Shaver said again, the crowd surging with optimism for this vision of the future, "we'll see that black men, and women, have all the rights whites have to respect."

As the call and response came again, there was some kind of disturbance off to one side of the stage. Shaver didn't seem to notice. "When we look backward from the tricentennial," he projected, "we'll see that–"

A single gunshot interrupted his words.

Edith gasped as Shaver clutched his midsection.

Julian tightened his grip on the sign pole.

Four armed men with a paramilitary aura rushed across the stage, led by a young white male with a bushy red beard. Shaver sank to one knee clutching the lower-left quadrant of his torso. "Oh, Lord," he moaned into the headset, sending the words reverberating across the field.

Edith pulled away from Julian, an expletive falling from her lips in surprise. He stayed rooted in place, instinctively pulling his sign from the pole, staples unzipping rhythmically as he analyzed the situation. The crowd was not yet panicked; a few enterprising souls were still recording with their phones as the red-bearded man shot the reverend in the chest. Shaver crumpled to the stage as two of the gunmen angled AR-15s toward the crowd. Individuals in the audience began to retreat.

The red-bearded man plucked the headset from Shaver's body, and spoke into it. "Reparations are theft," he proclaimed, gesturing wildly with a handgun. "Our caucasian forefathers didn't build this nation so you ungrateful bastards could rob us. This country was formed for the white, not the black."

As the leader began to rant, two of the men jumped down from the stage. The crowd teetered on the edge of a stampede. Julian watched the closest gunman; he was practically a boy, his pale features radiating nervousness, the handgun he clutched wavering unsteadily. "Let's go," Edith said, grabbing Julian's arm and tugging at it.

Crazily, Julian imagined what a perfect story this would be to tell in the future. *She'd only just met me,* he'd say, *and already Edith wanted us to run away together.*

The first screech of a police siren began to rise, and the boyish gunman turned to look for it as the red-bearded man cried out, "Now!" Julian shook off Edith's hand and began to sprint forward. Bursts of semi-automatic fire gave birth to screams and cries. Julian ignored them, rapidly closing on the boyish gunman. He gripped the end of the pole, gauging its heft, and swung it like a baseball bat. It connected solidly with the back of his target's head, sending him to the grass. Julian whirled his weapon again, this time in a high arc, and brought it down on his skull.

Julian knelt and plucked the gun from the man's lifeless hand, looking for a target. The other gunman who'd jumped down from the stage was firing an AR-15 indiscriminately into the retreating crowd; Julian took a deep breath and aimed carefully, squeezing the trigger three times in rapid succession before the man pitched forward.

Swiveling toward the stage, Julian saw he'd drawn the attention of another attacker. When the man fired, the impact tugged Julian sideways. It was as if he were underwater; the air seemed to resist him as he lifted his weapon. The twitch of his finger repeated until his own shots found their mark, and the man tumbled backward onto the stage.

The satisfaction was short lived. His gun empty, Julian shifted his focus to the boyish gunman, kneeling to pat down the still form, frenetically searching for another weapon, for ammunition, ignoring the sharp pain the movement triggered inside him, ignoring the wailing police sirens, ignoring the cacophony of panicked screams. Then one voice cut through the stew of sounds: "Julian! Look out!"

A glance at the stage revealed the man with the red beard striding toward him, piercing blue eyes filled with hate as he lifted his arm—the same arm, the same hand, the same gun that had pointed unhesitatingly at Reverend Shaver before he fell. Julian stumbled to his feet, clamping a hand to his side to staunch the splash of wetness. His gaze cast about like a searchlight, seeking something to duck behind, and he caught a glimpse of Edith. Lying prone on the ground, she was staring right at him. Their eyes locked as she screamed again, "Look out!"

The words echoed uncontrollably over the flurry of gunshots, and in that moment he glimpsed infinity, a blinding, chaotic expanse punctuated with lancing pain, the greatest of which was the injustice that he would never see Edith Bartlett again.

Part II

Where am I?
March 10–17, 2076

It may be through the negroes that the unadulterated message of nonviolence is delivered to the world.

— M.K. Gandhi

As I delved deeper into the philosophy of Gandhi my skepticism concerning the power of love gradually diminished, and I came to see for the first time its potency in the area of social reform.

— Martin Luther King Jr.

Chapter Three

"He's going to open his eyes. He had better only see one of us at first."

"Promise me, then, that you won't tell him."

The first voice was a man's, the second a woman's, and both spoke in whispers.

"I want to see how he seems," replied the man.

"No, no, promise me," persisted the other.

"Well, I promise," answered the man. "Quick, go! He's coming out of it."

Julian opened his eyes. After several long blinks, he could make out the beaming face of a man of about forty-five hovering over him. The broad smile was framed on his black face by a strong chin and closely cropped hair; it showed concern and satisfaction. "How do you feel?" he inquired.

Nothing looked familiar. "Where am I?" Julian demanded as forcefully as he could manage. His throat was like sandpaper; he wasn't even sure the words were recognizable. He felt sober now, but had he blacked out? Had he done something while drinking that the woman didn't want him to know about?

"We'll talk about it when you're stronger," the unfamiliar man said. "There's nothing to be anxious about; you're among friends and in good hands. How do you feel?"

Julian took stock. "Exhausted." A brief pause was all he could manage before the most pressing questions spilled forth. "What happened? Where am I?"

"There'll be time enough for explanations later, when you're better rested. Would you do me a favor and have a few swallows of this? It'll do you good;

CHAPTER THREE

I'm a physician."

Julian managed a nod, and the doctor held out a cup with a straw, bending it to accommodate the angle of his mouth. Several swallows of cool liquid relieved his dry throat and left a medicinal aftertaste with a hint of raspberries. It did nothing for his strength; he had no desire to move.

The doctor reviewed something on a digital tablet, almost as a formality. "Feel up for a few questions?"

Instantly, Julian was alert. He didn't have any health insurance, and whatever care he'd received while he was unconscious couldn't have been cheap. There was little-to-no chance he'd be able to afford it. He knew hospitals had to provide emergency care; it was the law. He'd heard it applied even if you didn't identify yourself. They'd probably cut him loose as soon as they figured out they wouldn't get paid, but maybe he could make it hard for them to come after his meager financial assets.

A jumbled memory from the rally at the Washington Monument surfaced. The doctor's questions could be for the benefit of the police. He knew from experience when they decided to go after someone, specific charges could be developed later. Was this an attempt to get him to incriminate himself?

Julian concluded it was best to say nothing. "Another drink, please," he said, making a mild production out of lifting his head up to sip from the straw. Maybe the confusion wasn't as much of an act as he supposed; there was something strange going on with the straw. The tube was tweaked at an acute angle, but there was no accordion joint at the bend. The taste of it on his lips wasn't plastic, either.

After a few gulps, Julian let his head sink back down. "Tired," he mumbled, closing his eyes.

"Of course," agreed the doctor. "There's plenty of time. Get some rest." The lights faded.

Eyes closed, Julian perceived the other man leaving but didn't hear any other background noise from the hospital. In the stillness, he thought about his options, looking, as he often did, for the situational angles that might help. His first instinct was still to refuse to identify himself until they released him, but it raised other logistical issues. With luck, his car was still sitting in the Metro parking lot outside the city and not in an impound lot, but it would be tough to find out without revealing his name. Tomorrow, he'd collect what information he could from the doctors and nurses and insist on leaving. Let them try to send a bill to John Doe, location unknown.

Julian rested, eyes closed, still thinking. The softness of the pillow beneath his head and the smoothness of the bed covering suggested he was in an upscale facility. How had he ended up here? He searched his memories of the morning, quickly arriving at an image of Edith. Her natural hair accentuated the roundness of her grinning face, its auburn highlights contrasting with the silver frames of her glasses.

He recalled watching her as she held up her phone to record Reverend Shaver's speech. Together, they cried out with the crowd, "Reparations are our right!" He pumped the cardboard tube holding his sign up and down, enthusiasm masking the weight of the lead pipe concealed inside.

The gunshot. He remembered the gunshot, its loud crack interrupting Shaver mid-sentence, and, like the bursting of a dam, the memories began to spill out, flooding over him, cold and wet.

Julian stared upward in the dark room, pondering his own mortality. His fingers strayed over his hospital gown until he felt the rough patches where the bullets had torn through him. He was lucky to be alive. Suddenly overwhelmed by emotions, Julian closed his eyes once more and tried to not think about anything at all, waiting for sleep to lay mercy upon him.

※ ※ ※

In the morning sun, the place looked even less like a traditional hospital room. The light filtering through the frosted glass of the broad windows revealed a flat ceiling, not a grid with recessed fixtures and interchangeable ceiling tiles he might have expected, and the medical equipment along the far wall was portable, wheels resting on the hardwood floor.

CHAPTER THREE

The doctor sat in an armchair, one leg casually crossed over the other, and he was engrossed in reading on a digital tablet. The sleeves of his light-blue shirt were rolled up, exposing smooth, dark forearms. Julian observed him for a few moments, reviewing his options, then gave an audible yawn. The doctor looked up with a calm and reassuring smile. "Good morning," he said. "How are you feeling? Well rested?"

"Sure," said Julian. "Thanks for patching me up, or whatever. How soon can I leave?"

The doctor chuckled. "Well, let's not rush things." He rose in a smooth motion and tucked the tablet under his arm as he approached the bed. "Let me introduce myself. I'm Doctor Raymond Leete. You were injured, and now you're in my care."

Julian shook the man's outstretched hand. "Okay," he replied.

Dr. Leete waited, perhaps expecting a reciprocal exchange of names, but then reviewed his tablet's screen. "Can you tell me how many fingers you see?" He held up three fingers.

Julian decided it was a safe question. "Three."

Next, Dr. Leete had him follow the motion of his index finger without moving his head, and seemed satisfied with his performance. "And can you tell me your name?" Julian's stomach clenched a little, but he just shrugged. After a moment, Leete looked up from the tablet and repeated the question.

"I feel fine. I'd just like to go home," Julian replied.

"If you don't remember your name, that could be a sign of brain damage," Dr. Leete warned. "Where is home?"

Julian shrugged, looking around the room that was much nicer than the one he lived in. A few pictures hung on the tan walls, including a black-and-white photograph of a smiling man holding a handful of grapes. There were two doors, and he wondered where they led. "You can skip that one too."

Leete stared back at this response for a long minute. "You don't know who you are or where you live, but you want to leave? Forgive me for saying so, but that doesn't seem like a good idea." Another pause. "What's the last thing you remember?"

He pictured Edith's panicked face screaming at him. Could he ask about her well-being without identifying himself? "I was at the reparations rally at the Washington Monument," Julian said. "I think I got shot, but I feel fine now. I'd like to leave, please."

"And what day was that?" the doctor prompted.

"Wednesday," Julian replied. Then, with a creeping suspicion, "What day is it now?"

"You were shot numerous times," Leete confirmed. "Today is Tuesday."

Startled, Julian sat up. There was a mild stiffness, but absolutely no pain. "I have to get out of here. Can a nurse bring my things, please?"

Leete demurred. "Not just yet," he answered. "Do you remember the date?"

"March 18."

"And the year?"

"The year?" Julian echoed. "How long was I out?"

"Please, will you lie back?" Julian decided this was a reasonable request and did so, his attention perfectly focused on the other man. "Today is March 11, 2076."

"For real?" Julian laughed. "What are you trying to pull?"

The doctor ignored the question. "You were placed into an emergency medical coma because of your injuries. When no other family members could be located, your body was placed, by a court order one week later, into the custody of Washington Memorial Hospital. That medical coma was then stabilized at an extremely low temperature. Have you heard of cryonics?"

"Is that like cryogenic freezing, like in *Idiocracy?*" Julian asked, recalling a low-brow comedy he'd enjoyed in high school. The name of the hospital sounded familiar, but he couldn't connect it with anything else.

"Close. Cryogenics just refers to the branches of engineering that deal with ultra-low temperatures. Cryonics is the process of preserving people for future revival; that's the correct term for what you've experienced. The idea has been around for a while; you're certainly not the first one revived, but you are one of the oldest success stories.

CHAPTER THREE

"One month ago, we started slowly warming you up. The vitrification fluid was replaced with new blood created to the specifications of samples taken from you in 2026. You now have a full complement of modern gut bacteria. Because your metabolic system was slowed way down, your body didn't atrophy too much, but it was a non-zero amount. We've also been exercising and stimulating your muscles, trying to get them reacclimated to physical use. From what we can tell, it's worked pretty well."

Leete tapped at his tablet and pointed one end in front of Julian. A holographic projection of his body, about one-quarter scale, appeared in the air. Most of it was colored green, with some pink and red spots in places. His brain was a yellow-green, which he interpreted to mean that there wasn't enough data yet. The casual use of the technology made a pretty convincing demonstration he'd slept for decades, and the label *West, Julian* on the projection revealed subterfuge was a waste of time.

Questions were bubbling up inside Julian. He managed to open his mouth, but no sound came out, so he closed it again.

Leete grinned, tapped the tablet a few more times, and the figure's orientation changed so it was upright. Julian noted his name remained in the bottom-right corner of the display. "Overall, Mr. West, you appear to be in good physical health, but it's difficult to get an assessment on your brain functions without your cooperation. We'd like to do a series of evaluations, looking for any gaps in your memory that may have developed over the last fifty years."

Julian scratched his cheek and decided resistance was futile. "Yeah, okay," he agreed. "There was a woman with me at the rally—Edith Bartlett. Do you know what happened to her? Did she survive?"

Dr. Leete seemed surprised by the query. "Well, I'm sure that's a matter of public record," he offered. He moved toward the door closest to Julian's head and tapped lightly on it.

"Fifty years," Julian echoed. "It doesn't feel like that. What's the world like?"

"Pretty good, compared to most of human history," the doctor answered. He gestured toward the window. "Would you like to take a look?"

Julian swung his legs off the bed and stood. The floor was cool against his bare feet, and Dr. Leete stayed by his side as he walked forward. At the window, Dr. Leete pressed a switch, and the translucent white haze on the floor-to-ceiling glass began to disappear like frost melting in the morning sun.

They were high in the air, and the view was stupendous. A river twisted below them, a lush island in the center, and on the other side was a great metropolis, easily identifiable by the Washington Monument–dominated skyline. The sleek structures around it gave insight into modern architecture; gleaming solar panels and rooftop gardens topped buildings clad in earthen materials.

Julian was still taking it all in when a door opened behind him. A young woman carrying a food tray stood there, staring intently at him as though he were a fascinating specimen under a microscope. "Mr. West, this is my daughter, Idabee," Leete said proudly. "We have a light breakfast for you, if you like. You've been on liquid nutrients; reintroducing solid foods is easiest with your cooperation."

Idabee looked to be in her early twenties and wore a muted green skirt paired with a blouse lacking frills or adornments. Its simplicity accentuated her female form. The tray she offered Julian after he returned to bed appeared to be metal, but the weight was insignificant. His food was on the softer side—applesauce plus a fruit-and-yogurt smoothie—but Julian welcomed it. "Do people still make jokes about hospital food?" he asked.

Dr. Leete gave his daughter an amused glance before answering. "They do, but you're not in a hospital. This is my home; you've been my patient, although somewhat indirectly, for many years. It was decided that reacclimating to life would be easier in a private residence."

Julian's face registered surprise. "Well, thank you," he said. "But who's paying for all this?"

"There's no one entity," Dr. Leete explained. "I'm employed by the hospital; they've scaled back my duties for these few weeks so I can spend most of my time here. The Department of Health pays them a fixed amount for your care; I can also get reimbursed for extra expenses. But please, don't worry about it. You're my guest."

"I think of this as his hobby," Idabee added, "helping sleepers wake up. It's been going on for years. People stay for weeks or months until they're ready to move on."

"You won't be surprised to hear the length of the stay depends on how long the sleeper was frozen," Dr. Leete said. "To help answer questions about what you've missed, I invited a friend, a historian, to visit us tomorrow. She was quite excited to learn you were from 2026. I'm sure she'll have questions about life after the COVID-19 pandemic. It triggered a great turning in American history."

Idabee had something she wanted to say; without objection from her father, she explained, "Mr. West, you were part of shaping that history. You were there at the reparations rally where Reverend Shaver's *Looking Backward from the Tricentennial* speech was interrupted. Your actions probably saved his life."

"Saved his life?" Julian echoed. "I saw him shot."

"Well, he survived—he's almost one hundred years old—and is internationally known." Idabee fixed Julian with an expression that was unreadable through the broad spectrum of emotions it held, and he struggled to decipher what this young woman was thinking. "I'm sure many people will want your perspective looking backward on life five decades ago. You'll get great publicity."

He would see that expression again fifty-one days later, when Idabee ended his existence in the tricentennial.

Chapter Four

"Stella should be here any minute," Dr. Leete said. They were in what Julian's host had referred to as the parlor; a room in his condominium dedicated to conversation with others, both physically and virtually present. Four chairs, a couch, and a loveseat sketched a loose oval around the parlor, intermingled with small tables, and the walls held a few pieces of art. Above them, the tray ceiling offered indirect lighting and, Julian supposed, hid the equipment that made virtual interactions possible.

Ray—the doctor insisted Julian call him by his first name, which Julian reciprocated—had explained their guest would be joining them via holographic representation. Stella Freedom, the author of several books about American history, was across the country in Seattle. With real time translations generated by artificial intelligence, the technology was used to facilitate discussions around the globe. The parlor setup had become standardized a quarter-century earlier; River Place Towers, the complex Dr. Leete lived in, integrated it into every unit's living space.

Julian settled back on the couch, still physically tired but mentally alert, while his host sat in a chair to his right. A brief tone softly announced Stella's arrival. Her female form began to flicker into existence next to Ray, stabilizing after a few seconds. Their guest was short and slender, with jet-black hair cascading to her waist over a crisp, white, button-up shirt.

Her sharp eyes took in the scene, quickly sizing up Julian before looking to his host. "Ray! Thanks for the invitation." Then, to Julian, "And you must be Julian West; it's a pleasure to meet you."

The illusion was marvelous. Although he noticed the faintest lag in the

CHAPTER FOUR

visualization of her speech, when she smiled at him, the genuine warmth came through in clear detail. "You too," he replied. "Thanks for taking the time to meet with me this afternoon."

"Still morning for me," Stella replied, clutching at an end table. Immediately, a mug appeared in her hand. "But don't worry, I'm on my second cup of coffee," she asserted, holding it out by way of demonstration. Julian stared in fascination as tiny wisps of steam curled up from the liquid. Stella took a sip, set the mug back on the table, and it vanished when she released it.

"Stella, Julian is the oldest sleeper I've ever dealt with," Ray said. "Politics from the twenties isn't something I know much about. I was hoping you could explain how things have changed, and about the American Union."

"The American Union?" Julian echoed the unfamiliar phrase.

Stella nodded and asked the two men, "Do you know the story of Rip Van Winkle?"

"A tale of a man sleeping for twenty years comes up fairly frequently in my line of work," Ray replied.

"I'll bet," Stella chuckled. "But an important plot point is that he slept through the American Revolution. He jumped right from living under King George the Third to President George Washington." She turned her attention to Julian. "You, my friend, slept through a revolution."

Julian raised an eyebrow. "I didn't realize there was an actual revolution. I'm not surprised. People were really pushed to the edge. Something had to change."

Stella settled back in her chair, grinning in anticipation. "Oh, this is great," she said, "getting your unfiltered perspective on the Second Gilded Age—the time of great inequality at the turn of the century. What are some reasons you aren't surprised?"

"Well," Julian began cautiously, "America had red states and blue states, you know? Republicans and Democrats? And they didn't get along. So the idea of a national divorce was to divide up the country."

Ray laughed. "That sounds incredibly impractical. Would states kick out everyone from the wrong political party?"

"I'm not sure how it was supposed to actually work," Julian replied peevishly. "The last couple of elections were pretty bad. January 6 and the other attacks on the political system showed people were willing to get violent. There were hundreds of millions of guns; mass shootings were all over the news. Life was broken for so many people, they were starting to snap.

"And Washington was totally dysfunctional," he said angrily, gesturing in the direction of the city. "It didn't matter how unpopular the Republicans and Democrats were; they always were reelected. We couldn't vote them out. So if it took a revolution to fix that, okay."

Stella listened calmly, with a hint of a smile. "Did you prefer one of the parties?" she asked.

"Democrats, I guess. But I voted for Cornel West last time, even if he wasn't going to win."

"Any relation?" Stella asked. Julian grinned like a cheshire cat and said nothing, so she continued. "There were years when Democrats had control of Washington. How'd it work out?"

Now it was Julian's turn to laugh. "Same way it always did. Nothing fundamentally changed. The rich got richer."

"That was one of the defining features of the Gilded Age," Stella confirmed. "What would you say was the roadblock to progress?"

"Lots of things. The Supreme Court started striking down a bunch of laws, rolling back rights, and people couldn't do anything about it. Then there was all the money in politics. Billions for lobbying, billions for elections; the rich had all the influence, and people like me had no say.

"Congress always had some sort of excuse why it couldn't get anything done. There were constant crises over the budget and the debt ceiling. There'd be a last-minute deal, Congress would rubber stamp it, and everyone would go back to bad-mouthing each other in the media and fundraising for themselves.

"The president tried to do some things with executive orders, but they didn't deliver much. So nothing happened," he concluded bitterly.

Stella struggled to keep a straight face. "Do you see a common thread?"

Julian considered, then asked, "The money?"

Ray answered a split second later, "It was Congress, wasn't it? That was the reason things were so out of balance back then?"

"You're both right," Stella agreed. "The Framers of the Constitution tried to set up a system of checks and balances, but money corrupts. Congress was distracted from its primary constitutional duty—setting public policy for the United States. The judicial and executive branches took up some of the slack, but the legislative branch had tied itself into knots."

"So we chopped the tree down," Julian said with a grin. His fist clenched with the same strength he'd applied to the lead pipe fifty years earlier. "I hope it made a nice bonfire."

Stella smiled back, thoroughly enjoying herself. "Julian, it was a nonviolent revolution, utilizing tactics Gandhi developed a century earlier."

"Gandhi?" Julian echoed. "The guy wrapped in a sheet?"

"The founding father of India," Stella agreed. "Yes, Congress' stagnation in setting policy was choking the country. But the American Union was able to sweep the gridlock aside and bring new life to the nation."

"How?" Julian demanded. "Any functional adults we had representing us had no power to get anything done."

"Didn't you see the roots of it at the time?" Stella wondered. "There were many organizations that empowered all people to participate. Had you heard of websites like Wikipedia?"

"Sure, it was a crowdsourced encyclopedia," Julian responded. "Anyone could contribute information in their area of expertise, and volunteers managed the process. It wasn't perfect, but it was free for everyone to use, and often had better, more up-to-date data than traditional encyclopedias."

Stella was nodding enthusiastically. "That was a good example of the model, yes. Did you ever use the Firefox browser?"

Julian nodded. "It was another nonprofit that developed an open-source internet browser. The big tech companies put out their own, but they would have trackers to spy on what users were doing. The developers of open-source web programs didn't put those features in."

"What about Open Office? Were you familiar with that?"

Again, Julian bobbed his head. "I used it on the computers at the community center when I was a kid; it was a free, open-source version of Microsoft Office."

"So," Stella summarized, "when people were dealing with entrenched interests that exploited users, who put financial barriers in the way of people having access to basic functions, or legacy institutions that used out-of-date information gathering techniques, what was the solution?" She waited expectantly for her student's reply.

"We crowdsourced it?" She nodded encouragingly for Julian to continue. "The American Union crowdsourced Congress?"

"Of course," Stella said. "There was nothing mystical about the legislative process; the members of Congress weren't high priests and priestesses communing with the spirits of the United States Code. By the twenty-first century, virtually all of the relevant information was accessible online. Artificial intelligence was able to do most of the legislative drafting, and there were many people who checked the results to make sure it would work.

"To return to the technological metaphor, the Constitution was the hardware the country ran on. There were limitations to what could be accomplished; to amend it and upgrade it was impossible by the time of the pandemic, due to extreme polarization. However, the software—the lines of code that determined how the country was run—could be changed relatively easily by a Congressional majority. A major update to the operating system was overdue, and the American Union crowdsourced the legislation that did it."

Julian pondered this, trying to think of some technical reason why this was impractical. "There were millions of pages on Wikipedia," he finally said. "A bill in Congress was a few thousand, tops."

"The passage of the American Union's first legislative package ushered in America 4.0," Stella said. "Are you familiar with the Phoenix Cycle?" Julian shook his head. "It's a pattern in American history. Every four generations, we upgrade the way our government works; who it serves and who it represents.

CHAPTER FOUR

"America's birth was the first cycle; we threw off the unresponsive government that brought taxation without representation. After the Revolutionary War, the Constitution established a framework for government—America 1.0. The Framers outlined five duties for Americans in the Preamble, and created a system of checks and balances to prevent any branch from having too much power over the others."

Julian snorted. "Maybe they should have put some checks on any men enslaving others."

"You're not wrong," Stella agreed. "The Framers were human, they were fallible, they were products of their time. Their intentions were not totally pure, but also not totally malicious. If we choose, we can see them in that context, as men who tried to make the world around them better and were willing to compromise rather than do nothing." Julian shook his head but didn't argue.

"Like a phoenix, the United States arose from the ashes of our colonial status," Stella said. "Those compromises over slavery, though, rippled forward through the decades, until the contradiction between the ideals in the Declaration of Independence and the racial injustice of slavery could no longer be papered over. When the Supreme Court issued the *Dred Scott* decision in 1857, establishing blacks had no rights, it started the next Phoenix Cycle.

"The election of Abraham Lincoln, as I'm sure you know, brought us the Civil War. It took the deaths of hundreds of thousands of Americans before Republicans and the Thirteenth Amendment ended chattel slavery. Reconstruction—America 2.0—brought civil rights to the formerly enslaved people, at least for a while."

"A brief moment in the sun," Julian said quietly.

"Another four generations later," Stella continued, "it was economic injustice that fractured our social contract. The wealth inequality of the Great Depression devastated America. This time, Democrats swept into power, and the New Deal brought us America 3.0. Harnessing new efficiencies in productivity, most Americans soon enjoyed a minimum wage, a forty-hour workweek, and the basic financial stability of Social

Security in old age.

"However, racial equality took a step back in the New Deal. Agricultural and domestic workers—technically race-neutral occupations, but predominantly held by people of color—were specifically exempted from the Fair Labor Standards Act, which passed on the heels of the Marihuana Tax Stamp Act. America was reborn again, but over the smoldering embers of racial injustice, which would flare up into the drug war decades later and engulf the criminal justice system." Julian nodded agreement.

"All of these problems returned by 2020—unresponsive government, racial injustice, and wealth inequality. When the global pandemic struck, it burned up what was left of the old social contract. Republicans and Democrats were unable to break out of the rut they had driven the country into. Like the previous cycles, it took a new political power to do so—the American Union. Are you familiar with the story of the Trojan horse?" Stella asked.

"Soldiers hidden inside a big wooden horse?" Julian replied.

"That's the one. For ten years, the Greeks fought against Troy. But it didn't work; the Trojans were well defended from a frontal assault. Finally, someone realized they needed to fight smarter. It wasn't necessary to overpower the entire army. Instead, they could persuade the Trojans to help them meet their real goal—getting inside the walls.

"Although various political parties had tried to defeat the Republicans and Democrats for two iterations of the Phoenix Cycle, their control of election machinery kept them well defended against any frontal assault. The American Union realized they didn't need to replace Congress. Instead, they could persuade Congress to help them meet their real goal by leveraging their votes."

"How exactly did they do that?" Julian wondered.

"Julian, the ultimate goal of all political reformers is to change government policy. First, a people's legislative assembly drafted a comprehensive package of solutions to trim back those recurring injustices. It included the American Union Jobs Program, and they expected Congress to pass it before the election in exchange for popular support."

Ray chimed in. "You might talk with Idabee. She's serving as a seated delegate in the assembly; she can explain the mechanics of how the people's congress works." He chuckled. "If you're not careful, she'll probably explain too much."

"Really?" Julian said, surprised and impressed to hear the young woman he'd met the previous morning had what sounded like an important role in the new political structure. To Stella, he asked, "Were there some election reforms that let the American Union gain influence?"

Stella frowned. "I don't believe so. I reviewed a few articles about the early days of the American Union, but they didn't get into the gritty details." Turning to their host, she continued, "Ray, I can put you in touch with a friend who specializes in voting science; she'd be happy to answer these kinds of questions." Julian nodded in appreciation.

"And what was the American Union Jobs Program?" Julian asked. "Could you explain that?"

"Everyone gets an American Union Job," Stella explained. "It's basically your share of ownership in the United States. The purpose of the American Union Jobs Program is to serve as the umbrella of benefits for a citizen. Unconditional basic income is your salary, plus there are health and wellness benefits, that sort of thing."

"So, it's like some sort of national service, where the man puts you to work?" With all the trouble he'd had in the past finding a job with health insurance, this might not be too bad.

"No, there's no strings, nothing," she answered.

Julian's brow furrowed in confusion. "Then why is it called a job program?"

"To remind us of our five constitutional duties, of course." At his blank look, Stella elaborated, "Every pupil knows them by heart. You might recognize them from the Preamble. We the people of the United States, in order to form a more perfect union, establish justice, insure domestic tranquility, provide for common defense, promote the general welfare, and secure the blessings of liberty to ourselves and our posterity, do ordain and establish this Constitution for the United States of America."

"I think I remember learning that in grade school," Julian said slowly. "And that was what the American Union ran on?"

"Campaigned on, yes, but only in part. Another key ingredient was framing the effort as a moral crusade, and building the organization on the principles of nonviolence. Are you familiar with the triple evils Martin Luther King identified?"

"Yes," Julian affirmed. "Reverend Shaver brought them up at the rally. Poverty, racism, and militarism."

"Right. It wasn't just the perennial problems of economic and racial injustice, but also what King called 'the greatest purveyor of violence in the world,' the US military. The peace vote has often been decisive in elections, because peace is popular. Incumbents like Woodrow Wilson and Franklin Roosevelt campaigned on their record of keeping the United States out of the world wars, although they reneged after they won, and Richard Nixon and Donald Trump both won narrow victories in part due to their promises to end unpopular wars.

"Poverty, racism, and militarism had interconnected roots, and so they could be addressed with a unified solution. With most Americans struggling—some reports say two-thirds of the country was living paycheck-to-paycheck—it was obvious the political system was failing the people of the country. Finally, they realized unionizing was the way to organize to bring about change."

"I'm not sure what that means," Julian confessed. "Labor unions were growing, winning better working conditions, but I never saw that as a permanent solution."

"A union is a group of people who engage in collective bargaining to improve their lives. Yes, labor unions are one of the best known examples, but student unions and tenant unions are others. They're useful for lopsided power arrangements, where a group of people with a common interest and insufficient bargaining power individually can cooperatively protect the interests of the whole. Voters who were fed up with a dysfunctional political system discovered they could do the same."

"But isn't that what political parties are? A group of voters with a common interest?"

Stella looked momentarily puzzled. "No, a union of voters can define what their interests are, instead of being forced to accept what candidates and parties offer them. The American Union broke through by doing the work Congress should have been doing. As Harry Truman is supposed to have said, 'It's amazing what you can accomplish if you don't care who gets credit.'

"By bundling up so many common-sense solutions into one package, the American Union was able to make Congress an offer it couldn't refuse—especially in the last critical weeks before the election. Anyone who objected had to defend the status quo. With so many problems festering, it was a tough argument to make.

"By appealing to America's collective conscience, they pulled together a critical mass of voters and empowered citizens to force real change. It wasn't just the tens of millions in poverty, the millions enmeshed in the racist criminal justice system, or the millions of peace activists. The American Union offered hope to everyone who'd lost faith in the power of the people, the power of nonviolence, and the power of the ballot.

"From the ashes of the old way of doing things, the United States emerged from the Phoenix Cycle reborn, Julian. Can you believe you only missed it by a few months?"

"What?" Julian asked, sitting up in surprise.

"You only missed it by a few months. The American Union of swing voters collectively bargained in the 2026 midterms and won us all a better social contract."

Chapter Five

"So, where are we going?" Julian asked, leaning against the cool wall of the elevator.

"There's a shopping level in the building," Ray explained as they descended. "Idabee's right, news of your awakening might lead to some publicity. We'll find you some new clothes and make sure you're looking good."

Dr. Raymond Leete lived on the thirty-ninth floor of a cooperatively run complex just across the Potomac River from Washington, D.C. In many ways, he'd explained, the four towers were self-contained villages. Each building in the River Place Towers complex contained community parks, gardens, and other amenities for the thousand condominiums within the structure. The individual units were all connected to a central kitchen, dispatching prepared foods on demand. The same system was used to deliver groceries and other purchases from the building's general store.

"And how are these clothes paid for?" Julian asked. It was better to find out the details up front.

The doctor waggled his left wrist, drawing attention to the smartwatch devices they'd put on before they left the condo. "Everyone has an account with the US Treasury," he explained, "except we're still waiting for yours to be set up. You'll get a monthly deposit into your account as part of your American Union Job, and you can use it to pay for what you want or need. Today, it's on me." By way of demonstration, he pressed his thumb to the watch face, which projected a holographic QR code. The grid of black-and-white squares was the size of a fist.

CHAPTER FIVE

"So everyone gets free money? How do you pay for it?" Julian examined the device on his wrist. Ray had called it a *doall*, a genericized version of the original brand name. He pressed his own thumb to its face. Nothing happened.

His host considered this. "Julian, did you know exactly how your cell phone worked? The frequencies used, the technology that made it possible, all of that?" Julian shook his head. "And I'll bet you didn't worry about it, because it did what you expected and more. That's how the government functions now. I can give you some of the details, but I'm not sure I'll get them all right. I do have a friend, an economist, who I'll bet would be happy to talk with you."

Julian accepted gratefully. "People used to say the problem was no one was paying attention to how the government worked. But," he ruminated, "a lot of people were paying attention. It just didn't seem to matter."

When the elevator door opened, Julian expected to see a large, open area like a mall, but instead found himself exiting into a hallway reminiscent of a hotel. It ran in both directions, with doors on each side. "There are thousands of different stores to choose from," Ray explained. "Every national chain and many local ones have facilities accessible here."

With a few taps, Ray called up a list of vendors from a panel mounted on the wall. The pair scanned the list. Julian recognized some names: Gap and Men's Wearhouse were still in business. Others he would never have associated with apparel; he could only guess what sort of outfits could be purchased at Mr. Peanut.

Ray pointed to Lord Hoot's listing. "They're a local business with a good selection. I think we should start with this one. Do you abstain?"

"Do I what?"

"Are you okay with that?" Julian was, and Ray made the selection, noting the number that appeared. "A4," he said aloud. "Lord Hoot's isn't actually located in the building, but they'll project a storefront and a clerk into room A4. We could do this in the parlor, if you knew what you wanted, but this way we'll have an expert to advise you on fashion. When you find something you like, it'll be custom made and delivered to us."

"This is like the conversation we had in the parlor?" Julian asked. "The store is just holograms?"

"Basically, except you don't have to sit down to have your physical appearance projected for the clerk. It's all automatic as soon as we walk in with these." Again, Ray waved the doall on his wrist. "We'll be able to see the outfits, and you can try them on virtually."

"Okay," Julian said, a note of skepticism in his voice.

Ray grinned. "Any other questions?"

"'Do I abstain?' What does that mean?"

"It's voting shorthand; yes, no, abstain. It's one of the ways we discourage binary thinking. When someone suggests you abstain, it welcomes you to raise an objection—no—but asks you to go along with the proposal."

Julian pushed back. "What's wrong with simple yes and no?"

Ray considered. "If we get back on the elevator, what are our options?"

"We can go up or down—it's a binary choice." He thought of an exception. "Unless we're on the top floor, or bottom."

"That sounds reasonable," Ray said. "But isn't there a third option? What would happen if we just stood inside the elevator and refused to choose?"

Julian conceded, "Someone else would come along and make a selection eventually."

"Correct. By declining to express a preference, we're actively choosing to go along for the ride. Yes-no-abstain voting is like that. It's okay to not be an expert on every subject." He nodded down the hall. "I am not an expert on fashion. Ready to check out the store?"

Julian took in the surroundings as he followed his host. Unlike a mall corridor, the floor was covered with a short berber carpet, a tasteful beige that went well with the light green walls. The letters A and B corresponded to opposite sides of the corridor, and about every fifteen paces they passed double sets of doors. All had identical handles, but the material of the door itself varied with the name of the establishment. The entrance to A2, The Exquisite Emporium, revealed shelves full of toys behind clear glass, but on the opposite side, blank doors appeared as solid mahogany, with a deep red stain that complimented the walls. He caught up with Ray

CHAPTER FIVE

and checked on B3; it showed the same thing. "If I wanted to buy some toys," he wondered, "could I walk into the Emporium? Or is it only for the person who called it up?"

"Anyone can enter, but you should probably expect the clerk to be helping someone else." Ray halted in front of Lord Hoot's; the doors showed an owl gazing outward with large, inquisitive eyes. Improbably, the animal wore both a crown and a bow tie. "Of course, there's no guarantee the clerk isn't busy inside this store either." He opened one door and held it for Julian.

Stepping inside, Julian found himself in an open room with four aisles, each with suits and other clothes displayed. There was a faint smell of fabric, and when he turned back to look at his host, he was shocked to see the doors they had just entered were glass—indeed, the entire front wall—and looked out on a busy urban street. Ray allowed the door to close behind him, shuttering the portal that revealed the reality of the hall outside in sharp juxtaposition to the cityscape.

A young man strode toward them, his crooked grin balanced between amusement and welcome. "Hello," he said, tucking the small tablet he carried under one arm before pressing his hands together in greeting. "Thank you for visiting Lord Hoot's; what can I show you today?"

Ray briefly explained to the clerk, who introduced himself as Sawyer, that Julian was a newly awakened sleeper and in need of a complete wardrobe. "What would you recommend?"

Steering them down an aisle, Sawyer stopped in front of three mannequins wearing similar outfits in slightly different styles and began to ask Julian questions about his preferences. Each response modeled a new array of choices, and Sawyer soon had some options he liked. "Ready to try these on?" the clerk asked.

Ray showed Julian to a changing room and instructed him how to use it. "In order to ensure a proper fit, the manufacturer needs the dimensions of your body. Strip down to your underwear, press this button, follow the directions on how to move about, and then get dressed. Come out and we'll see how the clothes look on you."

Julian did as instructed, but before dressing, examined his reflection in the mirror. He stroked his goatee as he stared into his own eyes, pondering the circumstances that had led him here. He ran a hand over his scalp, stubbled around the sides and back, smooth on top, and his gaze dropped to view the scars from the bullets that had nearly killed him. Julian touched each of the knots in turn and reflected he could stand to lose a little weight.

Ray and Sawyer were making small talk when he emerged. "Ready?" the clerk asked, and without waiting for a response, a full-sized version of Julian snapped into electronic existence.

"Woah," Julian marveled, walking around it. The digital doppelganger, tethered to one spot, sported the first choice of outfits Sawyer had selected and mimicked the movements he was making. Virtual Julian was wearing what would have been called business casual fifty years earlier. Sawyer cycled through the various ensembles, fine-tuning the colors and styles until all the men were satisfied.

With the major purchase out of the way, Sawyer showed Julian a selection of everyday clothes, from which he picked out a half-dozen outfits, including a long-sleeved green shirt. When they were ready to pay, Ray projected his QR code and the clerk touched his hands together in thanks for their business. "Your purchases should be delivered Friday," Sawyer informed them.

"Thank you for all your help," Julian said sincerely. He extended his hand to Sawyer. "I really appreciate it." The holographic clerk stared quizzically at him. Ray began to chuckle as Julian realized his mistake and withdrew his hand, feeling a slight flush in his cheeks.

Sawyer merely nodded politely. "My pleasure."

Ray shepherded him toward the exit as Julian gazed with wonder at the city through the front windows of the store. It was a meticulously crafted illusion, vivid and intricate, that showed colorful buildings and people bustling about. Although he knew intellectually it was a mirage, the complexity and completeness drew him in.

After following Ray out, Julian became distracted by the image of the bow-tie-wearing owl and his crown as they faded away from the door's

CHAPTER FIVE

exterior. "The store's gone?" He reached for the handle and pulled; it was locked. "What would we see if we could get inside?"

"Honestly, I'm not sure," Ray shrugged. "Maybe the four aisles?"

Another useless tug persuaded Julian to release the handle, and he fired another question at his host. "So, all money is digital now?"

The men meandered back toward the elevators. "No, but most of it. They have ATMs at post offices where you can withdraw Treasury notes. But it's an extra effort to spend paper money."

"Because you couldn't use them in a virtual store like this?"

"You can; there's a shredder you feed them into, which scans the serial number and credits the store's account. Wasn't that the case back in your time, though? Wasn't almost all money digital?"

Julian shrugged. "I knew plenty of people who still used cash. Some couldn't get bank accounts, and others were just tired of banks scamming them. The first year of the pandemic, Bank of America collected a billion dollars in overdraft fees. At least with cash, people knew where they stood."

"That's another problem that was solved. The Treasury can't discriminate against anyone; every citizen gets a free account, and it can't be interfered with. It's a cornerstone of our economy."

"And that comes with the American Union Job?"

"Like Stella said, it's one of your benefits as a citizen; yours should be set up soon. You'll also get to vote this year." Ray snapped his fingers. "That reminds me, I got in touch with her friend who can answer your questions about voting systems, a woman named Polly Sigh. I invited her for Saturday night. Idabee might be interested, any objection to her joining us?"

"It's cool," Julian said. "But Polly Sigh? Really? Like, her parents named her that, and she just happened to end up studying political science?"

"If I had to guess, it's probably not her birth name," Ray said. "So what? It's her identity now."

Julian held up his hands in surrender. "Okay, just checking. But why should I get to vote? I don't know anything about what's going on in the world, the candidates for office, and so on. I can't possibly be qualified."

"Do you really think the fate of the United States hinges on how you cast your ballot? It doesn't. One citizen, one vote; that's the rule."

After repeating the mantra to himself, Julian asked, "In my time, millions of people were excluded from the electoral process. Usually because of a criminal conviction, like a felony, but sometimes people who were mentally defective, too."

"That makes no sense," Ray said. "All citizens should have a say in how their country works. No taxation without representation and all that. Even if there's a non-zero number of people who can't meaningfully contribute to the decision-making process, what's the greater risk? Breaking the principle of universal suffrage, or the chance all the comprehending people will be so perfectly divided that a—what did you call them? mentally defective?—person will decide the outcome?"

"Look, I'm all for restoring people's right to vote after they've served their sentence," Julian said, nimbly dodging the question. "But are you saying incarcerated people still get to vote?"

"One citizen, one vote. End of story."

He shook his head in amazement. "What about immigration? It must be hard to become a citizen, with all the free money that goes with it."

Ray shrugged. "It's a fairly straightforward process; you could think of it as an unpaid internship. Anyone who wants to become an American can sign up when they arrive. They have to live here for a number of years—maybe seven? Then they're vested in the system, and can take the citizenship tests and get their American Union Job."

The older man leaned forward, almost conspiratorially. "Can I ask you something? I heard that back then, migrants and refugees would buy passage on crowded boats to get to their destination, or hike hundreds or thousands of kilometers and pay someone to smuggle them across the border, and they died all the time. Why did you block them from buying plane tickets? I've never understood that."

Julian had no defense to offer.

Chapter Six

The next night after dinner, for which Julian was served soft, easy-to-digest foods, he and Ray headed to the parlor. His host's economist friend, Teara Harper, was willing to chat with them about the American Union Jobs Program. After a moment, a middle-aged woman with caramel skin and hair pulled back into a tight bun appeared next to Ray on the loveseat. Her plumpness was shaped by her well-cut suit.

Ray made introductions. "It's a pleasure to meet you, Julian," Teara said. "I wanted to be able to address your questions about the economic transition, so I reviewed data from the twenties. Although relative poverty still exists—it's impossible for everyone's income to be above average—an estimated one hundred thirty million people lived in or near absolute poverty back then, including one in three children.

"That inequality was a hallmark of the Second Gilded Age. There was a euphemism for the growing economic insecurity, downward mobility, which one author compared to quicksand. 'Once it grabs you, it keeps constraining your options until it's got you completely.'"

Julian shifted on the couch. After spending a few days in this fancy condo, the statistic brought up memories of the littered streets of the neighborhood where he'd grown up, where the common struggle for solvency had been an integral part of the community fabric. Even if he didn't yet understand all the details of the tricentennial, Julian was grateful to have that behind him. "That's a good description," he said. "It was harder and harder to get ahead."

Teara wrinkled her nose. "It's an effective depiction, but I don't really like using it as an analogy because quicksand occurs naturally. The economy doesn't; it's strictly a human construct. The United States was touted as the land of opportunity, but those opportunities were maldistributed. Do you know what a fox hunt was?"

Julian nodded slowly. "I'm picturing horseback riders wearing red, chasing a fox across the countryside."

"In one of her books, Stella Freedom used it as an analogy for poverty," Teara explained. "I'll try to do it justice. Back then, fox hunting was described as a sport, which implies a contest where all participants have an equal opportunity to emerge victorious. In reality, it pitted one fox against a pack of dogs and men on horseback. To call it a sport trivializes the uneven stakes; the fox's life was on the line, while the worst a rider might generally experience was disappointment from an unsuccessful hunt.

"Theoretically, the fox could escape, maybe by climbing a tree or dashing through a stream to hide its scent from the dogs. Any mistake could mean instant doom, but even without an error, the animal was in a race against time. Eventually, the fox would become worn out, slow down, and be caught and killed. The rules and resources were all biased toward one side.

"It was theoretically possible to escape poverty too, and sometimes it happened, just like the fox sometimes got away. But the laws and rules of the United States, the political structure, even the very dollars that circulated through the economy: they were all biased in favor of those who already had money and property."

Julian gave a wry chuckle. "I wonder what the old foxes would have told the younger ones about fox hunts. 'I escaped, so you can too. Just try harder.' Because that was what we heard about poverty: work your way up to a better job."

"I don't understand," Ray said. "If an individual got a better job, wouldn't whoever took their place still be in poverty?"

Teara nodded. "The fact absolute poverty—not having enough money to meet your basic needs—existed in the United States was a policy decision by Congress," she said. "This was easily observable; in 2021, childhood poverty in the US fell to a historic low when Congress expanded the Child

Tax Credit. Congress took it away in 2022 and pushed more than five million children down into poverty."

A look of disgust flashed across Julian's face. "Did they expect the kids to go out and get jobs? Stella was telling us about how many problems in the United States were because Congress was failing to set good policy for the country," he said. "So what changed?"

"The American Union Jobs Program," the economist said. "Instead of pretending poverty was a personal failing—just try harder—the American Union recognized it as a societal failing. We the people were failing to look out for each other. The program's features included guaranteeing all citizens an unconditional basic income, which was often referred to by its initials, UBI.

"Every adult received enough money to start above the national poverty line—$16,800 when the program began, or $1,400 a month. Children—apprentice citizens—were credited one-third of that, $5,600, with half deposited into each of their parents' Treasury accounts. This virtually eliminated poverty in America.

"Promoting the general welfare is one of our constitutional duties, Julian. Do you know what the word welfare means?"

"Sure," he replied. "It's when people get money from the government."

"Well, you can use it that way," Teara said. "But the dictionary definition is quite specific—*health, happiness, prosperity; well-being.* Those are the things all Americans are supposed to promote, but especially Congress. The Constitution even repeats this responsibility in Article 1, Section 8, directing that Congress shall provide for the general welfare.

"The general welfare clause is one of the most important ones in the Constitution; it's the authority for universal healthcare, for example, providing for the general health of the country. Providing everyone with an unconditional basic income also promotes health, happiness, and prosperity."

Julian scratched his ear. "Sixteen thousand wouldn't be enough to live in most of Philadelphia," he offered.

"That's true," Teara acknowledged. "The national poverty line was an average. Every citizen received the same amount, and the freedom to decide what to do with it. If individuals chose to live in places with a higher cost of living instead of a lower one, they accepted the responsibility for making up the difference. You might know that Martin Luther King Jr. advocated for a guaranteed income. He wrote, 'the simplest approach will prove to be the most effective—the solution to poverty is to abolish it directly.'

"Because it was a universal program, Julian, it eliminated significant layers of wasteful bureaucracy. The Social Security Administration still administers the program. They've always had extremely low management costs—about one-half of one percent in your time. It was far simpler to put all Americans on the same program than to sort three hundred million individuals into worthy and unworthy."

"Everyone hated bureaucracy," Julian agreed. "I had friends who lost their jobs when the pandemic hit, but when they tried to collect unemployment, they ran into problems."

"Not only that," Teara said, "unemployment discouraged people from looking for a new job, since it was contingent on remaining unemployed. Many programs had similar disincentives. If a person's income reached a certain level, they often lost their benefits. It was completely backward. Unconditional basic income ensures everyone a regular amount of money, and everything people earn on top of it is theirs. People are always better off financially by accepting employment.

"From my perspective, the primary purpose of the bureaucracy back then was to minimize payments rather than maximize the number of people helped. A safety net, by definition, is full of holes, and tens of millions of people were falling through. It clearly wasn't working, so voters unionized to look out for each other. The real purpose of the American Union Jobs Program was to build a safety floor under every American."

"But that seems wasteful, too," he objected. "Not everyone needed help."

Teara shook her head. "The real waste was in human capability, Julian. A 2018 study found the lifetime costs of childhood poverty were over one trillion dollars for the cohort of kids born every year. Not only was UBI more cost effective, when the number of people using support services was dramatically reduced, agencies could better focus their time and resources on those who needed additional help.

"Most people back then were stuck in a mindset of scarcity. I saw pictures of the long lines at food pantries during the pandemic. Food was available in the supermarkets, but people whose primary income stream had been disrupted lacked money to purchase it. Rather than setting up a new distribution system, it would have been much simpler to give people the money to buy food directly.

"That's what the American Union Jobs Program does, and unconditional basic income helped shift people to a mindset of abundance. If you've ever been to a potluck dinner, you know the festive attitude that goes along with knowing there's plenty to go around.

"It also pushed money into impoverished communities," Teara continued, "where so much potential was being squandered. The effects of concentrated poverty had been known since the 1920s, when sociologists at the University of Chicago compared the economic zones of the city to the demographics. They proved that the cause of the crime and disease associated with slum life was social disorganization, not skin color or heredity.

"There were leveling effects in those communities; individuals didn't just have to deal with their personal financial situations, but the results of their neighbors' poverty as well. If one person came into some extra money, there was often a friend or family member who needed extra help, so it was incredibly difficult to build up a reserve of liquid cash that could be used to move away."

Julian nodded. Hard luck stories were always abundant in his neighborhood.

"Unconditional basic income transformed those areas by putting disposable income into the hands of everyone who lived there. Local businesses that had struggled for customers were able to flourish and grow. That's the prosperity Congress is directed to provide."

Julian nodded slowly. "Okay," he agreed. "But do you stop people from wasting the money?"

"What do you mean?" Teara wondered.

"Spending it on stupid stuff—expensive clothes, jewelry, electronics; like that."

"Oh. I was trying to picture how someone could waste digital dollars—maybe by withdrawing them as cash and setting them on fire? Julian, one person's spending is another person's income. Even if you had a person who bought stupid stuff, the retailer benefited from increased sales, and so did the manufacturer of the stupid stuff. The business taxes on their profits from the stupid stuff ended up reinvested back in the community. The economy—prosperity—was better off than if the money hadn't been spent.

"Sometimes those purchases were a way of sidestepping the leveling effects of poverty by buying status symbols or other displays of wealth. Julian, imagine you'd purchased an expensive pair of shoes, then learned your cousin was struggling to pay for a car repair so she could get to work. Donating one shoe wouldn't help. You were off the hook if you legitimately didn't have money, whereas someone who'd accumulated savings arguably had a moral obligation to help them.

"Most efforts to lift individuals out of poverty, while absolutely beneficial and worthy, didn't address the social structure that ensured others remained in it. The American Union Jobs Program changed all that. Instead of bringing buckets of water to a parched village, it rerouted the river for everyone's benefit."

Julian shrugged, not quite convinced. "I just think people'd make bad decisions."

"Some non-zero amount will, but the vast majority are responsible adults.[2] Any sort of government bureaucracy that put checks and balances on personal choices would have done more harm than good. Setting

---

[2] Studies find that people given the resources to make better decisions generally do just that. https://blogs.worldbank.org/impactevaluations/do-poor-waste-transfers-booze-and-cigarettes-no

up hoops for people to jump through and invading their privacy would discourage some people from participating, undercutting the goal of ending poverty.

"Trust, Julian. It was one of the things that we, as a nation, were struggling with back then. People didn't trust each other, in part because wealth inequality exacerbates distrust. The American Union was built on the principles of nonviolence. Trusting others and believing the best in them is an important component. Unconditional basic income is a statement of faith that each and every one of us can make good decisions.

"Another important part was equality; everyone received the same amount. Did you know anyone who struggled financially, but refused to ask for help? They didn't want charity?" Julian nodded, and Teara continued, "The American Union Jobs Program treated everyone the same; there was no stigma attached to it, any more than there was for driving on a public road, attending a public school, or going to a public library."

"Okay," Julian said. "But how was it paid for?"

"Good question," Teara answered cheerfully. "Do you know the difference between a regressive and a progressive tax?"

"Progressive is like the income tax? The more you make, the more you pay?"

With an affirmative nod, Teara continued, "And regressive taxes are the opposite; they hit low-income earners harder. The American Union Jobs Program came with new taxes, which clawed back most of the payments in ways that advanced public policy. But because these taxes were combined with UBI, they were progressive, not regressive. A family of four had to spend more than a quarter million dollars before they'd paid back their UBI through higher taxes. Over 80% of families came out ahead."

"What kind of taxes?" Julian asked suspiciously.

"One of the problems of the tax system in the Second Gilded Age was its reliance on income taxes. The wealthy had many mechanisms for making their income appear artificially low, such as borrowing against appreciated assets, the use of trusts and nonprofits, and claiming purchases as business expenses. The American Union Jobs Program was offset by a value-added tax: a broad-based consumption tax that ensured those who spent the most paid the most, regardless of how much income they claimed. There were also fees on the production of greenhouse gases, which addressed environmental issues by creating an economic incentive to pollute less."

Julian pondered the idea for a moment. "Had anyone ever tried this before? Giving everyone money?"

"The state of Alaska did, starting back in 1982. It was on a smaller scale and funded by taxes on oil production. Every resident of the state, of every age, received a check once a year. It was like a holiday; businesses would have sales to get people to spend the money. They also found property crimes went down in the weeks after people received their checks."

"But did the American Union Jobs Program really need to include everyone? I'll bet the wealthy didn't even notice."

"Did they notice the extra money in their bank account?" Teara asked rhetorically. "Almost certainly not, especially since they paid far more in additional taxes. But you know what they would have noticed? Being excluded. Everyone gets an American Union Job."

Julian glanced over to Ray to see if he had any questions, then shifted in his seat. "Thanks for explaining. But I'm still not clear on what the jobs were that people had to do."

"In short, be a better American," she answered. "The Preamble lists our five duties: establish justice, insure domestic tranquility, provide for the common defense, promote the general welfare, and secure the blessings of liberty to ourselves and our posterity. Do any combination of those things, however you like; that's your American Union Job."

"But how do people track what they're doing?"

Teara smiled. "Julian, the program is unconditional. You can't get fired any more than you can get fired from being a citizen. If there were any reporting requirements, it wouldn't really be unconditional.

"However, for people who do want to think about it, the rule of thumb is one thousand hours of productive work a year, or twenty per week, fifty weeks a year. The most generic of the duties is promoting the general welfare. For people who have paid employment, they're contributing to the prosperity of America; UBI is like a raise.

"Other people without employment perform different types of valuable work. Insuring domestic tranquility, for example, could include all sorts of domestic activities, such as being a homemaker or caretaker. Some people get involved in the political arena, working to secure our liberties. Still others might be stewards of the environment, preserving it for our posterity. At an absolute minimum, just spending that money into the economy promotes prosperity and the general welfare.

"Julian, there aren't really any wrong answers. It's not the government's place to micromanage people's lives," Teara said emphatically. "The American Union Jobs Program created a true right to work. Karl Widerquist wrote, 'The right to work without anyone else's consent is not the right to a job, but the right to direct, unconditional access to resources.' Unconditional basic income put cash in people's hands and let them guide their own lives. Are you familiar with Maslow's hierarchy of needs?"

The phrase prompted a recollection of a colorful poster that he'd seen on the wall of a community center. "I think so," Julian replied. "It's a pyramid, with food and shelter at the bottom?"

"Right idea, wrong shape," Teara replied. "Maslow never said anything about a pyramid. We show it as a ladder, with rungs the same width, so there's no implication that not everyone can make it to the top.

"The five levels are survival, security, society, self-esteem, and success. The American Union Jobs Program ensured everyone could meet their survival and security needs. When people are insecure, maybe unsure how they're going to pay their rent or put food on the table, it takes a toll."

Julian said nothing, but he remembered how he'd been uncooperative with Dr. Leete because of the fear of crushing medical debt, something that bankrupted hundreds of thousands of people annually in his time. What would it be like to not be afraid? Maybe that's what Teara meant when she talked about a mindset of abundance.

"We all have limited mental capacity," Teara continued. "There are only so many things we can think about, or concentrate on. Now, when part of your brain is worried about the security and shelter issues, it eats up mental bandwidth: IQ drops, productivity drops, people make more mistakes, and become worse at long-term planning."[3]

Ray spoke up. "What about the adrenaline boost people get from survival situations? Doesn't that help them think faster and sharper?"

"It's not sustainable," Teara explained. "Economic insecurity means never getting a chance to recover and recalibrate back to normal; it wears people down. That was the social cost everyone was paying for allowing most of the country to live paycheck to paycheck."

Julian nodded slowly. "Okay, that was the social cost, but what was the actual cost? It still sounds expensive."

Teara looked away for a moment. "Could we continue this next week? I have another meeting in a few minutes, and that'll take some explaining. Can I give you a homework assignment?" Julian nodded. "When were you born?"

"1992."

"Okay. That year, the United States had a national debt of four trillion dollars, and our GDP—gross domestic product—was more than six trillion dollars. That was the sum of all the goods and services produced across the country. But by 2026, the national debt was thirty-seven trillion. Julian, see if you can figure out how we managed to borrow five times as many dollars as there were circulating through the economy in the year you were born." Teara turned to Ray and said goodbye before her digital form disappeared.

"Where did we borrow thirty-three trillion from?" Julian echoed to Ray. "I can figure that out." His host gave him an encouraging smile. Feeling the thrill of the hunt, Julian began to think.

---

[3] For more on this phenomenon, see *Scarcity: Why Having Too Little Means So Much* (Mullainathan & Shafir, 2013)

Chapter Seven

Julian stared out his bedroom window at the Washington Monument. Illuminated by the afternoon sun, it drew his memory to the violence he'd experienced there a few days earlier. Other than Reverend Shaver's survival, he knew almost nothing about how things had turned out. How many innocent people had been hurt? Had Edith Bartlett been among them, perhaps targeted by the red-bearded ringleader for trying to warn him?

The whole incident still seemed surreal. Had he really killed three people? It had been unlike all the video games he'd played, the first-person shooters like *Call of Duty*. Julian felt his index finger twitch, recalling how he'd traded shots with the man on the stage and somehow prevailed. An intangible quality surrounded the memory. There had been no planning, no premeditation, simply an instinctive reaction to unfolding events. Only afterward did he realize how close he'd come to dying.

His mind replayed his movements with the pole. Julian's arms experienced the vibration as it connected with the boyish gunman's skull, first knocking him down, and then the second hit that halted the man's movements for all time. He tried to remember if he'd ever taken a life before: insects of course, and mice indirectly with traps and poison. Again, he heard Edith call for him: *Julian! Look out!* What had she thought when she'd seen him shot?

A light knock at the door jolted him back to reality. Ray peered in. "Hey, Julian. Dinner's about ready." Julian thanked his host and promised to join him in a few minutes.

He glanced back at the computer display projected in the air in front of him. Ray had provided him with his own digital tablet and set him up to browse the internet, which he hoped would help him get a better sense of what was going on in the world. There was a small charge to read each of the news stories, and since he hadn't been assigned a Treasury account yet, Ray had logged into his own in the browser.

The headlines were exotically mundane. An earthquake in South America had killed hundreds; while the name of the country wasn't one he recognized, the specifics of the disaster could have been plucked from his own time. The Department of Justice had blocked a proposed merger between two tech companies—again, whose names he'd never heard of. And a musician was concluding a farewell tour before entering rehab.

On impulse, Julian entered Edith Bartlett's name into the search field. As thousands of results appeared, he exhaled softly. Whatever information about Edith was out there, he wasn't going to find it at this moment, although he was confident answers existed.

In the kitchen, a young woman sat at the table, and he remembered meeting her three days earlier. It was Idabee, Ray's daughter, and she greeted him cheerfully. "Mr. West, hi!" Her smile stretched across her lean face, hair closely cropped on the side with tight natural curls rising a finger's length at the top. "How are you?"

Julian shrugged. "Fine, as far as I know." He surveyed the room; the open concept took advantage of bountiful light from the large windows on the far wall. A countertop ran most of the length of the west wall, and a window in front of the kitchen sink revealed the sun beginning its nightly descent.

At the large island, across from the sink, Ray was removing three steaks from the stove. "Smells good in here," Julian said. "Can I help with anything?"

Ray grinned. "Thanks… I think your digestive system is ready for a full meal now, so I thought we'd make an occasion out of it." He gestured toward the far end of the room. "You could grab sour cream from the fridge."

"I'm giving my own digestive system a break after this," Idabee said to Julian, "and starting a fast. It's always nice to share a last meal with family and friends."

Julian nodded absentmindedly as he looked around the kitchen for the refrigerator, not seeing the large appliance he was expecting. "Sure," he replied to his host, "if you can point it out."

"Right here," Idabee said, coming up behind him. She pulled open a drawer under the counter; it revealed an illuminated space lined with various condiments. "If you don't see it there, try the one underneath."

Julian touched the neat row of glass bottles inside; they were cold. A quick scan identified the jar of sour cream. "Interesting refrigerator," he said. "We used to have taller versions, where you could open up a door and see everything inside on shelves at the same time."

"How did you stop all the cold air from falling out?" Idabee asked.

Seeing the dumbfounded look Julian gave her, Ray began to chuckle. "I remember those," he said. "What an inefficient design." Perhaps challenged by his own words, Ray shuttled all three plates to the table in a single trip; each steak was accompanied by a baked potato, broccoli, and a dinner roll.

Something about the room's layout occurred to Julian. "That window over there," he said, pointing toward the setting sun above the sink, "isn't the hallway on the other side of the wall?"

Idabee twisted to see where he was pointing. "Yes," Ray admitted. "That's a faux window."

"A foe window?" he echoed, not understanding.

Ray spelled it out. "It's a hologram projected behind the glass, like we saw in Lord Hoot's. If you look closely, you can see the layers that help give it depth, but if you're not thinking about it, it's just a window. They're very popular; there are different channels you can tune into; all sorts of nature scenes. But I like having it match the actual view."

The table had seats for six; they took three together, with Idabee in the middle. Silverware clanked as they cut into their meals. Julian speared a piece of broccoli, roasted with slight charring, and popped it in his mouth. It was tender and crunchy, with a smoky and salty flavor. "Best food

I've had in fifty years," he said, savoring it with a smile. "Don't all these holograms use a lot of power?"

"There's plenty of electricity to go around," Idabee said.

He looked to Ray. "Teara said something about a pollution tax being tied to unconditional basic income? Didn't that make electricity more expensive?"

"Depends on how you define expensive," Idabee said. "Using fossil fuels on the scale we did at the turn of the century generated tremendous external costs. Everyone was affected by climate change; putting a tax on greenhouse gases undercut the structural convenience of pollution. It was an escalating fee; it went up a bit every year, so it created a strong incentive to divest from fossil fuels and invest in more sustainable sources of energy."

"Solar and wind power were getting pretty popular," Julian said.

"That's true, and they still are. To really strengthen the power grid, though, the United States began building thorium reactors. They were safer and more efficient than the old nuclear reactors, and had a big advantage when it came to global stability; they couldn't be used to facilitate the production of nuclear weapons.

"Energy is abundant today, Mr. West. If you're interested in learning more, I'm moderating a panel Monday that's working on a provision for consideration in the American Union's legislative package. You're welcome to come and observe."

Startled, Julian reappraised her. "Your dad said you were a delegate of some sort, although I don't really know what that means. Sorry, how old are you?"

"I'm twenty-six," Idabee said primly. "Maybe younger than average, but a people's legislative assembly is accessible for everyone. I happen to have earned a seat there at the moment."

"When I was twenty-six," Julian chuckled toward her father, "well, never mind. Sure, Idabee, I'd be interested in seeing how it works. And call me Julian."

"Julian, how's your steak?" Ray asked. "I don't cook them very often."

"Not bad; I usually prefer mine a little more well done." He hesitated, then added, "A cold beer would go down smooth."

The Leetes exchanged a measured glance, then the doctor said, "I didn't think of that, sorry. I do have a bottle of whiskey."

"I'm not really a drinker," Idabee said, "but, doesn't the alcohol numb your taste buds?"

Julian dismissed the idea with a wave of his hand. "It's supposed to make you appreciate the meal."

"You know what else you might appreciate about this meal?" Ray asked. "It's not from a cow—at least not directly. Lab-grown steaks. I wondered if you could tell the difference?"

Julian took another bite, pondering the texture and flavor. "I don't think so. Tastes like steak to me."

The doctor grinned. "Well, they say it's the same on the cellular level; I hope you don't mind me using you for a blind taste test. Find anything interesting in the news?"

Julian summarized the stories he'd found. "Paying for every article—that'll take some getting used to. In my time, news sites would run ads, but usually you could read what you wanted. Although, some newspapers would require a subscription."

"I know this one," Idabee chimed in. "Before everyone had Treasury accounts, private banks handled the payment system, and they had a minimum charge. But once micropayments were practical, websites could charge a few pennies per page, or ask for small donations."

Julian nodded. "Credit card fees were terrible! I had a website a few years ago," he said without thinking, then caught himself. His dinner companions grinned. "Anyway, it was twenty-nine cents plus a percentage of the payment. Free banking sounds better."

"FDR said, 'The American people should control their money; their money should not control them.' We've controlled ours for decades now, and it works pretty well," Idabee explained.

"Teara Harper will probably explain more next week, if you're interested in the details," Ray suggested. "How's your stomach feeling with the food?

Listen to your body; a non-zero amount of discomfort isn't a problem, but please don't overdo it."

"So far, so good," Julian said, deliberately stabbing another piece of broccoli with his fork. "You keep using that word, non-zero. What's up with that?"

"It's usually a way of emphasizing that while zero may be the goal, perfection isn't realistic. It can also be an acknowledgment the thing being measured is an insignificant number or percentage," Ray answered.

"It's commonly used with VOZ metrics," Idabee added.

"Vossmetrics?" Julian echoed the phrase.

Idabee spelled it out. "VOZ stands for variable-one-zero," she explained. "It's part of how we develop data-driven policy with the American Union. Basically, you reduce a metric to a number between zero and one, and track how the measurement changes. Is it moving toward zero, toward one, or is it stable? When you have a hard number, it minimizes legislating by anecdote. More importantly, you can usually find agreement about which way the trend should be going. If not, you can try coming at the problem from a different metric to see if you can build consensus around that one."

Julian nodded slowly. "Can you give me an example?"

Her face adopted a pensive look. "You mentioned the ads websites used to have. Did you see many commercials in different formats, or other ways businesses would promote themselves?"

"Yes," Julian groaned, "we were bombarded with advertising, hundreds of times a day."

Idabee raised a hand to her mouth as a giggle escaped her lips. "I assume it was a number you would have liked to see trend downward."

"Of course," Julian agreed.

"First, let's try and define that metric a little better, and then figure out how to apply nonary logic to it." Once again, Julian found himself asking for clarification of an unfamiliar term. This time, there was no spelling involved, and Idabee explained, "There are nine basic policies we can implement. For simplicity, let's call our variable the percentage of the day the average person is subjected to advertising. Our first choice is to decide if we want that number to go up, down, or if we're satisfied with where it's at."

Julian nodded. "So, like yes, no, abstain?"

Idabee beamed. "Exactly. Choosing to do nothing can be an active policy decision. In fact, it's really the goal—to steer things into a stable place. But in this scenario, you want to see the percentage of the day you're bombarded with advertising go down. Then there are two more choices: whether to try to influence the supply or the demand, and in which direction."

"I'm not sure I understand," Julian admitted. The amusement radiating from Ray's eyes brought to mind the friendly warning he'd offered about Idabee: *If you're not careful, she'll probably explain too much.* Julian decided to risk it. "How would that work?" he asked.

Idabee smiled brightly. "The easiest way to try to drive the supply—the quantity—of ads downward is to make them more expensive, usually with taxes or fees, so less of them will be produced. We've done that; advertising manipulates the public consciousness for private gain. Taxes acknowledge the societal costs it generates.

"To address the demand side usually takes more thought. What are the root causes of the behavior? In this case, how do we motivate those news sites to want to run fewer ads?"

"The micropayments?" Julian asked. "Give them a different way to generate revenue that's less annoying for their readers?"

She nodded. "Very good! The three choices have nine outcomes; that's nonary logic. By establishing clear goals and identifying which path of action we want to take, it's much easier to build consensus around solutions. Does that make sense?" Idabee waited expectantly.

There was a pause. "Julian, just say yes," Ray advised.

"Yes," he echoed. Idabee gave her father an annoyed look.

"If you really want to have a good time," Ray added, "ask her about parliamentary procedure."

"Father," she replied with mock indignation. "It's important."

"I know," he said supportively. "What do you think of Julian's new clothes?"

Idabee appraised him. Julian waited expectantly, and she bestowed a smile on him. "Looks good."

"He tried to shake hands with the clerk," Ray said, chuckling at the recollection.

Quickly changing the subject, Julian said to Idabee, "You said you're starting a fast after dinner? Like, no food?"

"I am," she agreed. "It's a tradition, part of the American Union, a group fast once a month. It's called the fast for peace."

Ray settled back in his chair. "I want to hear how you explain this."

Idabee shrugged. "You know what they say, Father. Fasting and compromise are two sides of the same coin—willingly giving something up." Then, to Julian, "It's a monthly reminder for people that if we want to work things out peacefully, we can. We have the capability. And because it's free and accessible to everyone, it serves as an opt-in for steering the American Union, Mr. West—Julian."

"I knew people who tried fasting," Julian said. "Does everyone give up food at the same time?"

"Pretty much," she answered. "It's on the fifteenth of each month, but people can choose their own twenty-four hours. I usually go from dinner to dinner. It was originally used by Gandhi in India as a way to bring Hindus and Muslims together."

Julian frowned and bit back the question he wanted to ask. "Stella Freedom said his tactics were part of the nonviolent revolution," he offered instead.

"I don't even want to think about what shape our country would be in if we had a violent revolution," Idabee said. "This month is when he did his first fast, during World War One, March 15 through 18. Some of us are fasting for seventy-two hours in commemoration."

"Three days without food sounds like a long time," Julian said skeptically.

"It's not too bad," she said brightly, "especially if you know up front it's only three days. Gandhi's was an open-ended fast, to help a labor union get a living wage, and after three days there was a compromise reached so he could eat again. But most people just do twenty-four hours for the fast for peace."

Ray gestured with his fork. "I'm going to disagree with 'most people.' You can support the American Union without fasting every month. Maybe it was necessary back in Julian's time as part of getting through the Phoenix Cycle. But it's not like that anymore."

"That's the point, though," Idabee countered. "It takes an active effort to keep society in balance; someone has to be responsible for it. Julian, how well did it work electing members of Congress to be the responsible ones?"

He laughed. "We were talking about this the other night; Congress was the problem."

"Exactly. Someone has to actually take responsibility. That's what the fast signifies—a willingness to accept responsibility for being part of the solution. It's an important component of being a delegate in the people's legislative assembly; we all fast for peace."

"And you're doing a fine job," Ray responded. "I just don't want Julian to get the impression that if you have a midnight snack, the United States will come apart at the seams. Things will work out."

Julian was thinking this over. "Twenty-four hours, huh?" Idabee nodded. "I think I could do that." He certainly wouldn't starve to death in one day, and he remembered the mirror in Lord Hoot's prompting him to lose a little weight.

Idabee's eyes sparkled and she beamed at him; it was a little disconcerting. "You can; it's just a matter of will power. No food or recreational intoxicants, and just drink water." Then she added, "You can join us too, Father."

Ray shook his head. "Not this month, thanks. Are you going to tell him about your other challenges, and try to get him to take cold showers for thirty days?"

Suddenly, a noise from the hallway interrupted their conversation.

Chapter Eight

The sound of a tone prompted Ray to look at the hands of the wall clock. "That's Polly Sigh," he informed them. He made no move to get up from the kitchen table. "Julian, election theory doesn't hold much interest for me; I just vote with the American Union. I'll sit this one out, if you don't mind."

Idabee was already rising from her chair. "Aren't you curious about the science of why it works?" she asked. Julian stood as well, unsure if he should clear his dinner dishes or continue keeping their guest waiting.

"Not that much," Ray admitted without the slightest trace of regret. "You two go ahead; I'll clean up." Julian thanked him as he followed Idabee to the parlor.

Polly Sigh was already sitting comfortably when they entered. She was a young white woman around Idabee's age, and her short hair was a vibrant purple. There were several rings in each of her ears, and one in her nose. "Sorry to keep you waiting," Julian said, making his way toward the couch. Polly ignored his statement, waiting patiently with her hands folded on her lap.

Glancing up at the corner of the room, Julian saw two red lights with a single green, and remembered how Ray had explained it took several seconds of sitting before the holographic recorders were activated. Only at that point would the light turn green to indicate others were viewing him.

"She can't hear us," Idabee said cheerfully, making herself comfortable on the loveseat. She kicked her shoes off, folded her legs up under her, and gave Julian a warm smile. As he sat on the corner of the couch closest to their guest, he cast an eye up at the trio of indicator lights. His twinkled green for five quick pulses; red pause; four pulses; red; and so on until the green pulse stayed steady and Polly was looking at them. "Polly, hi! I'm Idabee Leete."

Julian apologized again for keeping her waiting and introduced himself. Polly responded graciously. "I'd love to hear more about your impression of politics back then, but Stella Freedom said you had questions about how the American Union gained political influence."

"Yes, I do," Julian agreed. "I want to understand how it unstuck the political system. Stella explained the historical stuff—how the Phoenix Cycle dictated a new political power would rise—but she was a little fuzzier on how exactly it happened."

"Stella's an amazing historian," Polly gushed. "Can you explain what you mean by stuck?"

"Well, we were stuck with two parties," Julian said, "even though most people wanted more parties and half the country said they were independent."

Polly nodded. "It's called Duverger's law. It says that when you combine winner-take-all elections with single-member districts, you tend to get two parties. Which is exactly what happened. That dynamic applied across the whole country; in fact, Republicans and Democrats won more than 99% of the time. Because the two of them had a monopoly on getting elected, they were often called the duopoly.

"Another factor was the Electoral College, that thing the Framers made up to stop people from directly electing the president. The Constitution said if no candidate received a majority of electoral votes, the House would decide the president. So as a practical matter, the duopoly was sure to win the presidency, and the strength of the top of the ticket helped to support all their parties' candidates for Congress."

"But people wanted more parties," Julian insisted.

Polly shrugged. "And the Framers wanted zero political parties, which is why they left them out of the Constitution. Math doesn't care about people's feelings, Julian. The political system couldn't support a multiparty democracy because elections were a zero-sum game; a single candidate was elected and all the others lost. A two-party system developed immediately, because it's the most efficient model for winning a zero-sum game. George Washington saw it, and warned in his *Farewell Address* that 'the alternate domination of one faction over another, sharpened by the spirit of revenge' would lead to 'a frightful despotism.' The names of the parties changed over the centuries, but there were always two major ones.

"That's how the mathematical principles work out, but there were practical reasons as well. Power tends to accumulate, and by the twenty-first century, the Republicans and Democrats had developed a number of advantages to protect themselves from competitors. Classic behavior of a monopoly," Polly observed. "In the previous iteration of the Phoenix Cycle, the duopoly cooperated in enacting barriers to keep the Socialist Party off the ballot. Often that meant petitioning, forcing third parties to invest resources every election just to appear on the ballot.

"The two parties also benefited from network effects. The duopoly had databases of voters across the country; they had suppliers for their campaign materials; they had lists of donors, volunteers, and campaign organizers. Even law firms that dealt with campaign finance and election law catered to one party or the other. When the American Union started out, trying to disrupt the duopoly, lawyers refused to represent them, claiming a conflict of interest."

"Republicans and Democrats," Julian said with a scowl. "They were tearing the country apart. They'd fight over every little thing; everyone had to pick sides. And because of gerrymandering, it just got worse and worse. They'd make districts weird shapes, so one party's candidate was guaranteed to win. It was usually the incumbent, but if there was a primary, it'd bring out the most polarizing candidates."

"There's some truth to that," Polly admitted, "but didn't US Senate districts have the same problem with polarization? They couldn't gerrymander state lines."

"True, but people really wanted more political parties. We could have made it so votes for third parties weren't wasted," he suggested. "Because some states were trying to fix that with ranked choice voting, do you know what that was?"

"I do," Polly said. Then, to Idabee, "It let voters rank their candidates in order of preference. If no one received a majority, the last-place candidate was eliminated, and their voters' next choice was redistributed, and so on, until there was a winner."

"Then people could vote for third parties and not have to worry about spoiling the election," Julian added. "Lots more parties would have been viable that way."

"No, ranked choice voting doesn't lead to more political parties," Polly answered. "As long as elections are zero-sum games, Duverger's law still applies. Australia adopted ranked choice voting a century before any American states did, and they maintained a two-party system under it." Julian didn't say anything, but looked unhappy.

Polly continued, "Another barrier that protected the duopoly was the millions of dollars needed to effectively campaign for Congress. It was a very high bar for entry into a zero-sum game. Since people knew the duopoly won 99% of the time, campaign contributions to third parties were generally as wasted as their votes."

"Still," Julian insisted, "states adopting ranked choice voting could have made a third party practical. People were really fed up with the Republicans and Democrats."

Polly shrugged. "Changes on the state level could never actually threaten the power of the duopoly, because Congress has always had the constitutional authority to set national standards for federal elections 'at any time' under Article 1, Section 4. Anyway, any state laws that used it in federal elections were overruled by national reforms a few years later."

Julian shook his head sadly. "It's depressing to think we were stuck with a two-party system."

"Ironically," Polly added with a mischievous smile, "ranked choice voting would have actually strengthened the power of the duopoly, because it channeled third-party votes that might otherwise have been spoilers into electing their candidates. With it, there was little pressure for the duopoly to make any concessions because third parties could no longer spoil their way into relevancy."

"I'm confused," Idabee replied, rubbing her forehead. "Were the third parties running to win, or to be spoilers? And how exactly would they do that?"

"Let me try an analogy," Polly offered. "Imagine a huge map representing the political battlefield, one with all the issues people care about marked somewhere on it. Political parties were practical; they would stake out whatever positions would gain them the most ground, because the more territory they covered, the easier it was to win an election. Sometimes that led to contradictory policies within a party, but between the two, they covered almost everything.

"Idabee, to your question, third parties could find vacant spaces or create new ground around new issues. Yes, the principled goal of third parties was to have so many voters commit to those policies as to win an election. But the practical goal was to make that chunk of political real estate appear valuable enough that a major party would take it over, like a big company buying a startup that could otherwise turn into a competitor. One historian observed that the role of third parties was to sting like a bee, then die."

"And did that really work?" Idabee wondered.

"Yes," Polly answered, stretching out the single syllable so there would be no misunderstanding, "that's Duverger's law." When the other woman looked sufficiently chastened, she continued. "One of the best examples was the People's Party, formed during the First Gilded Age at the end of the nineteenth century. They had many specific reforms that they wanted to see enacted, like adding silver to the money supply, an income tax, the direct election of US Senators, and more government support for labor and agriculture.

"In the 1892 election, more than a million men and some women cast their ballots for the People's Party. They won five states and captured twenty-two electoral votes. Williams Jennings Bryan, a second-term Congressman from Nebraska, took note. Four years later, he won the

Democratic presidential nomination after his stirring *Cross of Gold* speech, vowing to bring prosperity to the farmers hurting from deflation with a policy of free silver."

"Free silver?" Julian echoed.

"Free, as in being able to freely turn the metal into US currency. This was one of the People's Party's signature planks. At their convention, strategically timed to take place after the two major parties', the delegates weighed the principled and practical choices for their presidential candidate. Julian, you can probably appreciate their debate after some of the close elections you lived through. What if they split the free silver vote and McKinley, the Republican, won as a result? Finally, after four days, the People's Party decided to go all-in and nominated Bryan as their presidential candidate too."

"I don't remember ever hearing about a President Bryan," Julian said.

"Well, Bryan lost, but that was mostly because he was outspent by a factor of ten to one. The People's Party devolved into state chapters and local groups and never again carried national influence. But," Polly said brightly, "their ideas percolated through the Democratic Party as a result of Bryan's move. They got the income tax, the direct election of Senators, and eventually FDR took the US off the gold standard in 1933."

Julian looked unconvinced. "That was a long time ago, though," he observed.

"There are plenty of examples," Polly said. "Richard Nixon was a Republican who ran for president in 1960 and lost to John F. Kennedy by two-tenths of one percent. Then, after JFK was assassinated, his vice president ran for a full term in 1964, and the Democrat won with the largest share of the vote in US history.

"But," Polly said, a glum note in her voice, "After the Civil Rights bills passed, George Wallace split from the Democratic Party and ran for president in 1968 with the newly formed American Independent Party. He won five southern states and forty-six electoral votes. Richard Nixon won the three-way race for president with less than 44% of the vote, and he was determined to get reelected.

"Nixon saw there was a 13% bloc of votes in opposition to civil rights, so his southern strategy included launching the drug war to target blacks in a way that was race-neutral on its face. It paid off; besides sweeping all five of Wallace's states, he had a 23% margin of victory in the popular vote. It was vindication for him after those close elections, and a permanent realignment in the policies of the parties. No longer were the Republicans the party of Lincoln and freeing the slaves; Democrats were able to take the black vote for granted for the next fifty years."

"Wait, what happened fifty years later?" Julian asked.

"The American Union," Polly said. Julian looked incredulous. "That was how members of the black community, along with other marginalized interest groups, seized political power; by being willing to walk away from both Democrats and Republicans."

Julian shook his head. "Didn't you just say we were stuck with two parties?"

"Yes, as two competing entities, but not as specific packages of policies," she explained. "The American Union staked out a principled set of policies and pledged to vote together to reelect members of Congress from either party, if they took action before the election."

"Stella called them the American Union of swing voters," Julian recalled. "But they're not a political party?"

"We're not," Idabee answered. "Once you accept that third parties don't work, it's obvious that swing voters—someone willing to vote for either of the major parties—hold the real political power in the country." She was smiling as she said it.

Julian adopted a mischievous grin as he stared back at Idabee. "Okay, I'll accept it. But if it's so obvious, why didn't anyone do it before?"

"Do you know how America adopted alcohol prohibition?" Polly Sigh asked, drawing his attention. "There was a broad coalition of reformers behind the idea. They pointed to the social harms alcohol caused, how it contributed to crime, poverty, and domestic violence. The Anti-Saloon League focused on legislation at every level of government and drew attention to the political corruption saloons fueled. Others supported it as a quid pro quo for adoption of a progressive income tax, which would replace the tax revenue lost by prohibition. And there were principled supporters as well, who thought all alcohol consumption was sinful.

"Still, the passionate people only made up a small percentage of the population. The Prohibition Party ran a candidate for president every four years, but it never received more than a few percent of the vote. Neither major party was interested in owning that particular piece of political real estate, and amending the Constitution is a very high hurdle.

"The way they won was that the Anti-Saloon League united them as swing voters. Prohibition wasn't a partisan issue, and wherever candidates for office had differing views on the subject, the prohibitionist candidate could expect an extra bloc of votes. Over the years, they elected representatives at the state and federal levels. The strategy was described as turning minorities into majorities, and in 1916, they achieved a critical mass in Congress to advance what became the Eighteenth Amendment."

"Turning minorities into majorities," Julian echoed, grinning broadly as he held out a fist for Idabee to bump. She stared for a moment, then gingerly touched her fist to his. "Minorities into majorities," he said again.

"Do you see the difference?" Idabee asked him. "The American Union accepted that we'd continue to have a two-party system but refused to play partisan politics. What we do is offer a set of legislative solutions to all the candidates for Congress and try to help them succeed in enacting it, without paying attention to party affiliation. On Monday, you'll see a bit of how we develop the legislation."

Julian shrugged. "I know this is your history, but I don't understand. One, politicians lie whenever their lips are moving. They would always make promises and not keep them. Why was this any different? And two, why wouldn't the American Union just be ignored, like the third parties were?"

"Because this isn't about asking candidates to make promises," Idabee answered. "We craft an actual piece of legislation and give Congress a binary choice: enact it before the election or accept the consequences for refusing."

"And third parties run candidates," Polly continued, "trying to take votes away from the major parties. The American Union is a union of swing voters, trying to give votes to the major parties."

"But if the American Union didn't get what they wanted, there'd be no one to vote for," Julian said. "Why wasn't that the same as just wasting votes with a third party?"

"Because," Polly said patiently, "they pledged to vote together for a Republican or Democrat anyway. That was the insight: the duopoly always wins and swing voters decide which half. If that power isn't wielded, it's wasted."

"But," Julian tried again, frustration creeping into his tone, "you said ranked choice voting wouldn't work because it channeled the votes into the duopoly, but without getting anything for it. Then you said the American Union pledged to vote for the duopoly, even if they don't get their legislation. It's exactly the same thing!"

"It's different because the American Union ignored party affiliation as a matter of principle," Polly answered. "Like what happened in Australia, ranked choice voting just shifts people's third-party votes to their lesser-of-two-evils candidate. Duverger's law still applies."

"No," Idabee contradicted. Both Julian and Polly stared until she explained. "Yes, Polly is correct, but Julian is using two different metrics. He's comparing electing candidates to enacting policy. They are two very different goals."

Polly conceded the point and then offered a summary. "The American Union prepackaged solutions and offered them to all candidates for Congress on the same set of terms. They demonstrated a commitment to voting together, and when candidates were willing to take up the demand for immediate passage, indicating support let them compete to win a decisive bloc of swing votes across the nation."

"Wait," Julian interrupted. "When you say 'demonstrate commitment,' 'take up the demand,' and 'indicate support,' what exactly does that mean?"

Idabee and Polly exchanged looks. "Sorry, I thought you knew," Polly said. "What year did you come from again?" He told her. "Right, an election year.

CHAPTER EIGHT

All Americans—especially candidates for Congress—willing to support the union's demands with their votes had the chance to unite on Muster Day, October 15."

"October 15?" Julian echoed. He looked to Idabee, remembering what she'd just told him about the fifteenth of the month, but waiting for confirmation.

She nodded, reading the question in his eyes. "That's how the American Union de-escalates elections, Julian. It's a fast for peace."

Chapter Nine

"Breathe in," Doctor Raymond Leete commanded. Julian, mildly amused they still hadn't invented a cure for a cold stethoscope, complied. The doctor listened, shifted the position of the metal disc on his bare chest, and repeated the routine twice more before pronouncing him in good health.

Julian was a little hungry after skipping breakfast, but not uncomfortably so, and Ray had kept him occupied all morning with a series of cognitive tests. He identified random objects on flashcards, read lists of various words, and went through a neuropsychological assessment. Some puzzles were entertaining, and others annoying. He worried about his errors, but the doctor confirmed everything was within the normal range for a man of thirty-four.

An electronic tone sounded in the background. Ray cocked his head. "Excuse me a minute," he said, "someone's calling in the parlor." He ducked out, leaving Julian to put his shirt back on, and returned a minute later. "It's actually for you," he explained. "Reverend Shaver would like to talk."

For Julian, it had been just a few days since the charismatic leader had preached a vision of a better future. Reverend Shaver had aged dramatically, his remaining hair now white as snow, but most surprising was that he was a fraction of his former bulk. His frame seemed almost to float inside a charcoal-gray suit.

Julian sank into the couch across from the reverend's projection, waiting to hear what the thin man had to say. Shaver was adjusting his cuffs, but promptly looked up, the expectant look on his weathered face softening into a radiant smile. After a pause, he spoke. "Julian West! It's so good to see you again. Welcome to the tricentennial."

Julian replied in kind and explained seeing the preacher shot was among his last memories. The scar tissue that knotted the left side of the nonagarian's face gave silent witness to the nearly fatal gunshots.

"Without your intervention, I might have been killed all those years ago," Shaver said. "I very nearly was, but you stopped those men from finishing the job. The reason I asked to speak with you is because I'm about to begin a fast—I'm going to give up food for three days. It's a fast for peace, and it has many aspects. One intention that I'm bringing to it, Julian, is atonement, and part of that is directed toward you. Would you, and Dr. Leete, do me the honor of having lunch with me on Wednesday, so I could break my fast with you?"

Julian didn't answer immediately; there was much to unpack in those sentences. Was Shaver asking for his blessing to do this, or was he just informing him? What was Shaver seeking atonement for?

"Of course we could," Ray answered for Julian. "My daughter, Idabee, told him about the fast for peace last night when she started her three days. She's quite the salesperson, apparently, because young West decided to skip his breakfast and lunch today."

"Oh," Shaver replied, then repeated, "Oh! Well, that's great; I look forward to seeing you in person in three days." He held up a small cracker before pushing it into his mouth. "Happy fasting."

"Happy fasting," Julian echoed.

"There's something else I'd like to ask," Shaver continued. "A reporter has been interviewing me for a story about the reparations rally. When she discovered that you'd recently awoken, she asked about getting some pictures of us together. If you're willing, I'll ask her to come by for a few minutes, nothing more."

"I guess that would be okay," Julian said. The nonagenarian looked pleased at his answer. *People will want your perspective. You'll get great publicity.* Idabee had warned him this might happen, but he didn't want to disappoint Reverend Shaver; the man's fame left him a bit starstruck.

What was Shaver's relationship to the American Union, which had sprung up after the rally, addressed the triple evils he'd called out, and that he was now fasting with, even at his advanced age? Julian made an immediately relevant inquiry. "You're doing this for the same reason Idabee is, because of Gandhi?"

"Did she tell you how it relates to the American Union?" Julian shook his head, and the reverend clasped his hands, eyes twinkling, and launched into the story. "On March 15, 1918, in Ahmedabad, India, Gandhi embarked on his first public fast. Tens of thousands of people worked in the textile mills there, and they were trying to form a labor union. A plague had struck the city the previous autumn, and the mill owners offered hazard pay of 70% over the regular wages to keep workers at their machines. By February, they planned to end the practice. The workers, meanwhile, had come to depend on it, especially since prices jumped during the disruption. A pay cut like that seemed disastrous, and they contemplated going on strike.

"In response, the mill owners shut down the factories for two weeks, claiming maintenance, and laid everyone off. The workers pledged they wouldn't return to work without a fair raise of at least 35%. But the owners only offered 20%, which wasn't enough to meet their needs. Softened up by the two-week furlough, many workers considered it because poverty wages and starvation little by little seemed preferable to immediate destitution. Gandhi was a man who accepted poverty willingly, but it wasn't voluntary for them.

"He encouraged the workers to hold out, to stay on strike, until they got the wages they needed. But it was hard. When a man defines himself by his work and is then asked to not work as a matter of principle, it creates a conflict, an internal dissonance. Failing to provide for their families, those workers must have asked themselves: Am I a man?

"When they gathered for a meeting on March 15," Shaver continued, "Gandhi rose to speak. He recognized things were at a tipping point, where they could roll forward into the future or backward into economic injustice. If they gave in, another opportunity to organize in Ahmedabad might not arise for years. Later, Gandhi said, 'It is our duty to strengthen by fasting those who hold the same ideals.' He accepted that duty and announced he wouldn't eat until they all received their raise. Essentially, he was willing to commit the rest of his life to their cause, if that was what it took.

"His fast—technically a hunger strike—inspired them, reinvigorated them. They were a union, and by the third day of Gandhi's fast, they'd been promised a 35% raise. The people of the city always remembered what he'd done for them. Decades later, during World War Two, one hundred twenty thousand people struck for months to protest Gandhi's indefinite detention by the British.

"A fast can be a powerful thing, Julian, because when done with pure intention, it carries moral authority. It's part of the foundation for the American Union for that very reason. As you remember better than most, our nation was struggling for direction fifty years ago. By claiming the moral high ground and holding firm to a commitment to addressing Martin Luther King's triple evils of poverty, racism, and militarism, we offered the people of the United States a sense of purpose, a sense of justice, a sense of what America could be, if only we worked together. Gandhi said that when hundreds of thousands of countrymen fasted together, it ennobled individuals and nations.

"The United States may be a more noble nation, but like all of us, it is still imperfect. By this fast, I hope to atone for an error I made long ago: my misguided contribution to the state of America." Shaver paused to focus his gaze on Julian before continuing. "That you're fasting today feels to me like validation; that you heard the call for peace and rallied to the side of justice. It speaks to your character, Julian. In solidarity, brother, we shall overcome." He clasped his hands together once more.

After a quiet moment, Ray spoke up. "Julian, I think you just had your own personal sermon by Reverend Shaver." The levity broke the tension, and the three men relaxed.

"Thank you for the very thorough explanation," Julian said, feeling a little more comfortable in Shaver's presence.

"Gandhi was quite thorough, too," the preacher said. "One of the reasons he was in that mill town was because he was looking for a spinning wheel, which would become an essential part of the constructive program he developed."

"Constructive program?" Julian echoed.

"It's a strategy like a tripod, where all the legs support each other in holding up the main idea," the preacher replied. "The American Union was modeled on it, addressing social, cultural, and political issues holistically."

Julian nodded, then plunged ahead to the question that he'd been holding back. "But, wasn't Gandhi a racist? I heard he hated black people, called them some African slur."

Shaver laughed—a deep, booming laugh that reverberated through the parlor. Whatever the sound system was in the room, Julian felt a hint of the bass thrum in his chest. After Shaver had regained his composure, he faced Julian, his eyes twinkling as he apologized. "I shouldn't have laughed at your question. Yes, there's a kernel of truth to what you heard. In the late nineteenth century, Gandhi went to South Africa, and yes, he referred to the native blacks by a common term that is most definitely a racial slur today. I had a few character flaws in my twenties, Julian, I don't know about you. But it's a fundamental law of the universe that we can always do better.

"At the time, Gandhi was focused solely on his own community, the Indians who'd mostly arrived in South Africa as indentured workers. But he came to recognize all of humanity was his community—his family—universally and unconditionally. That was the message that drew many black preachers to him in the 1930s and '40s. Do you know what Gandhi said to Reverend Howard Thurman on his Indian sojourn in 1935?" Shaver asked, perhaps rhetorically, since he didn't wait for an answer. "'It may be through the negroes that the unadulterated message of nonviolence will be delivered to the world.'"

Julian's expression must have appeared unpersuaded, because the reverend's eyes narrowed. "If Gandhi were really a racist, don't you think Dr. King would have picked up on it instead of saying he was the person who had the greatest influence on his life?"

"That makes sense," Julian admitted. "But, he wasn't a Christian, right? I'm surprised at how much inspiration you've drawn from him."

CHAPTER NINE

"He was a Hindu," Shaver agreed, "but very accepting of all religions. Gandhi read the Bible when he was a young man and found the *Sermon on the Mount* resonated with him. He saw a parallel with the *Bhagavad Gita*, the ancient Hindu scripture he studied throughout his life.

"Gandhi looked for the best in all religions; he would read from different sacred texts at his prayer meetings. If truth is the pinnacle of the mountain, each religion offers a different path to the top. Of course, he realized that since all religions were written down by fallible men, imperfections were bound to crop up—wrong turns and dead ends along the path. They had to be analyzed critically, combining the principles of the whole with practical observations of how the world actually worked. If there were contradictory parts, they should be ignored. That was why he criticized the Hindu tradition of discrimination against so-called untouchables."

Julian nodded slowly. "That sort of reminds me of something that came up last night, about the American Union staking out principled positions without paying attention to political party."

Shaver grinned. "There is definitely a parallel. The Constitution is America's sacred text, and the Preamble lays out our highest ideals. Congress steered us down some bad paths and abdicated their responsibility to lead, so the American Union reminded people of our constitutional duties and helped us make progress toward the mountaintop."

"And they use a fast to do it? Muster Day?"

"It's one of the parts, yes. Do you know Martin Luther King's *Letter from Birmingham Jail*?" Julian nodded vaguely, and Shaver elaborated, "He laid out four basic steps for any nonviolent campaign: collection of the facts to determine whether injustices exist, negotiation, self-purification, and direct action.

"The American Union, with the people's legislative assembly, spends most of its time on the first step, doing the hard work to determine injustices and crafting specific legislative solutions to address them. Before publishing the final legislative package, though, they negotiate with Congress. And then, on Muster Day, we engage in self-purification—the fast for peace."

"That's October 15?"

"Yes, a few weeks before election day, which is when we take direct action and vote as a bloc."

"The negroes delivering nonviolence to the world," Julian repeated. "Was October 15 chosen as Muster Day because that was when the Black Panther Party was founded?"

The reverend grinned. "I think that was just a coincidence."

There was a pause, and then Julian admitted, "I have to say, I'm surprised at how much weight you've lost since the last time I saw you. How much fasting have you done over the last fifty years?"

The nonagenarian gave a deep laugh. "Julian, this is actually my five hundredth fast for peace."

"Wow!" Julian replied. After a moment's reflection, he added, "That's an impressive number, but I guess ten times a year doesn't sound too bad."

"Once a year is plenty for me," Ray said. "You can count on me come Muster Day." He eyed the other man and informed Julian, "The reverend has completed some longer fasts as well."

Shaver ducked his head modestly. "It's been a long time since I've done a twenty-four-day fast."

"What!" Julian blurted. "Twenty-four days! That's–" Words failed him.

Reverend Shaver cast his eyes upward for a moment, cementing a thought in his mind, and then quoted, "'The fast was first for me and then for all of us in this union. It was a fast for nonviolence and a call to sacrifice.'"

Julian nodded with what he hoped was sagely reverence. "Is that Gandhi?"

"No, but it was one of his students."

"Julian," Ray said quickly. "I think one Sunday sermon from the good reverend is sufficient. He needs to conserve his energy."

Another deep laugh emanated from Shaver. "We'll have more time to talk later, I promise." They said their goodbyes, and as Reverend Shaver prepared to stand, he plucked an item from the loveseat next to him. A light-blue envelope, the color of a robin's egg, appeared in his hand for a second, and then he was gone.

Ray chuckled. "Are you buying this whole fasting thing?" he asked. "Does it make sense to you that just because a century and a half ago Gandhi started a fast to the death on this day, everyone should skip eating on the fifteenth forever after?"

"Well," Julian answered, "I know what America looks like when no one does. From what I've seen of the tricentennial so far, it's hard to argue with the results. Giving up food for a day, or even three, seems like a pretty good deal to get a stable country."

Ray's eyebrow rose. "You're not thinking of trying for all three days, are you?"

"No," Julian replied quickly. "But if Reverend Shaver did twenty-four days, I might stretch mine out a little longer than twenty-four hours. So don't count on me for dinner tonight."

Chapter Ten

In the morning, Julian decided to skip breakfast. He waited for hunger to pounce, to maul him into submission, but the sensation never appeared with any real substance. It left him a bit incredulous, questioning that which he'd never thought to question before.

About noon, Julian was grateful when Ray offered to show him to the room where Idabee's panel would be held. Although reasonably certain he'd have been able to manage on his own, the world of 2076 was different in subtle ways as well as flashy ones, and the former seemed more likely to trip him up. Before leaving the condo, Ray prompted him to put the doall on his wrist.

"Remember the shop we were in the other day?" Ray asked as the elevator descended to their destination. "Buildings this size have a variety of multi-purpose rooms. There are even two with stadium seating; people gather to watch sporting events. The legislative assembly uses a large conference room configuration."

The elevator opened to reveal two young women in their late twenties conversing in the well-lit corridor. "Good afternoon," one acknowledged Julian. Her light brown scalp gleamed, as did the bright white teeth her smile exposed. She and her companion turned and moved purposefully away from them, revealing a narrow strip of black hair running from the top of her head to the nape of her neck, tightly woven and falling halfway down her back.

Ray tapped the information panel next to the elevator, gathered his bearings, and pointed Julian in the direction the women had gone. The

CHAPTER TEN

hallway was wider than the shopping level had been, and grand entryways featured double doors flanked by information screens. After a short walk, Ray pulled open a door and motioned Julian inside.

The rectangular room was filled with indirect lighting and dominated by a large U-shaped conference table a car's length inside. About two dozen chairs ringed the outside, and at the open end of the U closest to them, a small table and two seats were set. To both the left and right of the doors they had just entered, a dozen chairs in two rows provided an opportunity for an audience to sit and observe.

What was in those chairs, however, was disconcerting. The people occupying them were overlapped, their holographic projections stacked three and four deep. Simultaneously, he heard multiple conversations, words mixing unrecognizably. "Ray," he tried to whisper, "What's real here?" His eyes darted back and forth between objects and people, attempting to see reality behind the curtain of technology.

"It's like the parlor," his host explained. "In general, physical objects resting on the floor are real. There's a handful of standard configurations, so each person in their own room can interact with the tables and chairs in precise locations. Most everything on the walls and ceiling is a projection." Ray strolled to the seat nearest to him and tapped it with his foot. "See? Real. You can sit here if you like."

Three faces looked up from the chair. Two wore masks, reminding Julian of the pandemic, and their expressions ranged from amusement to annoyance. One lifted a hand to his mouth, the tips of all five fingers pressed together. The avatar's fingers separated simultaneously, and the mask vanished. "We can hear you," a voice said.

Julian blinked. "That wasn't real?"

Ray apologized for the intrusion before explaining to Julian. "Holograms can be manipulated in real time. When someone is muted, the default is to give them privacy with a mask." His index finger made an X across his mouth. "This gesture is used to mute yourself, and this"—he repeated the starburst motion they'd just witnessed—"is to unmute."

The room bustled with mask-wearing people, and Julian shook his head.

"I remember hearing about how people panicked when they saw the first motion pictures: trains headed at the screen, ocean waves moving toward them, that sort of thing. I suddenly have more empathy for them."

Ray chuckled. "You'll get used to it."

Near the U-shaped conference table, Idabee waved hello. She was dressed in a simple, cream-colored suit and chatting with the two women from outside the elevator. If he hadn't just seen the pair, Julian marveled, he would never have guessed they were anything other than digital projections.

"Hi, Julian, good to see you again," Idabee said before introducing Andrea Nussbaum, who'd spoken outside the elevator, and her wife, Shirley, a tall white woman with short cropped hair. "How was your fast?"

He smiled back. "Still going! You and Reverend Shaver inspired me to give it another day."

Idabee studied him for a moment before responding. "Great! I'm glad you could be here; it's the deadline for committees to make recommendations on policy proposals for inclusion in this year's legislation. The full committee is meeting later in another room, but first I'm going to moderate an investigative panel on reviewing electric rates."

Ray mimed a yawn. "What does that gesture do?" Julian wondered out loud.

"It indicates to the speaker that you're not interested in their topic of conversation," Ray said, pleased his guest had taken the bait for his dad joke. Julian joined the three women in a short laugh. "I'm going to head back upstairs and let you all enjoy splashing around in the legislative minutia." Ray touched his hands together, nodded, and walked away.

They watched him go, and Julian looked around the room, taking it all in as he examined the faces of older black women. He had no serious expectation of spotting Edith Bartlett in the crowd or real confidence in recognizing her after all these years, but whatever the odds, they were a non-zero number.

Idabee was scratching her ear when he glanced back. "Are you wearing a doall?" he asked. The device was visible on both Andrea and Shirley, but

CHAPTER TEN

Idabee's wrist—indeed, every other wrist he could see—was bare.

Momentarily puzzled, Idabee answered his question by pinching her left wrist. A digital artifact squirmed beneath her fingers, the holographic technology toggling between competing impulses to display what she was holding and to edit out the device. "Yep! If you see one on somebody, you know they're physically present. So don't walk through them, or try to sit on them."

"Sounds like good advice," he agreed.

"I need to set things up now," Idabee said, "but the Nussbaums offered to answer any questions you have." She excused herself and began making her way around the conference table, greeting other people as she did so.

After finding three seats in the front row, Julian asked the women if they were delegates. "I am," Andrea replied, "but I'm not seated. We keep an eye on the General Welfare committee; that's where I'll ask to be assigned when I win one. I'm building up my support with a small show about the assembly, and this is one of the proposals I've been keeping an eye on."

The crack of a gavel snapped the room to attention. Idabee was efficient; from the head of the conference table, she called the meeting to order, informed the audience they'd been muted, offered a two-sentence summary of the proposal, and recognized a Delegate Prentiss for a motion.

"Delegate Leete likes to keep things moving," Andrea said. She spoke in a normal voice, which Julian instinctively thought was disrespectful to the people around them. Then he realized since they were muted, no one not physically present could hear them.

Delegate Prentiss was a middle-aged woman who was ready for the attention. "I move PP-76-2832 be recommended for inclusion, and I'd like to speak to my motion." Idabee called for and found a second, then recognized Prentiss to continue. "This proposal would review and reorganize the auction process for supplemental electricity contracts. The electrical supply board was created in 2048 on the principle that ensuring residential access to a clean and constant supply of electricity was fulfilling our duty to promote the general welfare."

As the delegate continued to speak, Shirley offered her commentary.

83

"The committee killed this proposal a few years ago. We think it has a better chance of making it into the American Union's legislative package this year."

"And then on Muster Day, you try to pressure Congress to pass the whole thing? How many Americans actually fast for that?" Julian asked.

Andrea shrugged. "Unless the year's package is especially controversial, about 20% to 25%." Julian looked surprised, so she continued, "Were you expecting it to be higher or lower?"

"I'm not sure." He calculated. "Is that like one hundred million Americans? That sounds insane!"

Andea chuckled. "And in the ballot box, we somehow overpower all the abstainers. Two billion Muslims fast each year for the month of Ramadan, you know."

"That's only on Muster Day," Shirley reminded him. "I think there's only a handful of registered delegates in this building. Believe it or not, most people aren't that interested in the nuts and bolts of crafting legislative policy."

"I believe it," he said. Delegate Prentis was explaining the details and deficiencies of the current bidding process for supplemental electricity. "I imagine it gets boring pretty quick."

Andrea shrugged. "As a civic institution, the American Union doesn't have to have the entire community involved to make a difference, just the critical mass of people willing to put in the effort," she said. "You're a sleeper from before the American Union, right? I thought democracy was breaking down."

"Representative democracy left a lot of people unrepresented," he conceded. "But not everyone's in the American Union, right? So aren't they still unrepresented?"

"Not at all," she said. "Every citizen has the representation the Constitution guarantees them. They're free to contact their members of Congress and try to sway them. But in a nation of almost five hundred million people, individual voters generally aren't very influential. That's why we unionized. If people would also like to be represented by the American

CHAPTER TEN

Union, it's cheap to join. We're pretty effective, obviously."

"Obviously," he echoed, and the women laughed out loud, but no one else heard them. It was almost voyeuristic, watching this hearing in person while remaining unobserved.

Delegate Prentiss delivered her closing argument. "In the 1930s, Congress built the Tennessee Valley Authority to control flooding in the region, and the systems of dams also generated electricity. While there were a variety of essential services where government was the provider of last resort, the TVA helped establish the principle that government did not have to be the competitor of last resort. The government-managed utility served as a check on the private suppliers because we had good data on what the actual costs of electrical production were.

"We have similar data today, and we're overpaying. This proposal will address that. Access to electricity promotes the general welfare; therefore I urge the delegates to support the motion."

"If adopted," Idabee asked, "are there any witnesses you'd like to request testimony from?"

"Yes," Prentiss replied, reading from a list. "The chair of the Electrical Supply Board or their designee, a representative from the Energy Producers Association, and an associate from the Institute of Economic Game Theory."

"Thank you," Idabee said, "the motion before the committee is recommended for inclusion. Discussion?" An elderly gentleman signaled for Idabee's attention, and she recognized him. "Delegate Eisenhower."

"Thank you, Madam Moderator," he began. "I'm going to vote against inclusion this year. The committee had an almost identical proposal a year or two ago, and it was turned down in the second session for two reasons. First, because the revised regulations we came up with didn't really ensure better competition, they just reduced the barriers for entry. Second, it's a small problem. Yes, it's possible to squeeze more efficiency out of the system, but the same effort could promote the general welfare in greater ways elsewhere. We should tackle broader issues, not narrow ones."

Prentiss signaled for Idabee's attention. "I thank the delegate from Ohio for raising these concerns," she said smoothly. "He is correct that a similar proposal was voted down two years ago, but because that work was already done, we can build on it this time. The qualified witness from the Institute of Economic Game Theory was requested specifically to ensure better competition. And I disagree with the delegate's appeal to scarcity; inclusion of this policy does not diminish any of the others."

A few other members had questions; one delegate suggested requesting testimony from bidders who had been rejected. Prentiss accepted it as a friendly amendment to her list. After several minutes of debate, Idabee brought it to an end. "The question before the panel is a recommendation of inclusion for PP-76-2832; please indicate yes, no, or abstain."

In the middle of the room, a large holographic display materialized. The names of two dozen delegates were listed, and as voting commenced, green highlights began to appear, along with a few reds and yellows. Andrea aimed her doall at the board as they continued to change colors, watching an image on the face of the smartwatch.

"Investigative panels survey their members for instant results," Shirley explained. "If you stick around for the full policy committee, they use asynchronous voting—everyone has twenty-four hours to cast their vote."

"I'd have to wait a day to find out the result?"

"Mr. West, one of the things the fast for peace helps us practice is delayed gratification," Shirley chided him gently. "Yes, you'd have to wait twenty-four hours, and it's the same for the full assembly."

"Well, I'm on my first fast," Julian said lightly, "so I'm still working on developing my patience. But I'm sure it'll get easier." The greens had a clear majority, and the display vanished as quickly as it had appeared. One name had been highlighted in blue, and Julian made a mental note to ask Idabee about it later.

"Oh, there are still plenty of impatient people. Sometimes it takes a day for votes on these small panels to work their way up as public records," Andrea said, peering at the image she'd recorded. "Now I've got a scoop for my show."

After announcing the vote total and offering a few concluding remarks,

CHAPTER TEN

Idabee gaveled the meeting to an end. Julian turned to see the mad rush of people toward the exit. Avatars overlapped and shapes commingled as all the individuals moved unobstructed through the virtual crowd. As each touched the door, they disappeared.

Julian waited patiently with the Nussbaums as Idabee worked her way toward them, thanking various delegates along the way. "If you're interested in seeing the full assembly in session on Friday, you two are welcome to come over to our apartment. We're on the thirty-first floor," Shirley said, repeating the suggestion when Idabee arrived.

"You're all still muted," she told the trio.

Julian made the starburst gesture. "Can you hear me now?"

Idabee gave him a thumbs-up as Shirley repeated the invitation a third time. "Always nice to share a session day with a fellow delegate," Idabee said as Julian nodded agreement. "We'll see you Friday."

The Nussbaums rose to make their exit, and Idabee slid into the empty seat next to Julian, passing through Shirley as she did so. "What did you think?" she asked him.

"Interesting," he said diplomatically, "but I have a bit of a headache."

Idabee touched her hands together and ducked her head in admiration. "You're doing quite well with your first fast; I'm impressed."

"Thanks," he said. "I could eat, but I'm not hungry. Too much to see and learn."

"A word of warning on your fast, Mr. West," Andrea said. "If you stand up and feel faint or lightheaded, take a knee until it passes. Your body really wants adequate blood pressure in your brain, and if the only way it can do that is to lay you out flat on the floor, it will."

Idabee nodded. "Listen to your body, Julian, that's all. I've never fainted, but I've heard of it happening." He nodded soberly to the women, appreciative of the advice, and thanked the Nussbaums for their company as they left.

Julian looked around the room; it was much calmer than when he'd first walked in. "How did you end up working on this?" he asked Idabee.

She scratched her ear. "I joined the American Union as a teenager and then became an organizer and delegate for a few years. After the last election, I was seated in the legislative assembly."

"Power to the people," Julian grinned, lifting a fist for her to bump. He immediately realized his mistake.

"Power to the peaceful," Idabee echoed. "The Nussbaums are nice, aren't they? Andrea interviewed me for her show last year. Did you have more questions?"

She smiled encouragingly, prompting him to ask, "What's the agenda for the next session?"

The sigh Idabee released before answering was seasoned with a dash of frustration. "The full committee is meeting to discuss and vote on policy proposals recommended for inclusion—I know there's at least twenty that have to be dealt with today, including mine, because of the deadline. More than a thousand were assigned to our committee, but most are lumped into one motion and killed. Members throw some wacky ideas out there. It's going to take at least three hours."

"You have my sympathy," Julian said sincerely. "Will Delegate Eisenhower try to challenge the policy again?"

"Probably," Idabee replied. "He used to work for one of the energy companies that's doing pretty well under the current system. I've already told Delegate Prentiss to be ready to answer."

A wave of outrage washed over Julian, then receded. "How does the American Union deal with conflicts of interest?" he asked neutrally.

"Julian, what's the conflict of interest you see?"

"Advocating for a former employer seems corrupt; you feel me?"

"Why? The facts spoke for themselves, and the policy was recommended. He has expertise on the subject matter; I specifically asked for him on the panel. And the reason we know about his former employer is because he disclosed it."

"Still," he pressed, "the corruption in Congress was out of control; corporations were buying influence with campaign contributions. They got their money's worth—like the pharmaceutical companies spending hundreds of millions lobbying Congress each year and getting billions in extra profits. Why doesn't the same thing happen now?"

"Well, a couple reasons," Idabee said. "First, there are so many delegates, it would be pretty tricky to bribe us all. And since we're essentially volunteers, we're not really in it for the money in the first place." She flashed a quick grin. "Since the American Union has dues, you could even say we're paying for the privilege of being here. People who do things they're passionate about generally want to see them done well. Last, of course, if the process looked corrupt, Congress can always veto our legislation."

"And what happens then?" Julian asked. "You knock them out of office?"

"Maybe," Idabee said. "There was a package a decade or so ago—'63, I think—that Congress refused to enact. Every member of Congress faced a primary challenge, and lots of them lost. The assembly negotiated the removal of a few provisions, and when the package went back to Congress in the general election, it passed."

Julian considered this for a moment. "Did the members who'd vetoed it get reelected?"

"If they helped put it on the president's desk before the election, of course. The primary purpose of running challengers isn't to get them elected, but to build the necessary leverage for legislative action. Because if you're not actually setting policy, then what's the purpose of elected office?"

"Uh..." Julian floundered, "I don't know."

"In your day, it had other perks, right? Like fame and prestige, and lucrative offers for those looking for money. But Congress wasn't legislating. The American Union put their focus on getting it done."

"Like the Greeks with the Trojan horse," Julian said, remembering Stella Freedom's analogy.

"Right. The real goal is to pass good legislation, so an election challenge is about persuading the incumbent to vote for the legislative package. It's a strategy that relies on principled nonviolence."

"How exactly does it do that?"

"Uh..." It was Idabee's turn to flounder. "I'm not exactly sure; I was quoting something I read. I think it has to do with creating win-win scenarios." She appeared to ponder the question, but the veneer of nonchalance made him wonder if she had intentionally steered the conversation to this point. "I'd love to introduce you to someone who can answer the philosophical stuff."

"Okay," Julian agreed. "You try and get candidates to fast for peace instead of fighting over the election."

"Cooperative democracy, Julian. Just because it's possible to fight over things doesn't mean it's the best option." She smiled at him. "Of course, somewhere along the line, there has to be people splashing around in legislative minutiae."

"And you volunteered."

The smile widened. "I did."

Julian returned it, and their eyes held for a moment. Was he seeing something more in her gaze? He looked away from the younger woman.

A white rectangle suddenly materialized in the middle of the room, which Julian turned to read. In large block letters, it announced that the room would close in ninety seconds. A timer began to count down: eighty-nine, eighty-eight. "What does that mean?" he asked. "We're getting kicked out?"

"That's our cue," she agreed, rising from her chair. "Thanks for coming, Julian. I hope the rest of your fast goes well."

"I thought I'd feel hungrier, you know?" he said. When he stood up, tiny stars danced in front of him, and he quickly sat down again.

"Julian? Are you okay?" Idabee said with concern.

"I'm fine," he said defensively. "I'm fine. You go on ahead."

"If you need help, I can call my father," she offered.

"I don't need help," he said firmly. "I was just lightheaded for a second; it's fine. I'll see you Friday, okay? Go ahead." Idabee looked around. There were still a dozen people in the room, casually working their way toward the door with a minute left on the countdown. "Go on," he repeated.

Idabee bit her lip and walked four paces toward the door before hesitating. Julian stood up again, left arm gripping the back of the chair for support while his right hand sketched a wave. "I'm fine," he repeated. He was a touch lightheaded, but it was no longer concerning. He waved goodbye again. She took the hint, touched the exit, and disappeared.

CHAPTER TEN

There were still forty seconds left on the timer as Julian released the chair. Now that the moment was past, he thought of other times he'd become lightheaded after standing up suddenly. He took one more survey of the room, wondering what it would look like after the timer reached zero.

"Julian West," said a voice from the row of seats along the back wall, snagging his attention. An older white man, neatly dressed, moved toward him.

"Do I know you?" Julian asked, studying the contours of the man's weathered face. He was clean-shaven, bald on top, with wispy gray hair. Julian tried to picture a younger version but couldn't match it with anything in his memory.

The man's grin showed too many teeth. "We have unresolved business."

"What's that?" Julian asked distractedly, glancing at the few seconds remaining on the timer.

"You really don't remember?" The man's blue eyes flashed annoyance as he took a deep breath, preparing to speak. "You–"

With an audible snap, the mysterious figure disappeared. The rearmost row of lights in the room banged out, then the next, and the next. Before the darkness could engulf him, Julian pushed against the door and plunged out into the hallway.

Chapter Eleven

Although no alarm woke him, Julian still felt tired when he opened his eyes the next morning. Sitting up took extra effort, and he realized he was ready for breakfast—to literally break his fast. There was a tiny twist of desire to return to bed, and he toyed with it for a moment before rising to his feet, beckoned by the morning sun streaming in through the windows. This brave new world was calling.

Two days without food! A week ago—subjectively speaking, of course—he'd have been shocked by the idea of giving up eating on purpose. Having accepted a spontaneous challenge, having surpassed his goal twice over, any temporary discomfort was offset by pride in his achievement. It was a prize of knowledge and ability that could never be taken from him.

After showering, he selected clothes appropriate for the day and padded out to find Ray in the kitchen. "Happy Saint Patrick's Day," Julian greeted him, radiating a verdant green from the shirt he'd chosen from Lord Hoot's. "Or is that not a thing in 2076?" His host, he was disappointed but not surprised to see, wore no green.

Setting aside the tablet he was reading from, Ray rose from his seat. "Good morning," he said. "Still on for breakfast?"

Julian patted his stomach. "I'm ready to eat," he said.

Ray motioned him over to the counter. "Let me show you the options," he said. Tapping at a spot on the wall, a handful of foods sprang to life in colorful holograms. "This is what the kitchen has this morning, although if you want something else, we can get the ingredients and cook."

"Corned beef hash," said Julian, pointing. "Everyone's Irish today. With

CHAPTER ELEVEN

eggs?"

Ray scratched his chin. "I remember St. Patrick's Day from when I was a kid," he said, "wearing green and all that. You might be right, though, because that's not usually on the menu." He made a few more taps. "Should be up in a few minutes."

Julian fixed himself a cup of coffee with cream and sugar and stood by the island. "You mentioned the other night at dinner that you had some whiskey on hand. How about breaking it out for St. Patrick's Day?"

Ray considered the idea for a moment, then opened a cabinet. "Well, as your doctor, I'm certainly not recommending this," he said, lifting out a glass bottle filled with amber liquid. "But it's your choice. There was a note in your file: you had a non-zero blood alcohol content when you were placed into the medical coma." He shrugged and set it on the counter. "In case you had cravings, I thought it best to have some medicinal stock on hand."

There was a soft chime. Julian's mouth began to water as Ray slid a panel open and removed a metal tray with his breakfast. "That smells really good," he said.

"Can I advise you to go slow?" Ray asked.

Julian picked up his fork and maneuvered both eggs and hash onto it, then spoke. "I don't know what the traditions are for breaking a fast. But since Reverend Shaver asked if he could end his with me, there must be a non-zero amount of significance to it." He smiled inwardly at working the new phrase into conversation. "Anyway," he toasted with his fork, "thank you for waking me up in 2076. It's pretty amazing so far."

His mouth exploded with flavor. The silky-smooth scrambled eggs blended with the crisply fried corned beef hash, their tastes forming a divine combination that lingered on his tongue afterward. Julian closed his eyes and grinned.

"Sixty-three hours," he heard Ray observe. "My compliments."

"Thank you," he replied. "I'd always heard breakfast was the most important meal of the day; it never occurred to me I could skip a couple of days and still feel good." He remembered what Idabee had told him about the fast. "Ray, you said you usually only fast for Muster Day, for the American Union?"

The older man nodded. "I can fast. I just don't have any interest in doing it regularly."

"You're a doctor; is it bad for your health?"

"No, just the opposite, really," he said, "in moderation." The last two words were emphasized. Julian waited for him to continue, taking another bite. "I get it; it's good for our bodies to take a break from digestion now and then, and when you get into autophagy, your body scavenges protein buildups, doing a deep clean you don't really get any other way. There are benefits for your heart and brain, and it improves your insulin sensitivity. And I appreciate it's easier to keep up the habit by doing it as a group, and I mostly approve of the changes the fast for peace has brought about. Don't get me wrong—it's a good thing overall, but just not really for me."

"You've never had any interest in being a delegate to the people's assembly?"

Ray shrugged. "It crossed my mind once or twice when I didn't like their proposal and thought I could do better. I don't know what you saw with Idabee, but while they do their due diligence, it's not a perfect system."

"Can you give me an example?"

"About a dozen years ago, the legislative package was going to bring back prohibition. The backers claimed it was sinful or something. Muster Day had the lowest participation rate in a generation. Congress didn't pass it, and while some challengers supported it, there was a bit of a backlash. Prohibition cost a lot of lives; we don't need to try that experiment again."

Julian brought the whiskey bottle over to the table. "I'm glad they didn't succeed; should we make our coffee Irish this morning?"

The doctor fixed his attention on his patient. "Julian, this seems important to you, and I'm curious why. But, to answer your question, I decided last week I was willing to have a drink, singular"—he held up his index finger for clarity—"with you if needed. While I don't think it's needed, I'm still amenable to sharing the experience with you."

There was a brief pause, then Julian responded simply, "Cool." He

CHAPTER ELEVEN

uncapped the bottle, added a generous slug to his cup, and extended the neck toward the other man. Ray slid his own cup forward and received an abundant portion in return. Julian lifted his mug and held it halfway across the table. "To new friends," he said.

"To new friends," Ray repeated, and their cups clinked before the men drank. The doctor shuddered a bit. "I don't really see the appeal of a liquid carcinogen."

"A what?"

"Alcohol has been a known carcinogen for a century," the doctor explained. "We have some pretty solid cancer-fighting regimes these days, but why take extra chances?"

Julian sipped from his cup again, feeling it burn as it tumbled down his throat. "What better way to enjoy breakfast today than with a little Irish spirit?"

Ray grinned. "I'm not persuaded, sorry. But then I was never bombarded with alcohol advertising the way you were. The truth is right there in the root word of intoxicated." Julian puzzled this out, then frowned at the conclusion. "It's literally poison. But a little bit won't kill us."

"I can't believe they tried to bring alcohol prohibition back! Glad to hear you didn't support it." Julian took another bite of his food. The flavor was duller now, but he was enjoying the simple sensation of eating again after two days.

"Not just alcohol prohibition," Ray clarified. "Drug prohibition, too."

Julian froze with his fork in midair. "America got rid of the war on drugs?" Ray nodded. "Stella said addressing racism was part of the moral crusade; I'm glad that meant criminal justice reform. Especially the war on drugs."

"I don't think it was a criminal justice issue as much as a health issue," Ray said. "Drugs and alcohol were killing hundreds of thousands of people every year in this country. Remember how Idabee talked about nonary logic? Since trying to restrict the supply didn't work, it made more sense to address the demand."

Julian nodded. "You're right that it was bad; the pandemic really escalated things. But you're wrong that prohibition was a health issue," he said forcefully. "Richard Nixon started the war on drugs to appeal to racists."

"I don't know about that," Ray backpedaled.

"How do you not know?" Julian asked. "You know about slavery? About Jim Crow? The drug war was part of the new Jim Crow; there was a book about it."[4]

Julian wanted to be angry that the details of racial injustice in his time had been forgotten, but the feeling of peace his fast had cultivated made it hard for the sentiment to take root. The scrap of emotion floated away like a balloon escaping a child's grasp. Getting upset wasn't going to change the fact that Ray didn't know.

"You know how many millions of black men were sucked into the criminal justice system, ripped away from our families, from our lives, because of the drug war?" Julian continued. "It was a system of control to keep us down. They couldn't discriminate because of the color of our skin, but an arrest record or conviction was a scarlet letter. It made it okay to turn us away from jobs, for apartments, for all sorts of things.

"The war on drugs was a war on us, brother," Julian said, frustration leaking into his voice as his pulse raced. "How do you not know that?"

Ray held his gaze for a moment before responding. "Because the war has been over for a long time, brother. Peace."

After a brief moment, Julian flashed a grin. "Sorry. I just…" he gestured with his fork for a moment, then took another bite.

"No need to apologize," Ray said lightly. "I vaguely know how things were back then, but you lived it. I'm happy to listen if you want to talk."

"Not really," Julian said instinctively, but then began. "I spent a little time in prison. After, finding a regular job was harder, you feel me? I'd check that little box on my application that said I had a record and never hear anything back. Waking up here in the tricentennial is the best break I've

---

[4] In *The New Jim Crow: Mass Incarceration in the Age of Colorblindness* (2010), Michelle Alexander concludes: "If we become serious about dismantling the system of mass incarceration, we must end the War on Drugs. There is no way around it."

CHAPTER ELEVEN

had in a long time. I'll take an American Union Job."

"Now you have one," Ray replied.

"Hey, do those health benefits include dental?" Julian asked. "I've had this tooth bugging me for a while."

The doctor nodded. "As soon as they get your Treasury account set up, I'll show you how to make an appointment." Julian smiled with real pleasure and took another bite of his breakfast.

"As far back as I can remember," Ray explained, "recreational drugs have been legal, and the FDA—the Food and Drug Administration—sets standards for purity and labeling. There's a national sales tax, and states can add their own, too. If they want to essentially stop recreational sales, they can set it at 1,000%, but there's no tax on medical use, so doctors can prescribe them if it's appropriate."

"As far back as I can remember," Julian countered, "the government was pushing an anti-drug message, although states were legalizing marijuana. Oregon, too, tried decriminalizing personal use of all recreational drugs. I read four out of five Americans thought the drug war was a failure, so I guess you could predict the end was coming, but I didn't.

"From what I've seen, a lot of drug use is self-medication. The pandemic and the lockdowns stressed everyone out. Heroin overdoses spiked because it could be cut with fentanyl, a stronger opioid, and people wouldn't know what they were getting until it was too late." He looked away, running some mental calculations. "I knew a few people who died."

Ray nodded sympathetically. "Not that it helps now, but there's treatment on demand for anyone who wants it. The sales tax funds it." He turned the bottle and pointed to a place on the label. "People can connect any time."

"But once someone gets hooked, it's hard to stop."

"There was a study they did in Canada with rats that they taught us about in medical school," Ray said. "They kept them in little cages and gave them two water bottles. One was laced with morphine, and pretty soon, that was the only one the rats would drink."

"Sounds about right," Julian agreed. "Cages suck."

"But that wasn't the experiment," Ray chuckled. "Then, they moved them from little cages into an open space two hundred times bigger—a rat park. There were all sorts of things to do: wheels to run on, toys to play with, other rats to fool around with. Suddenly, their miserable lives weren't so miserable. When they had the same choice between the two bottles, you know what they drank? Plain water."

The doctor leaned forward for emphasis. "These rats put themselves through withdrawal voluntarily. Because when they had happier, more meaningful lives, drug use just wasn't appealing."

Julian nodded understanding. "So you can just order what you want and they'll send it up on one of these trays?"

"No, not here," Ray replied. "Part of Towers' policy is practicing right livelihood in our store. No transfers of alcohol or drugs; nothing inherently harmful. I made a trip to a physical store to buy the bottle."

"That seems restrictive," Julian said, "but it's better than my time." He gave a short laugh. "Some of the rules around public housing were pretty crazy. There were seniors who got kicked out of their homes because a grandkid used drugs."

Ray stared. "Were the grandparents involved? Collective punishment for drug use can't possibly be justice."

"There wasn't anything just about the war on drugs," Julian agreed. "But the Supreme Court said it was okay. Do you still have civil asset forfeiture?"

Ray repeated the words individually, then confessed, "I don't think I know what that is."

"It's when the police confiscate your stuff," Julian explained, "because they claim it's connected to a crime. Cash, cars, houses, pretty much anything—they'd be able to keep your property unless you could prove it was innocent. They were seizing more property each year than was straight-up stolen during burglaries."

"I've never heard of that. Didn't a person have to be convicted?" Julian shook his head. "I don't think we still do that."

"How about no-knock warrants?"

Again, Ray repeated the unfamiliar words. "How did the police let the person know they were serving a warrant without knocking? I'm almost afraid to ask."

Julian slammed his hand down on the table. "Bam! Smash the door and charge inside."

"Sounds like a good way for people to get hurt," Ray said, shaking his head. "But how could that be legal?"

"Lots of people got hurt," Julian verified. "In any drug case, the Supreme Court said police only had to wait fifteen seconds after knocking before breaking through a door, just in case evidence was being destroyed." Ray looked skeptical. "Police departments all around the country had these SWAT teams, special weapons and, uh, I forget what T stood for. A lot of their gear was military surplus."

"Was crime really that bad that cities bought military surplus?"

Julian snorted. "They didn't buy it; the military gave it away for free."

"Why would they do that?"

"I told you, the war on drugs was a war on us. Don't you know?" Julian demanded. In the silence that followed, a deep gastric rumble was heard. Julian stood suddenly, his expression pained. "I'll be back," he said, speed-walking purposefully toward the bathroom.

When Julian eventually returned, his host was reading his tablet intently, his face somber, his cup empty.

"Well, Doc, my digestive system is up and running again," Julian announced cheerfully. "That was the first time I ever used a bidet. Not bad."

"Seventy-five million," Ray said, waving his tablet, although Julian couldn't see the text. "That's how many people were arrested during the war on drugs. It's insane. Yes, you were right; black men especially were hit the hardest—more arrests, longer sentences, something called the crack cocaine disparity?"

"I was thinking about what Stella Freedom said the other night," Julian replied. "All those Supreme Court decisions, all those laws and rules, the millions of arrests, and all those deaths; it goes back to Congress. Congress sets national policy." He looked at Ray. "Crowdsourcing the process with that people's legislative assembly is really something."

Ray nodded. "The American Union encourages us to look out for each other."

"Is that why your building won't sell you drugs and alcohol?"

"When you talk with Professor Carlton, ask him about voluntary temperance," Ray replied. "The American Union doesn't run this building, but it is operated cooperatively. Everyone spends a few hours a week helping things go smoothly. Not dealing with intoxicants means no one has to violate their ethics."

Julian tilted his head, pondering. "When you said the kitchen had different things prepared this morning, do you mean your neighbors did the cooking?"

"To a certain extent," Ray said. "Some is automated or preprepared. But yes, there's human effort behind much of it; your eggs might have been under a chicken this morning. I'm going to put in a few hours after dinner. I'll probably be on dish duty."

"But why?" Julian asked.

"Why is it good for people to get out of their four walls and interact with others on a regular basis? Didn't we talk about that a little while ago?"

"Well... couldn't it all be automated?"

Ray shrugged. "Most of it is; I'll probably be loading the dishwasher. You can't be missing the point, Julian. Human interactions, connections, relationships—those are the things that add depth to our lives. River Place Towers facilitates relationship building; I work with the same people all the time. We're organized into twenty cohorts of about sixty residents each."

"But you already have a job at the hospital."

"Julian, this isn't employment, but it's still work. When I'm separating out food waste tonight for the compost and the chickens, that's valuable work. When Mr. and Mrs. Yang share stories about what their great-grandkids are doing, my listening has value to them. When I tell them about how my week is going, I'm adding strength to the relationships that hold this building together."

Julian shook his head, then stood again, picking up his tray and nearly

CHAPTER ELEVEN

empty plate. "What do I do with this?" he asked.

Ray pointed to the sliding door above the counter. "Put it back in there," he said. "The chickens will enjoy the scraps." Julian slipped open the wall panel that his breakfast had emerged from and placed the tray on the conveyor belt inside. When he closed the panel, there was a faint whoosh. Curious, Julian reopened it to see that the tray was gone. "Neat."

Ray was glancing at his tablet again. "Did you know there were more blacks in the correctional system fifty years ago than enslaved people at the time of the Civil War?"

"Yes."

"That America had the largest prison population of any nation?" Julian nodded. "That blacks received 20% longer prison sentences on average?"

"I told you, it was a war on us," Julian replied.

"The Constitution says we're supposed to establish justice," Ray observed, his expression troubled. "How did we get so off track?" He reached for the bottle and uncapped it.

Chapter Twelve

Quite pleasantly buzzed, Julian found himself alone in the kitchen a few hours later, mindlessly flipping through the holographic menu. He craved something salty and greasy—preferably deep-fried—to sate his hunger. None of the healthy options appealed to him.

Ray's strategy to limit himself to a single drink hadn't gone as planned. After expanding on the deficiencies of the criminal justice system in Julian's time, the men spent the rest of the morning trading stories of love and loss. As they worked on the whiskey, Ray offered up a rant about his marriage to Idabee's mother, which concluded when their daughter was ten, confessed an on-again, off-again relationship with the historian Stella Freedom, and a short, passionate fling with Teara Harper.

Julian, still coming to terms with his new surroundings, found himself complaining about wrongs many decades in the past. He vented about his own ex-wife and described his frustration with the reticent doctors who ostensibly treated his parents during the COVID-19 pandemic. Each tale required another toast, another portion of the intoxicating liquid. When the bottle was well dented, his host announced he was going to lie down for a while, staggering toward his bedroom and leaving Julian alone.

After puttering around in his room for an hour, Julian realized he was hungry and returned to the kitchen. Maybe he was in the mood for something sweet? Swaying slightly as he overcompensated for the holographic swipes, Julian wondered what Edith Bartlett might be doing now. Did she still have the picture they'd taken together? Recalling her smiling at him, he whispered, "Reparations now."

CHAPTER TWELVE

Perhaps when she was drinking with her friends, she told the story of Julian West as the one who got away. If she were alive, she would be in her eighties, unless she had utilized cryonics to skip some decades like him? He refused to ask Ray for help finding Edith, not after his first request had been so casually dismissed.

There was a noise in the hallway, and he turned. It was Idabee. "Hi, Julian," she said, strolling into the kitchen with a broad smile. "I thought I'd stop by and see how your fast went." There was a subtle floral pattern to the earth-toned maxi dress she wore, but the bone-white hoop earrings caught his attention.

Her spontaneous appearance required shifting mental gears before he could respond. Julian began to explain he'd had breakfast with her father that morning to break it, but when Idabee approached, her eyes glazed over and her nostrils flared. "Have you been drinking?"

Recalling the explanation he'd given Edith the morning of the reparations rally, Julian spread his arms to fully display his green shirt. "It's St. Patrick's Day," he said jovially.

She was less than impressed. Falling silent, Idabee swept the folds of her dress underneath her as she settled into a chair at the table, her gaze resting on the half-empty bottle of whiskey. "Are you still fasting?" Julian asked, continuing to swipe through the menu. Ordering food for them would demonstrate his growing proficiency in the tricentennial.

Idabee made a noncommittal noise, then explained, "Fasting until tomorrow; I already have plans with friends for an early lunch."

He stood there for a moment, frustrated with her for showing up randomly. "Aren't you hungry?" Julian asked.

There was a brief pause, but her desire to educate and inform won out over whatever disappointment she was feeling. "Do you know anything about biology, Julian?" Without waiting for an answer, Idabee continued, "For the first couple days of a fast, your body just runs on the last meal you've had. But around day three, your body switches over to burning fat, which is literally stored energy. That's where I'm at; I got some euphoria and extra pep in my step a few hours ago."

"But aren't you hungry?" he repeated.

"Sometimes," she admitted. "But it comes in waves, then recedes after a little while. Hunger doesn't necessarily mean you need food, Julian. Your body produces ghrelin four or five hours after a meal, no matter what. We call it the hunger hormone; next time you feel hungry, look at how long it's been since you last ate."

When the clock on the wall confirmed her explanation—it had been almost five hours since breakfast—he was both amazed and annoyed. Somehow, identifying the feeling made him want to assert control over it, especially under Idabee's gaze.

Julian excused himself and went to the bathroom. He splashed cold water on his face, pushing back the alcoholic fog that encircled him, brushed his teeth, and checked his appearance in the mirror. Slightly invigorated and with a clearer head, he returned to the kitchen, stashed away the whiskey, and joined the patiently waiting Idabee at the table.

"Tell me about St. Patrick's Day," she invited. Julian gave her a quick rundown of the festivities. "And why is it important to you?"

"Besides a reason for drinking?" Julian joked. Idabee's face remained placid, her eyes waiting for his explanation. "When I was a kid, I remember celebrating it with my dad," he said. "One time, I didn't have school, but Mom was working, so the two of us spent the day together. He put up green decorations, made green pancakes for breakfast, and we watched movies, laughing and joking and even singing along with them." He smiled at the recollection. "Looking backward, I'll bet it was just an excuse for him to drink all morning, because he fell asleep on the couch. Still, it was a good memory."

Idabee looked skeptical at the last bit, but thanked him for sharing the story. "Julian, I'm going to introduce you to Professor Carlton on Thursday. He runs a program for members of the American Union that qualifies them to serve in the people's legislative assembly. The friends I'm meeting tomorrow, Faith and Adon, are also delegates."

"What kind of program is it?" he asked.

"Carlton is a professor of nonviolence studies," Idabee explained. "The

CHAPTER TWELVE

American Union was built on the principles of nonviolence and used some of the tactics Gandhi did, like the group fasts. Anyway, Gandhi's autobiography was subtitled *My Experiments with Truth*; the thirty-day program is about experimenting with our own lives. The basic framework includes two twenty-four-hour fasts—the fast for peace on the fifteenth and on the final day—during thirty days of sobriety."

The last data point hung in the air. Julian ignored it. "I heard Reverend Shaver did a twenty-four-day fast," he said. "How long can someone go without eating?"

Idabee's desire to explain redirected her to the new topic. "It really depends on how much fat they have. For longer fasts, most people supplement electrolytes—salt, potassium, and magnesium. A person usually burns through about a kilogram each day." Seeing Julian's confused expression, she translated, "About a half pound. A week is my longest fast."

"That's impressive," Julian told her, and meant it.

For the first time since she'd smelled the alcohol on him, Idabee smiled. "Thanks. Julian, how did your fast make you feel?"

He shrugged. "I thought I'd be more uncomfortable, but it never really happened."

"Thank you, but how did you feel?"

"Oh. I felt good—like actually peaceful. My mother used to make me count to ten when I'd get upset, and it worked. This was like counting to ten for an entire day." He smiled at the thought. "And it made me feel good, like powerful? She also used to tell me breakfast was the most important meal of the day—that kind of thing, you know? I'm not saying she was wrong, but this was like the training wheels coming off." Seeing Idabee's confusion, he clarified, "Do kids still ride bicycles?"

"I've seen them in the movies," she said.

"Training wheels were an extra set of wheels you could attach to little kids' bikes, so they couldn't tip over. After they learned to keep their balance, the training wheels would come off, because once you know how to ride, you can't unlearn it. I learned I'm more capable than I gave myself credit for. Thank you, Idabee."

She nodded acknowledgment. Hearing himself appreciate what he'd learned from her, Julian decided Idabee deserved a fair hearing on the self-improvement program. Her face lit up when he asked her to explain how it connected to crowdsourcing government.

"Leading by example is one of the duties of nonviolence—be the change you want to see in the world," Idabee began. "To demonstrate a commitment to improving the country, we start by improving ourselves, thirty days at a time. Besides the basic framework, the fasting and sobriety, there are optional challenges we take on during the month.

"The optional challenges—the various experiments—generally fall into one of four categories: abstinence, stoicism, perspective, and betterment. Abstinence can be any aspect of your life you're willing to give up for thirty days. It could be diet-related, a pastime, or some other behavior. Stoic challenges usually practice willingly being uncomfortable, perspective challenges often try to reduce one's status to see how others experience the world, and practicing positive behaviors are betterment challenges.

"Carlton offers a handful of choices to the group so that we can have shared experiences, but self-directed challenges are encouraged as well." Idabee exhaled thoughtfully, scrutinizing Julian's face to see if he was following so far. "Both the fast for peace and these challenges are part of addressing the Boaty McBoatface problem."

"The what?"

She smiled, brown eyes flashing with amusement at his puzzled look. "Back in the early days of the internet, there was a contest to name a boat. The runaway winner was…"

"Boaty McBoatface?"

Idabee laughed. "Of course. And no, they didn't actually give the boat that name, but it's what we call problems that crop up where people across the internet do stupid things they know are stupid. There's a continuum of malice; sometimes it's more like peer pressure, other times it's a deliberate attempt to be disruptive. But when it comes to crowdsourcing government, it's important to get it right."

Julian nodded. "President Obama let people create petitions on the White

CHAPTER TWELVE

House website, and after enough signatures, they'd respond. They had to explain why the US wasn't going to build a Death Star." He decided it was his turn to explain. "It was a giant space station from a movie."

"Yeah," she said, "*A New Hope Rises*; I've seen it. But it only came out a few years ago, how did you know about it back then?"

"They remade *Star Wars*?" He waved a hand. "Never mind. Boaty McBoatface?"

"Mobs have always been a potential problem in society," Idabee began. "When the internet connected billions of people, it also created a new way for them to form. It also reduced barriers to doing so. Gathering in person carried certain costs in time and transportation; the world wide web was much easier.

"There are usually three components to the Boaty McBoatface problem: a low barrier for entry, anonymous or nearly anonymous participation, and the ability of clearly dumb proposals to move forward unchecked.

"Now, the American Union has a low barrier for entry, and that's on purpose. It's about making political representation available to all, so membership dues are one-half of one percent of your American Union Job. Everyone can enjoy the societal benefits without joining, but making dues a non-zero amount makes it an opt-in process.

"However, membership isn't anonymous. Only US citizens can join, and since dues are paid through a person's Treasury account, it establishes their identity and minimizes foreign interference. This is a barrier to the Boaty McBoatface problem, but not an insurmountable one."

"For real," Julian said. "The Ku Klux Klan was brazen, riding around at night under anonymous hoods, but lynch mobs still could form in broad daylight."

Idabee nodded as she continued. "Which leaves us with the last part—checks on bad ideas. When the Framers wrote the Constitution, they came up with the electoral college, so if a mob of voters elected someone unqualified, the electoral college was supposed to be the wiser heads that fixed the problem. They feared direct democracy.

"With the American Union, there's no technical obstacle that blocks us from demanding something crazy, like building a Death Star. But these thirty-day challenges put a philosophical obstacle in place. In order to take on higher roles in the American Union, like organizer or delegate, members have to complete them. The requirement for personal sacrifice helps weed out those who are motivated by greed, and it encourages mindfulness."

"That's not a characteristic mobs are known for," Julian observed.

"No, not at all. The sobriety aspect is also an important part of being a delegate, because we make better decisions sober." Idabee paused, possibly wondering if her father's absence could be explained by his participation in some day drinking. "If someone's asking for decision-making authority on your behalf," she continued, "then it's not unreasonable to expect them to do their best. Again, it's not an insurmountable barrier—Adolf Hitler didn't drink—but it is one that helps weed out bad actors.

"At the same time, going through the experience with a small cohort of people—guided by the principles of nonviolence—helps develop a shared perspective for those who want to get into policy setting and the legislative details. Those are the wiser heads that we want to prevail.

"Does that make sense? The thirty-day challenges are like a vaccine against the mindset that produces mobs. Boaty McBoatface can be a contagious idea in the real world, but the infection doesn't spread very well among the people who've put in the work to become delegates."

"It does," he said, "Thank you for explaining."

"Of course, Julian. I know things are different here in the tricentennial; I'm happy to help you get acclimated." Idabee hesitated. "You've demonstrated you can do the fasting; what do you think about a month of sobriety? The groups meet on the first and fifteenth of the month; you could come on April 1."

"Maybe," he said politely. They'd only met a week earlier, and Idabee was already trying to change him! He'd known zealots in his own time; being able to categorize this woman, inscrutable in other ways, was somehow comforting. "Right now I've got other things on my mind."

Julian explained he was having lunch with Reverend Shaver the next day, and a reporter would be there to ask a few questions and take pictures.

CHAPTER TWELVE

"After you told me about the publicity I'd get after waking up, I started thinking about Ota Benga." He scowled. "Have you ever heard of him?"

Idabee hadn't. "He was an African in the early twentieth century who was brought to America as part of a display for the World's Fair. After being exhibited at a museum, he ended up at the Bronx Zoo in the monkey house." Julian sighed. "Am I just a primitive savage from 2026 here to entertain millions of people in the tricentennial?"

The time it took Idabee to consider the question was unpleasant. "There's a non-zero amount of truth to that, Julian. But clearly, you're more than just a primitive savage. You're the hero of the reparations rally. Who knows how things would have turned out if you hadn't stopped those men trying to kill Reverend Shaver all those years ago?"

The warmth of her smile helped smother his anxiety. "Thanks, Idabee. I'll be glad when it's over, though."

"I'll bet you will," she agreed. "Julian, I'm curious about Ota Benga. Do you mind if I look him up?" Idabee withdrew her tablet from a pocket and unfolded it. Within a half-minute, a photograph of a smiling black man with pointed teeth was projected in front of them, framed by an orange and blue border.

"He never got to return to Africa," Julian explained. Idabee cycled through several more images, each outlined with the same colored border.

Julian asked about the colors. "These are pictures from the National Archive," Idabee explained. "Orange certifies the digital image is an authentic reproduction, not manipulated, and blue signifies it is in the public domain. They serve as a public repository of digital information. Julian, you mentioned you had a website. What was it? It might be in the Archive."

"It wasn't anything special," he said.

"Can we take a look?"

He couldn't think of any compelling reason not to give her the information. "It was just a blog I started during the pandemic," he explained. "Julian's Jottings. There were a lot of things on my mind after my folks died, and so I put them out there. But no one was picking them up, you feel me? So I quit adding to it after a while."

Amazingly, Idabee found a record of his website, and the image on the front page stirred up a whirlwind of emotions within him. Georgia and Walter West were seated together on a park bench, and Julian stood behind his parents, hands on their shoulders. "Wow," he said softly, his voice thick as memories flooded back to him. "I assumed everything from back then was lost." He preemptively blinked away potential tears. What else of his digital footprint might have survived fifty years in the sands of time?

"I can't imagine what it would be like to land in a different year, away from everything you've ever known," Idabee said. She bit her lip, then continued quietly, "I think you're very brave."

Julian noticed something else about the page; it had a green and blue border. He pointed. "Are my blogs in the public domain?"

"Of course," Idabee said. "The green signifies the work represents your opinion and shouldn't be assumed to be factually accurate."

He decided to let that pass. "I thought copyright lasted for a long time."

"It's up to an initial eighteen years now. We increased it in the last legislative package." Julian quirked an eyebrow, and she began to explain. "Remember how we talked about VOZ metrics? Identifying a variable and deciding which way we wanted it to trend? There are about twenty variables that we evaluate every year, and one of them impacts the length of time the original copyright term lasts.

"Intellectual property is a special right, Julian, given temporarily to creators as an incentive for them to add to the knowledge and culture in the public domain. Copyright used to last for almost a century, which was ridiculous. Would you have refused to write your blog unless you were promised a century worth of special privilege?"

"No," he said.

"No," she repeated. "You said you had ideas you wanted to share, so you did. There were no movie studios or publishers that went out of business when the system was reformed; instead, we had a whole explosion of creativity as characters and stories that had been in the public consciousness for generations became available for everyone to use.

CHAPTER TWELVE

"Are you thinking of doing any new writing, Julian? Any creative work that you want to copyright, you'll need to submit it to the Archive, it's no longer automatic. I think a book about your adventures might be popular."

Julian pondered that idea. "I'll give it some thought," he said. "I've always written a few things down, about what's going on. A journal, you could call it. Ray showed me how to use my tablet to record and write. It helps me organize my thoughts."

Idabee smiled. "I had no idea you were so creative," she said.

"Why would you?" he wondered. "A few years ago, my journal was lost." There was no need to explain that it had happened when he was incarcerated. "I started another one afterward, but now that's lost too."

Julian shrugged, then continued, "About this Archive; can I find information about Edith Bartlett? She was the woman who was with me when I–" Her frantic scream echoed through his head. "Ray said it was probably a matter of public record."

"My father told you that what happened to her at the reparations rally was a matter of public record?" Idabee studied him, her features placid except for the intensity of her gaze. She knew something, Julian realized. Had Ray been evasive rather than tell him Edith had been hurt or killed? What was being withheld from him?

Julian suppressed the urge to demand anything of Idabee. The young woman had impressed him so far, and he trusted that her conscience was his ally in whatever internal struggle was taking place behind her eyes. He adopted a plaintive look and waited for her to explain.

Finally, Idabee spoke. "It's true that it's in the public record, but Father knows exactly what happened to her. In fact, she's sat in that very chair more times than I can remember."

"This chair?" he asked.

Idabee glanced toward the hallway, checking that Ray was not in earshot of what she was about to reveal. "Julian, Edith Bartlett is my grandmother."

Part III

What do I want?
March 18–22, 2076

It is perhaps well enough that the people of the nation do not know or understand our banking and monetary system, for if they did I believe there would be a revolution before tomorrow morning.

- Henry Ford

All true ethics must at the same time be good economics. True economics stands for social justice, it promotes the good of all equally, including the weakest, and is indispensable for decent life.

- M.K. Gandhi

Chapter Thirteen

When he dressed for lunch with Reverend Shaver, the fit of the outfit from Lord Hoot's impressed Julian, especially considering he'd never actually tried it on. The black shoes were exceedingly comfortable, and the khakis rested lightly on his hips. His polo shirt, top button open, was tight across his shoulders but loose enough over his midsection that it cloaked his mild bulging. He would look good when the reporter showed up to take their picture.

Edith Bartlett was alive and well, Julian thought yet again. Not only was she Ray's mother, but Idabee had also shared that Edith was the doctor responsible for putting him into cryonic suspension. Equipped with that information, Julian had found numerous news articles—none of them recent enough to require payment—about Dr. Edith Leete, head of the cryonics department at Washington General Hospital.

There was silence as he and Ray descended in the elevator toward the underground parking lot. Julian considered confronting the doctor with his new knowledge, but Ray spoke first, explaining they would take a car into the city instead of his usual bus because of the walking involved. "I don't want you to overexert yourself today, before or after lunch." Julian nodded approval; he felt fine but recognized the doctor's experience was the best guide.

As they exited into the cavernous structure, two passengers, presumably residents, were disembarking from a light brown bus. Julian held the elevator doors open, and the pair thanked him as they entered. When the bus driver looked expectantly in their direction, Ray waved a dismissal,

CHAPTER THIRTEEN

and the bus lumbered away.

Ray didn't own a personal automobile, but River Place Towers maintained a community transportation pool. The small, two-person vehicle, which glided silently to the curb, was reminiscent of the old Smart cars. It was empty. "No driver?" Julian asked.

"No driver," Ray chuckled. "I'll be honest with you, Julian; I had to pass a basic driving course twenty-some years ago, but I'm not sure I've actually driven since then. Autonomous vehicles have been very safe for as long as I can remember." He walked around the car and settled himself into what Julian thought of as the driver's seat.

There was no steering wheel; the large dashboard was desk-like. Ray tapped more commands onto a center display, and after the men pulled seat belts across their bodies, the vehicle rolled smoothly forward, winding its way through the garage before emerging onto a surface street. Ray paid no attention to what was going on, but Julian was entranced by the self-driving vehicle and the world outside the windows.

Traffic was dominated by buses, but a fair number of individual vehicles were also headed into Washington. The whole scenario seemed calmer somehow. After a moment, Julian realized what was missing. "There are no traffic signs," he observed. Ray looked puzzled. "Speed limit, exit markers, that sort of thing."

"The car has all the necessary information," Ray explained. "Cities like Washington are under automatic traffic control; individuals don't drive."

"But what about the bus? I saw you wave to the driver that we weren't going to be taking it."

"That was the conductor; the bus is self-driving, too."

Julian thought for a moment. "So, they supervise a self-driving bus? That seems unnecessary."

Ray swiveled toward him. "When you say 'unnecessary,' what exactly do you mean?"

"If all the driving is automatic, it seems like a make-work job."

"There's some truth to that. If the conductor is unexpectedly sick, for example, the bus continues to run. But what is the purpose of employment except to add value to society? That was Fredrick that I waved to; he's been one of the conductors on that route for years. He might see a thousand people over the course of the day, most of them regulars. Facilitating connections between people is valuable work, even if you can't put a dollar amount on it."

"That reminds me; are we still supposed to talk with Teara Harper again tonight?" Julian asked. "I think I figured out the answer to her question, about how we borrowed all those trillions of dollars. It was from other countries, like China, because of our trade deficits. But I don't see why that explains how the United States paid for unconditional basic income."

Ray paused before responding. "Look, economics is not my area of expertise, but I can tell you that's not the answer Teara is looking for. How would China loan us our own currency?"

"Well, they'd..." Julian trailed off as he realized his error. "Oh. The dollars would have had to come from the United States in the first place." He scratched his goatee and sighed. "Dang, I thought I had it. So where did they come from?" Ray grinned and said nothing else.

Within a few minutes, they were crossing into the District of Columbia over the turtle-green water of the Potomac River. The Washington Monument jutted up from the horizon, tall and imposing on the skyline, just like the morning of the reparations rally. Julian's hand slipped inside his jacket, fingers searching, tracing the knots of scar tissue through his shirt. He recalled seeing Reverend Shaver brutally shot and wondered how the physical and emotional scars had affected the preacher. Still, Julian marveled he had survived at all.

"Hey, Julian," Ray said, picking up on the sudden shift in his patient's demeanor. "Everything's going to be okay; I know it's recent history for you, but it's been fifty years for everyone else. I'm sure Reverend Shaver will want to talk about his perspective of the rally." Did Edith Bartlett— Edith Leete, Julian corrected himself—figure into his story as well? "The reporter might have some questions, but you're not obligated to answer anything. Let her get some pictures so the people of the tricentennial can see you two together on a historic day, but just remember, you're safe here."

CHAPTER THIRTEEN

What about that old man who'd shown up at Idabee's hearing, muttering about unfinished business? "If you want to talk more later, we can just hang out, even kill the rest of that whiskey. Okay?"

Julian threw on a small smile to mask his uneasiness. "Thanks, Ray. I appreciate that."

"Idabee, too," he added. "She really wants you to feel welcome here."

"I get that," Julian said, explaining Idabee had visited the previous afternoon to check on him.

"I had no idea she came by; I slept right through it," Ray chuckled. "How sober were you?"

"Enough that I understood her explanation using variable-one-zero metrics," Julian answered.

Ray burst out into laughter. "She loves to explain things," he said. "Idabee always wanted to know how and why things worked."

This was a natural opening, Julian decided. "She also explained you knew what happened to Edith Bartlett."

Ray released a sigh of relief. "Julian, I was hoping you'd bring that up again. It was too much to go into when you first asked me, and then I didn't know if you'd lost interest. Yes, Edith Bartlett was my mother's maiden name. Did Idabee tell you she was the head of the cryonics department before me?"

Julian gave an affirmative nod. "Does she know I'm awake?"

Ray hesitated. "I believe so. During the holidays, she mentioned you were scheduled for revival this year, and the hospital announced it last month. But I haven't spoken to her in a while."

"The hospital announced it?" Julian echoed.

"Like births and obituaries, cryonic suspensions and revivals are generally shared with the public. I assume that's how the reporter knew you'd been recently awoken."

"Edith still lives nearby, right?" Julian said. Idabee had described her as a frequent visitor. "I bet she'd like to see Reverend Shaver again. Maybe she could meet us for lunch?"

The doctor radiated discomfort at the idea but nodded. His index finger moved across the face of the doall on his wrist, spelling out letters in sequence, until a tone Julian immediately identified as a ringing telephone was heard. Ray tugged at the doall, and it opened up. The silver-dollar-sized face was black underneath.

"Yes, Ray?" came a flat, neutral voice. Julian's heart quickened. It was Edith.

"Julian West would like to talk with you," he said without preamble. "We're on our way to lunch with Reverend Shaver, and he suggested we invite you to join us."

"Julian?" Edith asked. The icy crust had melted; her tone now conveyed the warmth of spring and the possibility of new growth.

"It's me," he confirmed. "Edith, can you come to lunch? Or can we talk sometime soon?"

"Where?" she asked. Ray supplied the name of the Italian restaurant that Shaver had suggested. "That's about ten minutes from me, but I don't think I'll be able to catch a bus for another half-hour."

Ray snapped the face of the doall closed. "How about we plan something with a little more notice?"

"Can you drop me off and pick her up?" Julian asked eagerly.

"I could," he admitted, "but I'm not sure I should leave you by yourself." Edith's voice was heard. "Hello?"

"Please?" Julian asked, testing the tenuous bonds of their friendship.

Ray sighed and reopened the doall. "I can come get you in fifteen minutes," he offered.

"That would be fine," she replied. "It's good to hear your voice again, Julian. See you soon."

Julian was grinning broadly as the call ended. "Thanks, Ray."

His host nodded, but said nothing else. Julian followed his lead, staring out the windshield at the city streets and replaying the conversation, Edith's voice echoing in his head. Something was off in the Leetes' relationship, but it wasn't his main concern at the moment.

He was going to see Edith again!

Ray broke the silence and pointed. "The restaurant should be just ahead," he said. "I think that's Reverend Shaver." Among the pedestrians was a thin man in a gray overcoat, wielding a cane with each stride, moving fairly rapidly for a man in his nineties. "I'll drop you off."

Apparently, double parking was still around in the tricentennial. Ray directed the vehicle to stop a few car lengths ahead, and Julian climbed out to intercept the reverend. Shaver recognized him immediately. "Julian West," he boomed, grinning broadly. It was infectious, and Julian found himself returning it instinctively. "At last, at last. It is so good to see you again."

"Likewise," Julian responded. Shaver shook his hand with surprising firmness, and the two men sized each other up. Again, Julian was struck by the reduction in the preacher's bulk.

Shaver's gaze flicked to his shining scalp and made a similar confession. "I picture you with locs," he said. Julian nodded agreeably—the news reports at the time must have found some of his old pictures on social media—and explained Ray's errand. When he mentioned their additional guest for lunch, Shaver stopped short.

"I think it would be best if you didn't mention Edith Leete to the reporter," the nonagenarian said, gesturing to a dark-haired woman with inquisitive eyes watching them. A silver drone hovered over her right shoulder, its eye trained on the two men. "The restaurant said pictures inside would disturb the other guests, so we'll talk outside for a few minutes." Julian nodded agreement, and they continued forward to the restaurant's entrance.

The woman introduced herself as Vickie Lane, and at first she seemed primarily interested in capturing images and video of the two men. She energetically posed them in the warm March sunshine as though they were wax figures: shaking hands, smiling, walking together. Julian complied with her requests, recalling the cheerful expression of Ota Benga as he entertained the people of the 1904 World's Fair, and waited for it to be over.

Questions followed. "Julian, you're one of the longest sleepers revived. What are your impressions of the world today? Has it met your expectations?" The drone floated an arm's length away, ready to capture his responses.

Julian licked his lips and tried to swallow his nervousness. "It's better than I would have believed possible," he said. "One of the last things I heard was a wild idea that America would finally address poverty, racism, and militarism. Dr. King's triple evils had been with us for a long time; I grew up in poverty—not sure I ever left—and racism was always a part of that world. Militarism… America was always fighting; we'd been in a war on terror since I was a boy.

"I couldn't imagine a way we could change. Reverend Shaver said something recently about how the ability to be better was a fundamental law of the universe." The nonagenarian nodded. "I guess he was right. To your question—does 2076 meet my expectations?—the answer is that it has far, far exceeded them."

Vickie basked in the praise for the civilization she'd been born into. "Your quick action at the reparations rally made you a national hero," she informed him. "Twelve people died and forty-three were injured, Julian. It would have been higher if you hadn't interfered with the gunmen. While you were sleeping, five schools were named after you, and a statue went up in north Philadelphia."

"I'm glad I was there at the right time." Julian hesitated, knowing he was supposed to be answering questions, not asking them, but continued, "What happened to the gunmen? Death penalty?"

Reverend Shaver shook his head firmly. "No. With the criminal justice reforms the American Union delivered, they were rehabilitated and released a decade or so later."

"Ten years? I knew guys who were serving decades over nothing."

"They wouldn't be, today," Shaver replied. The silver drone shifted its location to stare at the preacher, perhaps sensing he was about to launch into a monologue. "Incarceration is very different now. Criminal acts—breaking societal norms of behavior—are seen primarily as a mental health issue, so it's not the default response. In the case of the gunmen, something had gone wrong in their minds that made them believe killing was essential to their dignity. Addressing that error is integral to establishing justice. Sometimes incarceration is still considered necessary, as societal self-defense, but always with the primary purpose of rehabilitation, not punishment.

"Prisons and jails offer a wide range of services, such as education, job training, treatment for substance abuse, mental health services, and other avenues for promoting personal growth. They've developed along the lines of the successful models many European countries used back then. A modern prison is more like a college campus, which is a good example of how a person can transform themselves in just a few years. By treating people with dignity and support, prisons offer a similar path for transformation."

It was nothing like what Julian had experienced during his own incarceration. "Those sound like good changes to the criminal justice system," Julian admitted, although he was skeptical about the rehabilitation of the white supremacists.

Vickie Lane took this as a cue to redirect the conversation. "What would you say is the most fascinating thing about waking up in the tricentennial?"

"Honestly?" Julian said. "Waking up in the tricentennial. Everything went black, and I thought that was it, but then I opened my eyes, and fifty years had passed."

"You were put into cryonic suspension because of the injuries you sustained during the attack on the reparations rally?"

"That's right," Julian confirmed.

She continued to toss questions at him. "Did you choose 2076 as your destination because of Reverend Shaver's speech?"

Julian had no answer. "I don't think I made any decision about it," he said. "They just woke me up."

The reporter cocked her head. "They've been reviving patients for more than thirty years. Who determined you should be kept frozen until now?"

Julian had no idea. "I don't know," he admitted.

"Did you have surgery when you were revived to address your injuries?"

"I think that's enough," Reverend Shaver interrupted. "Julian's medical history is his own business. You have your pictures; if you'll excuse us, we're about to have lunch."

"I'm just trying to understand the order of events," Vickie protested.

"It was nice to talk with you again," Shaver said, firmly ending their conversation. He tugged open the restaurant's front door and held it for Julian.

He didn't know what had triggered the reverend, but Julian began to relax as he realized he was done with the reporter. Walking away, he offered one final clarification. "Look, my doctor can explain what happened."

"Can he?" the reporter asked. The drone's eye accused him of withholding information.

Once again, Julian had no answer to her question. Had he been forgotten? Abandoned? Why had he been left frozen for fifty years?

Chapter Fourteen

The restaurant was warm and inviting, scented by garlic, tomato sauce, and fresh bread. Sharing food together was a deep-rooted human tradition, and aside from a few high-tech flourishes, the business appeared much like every other eatery Julian had visited. The lunchtime crowd filled most of the tables, and conversation filled the air.

Julian sat silently, shifting his legs as he waited for Ray to return with Edith, still a bit awestruck in the presence of Reverend Shaver. The preacher leaned back in his chair, studying Julian but saying nothing. His scarred left temple was a reminder of the violence they'd both experienced at the reparations rally, and Julian cast about for a different topic to spark conversation. "How are you feeling after not eating for three days?"

The nonagenarian replied with an exhausted wheeze. "I'm tired, and I have a headache. Once I have some food, I'll feel better."

"Idabee—Ray's daughter—told me yesterday that she was feeling good after seventy-two hours. I hope you're not risking your health." Julian nudged the basket of breadsticks resting on the checkered tablecloth. "Please, eat something."

"When the Dr. Leetes arrive. A little longer won't hurt me." Shaver continued to study Julian.

"You said you were fasting for atonement?" Julian asked. He assumed it was a religious thing, but the reverend had told him three days earlier *part of that is directed toward you*. "I didn't quite understand why."

"I'm eternally grateful that you interfered at the rally. I believe God spared my life so I could press for reconciliation in the aftermath." Shaver's thin hands quivered slightly as they reached across the table and grasped Julian's warmly. "Thank you, thank you for what you did."

"Of course," he said, beaming with pride.

Shaver hesitated before continuing. "But I also believe the strife would have been avoided if I'd only listened to your message in the first place." Shaver began wringing his hands, pressing them tight to his chest, and his eyes filled with grief.

Julian nodded, but without understanding. He'd never spoken to the preacher until three days ago, so the only message he could think of was the sign he'd held at the reparations rally. Since Shaver had called out Edith's sign during his speech, it stood to reason that he'd noticed Julian's as well. *Know justice, know peace*, it had read. How would that have prevented anything?

He waited to see if Shaver would continue. The yeasty aroma of the breadsticks tempted him, but Julian was determined not to take food until the other man did. When the silence became uncomfortable, he confessed, "I'm not sure what you mean."

"I refused to help you the first time we talked," Shaver said. At Julian's blank look, he gestured at the side of his own head. "Before you shaved off your locs."

Julian's heart began to race, and when he nodded, it was with the clear understanding that the old man was confused. Obviously, Shaver had mistaken him for someone else. "Ah," he replied vaguely.

"I was prideful," Shaver resumed, but Julian's attention shifted. Raymond Leete had walked through the restaurant door, and striding confidently behind him was an elderly black woman, silver-haired and professionally dressed.

Their eyes met.

It was Edith.

She breezed over to their table with a regal air, placing a hand on Shaver's shoulder in greeting. "Hello, Alvin," Edith said without breaking her gaze from Julian.

"Edith?" Julian whispered as he stood to greet her. The decades had been kind, but as thinly sliced as the years were, the quantity still weighed on her features.

"It's good to see you again, Julian," Edith said warmly. "It's been a long time." Her smile shone through the lines of her face, and he caught a glimpse of the woman that he'd subjectively met the previous week. Edith opened her arms, and they drew together.

At first, he was only conscious of her age. But as she clutched him, a warmth began to grow between them, revealing a sense of déjà vu. Had there been other times, other places, where they had held each other? Julian knew intellectually it was impossible, but the emotion rode in on a wave of destiny, summoning remembrances of shared sorrow and joy. "Edith," he whispered.

"Julian," she said comfortingly, and he was at peace in her embrace. Finally, Edith released him, studying his face intently as she held him at arm's length. "Thank you for saving me," she said.

"Thank you for saving me," he echoed. The buzz of the restaurant brought him back to reality, and they took their seats.

A waiter approached to take the doctors' drink orders, and Julian scanned the menu. Prices were five times what he would have expected. "They must make good tips here," he commented when the man retreated.

Ray furrowed his eyebrows. Edith's laugh was musical. "Tipping! I haven't thought about that in—well, I don't know how long," she said.

Julian turned to Ray in confusion. "Idabee talked about it the other night; websites have tip jars for people to make tiny donations."

"They're called wishing wells," Ray replied. "Visitors can throw some change in, to wish the website well. But I remember my dad telling me about tipping." He pointed at the menu. "He said it was fraud, that the price advertised wasn't the customer's actual cost."

"Julian, expecting employees to work for tips was exploitation," Shaver added in a voice that was clear and authoritative. Whatever disorientation had possessed him moments earlier was gone. "It took off after the Civil War, when Southern employers resisted paying wages to emancipated people. Tips devolved from a European practice of a bonus given on top of normal wages into a subsidy customers were expected to provide.

"Congress later codified the practice in the form of a tip credit, which let restaurants pay sub-minimum wages, perpetuating an employment ecosystem that left people in poverty until the American Union Jobs Program came along. Building the beloved community Dr. King spoke of meant being unwilling to ignore the devaluation of others," Shaver concluded. "We cultivate *agape* love—selfless love—and look out for each other."

"Like you looked out for me in the past," Edith said, placing a gentle hand on Julian's arm. Her intense gaze was nothing like the last time he'd seen her, frantically screaming *Look out!* Instead, relief was in her eyes; they were together, and they were safe.

The waiter arrived with the drinks and took their orders, giving Julian time to think of how to redirect the conversation and prompt Shaver to break his fast. "We got reparations, right?"

Expressions transformed into grins. "We did," Shaver said. "After one and a half centuries of waiting, the legislation was signed one and a half months after the rally. The United States apologized for slavery and the other injustices inflicted on our people and set up a commission to calculate the economic damages."

Julian nudged the basket of breadsticks. "That seems like a good reason to celebrate. You should eat."

"I think that's sound medical advice," Ray added, plucking a breadstick and snapping it in two. Edith followed suit, then Julian, and finally Shaver.

"Thank you for joining me in breaking my fast," he said. His eyes were on Julian, but the tone encompassed the whole group.

"Let us celebrate our unity and the nonviolent nature of our movement," Edith quoted. She held her breadstick out to the center of the table, and the adults all touched theirs together.

"Reparations now," Julian said quietly to Edith, and she echoed their private toast as the table fell silent, devouring the slim morsels.

When Reverend Shaver was smiling again, Edith began to elaborate to Julian. "Alvin is downplaying his role," she said. "He gave another speech from his hospital bed and asked all Americans who wanted to see justice done to join a national day of fasting on April 15 as a way of pressuring Congress to amend and enact HR 40." Julian jerked. Was Shaver the origin of the fast for peace?

"It was one of the speeches she made me watch when I was young," Ray added. "An apology, a dollar, and an accounting."[5]

"A dollar?" Julian echoed.

"After the apology, the dollar acknowledged that there had been a non-zero amount of economic harm," Shaver explained. "The commission did the accounting, looking at all the national policies that helped us or hurt us disproportionately over the centuries. Adjusted for inflation, the sum worked out to about two trillion dollars."

"Of course, everyone had an American Union Job by the time they were done," Edith said with a smile. "It really was a transformative time."

"What made you call for the fast for peace?" Julian asked.

"In a sense, April 15, 1865, was the real end of the Civil War," Shaver said, delivering the response with polished ease, possibly because he'd answered the exact same question countless times over the last half-century. "Abraham Lincoln's death by an assassin shocked the country, and the world. His successor called on the people of the re-United States to observe a day of fasting in remembrance. In the aftermath of the violence at the reparations rally, it seemed an appropriate parallel."

"And that's where the American Union came from?" Julian pressed.

"He even received the Nobel Peace Prize," Ray confirmed.

"Establishing that Congress could be influenced by fasts of moral pressure created a feeling of agency," Shaver continued, as though Ray hadn't spoken. "There were many other injustices that needed to be addressed. So we organized, not behind any politician or party, but to crowdsource policy solutions around addressing poverty, racism, and militarism."

Edith spoke up. "It's amazing what you can accomplish if you don't care

---

[5] The text of the speech is reprinted in Appendix I.

who gets credit," she quoted.

"I'll go further," Shaver added. "We were able to accomplish more in Washington by deliberately making credit available to the people who wanted public accolades. The other thing politicians wanted was power, and when it came to elections, swing voters were essential. By unionizing, we had something they wanted, which enabled a win-win situation."

Julian looked back and forth between Edith and the reverend. "By threatening to vote for Republicans?" he asked. "Must have been a tough sell. I knew a guy from high school, Delroy Jackson, who was a huge Trump supporter, but other than that..."

"Blacks weren't the only part of the new coalition that made up the American Union," Shaver clarified. "Yes, most of the groups advocating for ending poverty, mass incarceration, and the endless wars were left leaning. But remember, most of the people in poverty were white, most incarcerated people were white, and most members of the military were white. Cooperation was in everyone's self-interest."

"Whatever you did, it seems like it worked," Julian admitted.

"It did," Edith said. "Julian, as your former doctor, I think you could use some fresh air and sunshine. How about a walk after lunch?"

"I'd like that," he replied.

Ray objected, apprehensive his patient might overexert himself, but Julian insisted he was fine. Stretching his legs and seeing life from ground level really did sound good, especially after a week cooped up inside Ray's building.

Edith also ignored her son's concerns. "I'll keep an eye on him," she said flatly. The tension between them had returned, and Julian braced himself for Ray's response.

Perhaps due to the presence of Reverend Shaver, Ray conceded. "Just have him back by six," he said. "He wants to learn more about economics and how the American Union Jobs Program was paid for."

Shaver's deep laugh drew everyone's attention and dissipated any hostility. "A trillion dollars a year—that's how backward we were," he said. "Dr. King observed that spending more on the military than on programs of social uplift was a path to spiritual doom. But post-pandemic, we began paying more interest on the national debt than we spent on the military-industrial complex."

"Is that how we paid for the American Union Jobs Program?" Julian asked. "Default on the debt and use the money we saved on interest?" Their mirthful expressions revealed that this idea was also wrong.

"I'm sure Teara will explain it all to you tonight," Ray said. "Or maybe you'll figure it out by then."

"He knows it was backward," Shaver insisted. "As backward as the way people looked at the Constitution. That was the real purpose of the American Union Jobs Program."

"What was?" Julian asked.

"To remind people that duties come first; rights don't exist without them."

"Hold up," Julian said skeptically. "Everyone has rights. Inalienable rights: life, liberty, and the pursuit of happiness."

The preacher was silent for a brief moment, as though gathering strength from the challenge. "If that were really true," Shaver countered with surprising energy, "Thomas Jefferson wouldn't have had to make the argument to King George. Natural rights were a bluff, but it was the right play to make at the time."

"A bluff?" he echoed. Was the nonagenarian confused again? "What do you mean?"

Shaver once again began reciting his answer in a scholarly tone. "The idea that 'all men are endowed by their creator with certain inalienable rights' had an enlightened ring to it. The phrase was not just an appeal to a higher authority than the king but also an appeal to the public, since Jefferson knew the Declaration of Independence would be widely read. For those suffering from the top-down power structure of European monarchies, the concept of natural rights could be used for protection from abusive authority from above.

"But attaching an authoritative label to something doesn't establish it as a fact!" Shaver said sharply, leaning into his topic. "That line from the Declaration is simultaneously one of the most famous and the most false.

According to the dictionary, inalienable means *not capable of being taken away or denied.* Since the Framers of the Constitution deliberately denied these rights to large swaths of the population, especially our ancestors, they knew these 'natural rights' weren't actually inalienable.

"Jefferson was bluffing, but no one called him on it, and the paradigm took off. Two hundred fifty years later, people were still framing political arguments that way, saying 'healthcare is a human right,' 'housing is a human right,' or, in my case, 'reparations are our right.' People had forgotten that so-called natural rights were an artificial construction. In their purest form, they're a blank check, claiming a debt without limitation or corresponding obligation.

"Rights are a figment of our collective imagination, but they're still a good concept, especially in a top-down power structure. Rights are a shield; the king, or the government, isn't supposed to violate people's rights. Enumerating civil rights also sets expectations for the way a society will function and for the way individuals should treat others and expect to be treated.

"But the American Union offered a different framework for government. It established a bottom-up power structure: by the people, for the people. That structure couldn't be built on natural rights—blank checks for everyone would have been a ponzi scheme of epic proportions. The foundation for a bottom-up power structure is duty. Duty turns the question around; instead of saying everyone owes me X, Y, and Z, it's what do I owe other people? The finished structures may look identical, but the way they're built is important.

"Fortunately, the Framers of the Constitution wrote a list of duties into the Preamble; they spelled out the responsibilities of the people of the United States and the purpose for forming a more perfect union. The American Union Jobs Program reminded us of those duties, individually and collectively, and helped flip the broken paradigm."

"Didn't they write the Constitution to protect their rights?" Julian interjected. "That's why we have a Bill of Rights."

Edith laughed. "I used to think the same thing."

CHAPTER FOURTEEN

"Despite the grand language about inalienable rights in the Declaration," Shaver continued, "none of it filtered through into the 1787 drafting of the Constitution. It was strictly a framework for government. There was nothing about rights except for giving authors and inventors an exclusive right to their work for a limited time." That seemed to match the explanation of intellectual property reform Idabee had described. "The Bill of Rights was a series of amendments that came later." Shaver concluded with a smile, his mirthful eyes resting lightly on Julian as he waited for the idea to sink in.

After a moment's hesitation, Julian said, "Duties come before rights?"

"You know it," Shaver affirmed jovially.

"And that's why you thought you needed redemption? For saying the descendants of enslaved people had a right to reparations after calling out all sorts of injustices we'd faced over the centuries?"

"Yes," Shaver answered. There was no doubt in his voice, no confusion, no hesitation. "An appeal to justice would have been appropriate, a request for help in fulfilling a shared duty. But asserting an obligation onto others wasn't. It was a misguided contribution to the state of America."

Julian rubbed his face, trying to make sense of the reversal, and gauged the doctors' reactions. Ray seemed indifferent, but Edith looked sympathetic to his internal struggle.

"Welcome to the tricentennial," she said.

Chapter Fifteen

Springtime in the nation's capital was embodied in Lafayette Square by the fragrance of cherry blossoms, the pink and white buds forming a lush canopy over the park bench where Julian and Edith sat watching the White House in the mid-afternoon sun.

"Happy anniversary, I suppose," Julian said. "Fifty years since we met. Seems like just last week." Edith smiled. The initial rush of pleasure he'd undergone at seeing her again had faded somewhat. The young woman he'd connected with so strongly was now a grandmother; her once-rich black hair was silver, and the wrinkles marking her cheeks were deep and abundant.

"For you, yes," Edith said. "For me, I feel every moment of those decades. An hour after you introduced yourself, all my expectations were upside down. Sirens wailing, people crying, you were lying on the ground bleeding. It was all I could do to keep you alive until the paramedics arrived." Her expression tightened. "I thought I was going to lose you."

"You felt it too, didn't you?" Julian asked, hearing the upswelling of emotion in her voice. "I could tell; the way you warmed up to me, the way you smiled. And you were out of my league; for real, I couldn't believe my luck." He chuckled.

"What about my luck? You protected me," Edith replied. A knot of teenagers floated past them on scooters, bantering in a language Julian didn't recognize. Edith waited until it was quiet again before continuing.

"You know, it's a strange experience for me to be sitting here with you after seeing your frozen body for all those years," she said. "I've played out

CHAPTER FIFTEEN

this conversation a thousand times in my head." She turned and reached out with her hands. Julian instinctively grasped them, feeling the warmth of the skin resting loosely over her aged bones. A wistful smile appeared on her face as she stared deep into his eyes. "I waited a long time for you, Julian. As the kids today say, 'I've been thinking about a physical relationship with you.'" When his expression betrayed him, she concluded, "But I know I've missed my chance to give you the thank you I'd imagined, even dreamed about, for being my guardian angel."

"Edith," Julian said as gently as he could, "we both missed our chance. I'm just glad you're safe, and things turned out well for you."

"I know," she said. The artificial cheerfulness in her tone suggested she wouldn't have been disappointed if he'd responded positively. "Ray told me your first question after waking was about me." Edith looked away and blinked rapidly. "His father was a good man, Julian. Don't think less of me for moving on."

"Of course not," he reassured her, releasing her hands. "If you hadn't, Ray and Idabee wouldn't be here now. That work she does for the people's legislative assembly is impressive."

"It is, isn't it? It's very gratifying, seeing Beebee follow in my footsteps," Edith said, deep pride for her granddaughter evident in her tone. "Ray was never interested; I guess it skipped a generation."

"You were a delegate?" he asked in surprise.

"I had a seat on the General Welfare committee," she said. "In my day, we didn't have holograms, fancy conference rooms, or AI-generated explainer videos. We had to make do with Zoom and a lot more human work. Helping guide real healthcare reform, turning sound bites into actual policy"—she allowed herself a small, satisfied smile—"was more my forte than being an organizer and growing the union. The problems with America's healthcare system were well diagnosed, but seeing the treatment through was a challenge. It took nearly a decade to transition to universal healthcare."

Something in her tone reminded Julian of his own grandmother and the way she unspooled treasured stories while reminiscing about the civil rights movement. He waited patiently for Edith to continue.

"Things from back then seem so crazy in hindsight; the patients I saw without insurance were the ones who needed healthcare the most. Whenever there was any type of reform proposed, the industries that profited from the dysfunction would scream socialism to scare people. And yet we were paying far more than other countries, and getting worse results.

"The American Union's first legislative package established a public option for insurance. Since employer-based coverage saddled businesses with a huge administrative burden and trapped one out of six employees in a job they wanted to leave, it was an incredibly popular provision. The federal government was already providing healthcare for four out of ten Americans; we gave everyone else the option to buy in and freed businesses from the obligation.

"It also included eighteen weeks of paid family leave—the US was almost the only country on the planet that didn't require new mothers receive paid time off. One in four went back to work within two weeks! It drove up our infant mortality rate; nearly two dozen babies died each day, never reaching their first birthday, because Congress refused to pass family leave.

"Julian, the real purpose of the American Union Jobs Program was to help people buy into the concept of universal healthcare. Because so many people had employer-based coverage, when they explained an American Union Job came with health benefits, it was a framework people could immediately understand.

"It made such a huge difference in the country's quality of life. Ray told me how you wouldn't identify yourself when you woke up, and he has no idea why." Her lips curled upward, but there was a deep sadness in her eyes. "He's never had to deny someone the healthcare they needed because an insurance company wouldn't cover a procedure—or because they didn't have insurance at all. But I have; I knew what you were afraid of. Things are better now, Julian, so much better. And you can actually appreciate it."

Julian grinned and touched his jaw. "I do appreciate it. I haven't been to a dentist in forever."

CHAPTER FIFTEEN

Edith had more to say. "One time," she began, "during my residency, it was a crazy busy night in the ER. If I told this to Idabee, I'd have to explain how many people didn't have any healthcare coverage, and they used the emergency room because they couldn't be turned away. I had a patient who'd been injured in a fight; the police brought him down to get checked out."

She hesitated. "He gave his name as Izzy Robynham, no present address. He insisted he was visiting from the year 2319, because he'd always wanted to see Washington, D.C." Julian laughed. "I didn't think much of it until I stepped out for a moment, and then he was gone. The windows in the room didn't lead anywhere; no one had seen him leave. He'd just vanished.

"Julian, it bugged me for a week. What if it were true, that he really was a time traveler from the future? I didn't put his claim in the chart; I was the only one who knew his perfectly reasonable–unreasonable explanation for disappearing.

"Finally, I went to security and asked to see the video from the night of his visit. He'd been fairly neatly dressed in a mismatched way that I normally associated with donated clothes, but it could have been a fashion sense three centuries ahead of its time. And there he was, strolling out of the hospital with such confidence that no one paid any attention. Izzy Robynham wasn't a time traveler." She looked at him carefully. "You're the only person I've ever told that story to in all these years."

Uneasiness danced lightly up his spine. "Why me?"

"We had something special, Julian," she replied. "I wish things could have been different."

"Me too," he said.

They sat there, together again, basking in the warm March sunlight. In the quiet, Edith shifted toward him on the bench, giving him a sideways glance that Julian understood. He put an arm around her, and she nestled her thin frame into him.

The contact opened up a sense of emptiness inside him. Theirs would always be a missed connection, a seed with the potential to blossom into a beautiful flower under the right conditions. But circumstances had intervened. Edith was twice his age now; she'd spent more years with Ray's father than he'd lived. If once they had been meant to be together, they now existed in two entirely separate worlds. Seeing her, being with her, offered him a sense of closure that had eluded him since awakening.

Julian shifted on the bench. "Mind if we walk over by the White House?" he asked, standing and offering his arm. Edith accepted, and the pair strolled down the path sprinkled with cherry blossoms.

She gestured to a spot across from the White House. "There was a Peace Vigil there for decades," she said. "They had a tent of sorts, surrounded by signs and flags, calling attention to injustices around the world and in the United States. A volunteer was always there, twenty-four hours a day, talking with tourists about how peace was possible.

"Back when we met, a man named Philipos was there most days. He was committed to the cause; it ran in his family like cryonics does in mine. But eventually victory was declared and the Peace Vigil shut down. There was a giant celebration; I brought Ray, although he might have been too young to remember.

"It must have been an amazing feeling for him, Julian. Dedicating decades of his life to a cause and finally succeeding. The American Union had reined in the military-industrial complex, the United States had become a force for peace in the world, nuclear weapons were on their way out, and global conflict was replaced by multilateralism from below. There was no longer a need to try and push peace in the face of the president, because the United States was pushing it in the face of the world."

Edith fell silent, lost in recollection. Julian, tethered to her arm, looked around the park. "It sounds great," he said.

"It was," she said absentmindedly. Then her focus shifted, clear and sharp, to Julian's face. "It was," she repeated, placing her free hand on his. "Everything changed. When you and I heard Reverend Shaver predict America would be born again, it sounded fanciful. But we did it, Julian. The American Union brought us through the Phoenix Cycle. Peace was possible; it was what people wanted anyway. We just needed a better way to organize for political power." A note of sadness crept into her voice.

CHAPTER FIFTEEN

"And you missed it."

"I only got delayed," he said. "Edith, I've been wanting to ask: how did I end up in cryonic suspension? Ray said something about a court order."

A guarded look fell over her eyes, and Edith tugged him into motion again, meandering toward 15th Street. "What did Ray tell you?"

"I'd just woken up; I don't remember the details."

Edith began to explain. "We looked for your family, Julian, but couldn't find anyone to accept legal responsibility for you. Something had to be done, and I wanted to see you again. I had to see you again. Can you understand that?"

"I think so," he answered. All week, he had been chasing the spark of hope Edith kindled inside of him that morning. Only now, after seeing her, had the match flame of possibility guttered and gone out.

"As head of cryonics, which back then was mostly a title that allowed the hospital to parade me before potential donors by dangling the possibility of life extension, I had a little political capital. When it didn't look like you were going to survive your injuries, Julian, I used it to get the hospital appointed as your conservator and then to shepherd you into the program. You were only the seventh patient I'd actually frozen, but the circumstances of your death were close to ideal, so I had high hopes for you."

Julian halted. "My death?"

Edith shrugged. "Before Congress passed enabling legislation in 2030, a person had to be declared legally dead before we could begin the vitrification process." Anticipating his next question, she explained, "That's a way of minimizing cell damage to a person during the freezing process. The crystalline structure of ice expands, but by adding cryoprotectants to a person's blood, it simply solidifies."

"So... I died?" Julian asked.

"Legally, anyway," Edith said. With an impish smile, she reached up and pinched his cheek. "It didn't take."

By unspoken agreement, they turned toward the Washington Monument, walking slowly south. Julian read the name on the building next to them. "This is the Treasury," he said. "Edith, how did the United States borrow thirty trillion dollars back then?"

"A few dollars here, a few dollars there," she replied. "It added up."

"You know what I'm asking," he protested. "Teara Harper said the whole economy was only worth six trillion when I was born. Was it inflation; was that how it happened?" He pointed at the Treasury building. "Money printer go brrrr?"

"I thought you were interested in where the money was borrowed from?" she asked innocently.

"Fine," he said playfully. "Whatever you did, it seems like it worked. I haven't seen anyone sleeping on a park bench, no tent cities, not a single panhandler asking for money."

"Are you disappointed?" she asked. "Looking for imperfections in the tricentennial?"

He repeated the answer he'd given the reporter: "It's better than I would have believed possible." Edith seemed pleased, and he expanded the idea. "I can't believe I only missed the American Union by a few months. Idabee invited me to a panel she was moderating yesterday, and Friday she's going to show me how the assembly sessions are run. It's incredible." He recalled the deep pride with which Edith had spoken of her granddaughter and concluded, "She's quite the young woman."

Edith's reaction was quick. "Young is right," she observed. "She has a bit more growing up to do, a little more to learn about real life. Those thirty-day challenges are fine for weeding out unserious people from the American Union, but they aren't real-world problems, you know."

The note of jealousy in her voice both surprised and annoyed him. "So playing matchmaker wasn't the reason you and Ray waited so long to wake me up?"

"Certainly not!" Edith physically recoiled at the suggestion. "Idabee isn't right for you, Julian."

"Then what was the reason?" Julian asked. "Edith, why didn't you revive me decades ago?"

The question hung in the air. "I was married," she said finally.

"Ray's father."

CHAPTER FIFTEEN

She nodded. "Marvin's wife was terminally ill, and she wanted an ambulance ride to the future. He visited her all the time, sitting next to the stainless steel canister in the basement of the hospital, peering through the glass and talking about his day. I often saw him when I came to look at you, waiting for the day when you'd be revived.

"We were two broken people, and eventually, we were visiting with each other more than our frozen flames." She shrugged. "I wasn't looking for love. It snuck up on me, and I'm glad it did. Marvin and I had been married for more than a decade when the first successful revival took place. What would we have told Ray? Most people who've had thirty-seven years of marriage would probably tell you they couldn't imagine any other life. But I could, I have, and I do." The look she gave him left no doubt about how he featured in that scenario.

"I told you I understood why you arranged the—what did you call it?—ambulance to the future," Julian said. "But it feels like you're not telling me something about why it was a fifty-year ride."

The silence stretched out so long that Julian was about to break it when Edith finally spoke. "I won't lie to you, Julian; there's a longer answer to your question about why you stayed in suspension. If you insist, I'll explain everything right now. But I also think it's not time for us to have that particular conversation; it's been a busy day, and it's not urgent.

"I'd like you to withdraw the question. Do you abstain? That means I'm asking you to consent to my proposal, but you're free to reject it."

Julian sighed. The day's aches were accumulating in his body, and whatever Edith told him about the past, there wasn't anything he could do to change it. And he did believe that there was a good reason. "Sure. I trust you," he replied.

"Thank you," she said.

He nodded and changed the subject. "That's where I saw you for the first time," he pointed. The Washington Monument was visible now, creeping above the treeline. "You were just what I needed to take my mind off my hangover."

"Julian, why were you carrying a lead pipe with your sign?" Edith asked.

"What were you hoping would happen?" They walked in silence for a moment, the question gathering weight. "Sorry," she said. "You can tell me another time, if you want."

"It's okay," he reassured her. "And hoping isn't the right word. But if things started getting crazy, I was down for anything. I didn't have a lot going for me, Edith. No family left, like you said. No formal education. A bogus criminal record that dropped my job prospects from slim to none. The reason I could come down to D.C. in the middle of the week is because the only work I could get was weekend shifts at a gas station. And really, I had no expectation that things were going to change.

"Reparations, that would have been something. Cash would have meant options. So if we needed to march on the Capitol, or the White House, or whatever to get the attention of the people in Washington, I was willing to be front and center.

"But there was something about you, Edith. The way you studied me, you made me feel seen in a way that no one else had in a long time. Life suddenly looked less bleak than it had when I woke up that morning."

"I woke up that morning looking forward to the day. Then I wasn't quite sure what to make of you," Edith admitted. "But I knew you had potential."

"Potential," Julian echoed. "Reverend Shaver's speech must have given you a vision of the future."

"Maybe it did," she replied with a smile. "Maybe it did."

Chapter Sixteen

Alone in the parlor, enveloped in silence, tingling slightly from the whiskey he and Ray had tossed down, Julian began to relax. What a day it had been! Meeting Reverend Shaver in person and hearing his assertions that natural rights were an epic con game. Reconnecting with Edith Bartlett—Edith Leete, he corrected himself again—and walking the streets of Washington. And now he waited for an economist to take holographic form and teach him more about the monetary system of the tricentennial. It was superbly surreal, and he began to chuckle.

"What's so funny?" Ray asked as he entered the room.

Julian inhaled deeply and slouched back in his usual spot on the couch. "Just thinking about everything that happened today."

"How was your walk?" Ray asked.

He sat back up. "It was incredible. You really ended poverty," Julian said. "Everybody said so, but I didn't really believe it until I saw it myself."

"I didn't personally have anything to do with it," Ray laughed.

"Your mom, she was a delegate, so she sort of had something to do with it, right?" Julian frowned. "But she wouldn't tell me how we borrowed all those trillions."

Ray's grin would have made a cheshire cat proud. "You have one more minute to figure it out."

"I also asked her why it took fifty years for me to be thawed out," Julian said. "When the reporter was quizzing me, I didn't have an answer."

"What did she say?" the doctor asked, humor draining from his face.

Julian hesitated. *I was married. What would we have told Ray?* As a boy, had Ray picked up on Edith's internal struggle? The appearance of a red indicator light in the corner of the room warned him Teara Harper was about to arrive. "I didn't really get a straight answer," he said.

"That sounds about right," Ray agreed.

The economist flickered into the loveseat next to the doctor, smiling broadly. "Thanks for meeting with me again," Julian said, touching his hands together.

"My pleasure," Teara replied. After greeting Ray, she turned straight to business. "Now, you were going to figure out how the United States borrowed more than thirty trillion dollars after you were born, despite the fact that in 1992 the entire economy only produced around six trillion worth of goods and services." She looked at him expectantly.

Julian squirmed under her gaze. "I don't know. My first thought was that we borrowed it from other countries, but Ray pointed out that any dollars they loaned us would have had to come from the United States in the first place. People talked about the government printing money, but if that were the case, why would they need to borrow it? And I doubt the wealthy had been sitting on thirty trillion, waiting to loan it out."

"Oh, people borrowed much more," Teara said. "Household debt was another twenty trillion: mortgages, credit cards, student loans, auto loans."

Julian tossed his hands in frustration. "I give up, Teara. Where did it come from?"

Her eyes twinkled. "The answer I was looking for," she said, "is that it was all made up."

"Made up?" Julian echoed. "By who?"

"Who could create new dollars?"

"This is what I don't understand," Julian replied, shaking his head. "It would have to be the government printing dollars, right? But then how could the United States borrow from itself?"

"If you wanted to borrow money to buy a house, how would you do it?"

"From a bank," Julian said.

"And where would the bank get the money?"

"From the deposits other people put into the bank," he replied. It sounded

CHAPTER SIXTEEN

wrong as soon as he said it, because most people he knew owed more money than they had in the bank.

Teara shook her head. "Nope. Banks had Congress' permission to loan out dollars they didn't actually have through a mechanism called fractional reserve banking, putting new money—bank money—into circulation. As we describe it today, these dollars were borrowed into existence."

"Borrowed into existence?" Julian echoed. "How could people borrow something that didn't exist?"

"You just hinted at the government printing dollars," Teara reminded him. "Why is one easier to believe than the other? It was all made up."

He sat there for a moment, pondering. "So banks printed money?"

She nodded. "Essentially. In your time, 95% of money was bank money, Julian. That was how the US could end up borrowing tens of trillions of dollars that didn't even exist when you were born."

Julian rubbed his forehead. "Then how was it supposed to be paid back?"

"It was never supposed to be paid back," Teara told him. "By 2013, the national debt was equal to 100% of the country's GDP, and the pandemic drove it up even higher. Can you imagine what would have happened if everyone stopped buying things for a year to pay off the national debt? Sucking all that money out of the economy would have been catastrophic."

"Congress let banks create new money," Julian said slowly, trying to understand it. "Then Congress borrowed that new money, thirty-some trillion dollars worth, and paid interest on it? And the plan was to keep doing that forever?" The economist nodded. "But... that's so stupid!"

Ray and Teara laughed together on the loveseat. "Reverend Shaver warned you," Ray reminded him. "Money was one of many things the United States was doing backward, and you were wasting a trillion dollars a year as a result."[6]

"But that's so stupid!" he said again. "What about healthcare, education, school lunches, environmental protection, roads and bridges... I just can't."

---

[6] In 2023 alone, the United States paid a record $1.03 trillion in interest on its debt, or around $3,200 per citizen. https://fred.stlouisfed.org/series/A091RC1Q027SBEA

Julian shook his head sadly. "How did the American Union solve this?"

"Martin Luther King Jr. recognized the solution," Teara said. "He wrote, 'The problems of racial injustice and economic injustice can not be solved without a radical redistribution of political and economic power.' The American Union of swing voters was the radical redistribution of political power, Julian, and the American Union Jobs Program was the radical redistribution of economic power."

"Because of unconditional basic income?" Julian asked.

"That was a big part," Teara said. "But also because the American Union Jobs Program required the US Treasury to reclaim its constitutional authority under Article 1, Section 8, to issue debt-free money.

"The same authority was used by Abraham Lincoln during the Civil War to issue legal tender, commonly known as greenbacks. They made it possible for the United States to win the war and end chattel slavery. Instead of bank money, greenbacks were what is called base money: a 0% interest, sovereign currency backed by the credit of the United States.

"The American Union Jobs Program pays UBI in base money, Treasury Dollar Bills. They were the idea of economist Robert Hockett and pegged to the value of a Federal Reserve Note, the bank money of your time. By 2040, the national debt was virtually paid off."

"You just said paying off the debt would have been catastrophic," Julian reminded her.

"If the money had been sucked out of the economy in order to do so," Teara reciprocated. "Instead, Treasury Dollars replaced the debt; bonds were paid off as they matured, and the trillions remained in circulation as interest-free base money.

"Even better for the economy, the former bond holders, looking for other ways to get a return on their money, often invested in America's productive capacity. Since everyone gets an American Union Job, it created a trickle-up economy. Have you heard of William Jennings Bryan?"

It sounded like a rhetorical question, but he recalled jotting down the man's name in his journal after Polly Sigh mentioned him. "He ran for president with the People's Party. Something about a cross of gold and stopping deflation?"

Teara reappraised him in stunned silence; clearly, he had exceeded her expectations. "Very good," she said finally. Julian beamed, sneaking a quick glance at Ray to confirm his genius had been noticed. "Yes, deflation was hurting the farmers; falling prices made it difficult to pay their debts. I was asking because I had a quote for you from his *Cross of Gold* speech. Bryan said: 'If you legislate to make the masses prosperous, their prosperity will find its way up and through every class that rests upon it.' That's what a trickle-up economy does."

"What about inflation, though?" he asked. "I thought printing money was supposed to cause that."

"It absolutely can, when you add more than is necessary to counteract deflation. We still target 2% inflation as a healthy amount. Prices stay relatively stable, but there's always a little extra money swirling around the economy, looking for new business opportunities.

"Inflation has five primary causes, and it's a whole conversation of its own." She ticked them off on her fingers. "Supply shrinkage, cost push, profit pull, artificial scarcity, and demand pull. Julian, I'll bet you're thinking of demand pull inflation; demand for a product grows faster than the supply, and the price goes up."

"Okay," he agreed.

"But how does the market determine prices have to rise because of new money in the economy?" she asked. This time, she didn't wait for an answer to her rhetorical question. "It's like a game of musical chairs; the first people to buy get the old price. They get the cheap seats, so to speak, but as that money spreads to other consumers, there's fewer and fewer chairs. The last people to buy end up with the highest prices, or maybe no chair at all. This is the *cantillon effect*, named for a French economist.

"Allowing banks to add money into circulation generally rewards the wealthy, Julian, because they are best positioned to borrow it into existence for investments and speculation. Meanwhile, those below them experience the negative consequences of the cantillon effect, exacerbating wealth inequality and generating more societal problems."

"The rich get richer, and the poor get poorer," Julian muttered. "When you used the fox hunt analogy the other day, I didn't understand what you meant, saying dollars themselves were biased in favor of those who already had money and property. How did we fix that?"

"Why do we need to wedge more money into the economy?" Teara asked him.

"I had the same question," Ray said. "Why not just leave it alone?"

"Doctor Leete," she replied to the man next to her with mock severity, "money is the lifeblood of the economy; its proper circulation is essential to well-being. Could you determine an optimal amount of blood for a human being, some fixed amount that would keep a person in good health during the course of their lives?"

"Of course not," Ray answered. "A baby is born with only a few hundred milliliters of blood. By age ten, the child has two liters flowing through its veins, and a healthy adult might circulate six. It would be medical malpractice to suggest the quantity should be a fixed amount."

"Likewise for the amount of money in the economy," Teara said, grinning at him. "It is economic malpractice to suggest that the quantity should be a fixed amount."

Her gaze swiveled back to Julian. "Do you know the answer to why we have to keep adding money to the economy?"

Julian thought hard. "Because there are new things to buy and more people to buy them?"

"Of course!" the economist said. "If the money supply didn't keep up with population growth and the expanding amount of goods and services available, we'd get deflation. Ray, what happens if a person can't produce more blood as they grow?"

"Well, you'd see the symptoms of aplastic anemia," he answered. "Insufficient red blood cells to carry oxygen around the body would make them tired, not enough white blood cells means a higher proclivity for infections, and a scarcity of platelets makes it harder for blood to clot. All sorts of problems would develop."

Teara nodded. "Deflation is just as unhealthy for the economy. That's what happened at the end of the nineteenth century on the gold standard. Farmers were especially hurt, and Bryan wanted to address it with the policy of free silver.

"Deflation discourages investors from borrowing, slowing growth; it encourages consumers to hold their money because their purchasing power is increasing, which slows demand; it pressures businesses to cut prices—deflation—to get consumers to spend; and to reduce their payroll, with layoffs, pay cuts, or both, in order to deliver lower prices.

"Most importantly, Julian," the economist said, ensuring she had his full attention, "deflation violates our fifth constitutional duty: securing the blessings of liberty to ourselves and our posterity. When the per capita money supply shrinks, it shifts economic power into the hands of those who already hold money. Since each generation has to compete with the previous ones for a share of economic resources, deflation is a systemic bias against the liberty of our posterity."

Teara smiled brightly at Julian as he absorbed all the information. "Let me get this straight," he said finally. "You have to keep adding money to the economy?"

"If you didn't, it would be a zero-sum game," she said. "The economist Milton Friedman advocated for increasing the money supply by five percent each year."

"And now the US Treasury does it by giving every citizen a share of new base money, as part of the American Union Jobs Program, as unconditional basic income?"

She nodded. "That's the proper way to minimize the cantillon effect. Since new money must always be wedged into the economy, the natural and moral spot to place that wedge is at the very bottom of the socioeconomic pyramid, so every citizen is lifted up equally.

"This was the real purpose of the American Union Jobs Program, Julian. The increase in the money supply is the profit from our growing economy, and the dividends rightfully belong to the citizens."

Julian laughed out loud. "The first time we talked, you told me the purpose was to build a safety floor under everyone."

Teara and Ray joined in his laughter. "Well, that's true too," she replied. "But that safety floor is built out of Treasury Dollars."

After a moment's consideration, Julian asked, "Do banks still borrow money into existence?"

She shook her head. "For a country reborn on the principles of truth and nonviolence, there was no place for allowing banks to loan out money they didn't actually have. And as a practical matter, if banks were allowed to add money to the economy, the amount of new base money being issued as UBI would have to be reduced in order to control inflation. The public good would be diverted into private profit.

"However, allowances had to be made during the transition. Fractional reserve banking was gradually abolished while the national debt was paid off; each month the percentage of deposits that banks had to keep in reserve was increased, until it reached 100%. Today, the Federal Reserve functions as a public investment bank. It holds trillions in assets and distributes them to twenty-three regional banks. In turn, they loan it out to businesses, guiding capital into productive purposes."

"Was that why the Federal Reserve used interest rates to manage the economy?" Julian asked. "Lowering them when they wanted people to borrow money into existence faster and stimulate the economy, and raising interest rates when they wanted people to borrow less?"

"That was the theory," Teara said. "The idea was that a central bank should be independent, so the legislative branch wouldn't be tempted to influence policy for political gain. But there were two major flaws. First, the Federal Reserve had no actual control over how much bank money the commercial lenders churned out.

"Second, the Federal Reserve wasn't really independent; it was very, very connected to the banking industry. Big banks had major influence over policy, which they steered in ways that would produce larger financial gains for themselves. By 2026, the corruption was obvious to anyone paying attention, so something had to change.

"It sounds like it," Ray chimed in. "But why did it take so long to figure out a better way?"

CHAPTER SIXTEEN

"The idea the United States could function this way had been known for a long time, Ray," she answered. "All the way back during World War Two, the Chair of the Federal Reserve Bank of New York gave a speech explaining how taxes for revenue were obsolete; a central bank could simply spend.

"Of course, there are very good policy reasons to have taxes; he listed four. The first was to claw back extra money from circulation and keep the purchasing power of the dollar relatively stable. Different countries had different goals for inflation; ours was 2%; other nations like India and South Africa aimed as high as 6%.

"The second was to express public policy around income and wealth inequality. These inequalities distort the economy; progressive income taxes were an attempt to address them. But since the wealthy were good at finding ways to disguise their income, consumption taxes were used as offsets for the American Union Jobs Program, so that those who spent lavishly paid the most.

"Third, taxes could be used to guide industries and other economic groups. The other big, new taxes were on pollution. A carbon fee created a financial incentive to use less greenhouse gases; the rate went up each year, which helped accelerate the transition away from fossil fuels. There was also a tax on plastic; it was causing widespread environmental harm. A fee on new production encouraged recycling, and a small, per-unit fee on consumer goods discouraged disposable and single-use items.

"The fourth reason was user fees: accounting for the cost of things. Think of how the gas tax funded the highway system in your time, Julian. The real insight of the speech was to think of taxes as policy questions, not revenue ones. What kind of country did we want to be?"

"One that ended poverty?" Julian answered. Remembering what he'd seen in the nation's capital today brought a smile to his face.

"We had that option for a long time," Teara confirmed. "Dr. King saw it, and we harnessed the power of the Phoenix Cycle to make it happen."

Chapter Seventeen

That night, after recording the day's highlights in his journal, Julian dreamed of the reparations rally.

He moved through the crowd, looking for Edith. Gun-toting white men were everywhere, and he had to warn her. His search became more and more frantic until he finally saw the hand-lettered sign proclaiming *Power concedes nothing without a demand*. But however he approached her, she refused to look at him. He called her name, but she turned her back to him.

The gunmen were getting closer, moving in like moths to a flame. He pleaded with Edith to come with him, only to be rebuffed. Finally, Julian sank to his knees on the grass, beating his hands against his head in frustration and begging her to listen.

Another figure marched through the crowd, old and thin, with hands held high. It was Reverend Shaver, and he gave Julian a deliberate wink. Behind him, driving him forward with the barrel of an AR-15, was the red-bearded gunman. He looked down on Julian with angry blue eyes.

Then Edith was kneeling with him. As young and beautiful as when he'd first seen her, she leaned forward to kiss him. The quick brushing of the lips hinted at more, and all thought of escaping the crowd flew from his mind. When she pulled back, her hands clutched the sides of his head as she stared intently into his eyes. "Is he robbing him?" Edith asked.

Julian leaned in to kiss her again, reaching out to hold her. They moaned as the kiss became more passionate, and he opened his mouth to hers. A warm fluid began to flow past his teeth, and he realized with horror that it was blood. He tried to pull away, but Edith held his head tightly, pressing

CHAPTER SEVENTEEN

her lips firmly to his. The thick, warm liquid filled his mouth, spilling down his throat as he struggled to breathe. He was choking, gagging, as Edith kissed him harder.

Gasping, Julian sat straight up in bed. His heart raced as he swallowed air greedily, but there was no impediment, and he fell back against the pillow with the dream already fading. He smacked his lips together and unconsciously repeated Edith's question to himself, the words slurring together as he slipped back down into sleep.

In the morning, none of it remained in his memory except the piercing blue eyes, prodding him from within. Julian lay in bed, letting his brain examine the idea. Where had he seen blue eyes like that recently?

His mind produced a terrible suggestion. It was like ice, freezing him in place, stopping his breath. The stalker, the old white man who'd approached him after Idabee's hearing, muttering about unfinished business, must have been a young white man in 2026. Had he been one of the gunmen from the reparations rally?

A search on his tablet revealed that two of the attackers had survived. Before long, he uncovered their mug shots. The red-bearded ringleader, Connor Sullivan, stared up from the screen, blue eyes boiling with hate, glowering at the camera with a look of annoyance that Julian thought he recognized as the same one the old man had given him in the virtual meeting room. Without conscious thought, his hand crept to his side, tracing the hard knots of scar tissue.

Within a few minutes, he found a more recent picture showing the killer clean-shaven, and then Julian knew with certainty.

Connor Sullivan was stalking him.

Chapter Eighteen

Julian glanced up at the indicator lights—two reds and a green—when he reentered the parlor on Thursday afternoon. Idabee's projection was there waiting, and he was about to sit in the chair next to her when a man's form began to appear. Stepping away in surprise, Julian settled on the couch instead and waited for the lights to turn solid green.

The arrival turned out to be a white man in his early seventies, with a full head of gray hair, big bushy eyebrows, and a neatly trimmed beard. His clothes were well worn and his eyes, Julian couldn't help but notice, were green. "Welcome, Professor Carlton," Idabee said, hands pressed together in greeting. "I'm grateful for your visit."

Julian was struck by a momentary incongruity; the visit was taking place in his—Dr. Leete's—parlor, not Idabee's. Then he realized this exact scene was playing out in her parlor as well as Carlton's. Did this mean he was visiting the other man's parlor despite having no clue of his physical location on the planet? Before Julian's mind could go too far down the linguistic rabbit hole, he realized the others were looking at him expectantly.

He pressed his palms together. "Thank you for joining us," Julian said after introductions were made. "I know a bit about nonviolence from Martin Luther King Jr.'s work, but I don't understand how a political system can be based on it. Idabee thought you could help explain."

"Of course! Dr. King's work is part of the foundation for the American Union," Carlton began. "You probably know he was a student of Gandhi's, one of the architects of the larger philosophical framework of nonviolence.

CHAPTER EIGHTEEN

Nonviolence carries certain duties, and the American Union used them to address the largest social problems America faced, the triple evils King identified as poverty, racism, and militarism."

"That was the first platform the American Union brought to the voters," Idabee reminded Julian. "End poverty, end mass incarceration, end the endless wars." The phrase brought a warm smile to Carlton's face. He looked at Julian and fell silent. Unclear if his gaze was scrutiny or if the gray-haired man was merely lost in reflection, Julian and Idabee waited.

"The United States was at a historic turning point," Carlton started suddenly. "Have you heard of the Phoenix Cycle?" Julian nodded cautiously. "It began with the Revolutionary War; years of fighting left such bitter feelings that three decades later, we ended up at war with the British again. Contrast this with Gandhi's methods in India's struggle for independence. It's said his genius was that he allowed the British to leave as friends.

"The second iteration brought about the Civil War. Hundreds of thousands of Americans died in the fighting. Yes, we abolished chattel slavery, but the violence in the way we did it left scars on our nation's psyche that took nearly two hundred years to heal.

"But," Carlton brightened, "America's rebirth during the New Deal was accomplished nonviolently! After the Great Depression hit and FDR was elected, a peaceful transfer of power and a supermajority in Congress let him take the reins of the nation and guide it to one where the general welfare of the nation was promoted like never before, ushering in decades of prosperity.

"When the pandemic struck, we were on the cusp of a new societal restructuring. The status quo was a sinking ship; there was no choice but to find an alternative. It didn't have to be a peaceful process, though," Carlton concluded. "I knew many people back then who thought there would be a civil war."

Julian nodded emphatically. "We were just talking about how polarized politics was. Neither party was going to get a supermajority like FDR; the system was broken." He confessed the extent of his frustration. "I was willing to fight to change it; I just didn't know how or where to start. Stella

Freedom said the American Union was pitched as a moral crusade to fight Dr. King's triple evils. But I don't see how fasting changes how politics works."

Idabee piped up. "Because politics requires compromise. Fasting and compromise are two sides of the same coin—willingly giving something up."

Carlton settled back in his chair and folded his hands. "The fast for peace has many aspects," he said, "and one of them is that it takes an intention. The monthly fast for peace helps manifest a shared intention to work together for a common goal—peace. King defined peace as 'not the absence of tension, but the presence of justice.' As that applied to the Phoenix Cycle, economic injustice, racial injustice, and the injustice of unrepresentative government all needed to be addressed again.

"Another aspect is the power of shared self-sacrifice. Do you know about the Birmingham bus boycott?" Julian did, but Idabee shook her head. "It was King's first big civil rights campaign. Seating on the city buses was segregated; you"—Carlton gestured to the young black woman—"were prohibited by law from sitting next to me. For over a year, blacks boycotted the buses, refusing to ride."

"Instead, they walked," Julian said. Then, realizing: "They willingly gave something up."

Carlton nodded encouragingly. "And it strengthened their bonds as a community. Group fasts can wield the same power; for example, the world's major religions have all utilized fasting. Because fasts have to be voluntary—willingly giving something up—they serve as a way for people to opt in to the set of rules the religions prescribed. The associations we make voluntarily are our strongest ones, and religions were among the most powerful forces for political, social, and cultural change in history.

"The American Union was strictly secular, but like Gandhi's use of national days of fasting in India, it created the opportunity for principled nonviolence to unite people around a better paradigm. Do you know what he said at the first one?" Carlton asked rhetorically. "He said, 'No country has ever risen, no nation has ever been made without sacrifice, and we are

CHAPTER EIGHTEEN

trying an experiment of building up ourselves by self-sacrifice without resorting to violence in any shape or form. This is *satyagraha*.'

"He didn't know that America had its own traditions with them as well, going all the way back to the seventeenth century. The fast for peace was an experiment to rebuild a crumbling country through self-sacrifice and nonviolence—and it worked."

"What's satyagraha?" Julian asked, stumbling over the unfamiliar word.

"Satyagraha is the technique of nonviolent action that Gandhi developed, often translated as soul force or truth force. The goal is never to defeat opponents, but to persuade them of the justice of the cause and win them over. This was principled but also practical: the British wouldn't let Gandhi's people vote on anything important." Carlton grinned. "We didn't have that restriction in the US.

"Another important aspect is that the fast is accessible; people can participate anywhere on the planet. Huge rallies can create the same sense of community and purpose, but they require a certain amount of privilege: the ability to take time off work, find transportation or childcare, and so forth. Observing a twenty-four-hour fast is free, and the flexibility in the start and end points empowers all those who want to create the shared intention."

"You said America had a tradition with national days of fasting?" Julian asked. "Can you tell me more about that? Because it doesn't really sound like the country I knew. Yes, fasting was trendy, but Americans were more known for being obese."

"Obese," Carlton repeated with a smile. "I remember that. Many American presidents promoted group fasts as a call for peace and justice. For example, when the British blockaded the port after the Boston Tea Party, Thomas Jefferson authored a resolution in Virginia calling for a day of fasting and prayer, to inspire Parliament with wisdom, moderation, and justice. George Washington wrote about it in his diary: he went to church and fasted all day.

"Presidents continued to issue similar proclamations. During the Civil War, Abraham Lincoln called for a national day of humiliation, fasting, and prayer."

"Humiliation?" Julian echoed.

Carlton chuckled. "From the root word, humility. This is another aspect of the fast for peace—to be humble and acknowledge that we can't solve every problem on our own. The fast was a way to ask for help from the rest of the union family. This was true for the politicians, from first-time candidates for Congress up to the President of the United States. Joining the fast for peace was a humbling admission they needed help to produce the result they wanted, whether their goal was simply to get elected or bring about legislative action." Julian nodded; asking for help wasn't really his style.

After a moment, Carlton continued. "Another important part of nonviolence is striving to create win-win scenarios," he said. "As we use it in our day-to-day lives, it means to avoid thinking in terms of a zero-sum game, where someone else has to lose in order for us to win. On the surface, it's a hard principle to apply to the election process."

"We learned about Duverger's law a few days ago," Idabee said. "How the US was stuck with a two-party system as long as elections were a zero-sum game."

"It was one of the biggest challenges in persuading people to adopt a political system based on nonviolence," Carlton said. "Voters were used to thinking in terms of winners and losers; it was an adversarial system by design. The American Union succeeded by building a new political identity: conscientious objectors to partisan politics who sincerely wanted to see Congress—as a whole, not any specific party or individual—succeed in solving the country's problems."

The gray-haired man stroked his beard in contemplation, possibly waiting to give Julian a chance to ask more questions. When none came after a moment, he fired off his own. "Do you know the origin of the monthly fast for peace?"

"Gandhi's first fast?" Julian replied, only to have Carlton shake his head negatively.

Idabee chimed in. "Reverend Shaver started it after the reparations rally, on April 15, to commemorate the death of Abraham Lincoln."

"Good guess," Carlton replied, "but no."

"Is it Martin Luther King's birthday, January 15?" Julian offered.

"No," Carlton said, settling in his chair as he began the story. "It comes from a challenge thrown down in August 1947. 'The fifteenth is the day of our trial,' Gandhi said. 'Observe a fast on that day.' His nonviolent war of independence had finally succeeded, but the British carved the Muslim nation of Pakistan out of India as they left. Gandhi didn't want to celebrate that, so he boycotted all the official proceedings and carried his message of peace east, to where there'd been religious violence.

"When he passed through Kolkata, the city leaders asked Gandhi to stay and help keep things calm. A year earlier, thousands had died in religious riots, and gangs armed with military surplus roamed the streets. He agreed, if the state's outgoing governor, Shaheed Suhrawardy, would share a house with him.

"One Hindu, one Muslim; they would live together unarmed, unprotected, under one roof, and observe the fifteenth as a day of fasting. They would lead by example and demonstrate that Hindus and Muslims could peacefully coexist. Acutely aware of the tension in the enormous city, Suhrawardy accepted the challenge.

"On August 15, 1947, the day India became independent, Gandhi, Suhrawardy, and everyone else who was willing to answer Gandhi's call, they fasted for peace. It worked. Thousands of Hindus and Muslims took to the streets, not to settle old grudges, but in unity, reminding some of the Christmas truce during World War One.

"When I first heard this story, Julian, it inspired me. Republicans and Democrats had the ability to declare a truce and celebrate the things all Americans had in common, which were far greater than our differences. And so I continue to answer the challenge each month. I observe a fast on that day; it's the day of our trial. Do we want peace? The verdict is yes.

"It took me a few years to realize the moral of the story. Gandhi wasn't the hero here. He was coasting on his reputation; he even took a medical exemption that day and drank juice."

Julian leaned forward, listening carefully, as Carlton continued, "The real hero was Suhrawardy. Why did he fast for peace? Julian, he was a man who lived a life that was the opposite of Gandhi's. He was a career politician who was in it for himself; he made exorbitant profits stealing and reselling grain during the famine a few years earlier, while millions—literally millions—of his countrymen starved. He slept with as many women as his wealth gave him access to, he drank alcohol in violation of his Muslim faith, he ate prodigiously and weighed three times as much as Gandhi.

"And now his time in India was at an end. He was headed to Pakistan; he was literally about to walk away from Kolkata, where many people blamed him for the killings the previous year. So why did he stay with Gandhi for weeks after independence and fast for peace?"

"Why?" Julian asked, curious.

"Because people are always, always, always capable of redemption," Carlton said, affixing his gaze on Julian.

The knowing look pierced him, exposing what he knew to be true about Connor Sullivan. The internal conflict was quickly smoothed over as Julian realized that while the white supremacist was technically capable of redemption, it didn't mean he'd actually achieved it, or that he was worthy of forgiveness for his actions. The contradiction thus resolved, Julian returned his focus to what Carlton was saying.

"I don't know why exactly he did it, but the peace in Kolkata worked because the people wanted peace," the professor continued. "And like America fifty years ago, all it took was an action to coalesce around, to manifest that shared intention—the fast for peace on the fifteenth."

Julian exhaled deeply, as though he could release the memories of past injustices. The fast had brought him a personal sense of peace, but no deep connection to anything larger. Still, he had no reason to doubt the veracity of the gray-haired man's claim.

When it was clear Carlton was done with the story, he had another question. "Dr. Leete said I should ask about voluntary temperance." He looked to Idabee. "Is it connected to the sobriety pledge you mentioned for delegates?"

CHAPTER EIGHTEEN

"Yes," Idabee replied, then gestured for Carlton to answer the rest.

"For most of human history," Carlton observed, "intoxicants were primarily for ceremonial and celebratory purposes. Eventually, growth in productivity, when safety and survival weren't a constant struggle, enabled widespread social use. Then, of course, their addictive nature made production and distribution a profitable business model. But more consumption didn't actually add value to society. Instead, it was a net negative.

"Alcohol was legal, but caused huge problems in America every single year—it cost hundreds of billions in lost productivity, it was involved in hundreds of thousands of violent crimes, including most sexual assaults, and it killed more than a hundred thousand people."

"Dr. Leete told me it causes cancer, too?"

Carlton nodded and continued, "People were starting to recognize the harm it inflicted, but the alcohol industry was spending more than a half-billion dollars a year in advertising. Street drugs had their own set of problems—another hundred thousand deaths, global violence from the cartels, and a destructive influence on the criminal justice system.

"In short, Julian, voluntary temperance is the philosophy that drugs and alcohol should be legal, but people shouldn't use them," Carlton explained. "As Gandhi wrote: 'The man who stops drinking under compulsion by law, and not as a matter of duty, cannot be called a virtuous man. It is the man who of his own free will avoids drinking that is really virtuous.'

"Voluntary temperance was a philosophy that addressed both sides of the problem: secure the liberty of people to make decisions about recreational intoxicants, but encourage them to make the best choice and not partake.

"Sobriety is also an important component of nonviolence in a couple of ways. First, one of the duties of nonviolence is to consume mindfully. Intoxicants are, of course, toxic, so their use is self-harm. Second, clouding our minds limits our ability to serve others. It's this part that ties back to the sobriety pledge for delegates during sessions of the legislative assembly; when delegates volunteer to exercise decision-making authority on behalf of others, it's a way of committing to doing the best job possible. Thirdly, sobriety has a component of self-purification."

"That's one of Dr. King's four steps for a nonviolent campaign, isn't it?" Julian asked. Idabee looked at him in astonishment, and he grinned with pride.

"It is," Carlton agreed, seeming pleased Julian had made the connection. "You can also look at it as self-sacrifice or self-improvement. Since the American Union was pitched as a moral crusade to address King's triple evils, advocating for sobriety and leading by example helped deflect any accusations that supporters wanted to end the drug war so they could get high."

"Wait, people had to embrace sobriety just to join the American Union?" Julian said skeptically.

"No, like the fasting, it's voluntary, but also embedded into the culture. Part of becoming an American Union organizer is completing an annual training program that includes thirty days of sobriety, like a Dry January. Events to promote the organization had to be sober ones, and people arranging local meetups were encouraged to find places that didn't serve alcohol."

"This is the self-improvement program I was telling you about, Julian," Idabee said. "You can come on April 1."

"If you're willing to commit to sobriety that month," Carlton clarified. "I lead the group because I find value in self-improvement, and have since I went through the program more than five decades ago. This is a way of paying it forward, but seizing the moral high ground for the American Union makes it win-win."

Julian nodded thoughtfully. "Legalize drugs, but don't use them," he said. "Everyone had to have liked at least half of that. Did it make drug use go up or down?"

"Remember," Carlton said, "just like Dr. King's triple evils, these solutions didn't exist in isolation. Ending the drug war went hand in hand with ending poverty; drug use went down, but there were many contributing factors."

"I talked with an economist last week about unconditional basic income.

CHAPTER EIGHTEEN

The data about all the problems poverty caused was pretty surprising." Julian reconsidered. "Surprising isn't the right word; it all made sense. I've always seen poverty; I've lived it. I just never really thought through all the consequences before."

Carlton nodded. "But did they explain to you why the program was universal when only about half of Americans were living in or near poverty?"

Julian agreed halfheartedly. "She said it was simpler—less bureaucracy. But in my day, there were three Americans"—he held up three fingers for emphasis—"who had as much wealth as the bottom half of the country. Three! If I were going to end poverty back then, I sure wouldn't have given them any more money."

"It was my day, too," Carlton said lightly. "What would you have done with their share of the money instead?"

"Given it to people who deserved it," Julian answered promptly.

"Wasn't that precisely the argument for all welfare reform? Some people didn't really deserve the money, and if they were excluded, there would be more for everyone else."

"It's not the same thing," Julian said.

"It was the same pitch, but to different targets," Carlton said, drawing imaginary lines in the air. "'If we divide America into these two groups, yours will be better off.' It's the old story of us versus them: divide and rule. You heard a practical reason for including everyone—simplicity—but there's a principled one as well." He leaned forward. "The real purpose of the American Union Jobs Program was to finally put everyone on the same side, universally. As a matter of principle, it refused to draw a line and instead insisted on a circle—one that included all Americans unconditionally.

"Nonviolence is built on recognizing the value in all of us. By establishing universality as a core principle of the American Union, that every American is deserving, it created a new paradigm of unity and addressed the social problems of division."

Julian shrugged. "I found the practical reasons more compelling. I can see how a universal program is simpler. But it's silly to assume everyone deserves it."

"Why?" Carlton asked neutrally. "If I conceded your point—a non-zero number of people are undeserving—why would it be silly to build a program on the assumption that everyone is worthy? Wouldn't you rather live in a society that believes the best in you instead of constantly reminding you that you might have the worst qualities?"

Julian struggled for a rebuttal, but a childhood memory surfaced. Carlton held his gaze in a nonconfrontational way, patiently waiting for a response, and when he could no longer let the silence fester, Julian spoke. "I remember sitting at the kitchen table when I was little—maybe six or seven? I was supposed to draw a picture of what I wanted to be when I grew up. My mother told me I could be anything I wanted, and I wanted to be an astronaut like I'd seen on TV. But my dad, he said, 'Georgia, don't lie to the boy. He can't be an astronaut.'

"Looking backward, I realize he was probably drinking. He kept arguing with her until finally I just scribbled over my picture. But he was right," he said, taking a deep breath before plunging forward to his conclusion. "I couldn't be an astronaut; it was unrealistic. Even so, I'd rather live in a society that believes in my potential than one that emphasizes limitations."

Idabee offered him a sympathetic smile, and Carlton pressed his hands together again, an encompassing gesture of gratitude, sympathy, and solidarity. "Well, now you do," he said warmly.

Chapter Nineteen

"They're like fraternal twins," Julian said wonderingly.

Shirley Nussbaum grinned as he stared inside the parlor. The dimensions were identical to Ray's, with the same seating arrangement in a loose oval, but the Nussbaums' walls were completely different. Murals splashed joyous color across them, displaying smiling animals and vibrant shapes. "Do you like it?" she said shyly. "I painted them."

"Thanks for having us over," Idabee said, gently prodding Julian to move through the doorway with a hand on his waist. Unlike yesterday's conversation with Professor Carlton, she'd physically arrived at Ray's condo, leading him through the building to the Nussbaums. They settled into adjacent chairs at the far end of the room.

"Always a pleasure to share a session day with another delegate," Andrea said, joining her wife on the loveseat. "We'll show Julian how the people's legislative assembly works. And thanks for inviting Polly Sigh to visit us beforehand."

A moment later, Polly's holographic form shimmered into the room. The purple hair she'd sported at their first meeting was now jet black, as was her suit. Polly looked around to each of the four faces, and introductions were made.

"Do you mind if I record our conversation?" Andrea asked. "Shirley and I have a small show commentating on the assembly, and I think our viewers would love to learn more about the mechanics of the American Union." Polly agreed, and one by one, everyone gave verbal confirmation. When Andrea's tablet announced that recording was underway, she rattled off a brief introduction of their three guests: Seated Delegate Idabee Leete, daughter of the Dr. Leete who'd recently awakened Julian West, hero of the 2026 reparations rally, and Polly Sigh, an expert in political science.

Julian leaned forward. "Polly, I appreciate how you explained why third parties weren't a way out of the political mess fifty years ago," he said, "but I'm still trying to fully understand how the American Union started as a union of swing voters. Things were so polarized, I have a hard time picturing a bloc of voters willing to vote for both Republicans and Democrats and ignore wedge issues."

"Wedge issues?" Idabee asked.

"Political issues that are used to wedge voters into separate parties, usually through a false dichotomy," Polly explained.

"Why would you want to do that?" Idabee wondered. "Politics is about setting policy, building consensus around solutions."

Julian exploded into laughter. "Building consensus? It was the exact opposite, politics was about keeping people divided."

The four women waited, bemused, for him to sober up. "Julian, do you want to try to answer Idabee's question?" Andrea suggested. "Why would you want to wedge people apart?"

"Money. The almighty dollar," he replied easily. "Get people worked up, and they'll donate money. Campaigns cost millions of dollars, so the more angry people you had contributing, the better your chance of winning."

"That's a good point," Polly conceded. "The other part, though, is polarization. Wedge issues generated single-issue voters that were essential to maintaining a stable political base. That wedge could be made bigger by demonizing the other side, promoting an us-versus-them mentality that creates party loyalty.

"Of course, there was a practical problem with consolidating voters around opposite sides of a single issue. The people who were the most passionate about an issue also tended to have the most extreme views, which produced a downward spiral of demonization and polarization."

"Because demonization is good for fundraising," Julian said.

"What about their constitutional duty to insure domestic tranquility?"

CHAPTER NINETEEN

Idabee asked. "Were they just ignoring that?"

"Yes," Polly and Julian said simultaneously; she motioned for him to continue.

"Two of the big issues were abortion and gun control," Julian explained, "so most people who said they were independent usually had a preference for one party. A true swing voter would have to be willing to elect a candidate who had the opposite opinion on those issues."

"It's interesting that you say opposite opinion, Julian," Polly said. "The American Union used data-driven metrics to build consensus around specific actions. Are you familiar with VOZ metrics—variable-one-zero?" Julian nodded. "Nonary logic was used to channel consensus into one of the nine outcomes. You mentioned gun control; tell me about that."

"Mass shootings kept happening," he said. "Schools, churches, stores, workplaces. Democrats tried to ban assault rifles. Republicans blocked them. Gridlock."

"Sounds frustrating," Polly replied. "Why did they want to ban assault rifles?"

Julian stared at her. "To stop mass shootings."

"Why?" Polly asked.

"Why?" Julian echoed, looking around at the other women. Their expressions held no clue to whether she was messing with him. "Why did they want to stop people from being killed?" Polly nodded. "To stop people from being killed," he repeated slowly.

"So the real goal was to bring down the number of gun deaths," Polly summarized.

"Well, yeah."

"And that's the data point to use for VOZ metrics," Polly began brightly, having tweezed the desired response from her student. "Everyone wanted the variable—per capita gun deaths—to trend lower. The next step in nonary logic is determining whether to target supply or demand. It was less practical to address the supply side—the hundreds of millions of guns. The American Union went after the demand side of gun deaths with the three planks of the first legislative package. I looked over the data, Julian, because I thought you might ask about wedge issues.

"Mass shootings were a small but highly visible portion of gun deaths, and unfortunately, they were not a new phenomenon in American history. During the previous iteration of the Phoenix Cycle, the United States suffered from what were then called rampage shootings, after wealth inequality and the Great Depression frayed the fabric of our societal bonds.

"The American Union Jobs Program established a safety floor under everyone, dramatically improving America's overall mental health. The majority of gun deaths were suicides, and common causes included financial problems, drug abuse, depression, and difficulties with relationships. Poverty, of course, exacerbated all of those conditions.

"Police shootings were also responsible for more than one thousand deaths every year. The criminal justice reforms included restrictions on no-knock warrants, an end to the program that dispersed military surplus to law enforcement, and a requirement for police training in de-escalation.

"A huge contributor to the gun culture was military glorification, which promoted violence as a perfectly acceptable problem-solving technique. By reducing the size and scope of the military, we further shifted our national mindset toward peace and nonviolence."

Julian nodded. "And it worked?"

"Of course, Julian; gun deaths started to fall even before people began getting UBI payments, because hope had been rekindled. That isn't to say gun bans couldn't have also reduced gun deaths, but when people passionate about reducing the supply of guns were offered specific, data-driven solutions to reduce deaths, they had to make a choice. They could continue to support politics as usual, or compromise and show that reasonable adults could work out their differences rationally—which was exactly the message anyone considering gun violence needed to learn."

"Okay," Julian said. "But what about abortion? That was one of the rights the Supreme Court took away."

The four women were silent for a moment. "Stella Freedom talked about this in one of her books," Polly said finally. "We have a different perspective today. First, it was Congress that had refused to set national policy for fifty

CHAPTER NINETEEN

years in favor of letting the Supreme Court do it. Second, abortion is not about rights, but duty. When a baby would be viable outside of the womb, we have a duty to secure the blessings of liberty for them—our posterity."

"Julian, remember we talked about how there are policy variables that get reevaluated each year?" Idabee asked. "One of them sets the survival rate of premature babies that determines the threshold where abortion is no longer allowed."

"No exceptions?" Julian asked.

"If the pregnancy puts the mother's health at risk, an abortion is self-defense, of course," Andrea answered. "Likewise, there are accommodations if she didn't consent to the pregnancy. There will always be a non-zero number of abortions, but with universal healthcare, unexpected pregnancies are infrequent."

"Like with gun deaths, there was always consensus that the number should trend lower," Polly added. "Since three-quarters of women seeking abortion back then said they couldn't afford the baby, addressing poverty was highly effective in driving down the demand. Mothers could also enroll babies in the American Union Jobs Program and start receiving the child's benefits."

"Wait," Julian said, "before they were born?"

Polly nodded. "It's automatic once they cross that viability threshold, but women can opt in sooner. Society asserting a duty to protect an unborn baby's well-being means committing resources to help them succeed. Abortion is safe, legal, and rare."

"That was the real purpose of the American Union Jobs Program," Shirley declared. "To bring down the number of needless deaths in the United States."

"Just like gun control," Polly continued, "people passionate about reducing the supply of abortions had to decide what their real goal was. The number of abortions fell dramatically, along with the infant mortality rate. Thousands and thousands more newborn babies lived to reach their first birthday, thanks to the enactment of paid family leave.

"By using nonary logic to address root causes instead of arguing over how best to treat the symptoms, the American Union was able to offer life-saving solutions directly to the voting public."

Julian looked around the room again. "I thought this wasn't direct democracy?"

"It's not," Polly replied, shaking her head. "There are still checks and balances; if the delegates' proposal is too polarizing or demanding, Congress can—and has—intentionally turned it down. Julian, you probably recognized the duopoly was the biggest barrier to enacting reforms because they benefited from the status quo. In your time, it had been more than fifty years since Congress sent a constitutional amendment to the states and had it ratified. The American Union could only succeed at delivering a radical restructuring of government by working within the existing framework."

"Unionizing as voters let us look out for each other," Shirley offered.

"That's true," Polly agreed. "But game theory is an important part of how it works. Julian, you may have heard of the prisoner's dilemma, where two parties can each rationally conclude they are better off only thinking of themselves, even if their best outcome comes from cooperation. It was a thought experiment based on the way the criminal justice system used to function."

"What is it?" Idabee asked.

"Two men get arrested and accused of committing a burglary the previous night," Polly explained. "They're held in solitary confinement, so they can't communicate, and the prosecutor comes to each to offer them a plea bargain if they'll testify against the other."

"Wait!" Idabee objected. "Why were they still being held? How would a prosecutor talk to them directly without going through their lawyer? What was the reason they were in solitary confinement?"

"It doesn't really apply any more," Polly admitted.

"I want to hear more about how the criminal justice system works now," said Julian truthfully.

Polly held up her hands, appealing for order. "The American Union wasn't the first political reform to use game theory. When the Framers wrote the Constitution, they dictated that members of the Senate would

CHAPTER NINETEEN

be elected by state legislatures. During the First Gilded Age, the People's Party wanted the direct election of senators, to fight corruption and let voters hold them accountable. But until the Seventeenth Amendment was adopted, Oregon developed a workaround using game theory, and other states followed suit.

"The state would hold an election for US Senate—really, a referendum, since it was nonbinding. Each candidate for the state legislature was given the option of pledging to vote for the Senate candidate who won the referendum. The pledges appeared on the official ballot, increasing their appeal to the voters and their chance of winning the election.

"In 1894, before he ran for president, William Jennings Bryan campaigned across Nebraska for the US Senate. With the backing of the Democrats and the People's Party, he received more than 70% support, but the Republicans won a majority in the state legislature and sent their own candidate to Washington.

"By 1910, however, Nebraska had adopted the Oregon system, and Republican George Norris won the referendum for the Senate seat. That year, the Democrats controlled the legislature, but they kept their word and sent him to Washington instead of their own candidate. This system maintained adherence to the letter of the Constitution until 1913, when Bryan, who had become Secretary of State, certified the ratification of the Seventeenth Amendment.

"The best outcome for the men in the prisoner's dilemma is achieved when neither takes a deal, but each can rationally conclude it's in their best interest. State legislatures could have held onto their power if everyone refused to take the pledge, but individual candidates rationally concluded they were better off taking the deal. And so the people of their states came out ahead."

"And the American Union used game theory so the people of the United States came out ahead?" Julian asked.

"That's right," Polly confirmed. "When Muster Day came around, enough people were willing to pool their votes with the American Union."

"With the fast for peace?" Julian said.

Polly nodded. "For the general public, the twenty-four-hour fast is a personal choice and can be a private one. But for the candidates for federal office, Muster Day is a take-it-or-leave-it offer. They either join the fast for peace and publicly support immediate passage of the year's legislative demands, or they're recorded as being in opposition. This roll call vote, along with whether Congress actually passes the legislation in one week, is how the American Union endorsements are made."

"Well," Julian replied, "the obvious question is, what happens if none of the candidates take the offer?"

All four women smiled. "Julian, there's a logical solution," Polly said, "but I suspect that, like the nonviability of third parties, it'll take a little while before you accept it. I see Andrea's looking at the time; the legislative session is almost ready to start. Want to continue this another day?"

"Sure, that'd be fine," he agreed. "But is it that the American Union doesn't endorse anyone?" The chorus of chuckles quickly shot down his theory. Polly said her goodbyes and then disappeared.

"It's starting soon," Shirley said. With a few taps on her tablet, the parlor produced a large video screen in the air. It was not parallel to anything else in the room and was angled in such a way as to provide the best view for the four of them. Julian felt an urge to change seats, just to see if it shifted.

"Julian, this session will run for hours," Idabee cautioned. "When you get bored, just head back to my father's."

"We won't be offended that you don't want to spend the afternoon with us," Shirley teased.

The static logo on the video screen showed a phoenix wrapped around a capitol dome. It dissolved to reveal a middle-aged woman, who appeared to be of indigenous ancestry, standing at a podium. Chief Moderator Orenda rapped a gavel lightly before speaking. "Welcome to the session for March 20, 2076. Please join me in reciting the Preamble to the Constitution."

In the parlor, the three women began to deliver the words in unison. Julian joined in at the start, stumbled through the middle, and solidly nailed the last five words. "We the people of the United States, in order to form a more perfect union, establish justice, insure domestic tranquility, provide

CHAPTER NINETEEN

for the common defense, promote the general welfare, and secure the blessings of liberty to ourselves and our posterity, do ordain and establish this Constitution for the United States of America."

After a few announcements, Chief Moderator Orenda introduced the first policy of the day recommended for inclusion in the 2076 legislative package. Then she disappeared, and a video began to play. "What's this?" Julian asked.

"Each report has a short explainer video that lays out background information around the proposed policy," Andrea told him. The video's content related to healthcare; statistics about patient costs and outcomes appeared, narrated by a soft baritone voice that spoke smoothly and quickly. "It helps establish the facts, so there can be informed debate."

"Who makes these?" Julian asked, watching with great interest. The policy number, PP-76-1835, remained stationary in the bottom corner of the video.

"They're generated automatically by artificial intelligence, based on the discussions of the investigative panel and the policy committee that recommended the proposal," Andrea explained. "The audio runs at one and a half times normal speaking speed, and the video portion helps comprehension, making them more efficient than a delegate simply reading a report."

Shirley took notes on her tablet as they watched the rest of the video. It concluded with a summary of the policy being recommended for inclusion, and Julian was impressed. "I feel like I actually have some understanding of what they're talking about. It seems reasonable to me."

The video concluded, and Orenda appeared again. She read a question out loud, and a delegate rose to answer it. "Aren't there thousands of delegates?" Julian asked. "How can you possibly answer all the questions they have?"

"Hundreds of thousands, and we've crowdsourced the process," Andrea replied. "After the calendar comes out at the beginning of the month, discussion forums generate all sorts of questions and answers. If enough delegates think a specific question needs to be addressed during the session debate, they can petition to have the Chief Moderator bring it before the body. It's uncommon, though. Mostly, the debate is summarized by these informational videos."

Julian shook his head in wonderment. "There were so many internet forums where people with specialized knowledge helped others troubleshoot problems. And the American Union applied that technique to the country as a whole?"

"That was the real purpose of the American Union Jobs Program," Andrea said emphatically. She flashed a smile at Shirley, knowing her wife had a different opinion. "To empower all Americans to meaningfully participate in the political process."

Chief Moderator Orenda announced that voting was open, then promptly introduced the next proposal. The three women recorded their choices on their tablets. Julian asked, "Can we see how everyone's voting?"

The women were silent for a moment, watching the screen, before Andrea answered. "No, the assembly uses asynchronous voting. Delegates have twenty-four hours to vote; they can review the videos and any debate as it fits into their schedule. After that, the results are publicly tallied."

Julian nodded; it made sense for a national assembly. "And how often are these sessions?"

"It varies, depending on how much work there is to be done," Idabee explained. "The Chief Moderator announces how many there will be in the monthly calendar. They start on the sixteenth of each month and take place every other day; this is the third and final session for March."

"And all the delegates fast for peace and take a sobriety pledge?" he asked.

"No recreational intoxicants during the month until you're done voting in the final session," Idabee explained without looking at him.

"That's for delegates," Shirley clarified. "Say you're a regular member and there's an issue that's really important to you, and you want to make sure your proxy holders don't dilute your power. We can get qualified to vote directly that month by notifying the Assembly Clerk. It's basically the same thing, except the sobriety pledge doesn't start until the notification.

CHAPTER NINETEEN

And that can be the night before the fast." Julian nodded as though he had followed all of that and decided not to ask for clarification; the women were deep in the legislative minutiae, focused on the steady barrage of questions the Chief Moderator put before the people's legislative assembly.

The novelty wore off after a half-dozen videos. Julian determined he'd observed enough to record his impressions in his journal and politely excused himself.

Walking alone through the halls back to Ray's, he reflected on the four young women and contrasted it to the politics he had known. Politics then largely focused on elections, candidates, and their campaigns: Who was the best person—or worst person—for elected office? Thanks to polarization, what passed for debate usually revolved around the latter.

In the tricentennial, politics seemed to focus on policy: What were the issues citizens wanted addressed? Crowdsourcing Congress had clearly created a way for them to have a voice, and the American Union had provided tools for building consensus around legislative action. But in his time, popular support wasn't enough to cut through the gridlock in Washington.

What had Professor Carlton said about satyagraha? *The goal is never to defeat opponents, but to persuade them of the justice of the cause and win them over.* Julian supposed ideally, candidates would be persuaded of the righteousness of the American Union cause; second best would be for them to support the legislation just to improve their chances of winning; and third best would be for incumbents to enact the legislation solely to escape the consequences of refusing to act.

But what happened when persuasion didn't work? How did the American Union use game theory and nonviolence to gain leverage over Congress? Julian pondered the question all the way back to his room.

Chapter Twenty

The Virginia landscape unrolled outside the car's window. It was a sunny Saturday afternoon, and Julian was grateful to get away from River Place Towers and away from the city. Idabee had picked him up in a vehicle permeated by the smell of fresh bread, her gift to the family they were visiting.

With his Treasury account set up, Julian had searched for local apartments and quickly learned places like Dr. Leete's were far outside of his budget. He'd wondered to Idabee the previous day how people lived on the money from the American Union Jobs Program, and she quickly wrangled an invitation from some friends who did just that.

Faith and Adon were also delegates in the people's legislative assembly, and she'd met them through Carlton's self-improvement group. They lived with their two kids—Idabee vouched for their awesomeness—in an apartment complex owned by the American Union.

"That seems odd," Julian said. "Why would a political party be a landlord?"

Idabee's eyes twinkled. "The American Union is not a political party. True, it influences elections, but you could also think of it as a movement, a philosophy, and yes, a business enterprise. Professor Carlton says the American Union was designed as a Gandhian constructive program to address many problems with integrated solutions, and the lack of affordable housing used to be a problem."

As the car exited the freeway, Julian spotted a billboard. It was the first one he'd seen on the trip. Idabee had said advertising was taxed because of the societal costs it generated, and he realized how tranquil the drive had seemed without garish signs clamoring for his attention. He thought about commenting on it, but instead asked, "Does everyone there belong to the American Union?"

"No," Idabee answered, "no one has to be a member to rent there. It started in the early days; supporters bought up homes in swing districts. An American Union organizer would manage the house, and volunteers from around the country would come to help the campaign grow the bloc of swing voters. In the off-season, they rented out the rooms.

"Once the program was fully underway and every citizen was receiving money on a regular basis, the American Union started constructing self-contained buildings where land was cheaper. Cities have advantages, but for individuals and families who were tired of struggling financially, the American Union Jobs Program empowered them to move to places with a lower cost of living using their guaranteed income. Ironically, city rents dropped when landlords suddenly had to compete to fill empty apartments.

"The exodus also generated communities based around shared interests. The American Union encouraged this by allowing groups to reserve an entire building, which usually houses about thirty people. Virtual communities suddenly had a way to coalesce in the real world, and buildings filled up as fast as they came available."

Julian chuckled. "I can think of a lot of niche groups that would go for that. Why settle for an annual convention when you could live the life twenty-four/seven?"

Idabee nodded. "There are some that are entertainment-themed. But most are more focused on productive practices; do you know any foreign languages?" Julian shook his head. "If you want to become fluent in Spanish, for example, there are buildings that create an immersive experience—a mix of native speakers and students. Or if you're interested in learning yoga, martial arts, hunting, or eighteenth-century French poetry, you can find a community that does that. Creative arts are also very common: writers, musicians, photographers, painters, graphic artists. One year I lived in a building that did quilt making."

"For real, you made quilts?"

She smiled at the memory. "We did. The flying geese quilt I made was my favorite; it keeps me warm every winter. And I still keep in touch with some of the people." Idabee became serious. "Julian, this was the real purpose of the American Union Jobs Program. Instead of depending on employment for survival, everyone gained the freedom to pursue their passions and interests. It unlocked so many opportunities. Millions used the basic financial stability to take risks, to start businesses, or to invest in their own education or personal growth."

"I'll bet there were startups that took advantage of this model."

Idabee nodded. "Lots of creative co-operatives, sure. Video game studios, filmmakers, software designers—they could get a critical mass of people in one place and develop their product. But lots of it took place on a smaller scale. A handful of friends might rent a house to work on their own projects.

"The American Union also has a network of tiny homes. You have your own space but still benefit from shared amenities like community gardens. There are parks around the country, many with common themes. Lots of sustainable living and other outdoor activities. Communities usually manage themselves; the American Union has a standard agreement that each group can customize."

"Cool," Julian said, impressed. "It sounds worth looking into. Is it part of promoting self-improvement?"

"Well, yes. But, in fairness, there are a non-zero number of buildings that are oriented around more... adult interests."

Julian raised an eyebrow. "I'm not sure I want to know all the details."

Idabee laughed. "I'm not sure I'd want to explain them. Let's just say that creating the freedom for individuals to pursue their passions and interests extends to the bedroom as well."

"Why stop at the bedroom if you can pursue a whole building full of passions?" Julian joked, watching for her reaction.

Idabee met his gaze, smiling softly, dark eyes sparkling as if inviting him closer. Her lips parted sensually, and she said, "We're here." Idabee's eyes flicked toward their destination; Julian turned to look.

CHAPTER TWENTY

It was a cube.

There was something imposing about the stark simplicity of the design, a modernist style taken to a minimalist extreme. There were no decorative elements, which hindered Julian's ability to judge the size. It grew and grew as they approached, the car gently braking to a stop in its shadow.

Julian ducked his head down, trying to take in the structure's scope through the vehicle's window. "That's a–" he began, but was unable to finish. This building—the sharp straight lines jutting up from the earth, the perfect symmetry in its proportion—conjured a feeling of awe. Although he'd never actually seen *2001*, he was reminded of the black monolith he knew the film featured. The cube broadcast an unambiguous message to all who set eyes upon it; intelligent beings did this.

Finally, he looked back to Idabee, who was watching him with barely concealed amusement. "That's incredible," he managed.

She let out a chuckle as she opened her door. "Glad you like it. I think they could have dialed down the simplicity just a tad."

❋ ❋ ❋

"You made it," Faith greeted them excitedly. "Get in here!" Still slightly out of breath from two flights of stairs, Julian followed Idabee inside the apartment, where their host welcomed them with warm hugs.

He hadn't been sure what to expect from Idabee's description of the building as affordable housing. In his experience, affordable was generally a synonym for substandard. But at first glance, his expectations were exceeded. The common area they stepped into was long, with large windows along the length of the exterior wall. Two kids looked up from where they lounged on a corner sofa as Idabee greeted them, and at the far end, he saw a table set for six.

Adon strode over to greet them. Julian found their host was slightly shorter than him and felt a pang of nostalgia at the black man's locs. "Glad you could join us," he said, shaking Julian's hand firmly before introducing the children, Maggie and Alvin, who waved politely.

"Would you like a quick tour?" Faith offered.

Maggie, who looked like she was about nine, tugged at Julian's hand. "Come see my room," she said. The adults followed her into the dining room, where two doors stood against the far wall. An island with a granite countertop demarcated the L-shaped kitchen, and Adon returned to the stove, stirring a pot emitting a spicy aroma.

The girl's room held a twin bed pushed against one wall, a desk near the windows, and bookshelves along another wall. A colorful rug in the open area invited play. "All the bedrooms are the same size, about three and a half meters square," Faith explained.

Maggie introduced Idabee to a half-dozen tetras swimming in a tank on her bookshelf. "That's Jewel, Finn, Aurora, Strawberry, Harmony, and Bubbles." Julian recognized some castles made from little bricks; apparently Lego was still in business. The child pointed out the books on her shelves and rattled off the names of her stuffed animals.

When Julian noted there were no curtains on the windows, Faith touched a control on the wall. The windows became translucent, then opaque, momentarily leaving the room dark except for the light from the doorway. "The windows have solar cells embedded in the exterior layer, which provide electricity for the building." She dialed them back to full transparency.

Maggie flopped on the bed as Faith led them out of the room. Idabee nudged Julian and pointed to the quilt. "That's a bargello pattern," she said nonchalantly.

Now that he'd seen the bedroom, Julian recognized that the living room and dining area were each the same length, although narrower because of a closet along the interior wall. Like the building itself, the sections of the apartment were composed of square footprints. The door at the back of the kitchen led to the bathroom, he decided.

The adults milled around the kitchen island, and conversation quickly drifted toward the people's legislative assembly—Julian was impressed all three were delegates—and the voting he'd observed yesterday. "It's been twenty-four hours," he said. "They've counted up how many delegates voted for and against all the proposals and posted the results, right?" Silence met his question. Clearly, he'd misunderstood something.

"They didn't use liquid democracy back then, did they?" Adon asked. "It's more than just counting how many people are for or against something, because each delegate represents a different number of members."

"Liquid democracy?" Julian echoed.

"When you think of democracy," Faith explained, "I'll bet you think of representative democracy. Everybody gets one vote, and whichever candidate gets the most is elected to represent everyone for a few years. It was certainly a better system than what it replaced, where citizens didn't get to vote but still had people making decisions on their behalf—taxation without representation. It also worked reasonably well in the eighteenth and nineteenth centuries because, when almost everyone worked on farms, people's interests had a lot of overlap. But by the twentieth century, occupations and lifestyles were much more diverse, and one of the problems with representative democracy is that anyone who didn't vote for the winner often didn't have their views represented in the legislature.

"Liquid democracy is a twenty-first-century solution. Every member of the American Union gets to decide exactly who wields decision-making authority on their behalf; they get one vote to assign to delegates in the legislative assembly, and their proxy can be divided into hundredths."

Adon saw his confused expression. "Julian might appreciate some visual aids," he said to Faith. Explaining that dinner needed another half-hour, he suggested the others regroup in the living room while he finished cooking.

Faith settled in on the couch next to her son and whispered a request to him. As she used a digital tablet to log into the American Union's website, Alvin retrieved a device about the size of a loaf of bread from the closet. From the floor, it projected her screen into the air. The holographic display in the Nussbaums' parlor had automatically adjusted to give everyone in the room the best view, but Alvin swiveled the device to accomplish the same result before returning to the couch.

Projected in front of them was a complex pie chart, dominated by one large section and many small pieces. "This shows how I've assigned my vote," Faith explained. "I've kept 62% of it, 9% is designated for Adon, and these 4% blocks each go to Idabee and three other delegates I know. Then there are thirteen 1% pieces; ten go to other delegates in our district, and the rest to some national delegates."

Julian absorbed the graphic's details as Idabee, who once again was sitting close on his left, gave him a supportive smile. "Why do you give 1% to so many people?" he asked.

"A couple reasons," Faith said. "I delegated 1% of my voting power to ten of the most popular delegates in our district—that includes the seven seated delegates—so they'll listen to me as a constituent on important issues. Another 1% went to three of the candidates for Chief Moderator, because the delegate who holds proxies from the most members becomes the presiding officer for the assembly." Faith navigated to another page. "Let's take a look at how my vote turned out in yesterday's session."

"Everything's recorded on a blockchain for transparency," Idabee added.

Rows began to scroll upward on the display, each with a segmented bar containing four colors—mostly green, with small portions of yellow, red, and blue—and labeled with a proposal number and short description. "For this one, 3436, relative to amateur radio service, the committee recommended it for inclusion," Faith explained, "and 88% of my vote went to support the motion, 3% abstained, 5% opposed it, and 4% was recorded as not in good standing."

Julian turned to Idabee. "Is this what Shirley Nussbaum meant when she talked about proxy holders diluting voting power?"

"Yes. Look at 2860, relative to labeling of buffalo meat," Idabee said, pointing. The colored bar was dominated by red. "Faith voted against the committee; her vote was recorded as 21% yes, 70% no, 5% abstaining, and 4% not in good standing." She grinned at her friend. "Adon and I canceled out part of her vote, meaning less than half of her voting power influenced the outcome in the way she wanted."

"I wasn't persuaded there's an actual problem," Faith explained.

"Truth in labeling is important," Idabee said.

CHAPTER TWENTY

"Securing the blessings of liberty is important too," Faith countered. "We don't need to micromanage everything people could possibly say."

Julian looked back and forth between the women. "This is really how delegates spend their time?" he asked. "Debating the merits of labeling buffalo meat?"

From the kitchen, Adon laughed loudly. "It's exactly as exciting as you think it is," he called.

"Julian, I know it seems silly to you," Idabee said. "But it's important to some American Union members out there. They brought the idea forward, formed an investigative panel, and did the research. A subcommittee reviewed it, and a policy committee recommended it. What kind of union would we be if the members couldn't get their concerns heard?"

"For real, this is incredible," Julian said. "In my time, there were lots of virtual communities with specialized knowledge. Organizing a people's legislative assembly is beyond anything I would have imagined."

Faith was calling up another page. "If I don't like the way my proxy holders have voted, I can send them a note." She typed, *Is this really a problem that needs a legislative solution?* into a box, read it over quickly, and hit send. When the missive disappeared, Faith passed the tablet to Idabee.

Her friend logged in to her own delegate account. From the dashboard, Idabee retrieved Faith's message. "When I get messages from constituents, I can see how much of their vote they've assigned to me and how long ago. This helps me judge how valuable their feedback is. Faith assigned me 4% back in November '74, when I earned my seat."

"Julian, Idabee says you're thinking about joining us in Carlton's group in April, qualifying to be an organizer," Faith said.

"Maybe," he replied. "In those rows you showed a few minutes ago, the blue color? What does that mean, not in good standing?"

Idabee adopted a thoughtful look. "They didn't observe the most recent fast for peace, or they haven't kept the session pledge of sobriety."

"How do you know?" Julian wondered.

"Because they said they didn't," she answered.

"But how do you know that everyone who says they did, did?"

"Technically, we don't. Fasting is on the honor system," Idabee continued. "However, I think we've all raised that same question at some point." Faith nodded. "The best answer is another question: Are you proposing that every delegate be kept under constant public monitoring for twenty-four hours to ensure they don't eat anything and only drink water?"

Julian squirmed. "That doesn't seem practical."

"It's not," Idabee affirmed. "However, the Qualifications Committee looks into allegations of delegates breaking their vows, and they can recommend expulsion. The ban lasts for the election cycle, but after that, the person can rejoin the American Union with a clean slate." Julian gave a mental thumbs-up to automatic redemption.

"No one's perfect," Adon announced, wiping his hands on a towel as he wandered into the room. "I blew off my fast last June; it was a beautiful Saturday afternoon, I had plans with friends, and I decided being social was more important than completing it."

Julian scratched at his goatee. "It's any twenty-four hours, right? Couldn't you have finished your fast before the afternoon?"

"Yes," Faith answered. "But he didn't."

"There's an app for your tablet, Julian," Idabee explained. "We get a reminder on the thirteenth, and when we're ready to start the fast—to put that intention into our lives for twenty-four hours—there's a timer. We can see how many other people are fasting that month, and there are buttons to claim a medical exemption or to break it early. After a day, the app prompts you to indicate if you completed the fast."

"Which I didn't," Adon said. "So I reported I wasn't in good standing that month. I'm proud of being a delegate, Julian; if I lied to do it, how could I be proud of that? The system is set up to cultivate good intentions; sure, there might be a non-zero amount of weeds, but not enough to even consider that the garden isn't worth keeping. People are trusted by default.

"Anyway, missing one month isn't a problem, but skipping two in a row is grounds for losing your status as organizer or delegate. You can appeal to the Qualifications Committee; they rubber stamp any sincere pledge to get back on track the third month." That seemed to fit with the vision of

CHAPTER TWENTY

self-improvement and redemption.

"Reverend Shaver said this month was his five hundredth fast for peace," Julian told them. "Averaging ten a year means he misses a few months, too."

"He does that on purpose," Alvin interjected in a deep post-pubescent voice that didn't match his size. "Intentionally being imperfect as a show of humility." Julian turned to look at the young man, wondering if he was named for the reverend. Adon smiled at his son before disappearing back into the kitchen.

Faith put a proud hand on Alvin's shoulder, thanking him for his contribution to the discussion. "Skipping December's fast is also pretty common," she added. "There's not really much going on. Then we start the new year fresh."

"On Martin Luther King's birthday," Julian said.

"Setting our intentions for the year," Idabee replied.

"And how exactly did you all get to be delegates?" Julian asked.

"First, by becoming an organizer—leading by example," Idabee answered. "Complete the thirty-day challenge once a year, plus the monthly fast for peace. Dues are also higher than basic membership: instead of one-half of one percent of your UBI, contribute two percent. For organizers to qualify as delegates, complete the challenge twice a year and notify the Assembly Clerk that you're willing to serve, so members can assign their proxies to you. That's it."

"That doesn't sound too hard," Julian said. "So, if I commit to being sober in April, I could be an American Union organizer in May?"

"You could. And it's not supposed to be hard; it's supposed to require an intention," Idabee said with a warm smile. "Remember Boaty McBoatface. There are about a half-million Americans registered as delegates. Some hold tens of thousands of proxies, others a mere fraction of a vote."

Julian was silent for a moment. "That sounds like a huge number, but there were massive multiplayer online games with millions of users each day."

"That's sort of the point," Faith said. "The people's legislative assembly can only exist virtually. We're a unicameral chamber; it's simpler and promotes accountability. You might know some of the colonies had them, but when the Framers wrote the Constitution, the big states and the little states didn't trust each other. They made Congress a bicameral legislature specifically to codify that distrust."

"And Idabee gets a virtual seat because members gave her the most proxies?" he guessed.

Adon laughed from the kitchen. "Faith and I aren't anywhere close to winning an actual seat."

"Yes, but," Idabee answered. Julian waited for her to explain the fine print. "To determine the seven seated delegates in a district, each month the Assembly Clerk adds up the proxies directly assigned by local members, plus out-of-district proxies up to that number."

Julian played it out in his head. "Is that so delegates with large national followings can't crowd out the local ones?"

"Exactly," Faith answered. "Delegates are organizers first, and as a union of swing voters, it's important to actually be connected with the people in the congressional district who'll deliver those votes in the election."

"In session, there are at least a dozen delegates from my district with more voting power than I have," Idabee added, "but they're not seated. That means they can't sponsor investigative panels, serve on policy committees, or speak in the full assembly. Seats don't come with long-term leases, either. With liquid democracy, members can change their minds about who they want to represent them at any time."

Julian was still figuring out all the ramifications when Maggie appeared. "Dinner's almost ready," the girl announced. "What does everyone want to drink? Water, milk, coffee, tea, or kombucha?" The adults listed their preferences, and she disappeared into the kitchen.

"I hope you're hungry," Faith said to her guests as she stood up. "Adon always makes too much food."

Chapter Twenty-One

Dinner was served family style, and Julian scooped a healthy portion of the curry onto his plate. Potatoes, kale, and garbanzos swimming in a rich brown sauce stared up at him. Maggie had insisted on sitting next to him, and so he offered to serve her. "Not too much," the girl said, "it's spicy."

Idabee accepted the bowl from him with a look that said she approved of his being polite to little girls. He thanked her with a small smile before taking a dish of brussel sprouts, gleaming with melted butter, from Alvin.

"This looks really good," Idabee said, taking a bite. "Wow, it is spicy!"

Faith swallowed her mouthful and reached for the water pitcher. "It's a recipe from Adon's mother. He makes it for special occasions."

"Thank you for having us," Julian said, "and showing me your apartment. The future is not like I expected. It really is amazing that you can live like this without working." From the reactions around the table, he realized he'd made a faux pas but pressed on, "And this food is delicious." Julian took a big forkful to make himself shut up. Was it rude to imply that someone lived off the wages of their American Union Job? It had been the whole reason they were invited.

Alvin broke the awkward silence. "Mom works. She's writing a book."

"What I think Julian meant to say," Idabee offered diplomatically, "is what an amazing life you have without employment." She turned to him: "Julian, all employment is work, but not all work is employment. They are not synonymous."

Julian quickly swallowed and blurted out agreement. "I see that now. Yes, that's what I meant."

"No, this is interesting," Faith said. "Julian, in your experience, what does work mean?"

Julian thought for a moment, trying to articulate the concept. "I suppose it's an activity that requires effort or skill, done for a specific purpose. I assumed that earning money was part of the purpose, but it doesn't have to be."

"That's a pretty good definition," Faith said. "Doesn't look like your brain got any freezer burn." There was a quick chuckle around the table, followed immediately by Maggie's girlish laugh. "The American Union Jobs Program values all work, whether it's paid or not. Like this delicious meal Adon made," she said, putting a supportive hand on his shoulder.

"And the delectable bread Idabee baked," Adon continued, holding up a thick slice slathered with butter as he looked to Idabee. "Good work."

"I don't get paid to take care of my fish," Maggie added.

"Living a frugal lifestyle translates into extra work," Idabee observed. "It means doing tasks yourself instead of employing other people to do them."

Julian mulled this over. How many times had his cousin Greg said he was working on his car? Now he started thinking of other examples of unpaid labor—housework, yard work, even volunteer work. "Sorry," he said, "let me see if I have this straight. An American Union Job just pays you for whatever work you're already doing?" He felt like this had already been explained, but now he had better context.

"That's the real purpose of the American Union Jobs Program," Adon told him. "To recognize the value of all work, completely unrelated to employment."

Julian nodded with better understanding. "And if you or Faith accepted employment, you'd still get the same amount?"

"There's no disincentive to getting a paying job," Faith answered. "Anything you earn on top of unconditional basic income is yours. But it's also a reminder of our duties as Americans." She looked to her children. "And what are those?"

"Establish justice," Maggie chirped. "Insure domestic tranquility, provide for the common defense, promote the general welfare."

CHAPTER TWENTY-ONE

"And?"

"Secure the blessings of liberty to ourselves and our posterity," Alvin recited. "Except we don't have any posterity."

"That's very good," Idabee said, and then asked the kids what else they'd been learning. The conversation continued to flow among everyone at the table until stomachs were full and plates were empty. The children finished first and brought their dishes to the kitchen sink; Maggie disappeared into her room while Alvin returned to the living room to read on his tablet.

"You men go make yourself comfortable," Faith directed. "Idabee, will you give me a hand?"

Julian offered his help. "Don't bother," Adon said, clapping him on the shoulder. "You'd be interrupting their girl time." Faith's smirk confirmed her husband's observation.

Adon ushered Julian back into the living room, where they settled on the couch. The last rays of the setting sun cut across the room, painting the room with a mellow glow. "Thanks again for having us for dinner," Julian said.

"Our pleasure, really." Adon leaned forward. "Idabee's a friend of ours, Julian. She has a little crush on you, the hero of the reparations rally. If you're interested, you should tell her. If not, don't lead her on. We don't want to see her get hurt."

Julian glanced over to where Alvin was pretending not to listen. "Idabee's incredible," he admitted. "It's just been a crazy two weeks; there's been so much to adjust to. What do you think I should do?"

"Sorry, brother," Adon said, "only you can decide."

Julian was silent for a moment, thinking of his doctor's daughter. He recalled the laughs they'd shared, her confidence leading the subcommittee, her knowledge of history, her desire to improve herself, and the terrific bread she'd baked. Idabee's competence was intimidating, as was her age, but he could picture himself falling for her.

Laughter from the kitchen interrupted his thoughts. "You look like you figured something out," Adon observed.

"I think so." Julian smiled. Yes, if Idabee was interested in him, the feeling was mutual. "How about you and Faith—how did you get together?"

"She was a psychology major, and recruited me for an experiment she was doing on economic coercion."

"What's that?" Julian asked, intrigued.

"Using money or financial power to control or manipulate someone else. She was testing for a relationship between income levels and the amount of cash it took for people to behave irrationally."

"She was looking for people who behaved irrationally, and that's how you met?"

"Easy," Adon warned him with a grin. "But yes, we hit it off."

"What was the experiment?" Julian wondered.

"Can I show him?" Alvin asked, dashing toward his room even before his father finished nodding.

"What did you do to that boy?" Faith asked, approaching with two mugs. She handed one to her husband and lithely folded herself against him.

"He's going to show me an experiment," Julian explained. Idabee sat beside him, leaving a hand's width of space between them.

Alvin raced back into the room and skidded to a stop on the floor in front of Julian, holding a silver coin. "Imagine you could bet one dollar on a coin flip. If you call it, you win ten dollars. Would you do it?"

"Of course," Julian said instantly. "Ten-to-one odds on a fifty-fifty chance? You'd have to be crazy to turn that down."

"That would be irrational," Alvin affirmed as his mother chuckled. "Okay, now imagine I give you a hundred thousand—more than double your American Union Job." He balanced the silver dollar on his fist, Martin Luther King's profile staring upward. "If you win, you get a million dollars, but if you're wrong, you lose every penny. If you're willing to bet, call it."

Julian paused, although intellectually he recognized he was being tested. He struggled to decide, to verbalize a prediction that would send the silver disk spiraling upward. A hundred thousand represented financial stability. The coin quivered as Alvin prepared to thumb it into the air, the room silent and expectant. Somehow, the idea of gambling everything on a coin flip no longer seemed appealing.

CHAPTER TWENTY-ONE

The good-natured laughter began with Adon and was picked up by the women. "And that's economic coercion," Faith said. Julian chuckled as well, and a beaming Alvin joined the adults' merriment. "The math didn't change, only the amount of money, but it altered your behavior."

"Fair enough," Julian admitted. "How irrational does that make me?" Idabee's look suggested he was just the right amount.

"Average. For the vast majority of people, there's some number that tips the scales of their risk–reward ratio. But imagine someone like"—Faith scrounged for a name Julian would recognize—"Oprah Winfrey. Wagering one billion dollars to win ten billion wouldn't have impacted her lifestyle either way."

Julian nodded. "I heard about a study that found happiness didn't increase much after people earned seventy-five thousand dollars. What was the definition of economic coercion again—using money or financial power to control or manipulate someone else?"

"Yes. Thomas Jefferson called it peaceful coercion—as if tacking on an appealing adjective made it okay," Faith said with disgust. "As president, he used the Embargo Act to put pressure on British commerce, believing if he could disrupt their economy, they would voluntarily agree to American demands. When it failed, he learned coercion between rungs on the economic ladder usually only works in one direction."

"Down," Adon said emphatically, and the others nodded. "I'm cynical sometimes, so I wonder if he was thinking ahead to the abolition of slavery. If legal and physical coercion were taken away, peaceful coercion could be an alternate way to control our ancestors."

"Like sharecropping," Faith added. "By 1890, 70% of Southern farmers were sharecroppers. Lots of formerly enslaved people were working the land and trapped by debt to their landlords, so they couldn't leave and seek better opportunities.

"Debt used to be a powerful tool of oppression, especially when we used to create money that way, but it's not an essential element. When we did this study, Julian, we found a linear relationship between people's income and the point where people stopped behaving rationally."

"Like the story of Gandhi's fast for the union," Julian said to Idabee. "The mill workers knew the 20% raise wasn't enough to live on, but they were tempted to take it anyway, because otherwise they'd have nothing."

She smiled at him. "Right. Of course, they were trying to use coercion up the economic ladder with their strike. It's harder in that direction—strikes, boycotts, divestment—those activities generally take coordination, but it can be done."

"That was the real reason for the American Union Jobs Program—to minimize economic coercion," Faith said vehemently. "The United States prided itself on being a free country, but people had been exploited since the very beginning. With a guaranteed income, everyone had the freedom to say no. They could never be threatened with destitution again."

"It wasn't just exploitation that went down," Idabee said to Julian. "Eliminating poverty reduced crime, healthcare usage, suicides and other deaths of despair, abortions…" She looked expectantly to her right. "What else?"

"Homelessness, obviously," Adon added. "And domestic violence. Besides the fact that economic stress dropped, people—women mostly—had the ability to walk away from abusive situations."

"The freedom to say no," Faith repeated.

"It doesn't have to be just cash, right?" Julian asked. To Idabee, he elaborated, "Edith told me that before the American Union organized, one in six employees stayed in jobs they wanted to leave because they were afraid of losing health insurance." Nods from the adults showed he'd understood correctly.

"Some industries took a big hit, too," Adon continued. "like sex work and plasma donation."

"I believe it," Julian said. "I've done that a few times for extra cash—the selling plasma. And then America decided to end poverty." He shook his head, still amazed by the idea.

"Kids were the biggest beneficiaries," Adon said, prompting Alvin to look up. "There was a big boost in child development. Obviously, housing and food security played a major role, but another significant influence is the

CHAPTER TWENTY-ONE

amount of talking that you do with them. Adults under economic stress are less talkative. Not to mention parents who quit their second jobs had more time to spend with their families."

Julian was struck by the enormity of it all. After he and his family had struggled for so many years, it was hard to imagine a world where people weren't constantly wrangling to make ends meet. "And your family is living off your American Union Jobs?"

Faith nodded. "We live frugally but comfortably, even with how much Alvin eats these days. Julian, I don't want you to get the idea that unconditional basic income solved all of everyone's problems. Economic inequality—relative poverty—still existed, especially in the cities, but it was significantly reduced. Abolishing absolute poverty was a huge step forward in terms of social justice."

"And does everyone in this building live the same way? No one's employed?"

Adon seemed surprised by the question. "Oh no," he said, shaking his head. "There are plenty of people here with traditional jobs or side hustles. But it's their choice, not coercion."

"Are you familiar with agape love?" Faith asked.

"Selfless love?" Julian said. Reverend Shaver had mentioned it recently.

Faith smiled. "Unconditional love for all people solely on the basis of their humanity. There's no dividing people into worthy and unworthy. American Union Jobs are like that: unconditional, no strings attached. Strings equal coercion."

"That's the principled reason, anyway," Adon added. "As a practical matter, when Treasury Dollars are created, they're required by law to go to all citizens." Julian nodded knowingly, thanks to his conversations with Teara Harper, and when he offered a brief summary of the cantillon effect, he could feel Idabee radiating enchantment.

The room fell quiet for a moment, and Julian realized what made this Saturday night different from almost every other one he'd experienced in his life. When the state of the world was discussed, there was no undercurrent of frustration, no irritation with the status quo. Instead, the people around him possessed a sense of agency; the world was imperfect, of course, but it could be reshaped for the better.

The silence could have been oppressive, an attempt to pressure him into conformity. Instead, he felt supported by new friends willing to help him succeed, if that was his intention.

Could he commit to a month of sobriety? There really was no reason he couldn't. Two months would let him become a delegate. Julian broke into a grin as he remembered complaining to Ray that he shouldn't yet be allowed to vote. Now he was considering taking part in influencing the policy decisions of the United States.

"Okay," he said. "Sign me up; I'll be there April 1."

Nonviolent action seemed to be a lot more effective at delivering political change than a lead pipe ever would have been.

※ ※ ※

After saying their goodbyes, Julian followed Idabee back down through the building, heading outside to retrieve their car. It had been a great evening with Adon's family, and the conversation had driven home so many possibilities.

The moon was full and bright as they stepped outside. Idabee turned to look directly at him. "So, what did you think of them?" she asked.

"I feel lucky," he said. "Lucky that I survived all those years ago; lucky that I met Adon, Faith, and their kids." Julian looked close into her eyes; she held his gaze as he spoke with conviction. "Mostly, I feel lucky to have met you."

Alvin had offered him a theoretical opportunity to press his luck with a coin flip—a fifty-fifty chance that would change his life. The smile Idabee gave him was an inviting one, sending his heart racing. He liked his odds.

Julian leaned in for a kiss, feeling a surge of electricity run through him as he pressed against her warm, soft lips. Idabee's eyes widened with surprise. She pushed him away: not angrily, but firmly and without hesitation.

CHAPTER TWENTY-ONE

"What are you doing?!"

Confused, he stammered, "I thought… Adon said…"

"Julian, no!" Idabee shook her head in exasperation. "Just get in the car. Get in the car!" Their vehicle had rolled up silently, and without another word, she marched over to what he thought of as the driver's side door.

His cheeks suddenly burning, Julian meekly followed her directions. It was going to be a long ride back. How had he called it wrong?

Chapter Twenty-Two

The car ride had been dead quiet for five minutes; a thick fog of silence enveloped them. Julian could feel the frustration rolling off Idabee like waves of heat. Part of him was angry at her for pushing him away when their lips touched. He'd been confident in the signs he'd seen, and Adon's description of her as infatuated had been sincere. Women could be so fickle!

He tried to make sense of it; it had been a perfectly romantic moment in the moonlight. The kiss would have been a perfect ending to their dinner and perhaps the beginning of a passionate night. Every time Julian thought he was getting closer to understanding how he'd misinterpreted things, his thoughts slipped away like soap in a bathtub.

Once again, he considered the possibility that he was doomed to live out his life as a primitive savage from 2026. Idabee was supposed to be his guide, and if he'd blundered, certainly she shared some of the responsibility—he shouldn't have to ask for help understanding courtship rituals in the tricentennial. Julian gazed out the window, watching the world pass by in a blur of blue and gray.

"What do you think meeting Abraham Lincoln would be like?" Idabee said. Her words were conversational but guarded, and she stared straight ahead as the road unfolded before them.

Julian exhaled softly as Idabee broke the silence. Were they to pretend that nothing had happened? He cleared his throat, grateful for the opportunity to steer the conversation away from the botched romantic moment. "Hmm, that's a tough one," he said nonchalantly. "I think he'd

CHAPTER TWENTY-TWO

probably just lie there."

Her eyes still fixed on the road, Idabee stifled a chuckle. She paused for a beat, then continued as if he hadn't spoken. "Imagine that he showed up in 2026, and you gave him a tour of Washington, D.C." With a sinking feeling, Julian realized he was going to be the subject of this analogy. "He's impressed the Washington Monument was finally finished, so you go up and look out on the city. You point out the Lincoln Memorial and walk together alongside the reflecting pool. He tells you stories of Frederick Douglass elbowing his way into the White House to demand equal pay for black soldiers. And when your tour is finished, he looks at you sincerely and says, 'Thank you, boy.' He doesn't see you as an equal; you're just a person who has no rights that he's bound to respect. How do you respond to him, Julian?"

Even though he'd recognized what was coming, it still stung. "You mean, do I explain to him what he did wrong? Well, Idabee, I think I'd have to take stock of what I know of him as a man. Was he stuck in his ways, or had he demonstrated an ability to change his mind?" As he spoke, replaying her words in his head, he thought he detected a condescending tone, and an angry note crept into his. "Also, Idabee, it would depend on my behavior; had I clearly established that race relations had changed, or was I expecting him to pick it up from context clues? And finally, Idabee, it would depend on what kind of person I was. Because if I were the kind of person who promoted self-improvement, I think it would be pretty hypocritical for me to assume that someone was incapable of it." He was tempted to add an additional parting shot but remained quiet instead.

The silence returned, but only briefly. She shifted in her seat, leaning against the door as she stretched out her arm. "Julian, I'd like to hold your hand." His smile flashed in the dim light as he reached out to her, but just as quickly, she pulled back. "Silence isn't consent. Plus, it's more romantic if you say it out loud."

"Idabee," he began slowly, relieved that she'd reverted to offering explanations, "I would like to hold your hand, so our fingers can intertwine, seeking every square centimeter"—was that the right unit, or should he have said millimeter? Damn metric system!—"of contact between us, as we look deep into each other's eyes, and you teach me how to court a woman so lovely, so kind, so intelligent as yourself." He offered his left hand.

Idabee's look melted into a smile, and she eagerly grabbed his hand with her right. Fingers interlaced. "I get the feeling you're going to be a quick study," she said in a sultry tone, her skin warming under his touch.

Now he was picking up some context. "Idabee, may I kiss you?" Julian asked.

He could see her considering it, but then she wrinkled her nose and shook her head. "Not yet. After class, ask me again."

"I promise," he said quickly, and their laughter whisked away the last of the tension. The physical contact, as it had with Edith weeks earlier, kindled feelings of hope and possibility. Part of the power of their connection at the reparations rally had come from its random nature, but tonight, with Edith's granddaughter, it stemmed from making an informed decision. He'd ignored Idabee at first, a young woman almost a decade his junior. Only after they'd spent time together was he able to look past her youth and see the potential for a partnership.

"What did Adon say to you, anyway?" Idabee wondered.

"Um..." Julian realized that he didn't want to get his new friend in trouble. "He said that if I was interested, I should tell you how I feel."

"Those were his words? Tell me?" Julian nodded. "Then why did you think you should just walk up and kiss me like that?" she asked in an exasperated tone.

"Didn't it let you know how I felt?"

Idabee groaned. "I can't believe that was our first kiss."

"The next one will be better," he promised. "But you haven't told me how you feel."

"I was planning to, during this ride. But you botched things." She sighed. "You know, it's a strange experience for me to be sitting here with you."

The admission startled him because it was almost the same phrase Edith had used on the park bench. He quickly recovered. "How is that?"

She smiled. "I must have been all of ten years old when I first saw you.

CHAPTER TWENTY-TWO

Father took me. You were stretched behind glass and looked exactly as you do now."

"I would think it a somewhat chilling sight for a ten-year-old youngster."

The joke fell flat, Idabee entranced by her memories. "To the contrary, I thought it very romantic, the whole story. I thought of you as a handsome, charming prince who would someday awaken and–"

"And?"

"And take me away with you. You see, I've had a terrible crush on you ever since I was that little girl." She rotated their hands so his was on top and began tracing a figure eight over his skin, her finger barely grazing his flesh, her gaze tight on him, eyes dark with desire. "It even grew, when I reached my teens."

Julian returned her look, contemplating. "Wow," he said, "I hoped it was just my usual charming self that attracted you."

Idabee laughed, but her smile faltered and she shifted in her seat. "I know, it's silly, right?"

"Not at all," Julian said reassuringly, giving her hand a squeeze. "As long as you're going to give me a crash course in modern relationships."

"Right," she agreed. "Julian, why did you kiss me?"

"Because I thought you wanted me to."

"But you didn't know, and you did it anyway. It's a little barbaric, really." Idabee cast about for an analogy. "Remember the other night at dinner, how we were talking about yes-no-abstain voting?" He nodded. "Yes and no are clear indications of preference. Abstain isn't; it's neutral, and in the assembly, we interpret it in different ways depending on the legislative situation."

Julian had to stifle a chuckle as she continued to explain. "Amending an existing provision only requires more yeses than noes; abstaining is indifferent. On a motion to delete a section of the legislative package, though, abstentions are grouped with the no votes. True majority support is required for positive action."

"I love it when you talk about parliamentary procedure," he heard himself say.

Idabee continued, "It's the same way with physical relationships, Julian. You do not get to assume that someone wants to be kissed or anything else, just because they haven't explicitly said no. Unanimous agreement is required for action."

"Do I have to ask to be recognized by Madam Moderator first?" he teased.

"You do not," she said primly. "But you may state your motion."

"I move that we both lean forward for a kiss. Do I have to specify if there's tongue?"

"Great question," she replied. "What do you think?"

Julian laughed. "I feel like you're taking all the spontaneity out of things."

"I feel like you're not taking this seriously. Spontaneity," she said, "is an undetermined course of action, and I just told you unanimous agreement was expected. Julian, in your time, did you really feel entitled to a woman's body until she formally objected?"

He shifted back in his seat, uncomfortable. "It wasn't like that," he protested after a moment. "I wasn't like that; maybe some men were."

"Maybe?" she said incredulously. "My grandmother told me about what men used to be like back in your time; she was almost raped."

The knowledge stung him. Before Idabee could continue, Julian interjected. "You're right. There's no maybe about it; some men were like that. And if you dreamed that I were some perfect, frozen prince, I'm obviously not. But you can't blame me for everything that happened back then. I'm here now, Idabee, willing to learn from you so that I can enjoy and appreciate this world I woke up in. And, so I can enjoy and appreciate getting to know you, with your consent." Holding her right hand in his, he asked, "May I kiss your hand?"

Idabee looked delighted and nodded firmly. Julian was expecting this and made no movement; he simply continued to stare seriously into her eyes. The moment stretched out, not uncomfortably, and finally her acquiescence broke the silence. "I'd like that."

Julian tweaked a smile at passing her test, and without breaking eye contact, he lifted her hand to his lips. "Thank you," he whispered.

CHAPTER TWENTY-TWO

"You're welcome," she replied softly. In the silence, Julian continued to hold her hand, basking in the warmth of victory.

"So, back to class," Julian said. "What else has changed in fifty years?"

"I forget exactly; did you have marriage equality then?" Idabee asked. He nodded. "Marriage is much more flexible; it's more of a private contract than a civil one. Consenting adults form whatever relationships work for them."

"What happens if Faith and Adon decide it's not working?"

"First, they'd try marriage counseling. Like all forms of therapy, it's freely available. But if they really can't smooth over their issues, they'd stop being together; their counselor would try to help them make the process as peaceful as possible, especially for Maggie and Alvin. They might agree to have separate apartments in the same building, so the kids could go back and forth."

"How did you handle it when your parents divorced?"

He felt her stiffen. "Did Father tell you about it?"

"There may have been an alcohol-fueled rant about his ex-wife."

Idabee let out a sigh that morphed into a dry chuckle. "There were some alcohol-fueled rants while they were together, too. I was a little older than Maggie when they finally split up, and I was furious with both of them. So I ended up living with Nana for a few years."

"Edith?" he clarified.

Idabee nodded. "She took me in; I'd visit my parents, stay with one or the other for a day or two, then come back home. Ten years ago, when I was sixteen, I emancipated myself and started collecting full wages from my American Union Job. Nana asked me to stay with her, but I wanted a place of my own."

"Seems like you reconciled with Ray."

"We always kept in touch, but eventually I realized that holding onto that anger wasn't helping anyone. We've had our ups and downs, but I think we have a good relationship now."

"Looks like it to me." Julian squeezed her hand. "I guess I was lucky. My parents were always together. They died three days apart, in the pandemic."

"I'm sorry, Julian. They looked like a happy couple in that photo on your website," she said.

"For the most part," he agreed. "My mother was upset when I got divorced; she told me I should try harder to make it work. Dad understood better, I think."

"You were married and divorced?" Idabee asked. "I didn't know that."

"Why would you?" In the dim light, Julian could feel her eyes crawling over him, reevaluating him. "Idabee?" His stomach clenched. Was he being judged against whatever perfect, frozen prince the young woman had imagined?

Finally, she laughed. "Why would I? You had a whole life outside of saving my grandmother at the reparations rally. It's my mistake."

He looked around, peering at the screens and switches inside the vehicle. "Is there some AI you want me to talk to; make an explainer video so you can decide how to vote?"

"Too late," she replied with mock seriousness. "I already decided."

"Yeah?" Julian searched her face. "How about that kiss?"

Their gaze held in the dim light, and in a teasing tone that called up his comments about parliamentary procedure, Idabee said, "You may proceed." The pairing of formality and consent freely given excited him, and he leaned forward to capture her in a kiss. Soft at first, Idabee's lips yielding to his own, it deepened as they both became more passionate.

The certainty made it all the more arousing. They were both panting slightly when they broke apart. "Wow," Julian breathed as he sat back, taking in Idabee's smile, her eyes glinting mischief. "That was worth waiting for." The air crackled with the excitement of possibilities.

"It's been what, thirty minutes since you tried to kiss me? I've been waiting years, Julian." The fingers Idabee pressed gently to her lips did nothing to hide the radiant smile on her face. "And yes, it was worth waiting for."

"Are you surprised?"

"I am not," Idabee replied. "But I'm sure we'll have a few more surprises along the way."

CHAPTER TWENTY-TWO

Julian nodded slowly and placed another hand over Idabee's. "There's something else you should probably know about me," he said soberly. Idabee nodded, giving him her full attention. Julian looked around as if to verify no one was listening, and then delivered his news as though revealing state secrets. "I snore."

Her eyes leaped with laughter. "I will file that away for future reference," she said in a prim tone that reminded him she'd been practicing self-control and delayed gratification for the last decade. It wasn't the response he'd been hoping for, but then she continued, "The car is currently heading back to my father's place, but there's a spot outside the city with a great view. Would you like to stop there for a while?"

"We should," Julian agreed with a smile. "Unless it's going to cause problems with your father if I don't get back until later tonight? He'll probably put two and two together, and I'm not quite ready to get kicked out."

"I'm sure he will—put two and two together. My feelings are very well known in the Leete family; I made him promise that he wouldn't tell you."

The admission stirred a recollection of the conversation he'd heard when he first began to wake. "I think I caught part of that." Idabee looked away, embarrassed. "Can you explain where we stand on consent at this point?"

"More is always better, Julian, and it can be quite romantic." She hesitated, then leaned forward. Julian listened with delight as she whispered in his ear.

"Yes," he said quickly when she finished. "Can I kiss you again?"

"You may proceed," she agreed with a playful smile. It was a phrase that would be repeated with great pleasure throughout their short time together in the tricentennial.

Part IV

What have I done?
March 28–April 3, 2076

We can't solve problems by using the same kind of thinking we used when we created them.

- Albert Einstein

The mightiest government will be rendered absolutely impotent if the people realizing their power use it in a disciplined manner and for the common good.

- M.K. Gandhi

Chapter Twenty-Three

Gently ascending to the thirty-ninth floor, alone in the elevator with his thoughts of Idabee, Julian smiled. They'd just spent Saturday afternoon exploring the National Air and Space Museum, which included life-size replicas of living spaces from the first Mars colony. He invited Idabee to come up for dinner, but she declined, reminding him they'd see plenty of each other the next day.

The transformation in his life—and his country—over a subjective month had been incredible. Was he falling in love? Was that the force that kept pushing up the corners of his mouth at random moments? It was too soon to say with certainty, but Idabee's decade-long crush certainly put her feelings in an advanced state. Julian's grin widened, remembering their passionate goodbye.

Earlier that week, Idabee had helped him join the American Union using his Treasury account. He made a good-faith pledge to vote with them in November and listed Idabee as the organizer who'd recruited him so she could get a commission on his membership dues. They went through the process of delegating his voting power in the assembly—as a basic member, he couldn't assign any of it to himself. Julian divided it up among all the delegates he knew, with Idabee getting the lion's share. Then Professor Carlton asked to meet with him before starting the organizer program, and they made plans to talk this evening.

So much of his existence had been constrained, his options limited, but in the tricentennial, Julian felt surrounded by possibilities.

When the elevator doors opened, Julian strolled into the hallway and

CHAPTER TWENTY-THREE

toward Ray's door. Today, he needed to have a conversation with him about his daughter. Julian knew the relationship wasn't exactly a secret, but felt a clearing of the air was important. Ray wasn't just his doctor and guide to the year 2076; Julian considered him a friend as well. He didn't particularly want to jeopardize that, but if Ray didn't understand, he knew he'd choose to keep Idabee in his life.

Julian gave a sharp knock on the door before thumbing it open. He believed Ray was expecting him, but some audible notice seemed appropriate. Taking a deep breath, he announced himself, "Hey, it's Julian."

"In the kitchen," Ray called. Julian found his host throwing fresh herbs into a pot giving off an earthy aroma. "Perfect timing," he said.

Dinner was a kidney bean stew whose coconut flavor was enhanced by ginger and garlic. Julian dug in; he was halfway through his bowl before he broached the subject. "Ray, Idabee is really something."

"You've been spending a lot of time together," her father observed.

A memory of Idabee's lips pressed against his brought a smile to Julian's face. "We are. I guess I should thank you for introducing us." Ray nodded. "Tomorrow, she's taking me up to Philly. We're going to scope out the neighborhood where I grew up and see what it looks like today." He hesitated. "We're going to stay over, so I won't be back until Monday."

"Sounds like you two are getting along well," Ray said. "I'll be headed into the hospital on Monday, so I may not be here when you get back. Idabee used to visit me there when she was young, and her grandmother would tell the story of how you saved her at the reparations rally. So I feel somewhat responsible for her infatuation with you." He grinned. "Of course, if she decides not to keep you, there's a whole bunch more where you came from."

"Did I come with a money-back guarantee?" Julian laughed. "You know, I asked Edith if you two were playing matchmaker, waking me up now. Were you?"

Ray quickly sobered. "According to the records, you requested to be removed from cryonic suspension on February 15, 2076. I admit I had some flexibility whether to start or finish the process then, but I followed your instructions."

According to the records? "Ray, I didn't make any request. I got shot, then I woke up here." Julian gestured down the hall to his room.

Ray said nothing.

"Why was I frozen to begin with? Was I that close to dying?"

"I wasn't even born then," Ray said, "so you'd have to ask my mother why you were put into cryonic suspension. But in my professional opinion, no, there wasn't anything seriously wrong with you."

The admission hung in the air. "You know what this means, don't you?" Julian replied. The doctor put his fork down and watched him with a humorless expression.

Suddenly, Julian began to laugh. He spread his hands to indicate his body. "It means your mom let this get away! Man, I thought I had better game." Ray looked away to hide his grin. "Although, she was wearing glasses, maybe that was why. Nah, no question about it." He plastered a serious expression on his face. "What your mom did to me was cold." Julian exploded into laughter again, and Ray couldn't help but join in.

"I'm glad you're taking it well," Ray said seriously. "Let me take off my Leete-family hat for a moment, so we can talk doctor–patient. Do you want to make a complaint? If you do, I'll assign someone to make a fact-finding inquiry into the circumstances, and the hospital will try to get to the bottom of this."

Julian dismissed the idea with a wave of his hand. "We're good; that was a long time ago. It's like this was supposed to happen. You feel me?"

"I don't, but it's your decision. Let me know if you change your mind," Ray said.

"Edith promised to explain," he confided. Ray's assertion there hadn't been any life-threatening danger directly contradicted what Edith had told him. Whatever the reason, the truth was that he was alive and well now. "I'll let you know if there's a problem."

That resolved, the pair talked about other ways that Julian was integrating himself into the tricentennial. Ray had guided him through scheduling a dentist appointment. Employment opportunities were varied. The doctor

CHAPTER TWENTY-THREE

also offered to help him find work at the hospital, where he'd be resuming more duties next week, and Julian promised to consider it. Exploring and understanding the American Union held his interest for now.

The parlor played a note announcing Professor Carlton's arrival; Julian realized he'd lost track of time. The gray-haired man was waiting patiently, hands folded, when Julian took a seat across from him. When both indicator lights were green, he touched his palms together in greeting. "Sorry that I'm late," he said.

Carlton returned the gesture. "If you want to experiment with being on time, there's a punctuality challenge you could try," he replied, his tone light. "I'm glad you decided to join us next month. I'm confident you're capable, but before someone starts the organizer program, there's always a brief one-on-one. You're in a unique situation, Julian; everyone else has lived with and benefited from the American Union for decades. One of the duties of nonviolence is to empower meaningful consent, so I want to make sure you understand the framework."

Julian thanked him. "People keep talking about duties," he said. "Reverend Shaver said duties come before rights, and the American Union Jobs Program was about reminding people of that."

"It's quite a different paradigm than when we grew up," Carlton agreed, "but the man who explained it to me pointed out that it really stems from the golden rule: do unto others as you would have them do unto you. That maxim—that duty—can be found in every religion; it's the truth at the pinnacle of the mountaintop. To help others get there, organizers lead by example—another core duty."

"I like rights," Julian said forcefully. Then he laughed. "Maybe I'm just more willing to argue with you instead of Reverend Shaver."

"Rights are good," Carlton agreed. "They're so good that people would fight for them if they weren't getting what they felt they were owed. You remember what happened during the COVID-19 pandemic; how some people fought over wearing masks? It represented this debate in a nutshell; they claimed a right to not wear one trumped any duty to look out for others. Duty works the other way; when I feel I owe you something, there isn't much to fight over.

"And for large parts of American history, people did recognize the importance of duty. Perhaps you recall how President Kennedy said, 'Ask not what your country can do for you, but what you can do for your country'? How could the common good be improved? This was the tension Dr. King and the civil rights movement brought to the surface. It forced Americans to wrestle with the question of what their country could do to address the injustice of segregation.

"But the narrative began to change a decade or two later." Carlton leaned forward in his chair to emphasize his point. "America started to develop a culture of greed. With that came a greater focus on rights, a focus on self; what am I entitled to? Whereas a duty-based society is focused on others.

"Addressing this cultural problem was part of the American Union strategy, the Gandhian constructive program. It was another aspect of the fast for peace, Julian—shaping or reshaping the culture to address greed. Willingly giving something up on a regular basis helped people question their basic assumptions about what they actually needed. As Gandhi said, 'There is enough for every man's need, but not for every man's greed.'"

Julian nodded understanding—his own experience had raised such a question—and broke into a smile at the memory of accomplishing a two-day fast. "So organizers lead by example and promote the fast for peace each month, and it culminates on October 15 each year; Muster Day? You were there at the beginning. I'm still trying to picture exactly how the American Union got started."

"Part of it was timing. The Phoenix Cycle guaranteed transformative changes were on the way; the American Union just used the principles of nonviolence to make sure they were positive. I wonder, have you been back to see the neighborhood where you lived before? I'm sure that would drive home the changes."

Julian explained Idabee had had the same thought, and they would be visiting the next day. "They put up a statue of me; can you believe it?" he said. "It'll be a trip, seeing that. But what happened on the first Muster Day?"

CHAPTER TWENTY-THREE

Carlton nodded. "Reverend Shaver started a fast as he presented the legislative package to Congress on September 21, the International Day of Peace. End poverty, end mass incarceration, end the endless wars—all rolled up into one take-it-or-leave-it offer. No one liked everything in it, but the majority of Americans liked the majority of it.

"For the next three weeks, he called on all Americans to come together on Muster Day in a *hartal*–"

"A what?"

"A hartal; it's an Indian word that basically means a one-day general strike plus fasting. The slogan we used was, 'Don't work, don't shop, don't eat—take to the street.' The reverend went without food through Muster Day, holding daily press conferences and asking people who wanted peace, justice, and prosperity to join him on the twenty-fourth day for twenty-four hours."

Julian shook his head in wonder. "Twenty-four days. You did say leading by example was one of the duties of nonviolence."

"On Muster Day," Carlton continued, "the hartal went smashingly; millions of Americans refused to work and turned out in the streets to hold mass meetings, at least one in every congressional district. They flooded social media with the hashtag #fastforpeace, and members of Congress were inundated with phone calls and emails, demanding they act.

"There was no doubt that, as a bloc of swing voters, the American Union was going to decide numerous races across the country. Congressional leadership read the writing on the wall; seeing the opportunity to stay in power and go down in history as the most transformational Congress in generations, they greased the wheels of legislative machinery. On October 30, 2026, the president signed the legislation and gave Reverend Shaver the pen." Carlton settled back in his chair, deep in reflection.

Julian thought it over; he couldn't imagine the Speaker of the House or any Majority Leader willingly handing control over to the opposing party. Big corporations and the rich had influence over Congress precisely because they doled out large amounts of cash. That was what party leaders used to fund elections and vie for power. But since those elections were ultimately decided by votes, not dollars, a national union of swing voters let the marginalized outbid the deep pockets for legislative influence.

"Being part of that campaign was one of the greatest times of my life," Carlton said. "I knew so many people who'd given up on politics—the perennial fighting that never produced any resolution. The American Union offered a completely different way to address the problem. I signed up hundreds of members, and I still remember the pitch—the pledge—they took to join.

"I am a citizen of the United States and want to join the American Union of swing voters in order to collectively bargain for a better social contract.

"I demand Congress pass the legislative package with the American Union's demands, and end poverty, end mass incarceration, and end the endless wars.

"I will respond to polls for federal office—House and Senate—that I am a true swing voter who will only vote for the American Union–endorsed candidate in the November election.

"I pledge, in good faith, to vote for the American Union slate of candidates for Congress, but reserve the right to withdraw if the final legislative package is unacceptable.

"I will donate no less than seven dollars each month to the American Union PAC in support of these goals."

Carlton smiled at the memory. "It was an amazing time, Julian. Through the fast for peace, America reinvented itself as a nation."

Julian wore a pensive look, mentally replaying the words, then spoke. "But there wasn't anything about fasting in there."

"No, like we talked about the other night, fasting has to be voluntary. Members are under no obligation to participate; they can still assign their proxies in the legislative assembly to weigh in on policy. But to become involved in the American Union, we had to volunteer. We had to willingly give something up." The gray-haired man scrutinized him. "Are you sure you want to do this? It's not too late to change your mind."

"Pretty sure," Julian admitted. "Idabee explained the types of optional challenges to me; I think I'll pass on those, though. At least this month." He

CHAPTER TWENTY-THREE

recalled the quote the professor had shared the other day. *We are trying an experiment of building up ourselves by self-sacrifice without resorting to violence in any shape or form.* With luck, he would never need to resort to violence in the tricentennial. "At the beginning, wasn't it hard to get people from different political parties to work together?"

Carlton stroked his beard. "Of course. The animosity between Republicans and Democrats—and against both of them by third parties—was on an epic scale back then, as I'm sure you remember. A zero-sum game means one winner and everyone else loses.

"If you recall, polarization had pushed many policy issues toward their extremes because black and white are easy to describe. But very few issues are all on one side; VOZ metrics helped build consensus around gray. Nonviolence, as Gandhi saw it, didn't even mean total abstention from violence. Sometimes it was the least bad solution, and duty required action."

"Wait, for real?" Julian interjected. "Nonviolence can include violence?"

"Physical force is a better term," Carlton admitted. "But, yes. Gandhi described himself as a practical idealist. One of the duties of nonviolence is to reduce unnecessary suffering. Are you thinking about your actions at the reparations rally?" Julian nodded. Although he sat very still, waiting for the professor to continue, his hands echoed with vibrations from the pole he'd swung.

"To use physical force through a nonviolent paradigm, certain conditions must be met. If you hadn't acted, there certainly would have been more people hurt; there were no real alternatives. Have you been glorifying your actions?" Julian shook his head. "And I don't think you acted out of cowardice. You were willing to sacrifice your own life—and nearly did—to prevent harm to others."

"So I did the right thing," Julian said. His shoulders slumped as the tension he'd unknowingly been carrying unraveled.

"No," Carlton said. His voice was gentle but firm. "You failed. You allowed circumstances to develop where using physical force was necessary, where those men believed killing innocent people was essential to their own dignity."

"What?" Julian gasped. "I had nothing to do with that! It wasn't my fault!"

"Okay," Carlton agreed calmly.

Julian seethed. It was wrong to put hundreds of years of America's problems on his shoulders, as if there were a magic wand he could have waved to fix everything! He waited for Carlton to refresh his challenge, but the old man simply sat patiently.

He pushed back again. "The only people responsible were the gunmen."

"Okay," Carlton repeated.

Then Julian recalled Reverend Shaver's motive for his recent fast: atonement because of his contribution to the general state of America. The statement had struck him as ludicrous at the time, but now, talking with Professor Carlton, he could suddenly see Shaver's perspective, even if he didn't agree with it. But believing he was right didn't mean the other men were wrong. Shaver's mindset could still be valid; their truths weren't mutually exclusive.

Julian grinned. Truth wasn't a zero-sum game.

"Political polarization?" he prompted.

Carlton picked up where he'd left off. "Partisan people weren't ready to join hands and sing kumbaya, but it was possible to offer an armistice. The fast for peace staked out a middle ground; welcome all those who shared in the self-sacrifice. For political adversaries, the fast was like declaring a truce for the duration of the election cycle to advance common policy goals based on VOZ metrics and nonary logic."

"Still, there were some pretty extreme members of Congress that I'd never want to see reelected," Julian said.

"Building a nation where all people have the foundation to succeed couldn't be predicated on seeing some people fail—even those as generally disliked as the members of Congress. Creating that opportunity for a win-win scenario was important." Julian probably appeared as unconvinced as he felt because Carlton continued, "How important was it to you that they lose? Would it be worth keeping the status quo to violate the principle that

CHAPTER TWENTY-THREE

every human is capable of self-improvement and worthy of redemption?"

After a moment's reflection, Julian seemed to crumple. Slowly, he shook his head.

The professor smiled warmly. "I think you've just demonstrated self-improvement. I look forward to seeing you next Wednesday."

Chapter Twenty-Four

Idabee's legs—wrapped in tight jeans, shod with sleek black boots, one ankle on top of the other, toes pointed upward—stretched out in front of her as she reclined on the train. Julian extended his from the seat beside her, their paths nearly converging, and a slight twist of her boots was enough to tap against him and demand his attention. "You're smiling again," Idabee observed.

Julian turned away from the window—there wasn't much to see in the tunnel, not at the speeds the bullet train was achieving on its northwestern sprint—and looked at her. The angle of her lower lip pulled her face into a pout while her eyes conveyed incomprehension that he could possibly find anything else interesting when she was sitting next to him.

"Must have something to do with you," he replied. Stroking her cheek with the back of his fingers rearranged her mouth and tallied an additional pleasing curve on her body. Julian slung his arm around her and leaned in, bringing their faces tantalizingly close. He could see the desire in her eyes and waited to see if she'd request a kiss. Her breath was warm as she licked her lips, inviting him to ask. The tension built deliciously.

This was very much a non-zero-sum game.

The previous Sunday—only seven days ago—they'd parked overlooking the city and demonstrated that car windows in the tricentennial could still be fogged up. In Julian's experience, it happened quicker than in his time. The smaller volume of air seemed like the most likely explanation, but in the interest of science, they replicated the results on four other occasions. Idabee steered his expectations for modern relationships with firm vetoes

CHAPTER TWENTY-FOUR

and enthusiastic approvals, charting a path to steamy make-out sessions.

Despite the denials of matchmaking from Ray and Edith, Julian was grateful for whatever actions had guided him to this time and place with Idabee. Her competency and mindfulness continued to awe him. Three days ago, she'd suggested this trip to Philadelphia with an overnight stay; when he agreed, she demonstrated how to share the relevant information from their health profiles to show they were clean from sexually transmitted diseases.

As he'd stored their bags above their seats, Julian debated whether he was more excited about seeing the neighborhood where he'd grown up or checking into the hotel.

Idabee was tired of waiting. "Kiss me, Julian," she whispered, and he did. It was thorough but brief, and when he broke away, she moaned.

Julian grinned. "May I kiss you, Delegate Leete?" he asked, ready to re-engage with her soft lips.

"You may proceed," she replied, running a hand up his back and pulling him close. This time, the kiss lasted much longer. "And that's Seated Delegate Leete," she said huskily.

"And a very nice seat it is, too," Julian teased. She tsked in mock offense as he placed his mouth close to her ear. "Seated Delegate Leete, I move that Julian West..." His voice dropped lower as he made a new proposal. Idabee's breath hitched as he described sensuous acts, wildly inappropriate on the train, with tantalizing precision.

She listened to the delicate details in full; Julian grinned when he met her gaze to receive his rejection. "Julian, we're in public!" she protested.

"That's true," he admitted. His hand dropped to her hip and placed an exploratory finger under the hem of her white pullover. "May I proceed?"

Idabee wrinkled her nose endearingly. "I'm going to veto that," she replied. She gripped his hand just as they felt the train's inertia shift. "Besides, we're almost to our stop."

"Your call," Julian said agreeably. There was pleasure enough in her slightly flushed look and the primal sheen in her eyes.

Idabee put a hand on his chest as she stood up to retrieve their bags. "But

I'll entertain a motion for reconsideration later, okay?"

When they stepped out on the platform underneath the Philadelphia International Airport, Julian saw it was only eleven o'clock and shook his head in amazement. Less than an hour earlier, they'd been waiting for the bullet train to slide into Washington with passengers who'd left St. Louis that morning. The network of maglev trains crisscrossing the country had proven safer and more efficient than other forms of long-distance travel for decades, and their ride had been incredibly smooth.

Idabee procured a car, and it carried them north into the city on the interstate. When the Philadelphia skyline breached the horizon, Julian leaned forward in awe. He recognized the Comcast Technology Center that had once dominated the cityscape, but now it was just another gleaming skyscraper among many. Even City Hall, with its tower topped with a statue of founder William Penn, was obscured from view. It was no longer the city he'd grown up in.

The difference in traffic flow was dramatically different as well. Fifty years earlier, there would have been cars competing to get ahead, looking for any opportunity to maneuver for their own advantage. He'd done it himself on plenty of occasions, taking a certain pride in guiding his vehicle into open lanes and feeling superior to the slower-moving drivers around him.

In the tricentennial, communication made for a much smoother ride. Caravaning cars synchronized their speeds, traveling an arm's length apart, slipstreaming for greater efficiency. Space was generated whenever a new entrant came on the highway, and they were welcomed into the line. Cooperation had trumped competition.

Idabee called up a map, and he directed them northward along surface streets toward the neighborhood where he'd grown up and the statue they'd come to see. As the car carried them along, he recognized how much had changed, which made finding the occasional store or restaurant still in the same space a treasure.

"The neighborhood was just permeated with poverty, Idabee," he explained. "Teara Harper's been talking with me and Ray about the economic problems when money doesn't circulate. It just seemed like there was no way to turn things around; when people climbed out, they left everyone else behind." Julian shook his head, remembering faces that disappeared after high school and never returned—the foxes who'd escaped. "Unless they came back years later, when things got tough."

"It's possible to change rungs on the economic ladder, up or down," Idabee said. "But if you slip, you're most likely to end up on the rung your parents were at."

"That feels about right," he said. "One time, in high school, we went to a concert in Baltimore: this girl I was seeing, plus her cousin and her husband. The four of us were coming back after midnight, a little drunk, a little high, and he hit something in the road. Bam, a tire blew out, and we ended up on the side of the highway. I was freaked out; I didn't know how we'd get a replacement at that time of night.

"The dude called Triple A—this roadside service you could buy—and it turned out his mother had him on her Plus Plan. They towed us and the car all the way home, no charge. I don't know how it would have turned out otherwise."

"Failing to the level of your parents," she said. "I know they died in the pandemic; I guess that didn't give you much to fall back on. Thanks for sharing that story with me, Julian. I've looked at you for so many years, but without really knowing you. I think we might have something good."

"Me too," he said, and meant it.

"You're smiling again," Idabee teased.

They turned east on 65th Street, Julian marveling at the neighborhood's evolution. The distinctive cubes of American Union housing jutted up where the reservoir had once been. Idabee directed the car to find a parking space near Sturgis Park, and Julian peered through the windows for his statue. He caught a glimpse of the bronze form holding a sign on a tube, but was distracted by what was in front of it. "Did you set this up?" he wondered in amazement. A small crowd of people was gathered underneath a *Welcome Back, Julian West* banner. "This is why you wanted to visit today?" he asked, grinning broadly now. "Thank you."

She took his hand. "Julian, I don't know anything about this." The car maneuvered smoothly against the curb and stopped. "Really."

"So, it's either a coincidence or there's always a crowd wanting to see my hard body and big pole," he replied.

A single *ha!* escaped Idabee's lips before she could clamp down on its friends. Instead, she rolled her eyes; Julian mirrored her motion but concluded with a pointed glance at the two overnight bags behind them. Idabee had booked them a room with a view of the city, although he didn't expect to spend much time looking out the window. "Either one sounds plausible to me," she said, still amused, and pushed her door open.

When Julian stepped out of the car, the familiar contours of the park brought another wave of nostalgia. The trees themselves beckoned, their branches forming a canopy over the sidewalk, and in the background, he heard the rhythmic dribbling of a basketball on the courts he'd spent so many hours on.

Together, the two of them walked toward the dozens of people gathered in the spring sunshine, many dressed in their Sunday best. Julian was shocked to see that he recognized someone. "Delroy?" he blurted in astonishment. "Is that you?" A tall, lean man in a crisp white suit turned toward them, his mouth quickly widening into a smile at Julian's voice.

"Julian West! You made it!" Despite the webs of wrinkles that graced his dark skin, Delroy Jackson had an aura of vitality. The elderly man strode forward to embrace Julian in a hug of eternal brotherhood.

They broke apart, grinning wildly. "I don't believe this. What's going on?"

Delroy crowed. "You just won me close to four hundred dollars. Some of these suckers bet me you wouldn't show. But I believed in you, brother; I knew." He clapped him on the shoulder. "It's good to see you again."

"But how'd you know I'd be here today?" he wondered.

Delroy ignored the question in favor of his companion. "And this must be Miss Idabee! It's a pleasure to finally meet you."

Julian turned on her, confident the answer had been revealed, but Idabee's face was twisted in confusion. "How did you know who I was?"

CHAPTER TWENTY-FOUR

With a wide smile that displayed gleaming white teeth, Delroy reached inside his suit and removed a robin's-egg-blue envelope. "This is for you, young lady." He handed it to the stunned woman; Idabee's name was clearly printed on the outside.

Julian's stomach clenched as he recognized his own handwriting. The color, too, jogged something in his memory, but he couldn't place it.

Gingerly, Idabee accepted the envelope. "Should I open it?" she asked.

Delroy surveyed the scene; their arrival had drawn the crowd's attention. "Later would be better," he pronounced. "Let me introduce you." He guided them into the fray, presenting them to neighborhood residents old and new. With polished ease, Delroy delivered stories of his time with Julian on the high school basketball team. The strangeness of the circumstances aside, Julian quickly began to enjoy himself. After he'd become famous at the reparations rally, he realized exploits from his younger days had evolved into local legends.

Even Idabee began to relax. "Any exes here I should know about?" she whispered.

The statue erected at the center of the park was a surreal sight. The afternoon sun illuminated Julian's bronze form, standing tall and gripping a pole which was just as solid as the one he'd wielded fifty years earlier. The sign it held spelled out *KNOW JUSTICE, KNOW PEACE* in raised letters.

"I always thought that was profound," Idabee said, running her hand across his back. Julian laughed and confessed that Edith had modified his sign. Idabee was aghast. "And she never told me? I wonder what other secrets she's been keeping." She leaned forward for a quick kiss; he would remember it later as the last moment of normalcy before their world turned upside down.

"Speech!" someone yelled.

Delroy prodded him; Julian gathered his thoughts, took a deep breath, licked his lips, and turned to the attentive faces. "I'd like to start by thanking everyone who made today possible." Both Delroy and Idabee received a direct look while the audience clapped. "It's an honor to still be remembered here after all these years. While I may technically have spent those years frozen in a hospital basement, in my heart, I never left.

"This community shaped me; it made me the young man that I was. I was imperfect, and I've heard a few stories today that reminded me of that." A spate of laughter. "I was filled with passion and anger at the injustices of the world, and sometimes that's what the world needs. But it also needs community, and I'm proud and amazed to see it's still strong here."

There was a round of applause and cheers, and Julian continued. "I didn't ask for any of this; fate has a lot to say about how our lives turn out. But as Delroy told me when we played basketball, when you see the opportunity to take your shot, don't hesitate. I'm grateful I was in the right place at the right time all those years ago. But for those that weren't as fortunate, for those who were in the wrong place at the wrong time, I think we should have a moment of silence."

The crowd bowed their heads. Julian had no idea how to end his remarks, but fortunately, a woman's voice offered a prayer. "Heavenly Father," she began, "we thank you that Julian, our prodigal son, has returned to us today. His memorial has stood here for many years, reminding us of your commandment in Deuteronomy: 'Justice, and only justice, you shall follow.'

"We ask you to watch over all who stand up against oppression and inequality, and we ask you to remember those who have made great sacrifices in that pursuit. Bless us, remember us, and keep us, oh Lord. In Jesus' name, Amen."

The gathering chorused the final word, and Julian felt a sense of peace wash over him. He had come a long way from the angry young man he once was.

As the crowd began to disperse, Idabee approached, her face contorted under layers of inscrutable emotion. "What's going on?" she demanded. "I thought it was my idea to come up today, but I can't understand how this happened." Her right hand clutched the light-blue envelope.

Julian caught Delroy's eye, and the older man strode across the concrete to join them. "Del, I think it's time you explained all this," Julian said.

"It's some kind of joke, right?" Idabee said, waving the envelope. "Julian passed it to you; maybe stuck it in your pocket when he hugged you? Is

CHAPTER TWENTY-FOUR

that it?"

"It's got my handwriting on the outside," Julian said. "Where'd you get it?"

Delroy nodded sagely. "You gave it to me a long time ago, plus another handful like it, with different names and dates you wanted them delivered. You told me to meet you here today, March 29, 2076.

"The wife and I kept it private, like you said. I keep the faith with the fast for peace each month, I pay it forward into the community, and now I've delivered all the letters you gave me. Julian, sometimes I doubted you could predict the future, but when I saw you and Reverend Shaver in the news last week, I knew things were on schedule." He gestured around, grinning. "And here we are… although some people didn't think you were going to show."

Julian absorbed the story. "I don't remember that happening," he said.

Delroy cackled. "Like that time we got drunk on the bus back from Central and you woke up naked in Fisher Park the next morning?"

"No, not like that," he said, avoiding the look Idabee was giving him.

"Jules, there's no crystal ball that could give you vision like that, especially if you didn't know to come here today." Delroy appraised Idabee before continuing. "I've had five decades to think about it, and the only logical explanation is that you're going to go back in time. But you knew that, right?"

Julian reached for Idabee's hand in solidarity, but she pulled away. His stomach knotted as the ramifications mounted. "Fifty years?"

"Not buying it," Idabee declared, her face twisted with anger, waving the envelope at him. "I don't know why you're doing this, Julian, but it's not funny."

"Idabee, I've never seen that before in my life." He looked to Delroy for validation, but when none came, he gestured for Idabee to step to one side with him. "What did it say?" he asked. She glanced down, not deigning to look at him.

The silence was thick and oppressive, but he rose above it, riding the wave of peace he'd felt after the prayer, waiting, pondering the implausibility of time travel.

Finally, she met his gaze and spoke. "Coming up here with you was like a dream, Julian. It felt so right, like maybe we were going to build a life together." She paused, rebuilding her confidence. "Then, out of nowhere, we find people expecting your arrival. And I get this."

"What did it say?" Julian repeated.

She scoffed, and the emotion on her face crystalized. It was pain. "That's how you want to play this? It says that you'll always value our time together, but we have no future in the tricentennial."

"I didn't write that," he insisted.

"Right," she spat. "Because time travel."

He borrowed the phrase that Edith had used the previous week to describe her encounter with Izzy Robynham. "So we have a perfectly reasonable–unreasonable explanation."

"Fine," Idabee said. "Have it your way. I'm leaving." Delroy was watching them discreetly, his face blank. "And I don't particularly care if you come with," she announced, stalking toward the car.

Julian let her go, then approached his old friend. "That's one pissed off jawn," Delroy observed.

"Idabee wants to head out," Julian said reluctantly.

"Your call," Delroy replied. "Go after her if you think you should. But if you want to stick around and talk, I'll help you get back."

Julian watched Idabee storm away. An hour earlier, she and Delroy had represented his future and his past. Somehow, a blue envelope had scrambled their fortunes. When she looked back, Idabee's scowl helped him decide. Julian pointed to himself, then Delroy, and gave a thumbs-up. Her acknowledgment was a single finger, raised proudly erect, a finger adjacent to the one she would use in thirty-three days to end his existence in the tricentennial.

"Minnie passed eight years ago," Delroy said solemnly. "We speculated about who Idabee was—would be—for a long time. She was a romantic and believed there was a marriage proposal inside." The memory of his wife brought a smile to Delroy's face. "That Idabee was your one true love,

CHAPTER TWENTY-FOUR

and you were going to pop the question in a way that showed your bond transcended time." He shook his head softly. "She'd be pretty disappointed right now."

Idabee pulled away from the curb, the strings of his heart tugging after her before breaking, one by one. A question bubbled up, expanding to surround his life: past, present, and future. With equal parts curiosity and anguish, he asked, "Delroy, what have I done?"

Chapter Twenty-Five

Delroy Jackson's apartment in the Pennypack Retirement Community was a simple one-bedroom on the eleventh floor. "It's not much, but it's home," he said as Julian looked around the open area that doubled as a living room and dining room. The kitchen contained a humble stack of dirty dishes, but overall, the space looked well kept.

Pictures on the wall showed Delroy and Minnie over the decades, often with their daughter Alba. Julian smiled at an image from their wedding. "I remember this," he said, tapping at the frame. His finger struck the wall beneath, startling him. All the pictures were holograms.

"We were happily married for forty-seven years," the octogenarian said. "That's a pretty good percent out of fifty-four." The friends settled down on opposite ends of a couch that had seen a significant portion of those years, and Delroy's face became serious. "Julian, if I tell you what happened back then, will it change?"

"You know more about this than I do," Julian replied. "For real, I'm still not sold you're telling the truth. I wrote you from inside all those years ago. You could have copied my handwriting. But I can't figure why you would or how you'd know Idabee." He hesitated. "Plus, there are other things that don't square."

"We were happily married for forty-seven years," Delroy said again. "If it wasn't for you, it probably would have been three. Remember our old place on Sparks Street? You showed up at my door; I was half in the bag, fighting with Minnie, and you calmed me down. We sat on my front porch, and you explained I was the man to help with a long-term project, but I

CHAPTER TWENTY-FIVE

was going to have to get sober to do it."

"What, delivering envelopes?" Julian scoffed. "You don't have to be sober for that."

"You really don't know?" Delroy asked quietly. "You also wanted me to give up food for twenty-four hours. Not just food! But also"—the phrase was punctuated with air quotes—"recreational intoxicants." He waggled a finger at the younger man. "I was still buzzed enough that it sounded plausible."

Julian grinned. "The fast for peace. Idabee's the one who told me about it." His expression fell slack as he remembered how things now stood between them. "When was that?"

"Bastille Day," Delroy answered cryptically.

"What?"

Delroy cackled, a series of short coughs dripping with amusement. "Right? Why would we know anything about a French holiday? But when I pushed you on what this mysterious project was, you said it was Bastille Day and asked if I knew the significance."

"Did you?" Julian asked. Delroy cackled again. "What is it?"

"It's July 14, when the people of Paris rose up and stormed the Bastille, a prison fortress, to free the unjustly incarcerated. You said it was time to free the unjustly incarcerated here."

"It was long past time," Julian said. A fist bump emphasized agreement. "So we fasted together?"

"Minnie too; she'd been listening from the front room. Cooked us a fine meal to break it the next night, and after, the three of us talked for hours. You described how the American Union of swing voters would work—how it could change everything."

"The American Union?" Julian tried to make sense of it. Edith claimed to have put him in cryonic suspension months before it was founded in 2026. Had he left the hospital after the reparations rally, only to be frozen at a later point? He took a deep breath and asked, "What year was it?"

"It was 2023."

"I was locked up that July," Julian said. "Did you know that?"

"I'd heard. At first, I figured you were out on bail, and the Bastille thing was you saying it was time for an armed revolution. But we eventually cleared things up." Delroy gave one barking laugh.

Was it possible Shaver's recollection of talking with him before the reparations rally wasn't a mistake? "Did I have locs?" Delroy nodded. Julian ran a hand over his scalp. "I started shaving my head years ago because I was losing my hair. Was it a younger version of me?"

"No, you looked like you'd aged a few years. But Julian, there's this nasty-smelling cream you can get now; it'll grow hair on a cue ball." The octogenarian fondled the gray growth on his head. "Not that I've ever needed it."

"Time travel?" Julian said. The thought was gargantuan, clogging the flow of ideas through his mind as he tried to process it. "You're talking about things I haven't done." That didn't mean they couldn't be true, he realized. Truth was a non-zero-sum game.

Delroy shrugged. "Some Julian West did. You showed up at my door wanting to start a nonviolent revolution. When I offered you a beer, you laid that Annie Grace quote on me: 'Alcohol is the only drug you have to justify not taking.' Finally, you persuaded me to give the sober life a shot, and Minnie backed me up. We poured out all our booze that night and flushed everything else. Then you gave me twenty-five thousand in cash, asked me to find a lawyer who knew election law, and get the PAC set up. Eventually, I found one who didn't claim a conflict of interest."

"Delroy," Julian said, slowly and clearly, "are you telling me we started the American Union, and not Reverend Shaver?"

The octogenarian nodded. "He's just the one that made it go viral."

Julian rubbed his temples, trying to massage the concept into his brain. Delroy sounded truthful, and time travel explained the strange things that had happened. The mere possibility of returning to his own time brought an unexpected wave of homesickness. Ota Benga tried for years to cross the Atlantic back to Africa, a journey humans had routinely made for centuries. But how was it possible to journey into the past?

He'd learned so much in the last few weeks, gleaning information from

CHAPTER TWENTY-FIVE

a historian, an economist, a preacher, an expert in political science, a professor of nonviolence studies, and delegates in the people's legislative assembly. Armed with that information, there was nothing preventing the American Union model from working a few years earlier; Stella Freedom had even made its success sound inevitable. "But if we had the Phoenix Cycle on our side, why didn't it work in 2024?" Julian asked.

Delroy shrugged. "The internet was a noisy place. We tried, but the message never broke through."

"Are we stuck in a loop?" Julian wondered. "Will the same things keep happening?"

"Don't get me to lying, Jules. If you wanted me to know, you'd've told me."

Julian rubbed his hands over his face. Who knew about time travel? "Okay," he agreed. "What happened next?"

"Minnie and I started looking for more organizers. I even hit up some AA meetings," Delroy cackled. "There were nine people committed to starting the training program August 15, and you bailed on us; said you had a prior commitment. We did the best we could; six made it through the two fasts and a month of sobriety.

"I always thought of organizers like franchisees because they were selling the same solutions to voters all across the country, trying to build a brand: end poverty, end mass incarceration, end the endless wars. Did you know McDonald's had under one thousand locations when they started advertising nationwide? The fast for peace was the primary marketing on every level, a nationwide event month after month. Organizers tried to talk it up and help each other with cross-promotion." A wry smile twisted across his face. "It was a good system, Jules. Really weeded out the ones who wanted in for the money."

"The money?" Julian echoed.

"From crowdsourcing the revolution. The American Union didn't take any contributions from corporations or other organizations; it was the people of the United States who needed better representation. Basic members had to kick in at least twenty-five cents a day for dues."

"Seven dollars a month," Julian said, remembering the pledge Carlton had rattled off. "Sounds like a deal; it's up to sixteen now. And organizers get a commission?" Idabee had mentioned it when she signed him up.

Delroy nodded. "Organizers were a dollar a day, twenty-eight a month. Leading by example, right? But when they signed up members, they could take 10% commission, and if they signed up any new organizers, 5% of whatever contributions they brought in. A lot of people just let it roll over to the PAC, but for those who kept up with it, it could be a good side hustle."

"Hold up," Julian said. "It was a pyramid scheme? Multi-level marketing?"

"No," Delroy answered. "A small triangle, maybe; just one level. It wasn't about moving money up; it was about growing the pyramid's base as wide as possible. The Republicans and Democrats had a lot of dissatisfied customers, and when the organizers found enough voters willing to unionize, everybody would win."

He picked up a picture of his wife from the end table and gazed at it. "We tried, Jules," he said wistfully. "Minnie was good at listening to people and leading the thirty-day challenges. I made the books work out. We were a good team." The octogenarian looked up at Julian, his eyes moist with gratitude. "If you hadn't shown up at my door all those years ago, I'd have quit her. I'd have missed out on all those happy years, I'd have kept on drinking, I'd probably be dead now." When Julian accepted the recognition with a grave nod, Delroy tried to lighten the mood. "And I'd never have learned about Bastille Day."

"Except, if you hadn't told me about it, how would I have been able to explain it to you?" Julian wondered. "So what was it like, Del? When everyone got their American Union Job?"

Delroy took a deep breath and resettled himself on the couch. "It's hard to remember that far back. Decent jobs around here were scarce. I was keeping the books for Deacon's Garage and some other businesses, but the AI tax software was cutting me out. Minnie would pick up gig work sometimes, Uber, DoorDash, like that, depending on if Alba was in school. One of her friends had a little bakery, and she'd work there a few hours a week. We'd fight over money. It wasn't good, Julian."

CHAPTER TWENTY-FIVE

"I told Idabee the whole neighborhood was permeated with poverty."

"We spent 2024 working on the American Union, but after the election, everyone faded away, hunkering down for four more years of partisan fighting." Delroy scrutinized the other man. "Are you sure you want to hear all this?" Julian nodded, and he continued, "You got depressed when it didn't succeed; you stopped coming around. Minnie was worried about you, and eventually we came to visit. Do you remember that?"

"I do!" Julian said enthusiastically. "I hadn't seen you two in years, and then there you were at my door." He looked embarrassed. "I was a little messed up, though."

"You were not living a sober life," Delroy confirmed. "We had a vague idea you weren't the same person we'd been working with, since you'd been inside a minute. It was disappointing, for real."

"When I got out, trying to find a job?" Julian said. "A lot of doors were closed; you feel me? So yeah, I lost hope. That reparations rally, I thought that would be the change we needed."

Delroy raised a finger. "And that was the difference between the Julian we'd been working with and the wasted guy in that little apartment. What did 'the change we needed' mean to you? Who's the we?"

"Us, blacks, you know? The system had been biased against our people for a long time. Reparations would help make it right."

"And today, looking backward," Delroy asked with a crooked grin that said he enjoyed the role of wise elder, "what does 'the change we needed' mean?"

"Uh," Julian thought, "all Americans. The whole system was biased against lots of people in lots of ways, and that was what needed to change, so it worked for everyone."

Delroy nodded approval, and the two men sat in contemplation for a moment. "You asked me what it was like when everyone got an American Union Job," Delroy began. "When Reverend Shaver gave his speech, inviting everyone to fast for peace on the day Lincoln died, Minnie and I called the old organizers and put the band back together. Once reparations passed, he announced the American Union would bargain with Congress in the midterms.

"Everything took off. The old organizers got fired up and started training new ones. The PAC suddenly had enough money to run a real campaign: end poverty, end mass incarceration, and end the endless wars. Members of Congress decided not to throw themselves on the swords of a moral crusade, passed the legislation right after Muster Day, and the president signed it.

"The Treasury took about eight months to get everyone's digital account set up," Delroy explained. "Everyone got a debit card, and when they announced that it would go live on July 4, retailers unveiled huge sales." Teara Harper had said Alaska saw the same thing when residents got their oil dividend checks.

"Once everyone had unconditional basic income, life changed pretty dramatically. Crime fell along with poverty, and hundreds of thousands of people being released each year had an economic foundation to build on; recidivism dropped."

"I didn't feel like I was being set up for success when I got out," Julian admitted.

"Industries that ran on poverty wages had to reevaluate their business model," Delroy continued. "Workers had more bargaining power, and wages started to go up." *The freedom to say no*, Faith had called it. "I know a half-dozen families that decided they could raise their kids with one employed parent, so the other could stay home. That was the real purpose of the American Union Jobs Program: to strengthen families, because families are what hold communities together. Ensuring domestic tranquility, you could say."

"What could we do different, Del, to help the American Union break through in 2024?"

"I have two ideas," the octogenarian answered. "First, Reverend Shaver. He was the one who created national attention for the fast for peace and demonstrated to the country that we could work together when we wanted to. January 15, 2024, was the Iowa caucuses, Martin Luther King's birthday, and the first fast for peace of the new year. If he makes that a success, it'll

CHAPTER TWENTY-FIVE

frame the conversation for the rest of the election cycle." Delroy flashed a smile. "See if you can find a nonthreatening way to tell him if he doesn't cooperate, he's going to get shot."

Julian didn't have the heart to tell him about Shaver's apology—he'd already tried that idea and it had failed. Maybe there was some other way to break through to the preacher. Suddenly, he recalled where else he'd seen a robin's-egg-blue envelope like Idabee's. "Del, did you give one of those letters to Reverend Shaver?"

He nodded. "After the rally. It took two trips down to get it to him; he was in rough shape. When he made the speech a few days later calling for the fast for peace, Minnie and I knew what was in the letter."

Julian exhaled. He would definitely need to have another conversation with Shaver. "You said you had two ideas?"

Delroy grinned as he leveraged himself to a standing position and disappeared into his bedroom. He returned rolling a small black suitcase behind him. "You showed up with about forty-five grand to kick off the campaign, Jules. When we learned you'd been frozen, it seemed plausible that you'd wake up in the future, learn about the American Union, and bring the paradigm back to us." He motioned for Julian to open the suitcase.

Julian lifted it onto his lap and ran his fingers over the cold metal catches. When he flipped them open, more cash than he had ever seen in one place stared up at him. "Del, what's this?" he managed.

Delroy was beaming as he replanted himself on the couch. "Federal Reserve Notes, all 2023 or earlier," he said. "You never told me where the money came from, but this is for you. Close to one hundred thousand. Bring this and things will be different—money means options."

"Is this my commission? For recruiting Reverend Shaver?"

With an audible wheeze, Delroy settled deeper into the couch. "What kind of treasurer would I have been if I was writing checks to a popsicle? Sorry, brother, that all stayed with the PAC. You did earn it, in a way," he said. "Most of the cash is our reparations money, mine and Minnie's. You know about Treasury Dollar Bills?" Delroy slapped his knee. "Of course you do! Reparations were in Federal Reserve Notes, and we socked ours away for you. Paying it forward." He scratched his chin. "Or backward."

Teara Harper had mentioned Treasury Dollar Bills. "I was told they're base money. Which means the Treasury created them instead of banks borrowing dollars into existence—bank money?"

Delroy nodded. "Julian, you ever hear of a guy who ran for president named Ross Perot?"

With a laugh, Julian shook his head. "No. Tell me about him."

"Take notes, so you can tell me," Delroy cackled. "It was in the '90s, and he campaigned on balancing the budget. He convinced everyone that the federal government should only spend as much as it brought in in taxes."

"That's not right," Julian said. "If the economy and the population are growing, the money supply has to expand too. That means someone has to spend more dollars into circulation."

"You called it the Ross Perot fallacy," Delroy told him. "But he got a big chunk of votes, and after that, Republicans and Democrats worked together to balance the budget."

"I was just learning about this," Julian said. "That's what happens if a third party gets traction: a major party absorbs their popular policies."

"Well, in this case, both parties did," Delroy continued. "So no one seriously questioned the Ross Perot fallacy until the American Union Jobs Program proposed exactly what you said: don't balance the budget."

Julian fell silent, staring at all the cash in his lap. There was a lump in his throat as he realized what it could unlock for him in the early days of that summer—assuming the opportunity for time travel presented itself again. He exhaled deeply and closed the suitcase. "Del, what would you have done with this if I hadn't shown up today?"

The octogenarian rubbed his chin thoughtfully. "I don't really know. It's more money than I need. I live a simple life."

"Give it to charity?" Julian suggested.

Delroy laughed. "Charities aren't really a thing any more. They were there to help people who fell through the cracks in the system, and the American Union did a pretty good job of filling those cracks. One time, you made a joke about everyone whose employment depended on a steady

CHAPTER TWENTY-FIVE

supply of people needing help. You called them the charity-industrial complex because you were frustrated they weren't interested in actually fixing the United States. There's no need to run soup kitchens when everyone has cash to buy all the soup they want. We took away their customers and destroyed their business model."

"And you saved your reparations money?"

"For sure, Julian," Delroy cackled. "What do you think, Minnie and I spent our weekends staking out ATMs until a wealthy-looking dude withdrew cash and then robbing him?"

They laughed together for a moment, then Julian froze as the final words echoed through his brain. Where had he heard them recently?

"You okay?" Delroy asked.

The silence built until Julian answered, "I think someone else knows about my traveling in time. Does the name Edith Bartlett mean anything to you?"

"The doctor, right?" Julian nodded slowly, his suspicions confirmed. "I gave her a letter right after the reparations rally, even before I knew you'd been shot. You think she has something to do with this?" Delroy eyed his friend. "Did you travel back for her?"

"Del, I didn't know about any of this until you told me. When Edith and I met the morning of the rally, we had a connection." Julian swallowed hard. "She was the first person I wanted to see when I opened my eyes. But now, I think maybe when we met, it wasn't her first time."

"She still single?" Delroy inquired.

He offered up a wry smile in response. "A single grandmother, yeah. Her son is my doctor, the one I'm staying with, and you know her granddaughter, Idabee."

Delroy slapped a knee. "You like to keep things complicated, don't you? That Idabee, she special to you?" he inquired. Julian's old high school friend looked at him with fatherly concern. "The reason Minnie thought there might be a proposal in that envelope is because when you showed up at our door, you were wearing a wedding ring."

Chapter Twenty-Six

There were two good things about his trip back to Ray's. On the bullet train, a stranger engaged Julian in pleasant conversation about her grandchildren. *My listening has value to them*, Ray had said about his neighbors: It was win-win. Julian welcomed a distraction that grounded him in the present, shelving thoughts of the past and the future. Trying to unravel that tangle would have to wait.

He also proved to himself that he was capable of maneuvering through public transportation in the tricentennial. Julian retraced the path he and Idabee had taken that morning, identifying the correct bus to bring him back to River Place Towers. The empty seat next to him was doubly vacant, sharing occupancy with an Idabee who wasn't there. In her absence, he appreciated the many confidence-boosting explanations she'd provided that helped him succeed at tonight's challenge. Smiling softly, Julian watched the bustle of the city through the window.

He was weary but pleased when the elevator deposited him to the thirty-ninth floor—two months ago, he'd been a slab of ice. Julian delivered a quick knock on the door and thumbed it open. Music greeted him: a techno-African beat that swept him up with its pulses while communicating very clearly that his host was not expecting him. "Hey, Ray," he called loudly, "I'm back; the trip didn't work out." Cautiously, he stepped into the condo and let the door slide shut behind him, the wheels of the suitcase Delroy had given him clattering to a stop on the hardwood floor.

There was no response. Julian felt like an unwelcome stranger, and

CHAPTER TWENTY-SIX

remembered Ota Benga had eventually committed suicide. He hung up his jacket and counted to ten before approaching his bedroom door. The hallway gave him a clear line of sight to the kitchen table, but he didn't look—would he be interrupting something?

"Julian?" Ray appeared at the end of the hall, leaning up against the wall, bare arms folded across his chest with determined casualness. His tone carried concern: "Everything okay? I didn't expect you back tonight." A wine bottle and two glasses stood on the table.

"Sorry," Julian said, "I didn't know you had company." Ray wore a full-length apron proclaiming *Kiss the Chef*—and absolutely nothing else. Julian hooked a thumb toward his room. "I'm beat; I'll see you in the morning," he said. "Just pretend I'm not here."

Ray offered to lend a sympathetic ear, but Julian wished his friend a pleasant evening and disappeared into his room, closing the door gently. He rolled the suitcase over to the far corner and began to take stock. With the kitchen occupied—he heard a burst of female laughter—dinner wasn't an option. That was okay. He knew unquestionably he was capable of skipping a meal.

Julian kicked off his shoes and laid back on the bed. His muscles were tight with the day's tensions, and he pondered a nice, hot shower. Instead, he took a deep breath, willing himself to relax. Last night he'd gone to sleep looking forward to spending this day—and night—with Idabee. Instead, he'd inherited responsibility for saving Delroy's marriage and trying to start the American Union.

Time travel. It was absurd.

Idabee still had his overnight bag, so he was sans toothbrush and tablet at the moment. He wanted to record the day's events in his journal, but it would have to wait. He wanted to talk to Reverend Shaver about their earlier encounter, but it would have to wait. He wanted to hear Edith's extended explanation for his long sleep, but that would have to wait.

The lights in the room began to dim—it had been several minutes since he'd moved—and Julian took that as a sign that he should rest. He closed his eyes, ready to be done with this day. Voices in the hallway and the closing of Ray's door comforted him. At least someone was having sex tonight.

Drifting off to sleep, he realized there was something else Delroy hadn't told him. What had happened to the other Julian?

※ ※ ※

The rising sun nudged him awake.

When Julian opened his bedroom door, he discovered his bag slouched in the hallway. *You left this in the car*, Idabee's block print proclaimed. Julian glanced at the kitchen table as he retrieved it. The woman seated there had her back to him, but Ray gave him a hearty wave. "Good morning!" he belted out. Julian returned the gesture before retreating to his room, leaving the door ajar.

Brushing his teeth, Julian sized himself up in the mirror. Idabee had liked his head clean-shaven, the way she'd always seen his frozen body. Her passive-aggressive note inspired him to start letting his hair come in. Ray could certainly track down that regrowth cream Delroy had mentioned.

In the kitchen, it took him a moment to recognize the woman without her suit. Teara Harper, the economist, was wrapped in a royal blue silk robe and looked a little older, a little rounder, and much happier than she had in the parlor. "Good morning, Julian! It's so nice to meet you in person."

Julian ordered eggs and sausage—the meat substitutes no longer attracted his notice—and fixed coffee as he waited for his food to arrive. He demurred when Ray, clad in a flannel bathrobe, asked about what had happened with Idabee, instead apologizing again for interrupting their evening. "I was hoping to talk with you again," Julian admitted to Teara, "about Treasury Dollar Bills and how the transition came about."

Teara appeared less than enthusiastic. "That's a full conversation," she said. "We're just taking a breakfast break."

"Why are you so interested in economics?" Ray wondered, aiming a

CHAPTER TWENTY-SIX

wolfish grin at his breakfast companion. "Economists, I could understand." Teara giggled and reached over to pat Ray on the hand.

With a whoosh, Julian's food arrived. "Self-defense, maybe? Economics was always interested in me," he speculated, taking a seat at the table across from the couple. This wasn't the right moment to disclose he might be expected to explain all the details in his near future—or their far past. "Remember when you asked how the United States got so far off track when it came to establishing justice? I have the same question about the economy—the whole poverty-as-a-fox-hunt thing. How did I end up as one of the hunted?"

"It's not like anyone was out to get you personally," Ray said.

"Fine," Julian conceded, in the interest of harmony. "Teara, how did things go so wrong by the twenty-first century?"

Teara pulled her hand back and became serious. "Like inflation, there's no one thing you can point to and say, 'Aha! That's the cause!' The economy is a human construct, with ideas and concepts layered on over centuries." A sip of coffee gave her time to consider. "I'll give it a try, though. There was a philosophical tenet that connected many of the problems in the marketplace. Adam Smith's *The Wealth of Nations* was published in 1776 and influenced generations of economic thought. He told everyone that self-interest was what made markets function."

"Greed," Julian said flatly.

"There's an aspect of that," the economist agreed, "but Smith also described guardrails to prevent abuses. Anyway, one of the works he'd studied was by a thirteenth-century Muslim scholar who identified markets as being about mutual aid. Smith tweaked the concept from one of cooperation to one of competition, and the tiny shift in mindset accumulated over the centuries to pull us off course.

"The economy is built on humanity's intellectual infrastructure, Julian, but even all our accumulated expertise wouldn't allow an individual to produce everything they need from scratch. It's impossible to grow your own food and build your own shelter and weave your own clothes; cooperation is essential. Markets help us accomplish these complex tasks—

exchanging goods and services is mutual aid."

"You're saying that it's a non-zero-sum game?" Julian asked.

"Yes," Teara said, stretching out the word as though tempted to add some fine print. Instead, she skewered a piece of cantaloupe from her plate and began to chew.

"But isn't that supposed to mean win-win? Because the economy didn't look like that to me."

"Did you have to weave your own clothes, build your own shelter, and grow your own food?" she replied.

"Well, no."

"Julian, a non-zero-sum game doesn't mean everyone wins equally. The free market isn't free; it costs money to participate, and many factors can distort it. High wealth inequality, for example, means dollars are no longer of equal value for buyers and sellers."

"That doesn't sound right," Julian said. "A dollar is a dollar."

"Well, let's try a thought experiment," Teara suggested. "Imagine apples are one dollar each. It's a fair price; Julian, you pay ten dollars for ten apples. Now, Ray, let's say you have fifty apples already. Would you pay ten dollars for ten more?"

"I wouldn't need them, so no," he answered.

"This is the law of diminishing marginal utility," she explained. "Generally, the more you have of something, the less valuable each individual item becomes. There might still be a price Ray would buy apples at, but not one dollar each.

"Anyway, Julian, you have ten apples and Ray has fifty, and you'd both like an apple pie. I happen to have one I'm willing to trade; for the right price, I'll bake another one. Julian, you might offer eight apples, leaving you two to eat. How about you, Ray? How bad do you want my delicious apple pie?" Teara asked seductively.

"I could go for some pie," he agreed, playing along. "If I traded ten or fifteen apples I'd still have plenty."

"Julian, an apple is still an apple, but because Ray has far more than he needs, he's willing to spend a greater number. In your time, you might have noticed how wealth inequality drove up housing prices, contributing to rent increases and inflation.

"You might also have noticed what Ray was willing to offer: ten to fifteen apples. I was willing to trade for eight, so anything from eight to fifteen apples is our non-zero-sum game, where everybody wins. However, negotiating a price within that range is a zero-sum game—for every extra apple I get, Ray has one less, or vice versa." The economist smiled brightly and took another bite.

Julian rubbed his forehead. "I'm going to have to think about that last part, but I see how wealth inequality distorts things. You said that was one of the reasons for taxes, right?"

Teara nodded. "High tax rates on personal income after World War Two served an important function in reducing market distortions, and they're also an application of the law of diminishing marginal utility. In 1946, for example, the top tax rate of 91% applied to earnings over what was about three and a half million 2026 dollars."

Julian scoffed. "What's the marginal utility of one extra dollar when you already have millions of them?"

"Pretty small," Teara agreed. "And that same dollar invested in the nation's well-being produced a much greater dividend.

"You'd asked how things went so far off track by the twenty-first century—the industrial revolution also contributed. Factories opened up a structural gap in the economy; the wages workers earned were less than the cost of the goods produced. 1893 saw a major depression; factories had produced more than people could buy, so they laid off workers, which made it even harder to sell those goods. The recession contributed to the rise of American imperialism a few years later; using military force to expand into new markets helped shrink that economic gap, at least temporarily.

"In the twentieth century, that gap was bridged in two primary ways," Teara continued. "The first was consumer debt. After World War One, industrial production greatly increased. Automobiles, washing machines, refrigerators, and many other products were widely available but not widely affordable, so payment plans were popularized. This was a major change in American culture because taking on debt became an essential part of middle-class life, eventually reaching over twenty trillion dollars.

"The other primary method was deficit spending by the federal government. Congress putting extra money into circulation culminated in a thirty-nine trillion dollar national debt, and most of it went to the military-industrial complex.

"As you said the other day, Julian, this is why we have to keep adding money to the economy, because there are new things to buy and more people to buy them. Instead of bridging that gap with debt, the American Union Jobs Program filled it in by issuing everyone their share of the new money needed, which ensured that families could use the markets to meet their basic needs. Mutual aid."

"And the Treasury adds the trillions needed, plus enough extra to cause inflation?" Julian asked.

"Yes. The economy is always changing, Julian; different parts are moving in different directions. It's impossible to keep it stationary, so we give it a consistent direction by expanding the money supply; slow ahead."

"Wow, it's a good thing we're not having a full conversation about economics," Ray joked. His plate was clear, and Teara began energetically spearing the food on her own. "But you said the industrial revolution—factories—created a gap in the economy," he continued. "Couldn't factories have paid people more, so they could afford the things they were making?"

Julian jumped in while Teara chewed. "There was a chart that went around social media showing productivity had increased by a huge amount since the 1970s, but the average worker was only seeing a fraction of it in their pay."

"Then where did it go?" Ray replied.

"CEO pay," Julian said. "It was ridiculous."

Teara swallowed and pointed her empty fork at Ray to answer his question. "The gap would still exist, but it could have been smaller, like Julian said. The economist John Maynard Keynes predicted that by 2030, technological efficiencies in agriculture, mining, and manufacturing would allow everyone's absolute needs to be met with a fifteen-hour workweek."

Julian grinned, mentally contrasting the words employment and work. Picturing Adon's household living without employment, he knew there were plenty of hours of work that went on. Fifteen hours for adults plus one-third for kids—forty hours of work to meet a family's needs sounded better than what he'd known.

"Keynes assumed productivity gains would all be passed on to the workers, which generally hadn't happened," Teara continued. "As Julian said, part went to upper management. In 1965, the man who ran a large company was paid fifteen times what the average worker was. By the end of the century, it was four hundred times as much."

Ray gave a low whistle. "That's a lot of self-interest."

"Mutual aid is a healthier perspective," the economist agreed.

"CEO pay was ridiculous," Julian said. "How was it fixed? Did the American Union make it illegal?"

"Illegal?" Teara laughed. "No, but they made it unpopular."

"How?"

"The people's legislative assembly passed a resolution asking members to boycott the companies with the most lopsided ratios between CEOs and the average worker's pay. They were one-month boycotts; the Chief Moderator announced a different target in every calendar. That kept it fresh, so people didn't get bored, and generated press coverage as well."

"So the worst offenders were smacked down?" Julian asked.

"It was a huge incentive for businesses to proactively rein in CEO pay and raise employee wages. Wall Street made it worse—or better, depending on your perspective—when traders started shorting stocks of companies they anticipated would be the target of the next month's boycott." Teara popped the last of her food in her mouth and slid her empty plate to Ray.

"People being greedy—that was one of the cultural problems," Julian replied. "Idabee said the American Union was a Gandhian constructive program, addressing social and cultural problems along with political ones."

Teara nodded. "A century ago, the sociologist Daniel Bell observed how a culture of instant gratification was developing as a result of our economic system. Easy credit encouraged families to take on debt to help consume the products and services on the market.

"Reforming our monetary system had a positive impact in many ways, including on the culture. The Treasury still added roughly the same amount of money to the economy as the banks had, but because it was distributed at regular intervals instead of being borrowed into existence as lump sums, it encouraged people to save for large purchases."

"And delaying gratification is one of the things the fast for peace helps people practice. I see how it ties together," Julian said with a satisfied smile.

Teara shot a grin at him, pleased he'd made the connection, and then turned her smile toward Ray. The doctor had tucked the dirty dishes away and stood watching her expectantly, arms lightly folded across his robe. "Speaking of gratification," she said to him. "Did you want to show me that thing? In the other room?"

Ray agreed that he did, and Teara rose from the table, bringing their conversation to an end. "Nice to see you again, Julian; I hope that helped. We'll talk about Treasury Dollar Bills another time—next week is no good, but how about after that?" Julian thanked her as she took Ray by the hand.

"I'm still headed into the hospital later," Ray said. "You'll have the place to yourself in an hour or two. But I'll be back tonight; we'll talk more then."

Julian watched with wistful amusement as the economist tugged Ray down the hall to his bedroom. He should have been waking up with Idabee this morning, luxuriating in the crisp sheets of a soft hotel bed. He sighed. At least she'd brought his bag back—Teara had given him all sorts of ideas he wanted to record in his journal.

Markets were mutual aid. Didn't that describe unions, too?

Chapter Twenty-Seven

Edith strolled into Ray's kitchen, smartly dressed in a lilac pantsuit, tasteful pearls dangling from her ears. Julian looked up from his lunch. Ever since Idabee had explained about the hunger hormone, he'd taken a strange pleasure in recognizing the regularity with which his body prompted him to eat. Five productive hours after breakfast had helped him organize his thoughts.

"Mind if I join you?" she asked, striding to the counter and summoning the menu without waiting for an answer.

Her random appearance reminded him of how her granddaughter had pulled the same trick. "Ray's at the hospital," he said, still shifting mental gears. Julian had been struck by Edith's beauty, her fiery wit, and her fierce intelligence when he first met her—qualities that still shone through despite the accumulated decades.

"I know," she said, swiping through the holographic selections with her back to him. The indifference made him curious about what she was concealing.

"What do you know?" Julian asked. Was Edith the puppeteer pulling the strings of his life back and forth across the decades?

"I know that I talked with Idabee."

His heart leaped. If anyone could smooth things out between them, it would be Edith. "What did she say about me?" he asked excitedly.

Without turning, Edith replied, "She's pretty furious, Julian."

"At me for something I haven't even done?" Taking a deep breath, determined to get a reaction from her, he plunged ahead. "Or with you, for not warning her I was headed into the past?"

His cleverness drew Edith's full attention. She slowly twisted to capture his gaze and made her way to him without releasing it, her face emanating maternal pleasure. Her hand gently cupped Julian's cheek, tilting his face up to her. "I tried to tell you Idabee wasn't right for you," she said softly.

The warmth of her touch permeated his skin, and he experienced a deep swelling of pride. Edith had given him two clues across fifty years of time, and he had managed to recognize them and fit them together. "Is he robbing him?" he replied, enunciating all five syllables instead of allowing them to slide together into Izzy Robynham's name. Her look intensified, and he realized that his pride wasn't the only part of him beginning to swell.

"Julian," she whispered, her fingertip grazing back and forth over the tip of his earlobe. The faint hint of jasmine made him suddenly aware they were alone in the condominium, and she'd timed her visit for when Ray was gone. Edith's look conveyed a primal message, and he realized Idabee's features were faintly outlined in her grandmother's face. He was seeing what she would have looked like if they'd grown old together.

Only they wouldn't. Because time travel.

Julian cleared his throat, breaking the spell. "So what happens now?" he asked as Edith pulled her hand away wistfully. "Do you know how I ended up in 2023? Or will end up—I don't even know how to say it. When did we first meet? Tell me what you know, Edith."

Behind her, a whoosh announced the arrival of her food. "We never actually met, Julian," Edith answered, placing the colorful salad on the table as she seated herself next to him. "I met you, then you met me." She hesitated. "Obviously, it's reversed from your perspective. But as far as I know, the first time we interacted was August 15, 2023."

Edith waited to see if the date sparked recognition. When it didn't, she continued. "It was my thirtieth birthday, and I was out celebrating with friends at Fifth Edition, this little dive bar. Do you remember Charlotte?"

"I don't know who that is," Julian said.

"Right," Edith acknowledged. "Well, Charlotte remembers you walking

CHAPTER TWENTY-SEVEN

right up to me, saying we needed to talk." She dropped her elbow to the table and stared dreamily at Julian for a moment. "Out on the dance floor, we had about a minute together before you dropped the bombshell."

Julian waited.

"You told me you were there that night to stop me from getting raped, and warned me not to go home with anyone," she said, studying his face. "Why would you say that if it wasn't true? I slept alone that night, trying to decide if I was more grateful or pissed." Edith let out a laugh. "It was my birthday, and I really wanted to get laid!"

Through the lines of her face, Julian could see the roguish smile she'd given him at the reparations rally. It was easy to believe that Edith was a woman used to getting what she wanted.

"You wouldn't tell me your name," Edith continued, "but you were older, knew the secret about Izzy Robynham I'd never told a soul, and also claimed to know something very personal about what was about to happen to me. Before you left, Julian, you gave me the date we'd meet again—the first time for you—two and a half years later." Julian raised an eyebrow. "And you were wearing a wedding ring," she said. "It seemed pretty plausible that your knowledge and motivation were the result of being married to me in the future."

It seemed pretty logical to him, too, and it was disappointing that she couldn't solve this particular mystery. "I don't know anything about that, Edith," he said. She stared as though the veracity of his claim could be divined through the pores on his face.

"To your first question," she continued, "Your appearance and reappearance persuaded Charlotte that time travel was possible, and her breakthrough—she's a physicist—came a few years ago. It didn't make sense to revive you until she'd worked it out." A broad smile split her face, bursting with anticipation at the possibilities. "After lunch, we'll go see her."

Julian looked down at the remainder of his food without interest. "Now?" he asked. Delroy's suitcase was still sitting untouched in the corner of his room; he tried to think of what else he would need to bring. What would his new friends think of him if he just disappeared? "Edith, I need some time to think all this over. Don't I have any say?"

"You do," she insisted. "We're just going to talk with Charlotte. Nothing will happen today; she'll just explain the details."

Julian exhaled. "So what did Idabee say?"

"She's a smart woman," Edith admitted. "About three minutes into our conversation, she figured out that you and I had met before; time travel and the letter were quite real. After that... Beebee and I have been very close for many years. The hurtful things she said to me, well, I haven't really had time to figure out what's worse—that she feels that way or that her accusations might be true."

"What might be true?" he pressed.

"That I'm willing to jeopardize whatever you two might have now because of this imaginary life I've concocted for the two of us in the past. We had sixty-five seconds on the dance floor, Julian, and sixty-five minutes at the reparations rally before you were shot. If you prevent the attack, we could have sixty-five years together."

Julian laughed. "You practiced that line, didn't you?"

"I've had a long time to think about you," she grinned.

"Look, I told you I was married before, and I like to think I'd have done better a second time around. But sixty-five years? That sounds pretty optimistic," he said.

Edith lifted her chin and preened. "How many husbands get a chance to see what their wives will look like decades in the future?" she asked mischievously.

He let out a chuckle and spoke offhandedly. "I was just thinking that Idabee will probably end up looking like you." As soon as the words were out of his mouth, Julian regretted them. Edith's expression froze, the wound visible in her eyes. "Sorry, I just meant..." he began, but had no idea where to direct the sentence.

Edith spoke before the silence became awkward. "Her high expectations must have been contagious." She sighed. "I do feel responsible for her infatuation with you. When she was a girl, she'd visit me and her father in

CHAPTER TWENTY-SEVEN

the cryonics department. She always wanted to hear the story of the brave Julian West, the knight who rescued the princess"—Edith put a hand on her chest—"before succumbing to his injuries and falling into a deep sleep.

"I don't remember how old she was when she began saying she wanted to meet a man like Julian West. Of course, I was happily married at the time, so I couldn't very well tell her how badly I wanted you for myself."

"I'm sure she'll forgive you, Julian, for things you haven't actually done. In my case, she's understandably angry. I knew when you were revived, it would only be temporary. And I kept that from her."

She was still keeping secrets. "Do you know what happened to the Julian West you met in the past?" he asked. "Where did he end up?"

Edith fell silent at the question, her head drooping as though her salad was especially fascinating. He waited, dread building inside him, and when she looked up again, her eyes were deep pools of sadness. "You died," Edith said. "The night before the rally, trying to stop the white supremacists prior to their attack, you died."

A preternatural calm fell over Julian, even as her closing two words continued to echo in his head. Edith interpreted his silence as an invitation to continue. "The ringleader, Connor Sullivan, had a six-person team ready to attack the reparations rally," Edith said. "If you hadn't taken out two of them the night before, they might have succeeded in assassinating Reverend Shaver."

His mouth was dry when he managed to speak. "I really did wreck Connor's plan. No wonder he says we have unfinished business." Julian plunged his face into his hands and rubbed it vigorously. Edith was waiting patiently when he reemerged. "If I do this, I could be dead in a couple years?"

She shrugged. "There's a non-zero chance of that. Of course, you could get hit by a car crossing the street tomorrow."

Curiosity tugged his mind upward from the gloomy depths of death. "Really? Self-driving cars will run people over?"

"No, Julian, it's a figure of speech I thought you would recognize," she replied, amusement slightly edging out the exasperation in her tone. "If

I said you could contract COVID-68 tomorrow, would you be worried about a sudden demise?"

"I don't know. Should I be?"

"Julian, the point is to prevent the attack at the reparations rally," she said. "We know how you died before, and you'll be able to change things."

"You know what happened," he reminded her. "I don't."

Edith held out her hand for the tablet next to him, then called up the relevant news story within thirty seconds. Julian quickly scanned the text.

> *The Washington Post* (March 18, 2026) Police responded to an altercation near McGinty's Pub just after midnight. Witnesses indicated an unidentified Black male confronted a half-dozen patrons leaving the St. Patrick's Day festivities. When gunfire broke out, several escaped, but three men, including the assailant, were pronounced dead at the scene. Police are asking anyone with information to contact–

"That was the bar I was drinking at the night before the rally," Julian said slowly. It had been ridiculously crowded for the holiday. "Seemed like half the city was there. Anyway, I left before midnight and didn't get into any fights. Why do you think this was me? Or will be me?"

"It was you; I saw the body," Edith said firmly, her eyes flicking up to his bare scalp. "Except that Julian had some proud locs. The entire day was crazy; I hadn't even washed your blood out of my clothes when a messenger delivered a blue envelope with a letter from you that upended everything."

"So you know how Idabee feels," he observed.

She gave a smile and shrugged. "About unexpectedly going home alone, yes, I remember the frustration you can cause. But I sort of knew you were a time traveler from the beginning, so no, getting your letter wasn't quite the same. You apologized and told me to look for your older self in the morgue. You also volunteered your younger self for the cryonics program, which I had specifically not mentioned. Working with dead bodies wasn't

CHAPTER TWENTY-SEVEN

the first impression I wanted to make."

Julian's laugh shattered the pall in the room. "Good decision," he said.

"You told me that Reverend Shaver's survival was essential to the future," Edith continued, reaching out for his hand. "You told me we'd see each other again."

As Julian took her hand, he felt a spark of possibility ignite, just like the first time. "And here we are," Julian agreed. Under normal circumstances, Dr. Edith Bartlett would have been out of his league, but maybe if the past was malleable, that spark could turn into a raging fire. Who had that other Julian been married to?

"I want to help you stop Connor Sullivan," Edith said earnestly. "When you come see me on August 15, I want you to take me home. Tell me about the future, take me into your confidence, and let me help you so that we can have our decades together."

Now he recognized the date. Delroy had been very descriptive about how they worked together to start building the American Union in the year after his arrival, except that Julian West ducked out on that specific day, claiming a prior commitment. Protecting Edith explained why.

He knew what Delroy didn't: Julian West had had a conversation with Reverend Shaver, only to have his request for help turned down. Edith had given him a phrase to immediately earn her trust in 2023. Could Shaver provide him with something similar? If the American Union did succeed, all sorts of possibilities would be open, not just for him but for millions and millions of people. Edith seemed completely uninterested in that.

Although Julian's face remained composed, his mind was racing. Edith was still waiting for him to respond. The desire in her look was familiar; Idabee's features submerged beneath the lines of her face. Of course, if the past was fixed and couldn't be changed, he might not have to abandon Idabee and the tricentennial.

"I'll think about it," Julian said. "I promise." Edith smiled, and he squeezed her hand. "But now I want to hear what Charlotte has to say."

Chapter Twenty-Eight

Standing outside of the warehouse, waiting for Edith to open the door, Julian felt the vitality of the air flow through him, the fillings in his teeth emitting a metallic taste, the crackle prodding his eardrums in a thousand directions, the hairs on his arms standing, saluting, rising up in worship of the god of the twenty-first century, electricity.

Edith pulled the door open, revealing a dark portal by which to exit the bright spring sunshine. "Charlotte chose this place because it's adjacent to the regional substation," she explained. "We're going to need a lot of power to get you where you're going. Or should I say when?"

Julian followed her inside. As his eyes adjusted, he could make out rows of empty shelves, looming in the dimness like skeletons from a mythical age. They made their way into the interior, where Charlotte stood behind a large stainless steel bench, illuminated beneath a bank of lights. She was a white woman about Edith's age, wearing a stereotypical lab coat with her silver hair pulled back into a ponytail.

"Oh, my God, you look exactly the same as you did back then," Charlotte said as they approached, casually resting her hands on a contraption that dominated the bench, protruding off the front and back. "Which of course you should, because cryo girl knows her stuff, but it's amazing. Anyway, act surprised when you meet me again."

"If you're fifty years younger, that shouldn't be hard," Julian answered. The device had a triangular base, with the corners an arm span apart. LEDs flashed different colors on various electronic components. In the center, a disc about the width of his body appeared to be free-floating. "You invented

CHAPTER TWENTY-EIGHT

time travel?"

"This woman," the physicist replied, pointing a friendly finger at Edith, "swore up and down that the mystery man who walked into the bar that night was from the future. She was absolutely convinced that you'd meet again two years later."

"And we did," Edith said. It was clear from the banter that the women had had this discussion countless times over the decades.

"You were drunk; you weren't really a credible witness."

"Being drunk and right aren't mutually exclusive," Edith countered, beaming at Julian.

"She was right," Charlotte acknowledged. "And when that happened, I had to believe her. It was a fun side project, keeping my eyes peeled for any promising lines of research in the scientific journals. Had to keep it on the down-low because no one wants to get a reputation as one of those time-travel nuts at physics conferences.

"Finally, about a decade ago, there was an experiment that successfully manipulated time-flavored quarks within a high-energy field. Those quarks generally grip the stream of time, ensuring their atoms flow forward at the same rate as everything else. The experiment was able to shift them to a neutral state, raising the anchor, so to speak, but it took an incredible amount of power to keep them that way."

"If you had that much energy to waste, there were even applications in my field," Edith continued. "Why freeze a person if you could literally suspend them in time?"

"But for you, Julian, we want to move you against the flow of time, pushing you backward. And that's what this machine does." Charlotte spread her arms with a flourish, indicating the device in front of her. "I call it the timepad."

"She spared every expense in developing the name," Edith said.

"Glad you noticed," Charlotte replied. "I have a junior version that works for manipulating small objects, but this is the full-sized model." The octogenarian easily lifted the floating disc from the center of the machine, transferring it to an empty space on the bench and revealing a curved hollow underneath, where a short metal rod protruded upward.

"This is where you'll crouch for your trip," the physicist explained, running a hand over the gritty surface of the disc, "which should only seem like a fraction of a second."

"Please keep your hands inside the high-energy field at all times," Edith added.

"Yes," Charlotte said, "plus any other parts of your body that you want to preserve. The disc travels with you, and the base has two storage compartments." Charlotte flipped them open, revealing hollow spaces. "If you have anything that's electronically sensitive, carry it in here."

Next, she tilted the disc to reveal a hole in the bottom. The diameter matched the rod in the base of the timepad. "The disc stays balanced until just before the moment of travel, when the support rod snaps back and leaves it weightless. The energy field forms a sphere around you; we give it a good flick, and off you go."

"Okay," Julian said.

The women exchanged a grin. "Demonstration?" Edith asked Charlotte.

Metal scraped as Charlotte replaced the disc on the support rod. Reaching under the bench, she withdrew an orange. "A perfectly ordinary piece of fruit," she said, handing it to Julian. "I want you to toss it up in the air and see how long you can get it to stay there."

Julian complied, lobbing the sphere gently into the air, watching it through the high arc, and catching the fruit when it came back down a few seconds later. "Okay."

"Time is an aspect of gravity," Charlotte explained. "It's always pulling us down. What we needed was a way to stay aloft."

"Okay," he agreed. "Hot air balloon? Airplane? Did you invent anti-gravity?"

"All good guesses," Charlotte said, "but even simpler. We use the same principle that keeps satellites up. Gravity is always pulling them down, but forward momentum balances it out, and they stay in orbit around the Earth. This machine will theoretically push one hundred thirteen kilos of mass out of the normal flow of time, like you tossing the orange in the air.

CHAPTER TWENTY-EIGHT

Except, we're going to push you hard enough to put you in a time orbit, where you'll theoretically continue to fall backward in time until we drop you back down in the summer of 2023."

Julian held up his hands in surrender. "I'm going to pretend you didn't just say theoretically. Twice."

"Well, you definitely arrived there," Edith said cheerfully. She handed him a blue marker and gestured to the orange. "Write something on it," she directed.

Julian uncapped the marker and poised it over the textured skin of the fruit. "What should I write?" he asked.

"Absolutely anything you want," Charlotte said.

Nothing came to mind. Art had never been his strong suit, but with a few swift strokes, Julian sketched a smiley face on the orange, incorporating the navel as the nose. "How's that?"

Charlotte was grinning as she produced two more oranges from beneath the bench. She held the first one out; it wore a corresponding smiley face drawn in blue marker. "I think it looks good." The other she handed to Edith.

The appearance of the duplicate stunned him. "How did you do that?" he asked, comparing the two. They were eerily similar, but the one that he'd just drawn had a little crook at the end of the mouth line. "They're not identical."

"No," Charlotte agreed gravely. "What you drew wasn't destiny, but under the same circumstances, you're just very likely to make the same decision. You always have free will."

"So the past can be changed," he said, looking again at the fruit in his hand. Although he'd recognized his handwriting on Idabee's envelope and the stories he'd heard from Shaver, Delroy, and Edith had all held together, the pair of oranges were concrete in a way nothing else had been. His artwork had traveled through time. "Now we send this orange back to earlier today for the demonstration?"

"No," Charlotte said. "That one's for you."

"But if I eat this, how will you get that one? How can there be two?"

"Peel," Charlotte directed. Julian hesitated. Once he broke the skin, there was no way that the orange he held could end up as the other half of a demonstration for an alternate version of himself. "Julian, it's okay," the physicist reassured him. "The Charlotte who sent it sacrificed part of her lunch for you. Peel."

This time, Julian obeyed, spritzing orange zest as he dug through the rind. "And this is what it'll be like for me in 2023? They'll be two of me, right? Any warnings about destroying the space-time continuum if we meet or anything like that?"

Charlotte stretched to bump the two pieces of fruit into each other. Nothing happened. "See? But I still wouldn't recommend it. Do you know where your past self is?"

"I'll be locked up in PICC until fall '24. Just in time for the election." He hesitated. "Charlotte, if you have time travel, aren't there bigger and better uses for it in history?"

"Believe me, we've talked about it," Edith said. The air was rich with a citrus scent as she pulled a segment from her orange. "But it's not that simple."

"Getting you into a time orbit and returning you safely has technical restrictions," Charlotte explained. "There are certain windows, like on- and off-ramps of a highway, where the math lines up so you can get out of the regular flow of time and also merge back again safely. They're only about ten minutes wide and appear at regular intervals a little more than forty-two months apart."

"Wait, then when did this orange come from?" Julian popped a piece into his mouth. "It doesn't taste three years old."

"From a few minutes in the future," Charlotte said. "Without a window for time orbit open, it was pulled back down into normal time relatively quickly, just like when you tossed it into the air, except it's about a twenty-four minute trip. When it showed up twenty minutes ago, I knew you two were about to arrive."

Julian rubbed his head. "Except now you're not going to do that, but it showed up anyway. So who sent it?"

CHAPTER TWENTY-EIGHT

"A Charlotte in a parallel universe. These failed trips with small objects don't use quite so much power, so I've run many tests. When we flick something back in time, there are two possibilities: it arrives or it doesn't. A parallel universe is created next to ours, where the opposite occurs. It's roughly a fifty-fifty chance that we're in the universe where it lands; the rest of the time, whatever we sent is just gone." She pointed to the orange that Edith was eating. "I brought two oranges this morning to use for our demonstration; that way there was a 75% chance at least one would arrive."

"But now you're not sending either one," Julian said. "So, where did it come from?"

"The Charlotte who sent one, or maybe both, of the oranges back twenty-four minutes is in the universe where it no longer exists. Or at least yours doesn't." Charlotte smiled brightly.

"So that might happen to me?" Julian said with alarm.

"Except," Edith said sharply to her friend, "we already know that Julian did arrive in our past." She placed a supportive hand on his shoulder, leaving him somewhat reassured.

Charlotte let the point pass without arguing. "We can put you in early July 2023. Plenty of time to meet up with birthday girl." She looked fondly at Edith.

Julian had another question. "I talked with an old friend yesterday," he began, "who says I showed up at his door on July 14. But how do we know that's when I arrived?" he asked. "What if I went back another forty-two months, to the beginning of the pandemic, and hung around? My mother picked up Covid at bingo the last Friday in March. I could warn her not to go."

"You could also go back to 1998 and wait around to try to prevent 9/11," Charlotte said. "Or March 1981, to try and prevent the assassination attempt on Ronald Reagan. You're right, Julian; it's theoretically possible. Is that what you want to do?"

He considered possibilities. "How about the assassination of MLK?"

Edith shook her head. "The base that you travel with uses GPS to maintain your spatial location as your temporal location changes, so 1981 is the earliest Charlotte feels confident in predicting that you'll have a safe landing."

Julian looked down at the discarded orange peel, curls arcing upward from the metal bench. Fragments of blue lines showed where the smiley face had been. Charlotte's scraps had similar markings, made by a Julian West in a parallel universe. Both had existed together for a few minutes before being consumed.

According to Edith, the same thing had happened to him. For several years, two versions of himself overlapped in time until March 18, 2026, brought a hard stop to both lives. "Charlotte," he asked, "we know I arrived in the past, just like that orange did. But you don't actually have to send me for that to happen, any more than you had to send your orange. Is that right?"

"No, Julian," Edith protested. "You have to go, or nothing will change. Just like you drew something different on the orange, things won't end up the same. You'll make things better."

"You don't have to go," Charlotte said. Edith crumpled slightly at the contradiction. "Our past has already occurred, and it won't change. It's more likely that you would create a new, parallel universe that unfolds differently."

Julian nodded. "How long do I have to decide?" he asked.

"There's a ten-minute window at noon on May 1," Charlotte said. "After that, it's another forty-two months." She shrugged. "Edith thinks you were a few years older."

The past was malleable. If he could secure Reverend Shaver's help, everything would change. A month seemed like plenty of time to make arrangements. "Okay," Julian said. "Let's do it."

Sorry, Idabee.

Chapter Twenty-Nine

The parlor was quiet—too quiet—as Julian waited for Polly Sigh to appear. Although he could have looked up the answer to the question of how the American Union made endorsements when the candidates refused to support their legislative demands, he enjoyed these interactions with various experts, and Polly seemed to enjoy addressing his questions. More importantly, she might be able to answer a question that had never been asked in this universe.

Last night, after he had returned from Charlotte's warehouse, Julian talked with Ray about the events of the last few days. It cemented his legacy as the most interesting sleeper that the doctor had ever revived. Ray began listening sympathetically, waiting to hear what had gone wrong with Idabee, but his scientific mind rebelled at the concept of time travel and a multiverse. He refused to accept it.

Julian despaired. Ray good-naturedly agreed to his suggestion that they invite everyone—Idabee, Edith, Delroy, and Charlotte—over for dinner, where they could verify what he was saying. Then, one detail broke through and shattered his disbelief. Ray rose silently, paced back and forth, and retrieved the bottle of whiskey. After downing a stiff drink—Julian joined him in solidarity—he admitted remembering his mother being disturbed by a mysterious letter she'd received when he was a boy. Physical letters were almost unheard of, but what he recalled about this one was the color—robin's-egg blue.

"That's when she did it," Ray realized. "She altered your medical records to make it appear you'd requested revival in 2076. Since I'd heard your story many times, I couldn't make sense of how you'd requested a specific date when you were supposed to be in a medical coma. But when I confronted her a few months ago, she insisted the records were correct."

A gentle tone returned Julian's focus to the parlor, where Polly Sigh began to flicker into existence across from him. Julian grinned when he saw her. "I like the red," he offered after they made eye contact. Polly's hair was now shockingly bright, like a child might color a heart.

"Thanks," she replied, preening. "Where's Idabee?"

"She decided not to come," Julian said truthfully. Idabee's absence disappointed him. Her enthusiasm for digging into the mechanics of political science was one of her many charming qualities. He hoped she would accept Ray's invitation for dinner.

"We were talking about how the American Union makes endorsements, right?" Polly prompted.

Julian nodded agreement. "You said it's based on what candidates do on Muster Day—if they fast for peace with the American Union of swing voters to accept their demands?"

"Support the demand for immediate passage of the legislative package, yes," Polly clarified. "Incumbents always have first chance. Members of Congress are guaranteed the American Union's endorsement if they commit their support and deliver the legislation, without amendment, to the president's desk within one week. If they refuse, but their major-party challenger joined the fast, then the challenger gets the endorsement."

That seemed straightforward enough. "And what happens if they both do?"

"That's always the goal, Julian; it's a fast for peace. Then the American Union has succeeded in building consensus about what exactly Congress should be doing, but before the election, when voters—especially swing voters—have leverage.

"Remember, the challenger is a constituent, too. If they demand that their representative pass the legislation immediately and their demand is met, then they're expected to support the American Union endorsement of the incumbent. Persuading Congress to act before the election means

CHAPTER TWENTY-NINE

we all win. Sometimes challengers drop out of the race; others might do something as simple as issue a statement saying they'll be voting for the incumbent instead of themselves.

"If Congress doesn't enact the legislation, that's the same as the incumbent refusing—the challenger is endorsed and the incumbent is expected to support them since they couldn't get the job done."

Julian stared at Polly for a moment, then began to laugh. "Let me get this straight. The best chance for a candidate to win is to be willing to support their opponent?"

Polly allowed herself a chuckle. "Yes, it is. The game theorist Thomas Schelling pointed out that there's no rational reason to communicate in a pure zero-sum game. The hyperpolarization of your time exacerbated that; Republicans and Democrats often avoided working together—communicating—precisely to avoid giving any advantage to their opponents.

"The fast for peace overlays a non-zero-sum game on the regular election, so there's an advantage—the bloc of swing votes—to communication. Instead of voters feeling obligated to pick sides, they had a third option: focus on policy and let the candidates come to them.

"In one of her books, Stella Freedom says the problem with Congress in your time was that the marginal cost of doing nothing was zero. Members knew that people locked into the lesser-of-two-evils game wouldn't hold them accountable in the general election for failing to act. Martin Luther King's first principle of nonviolence was that it was a way of life for courageous people." Polly gave him a sly look. "That's a clue for you."

He nodded gravely. "Okay, but if neither candidate supports the legislation, what do we do? When I suggested not endorsing either, you all laughed, so that's not it."

"Nonviolence is active, not passive. Not only would that neutralize the power of voting as a bloc," Polly replied, "it would encourage negative campaigning because individuals would have to play the lesser-of-two-evils game."

"How about voting against all incumbents?"

"Then what's the challenger's incentive to get on board if they'd get the endorsement by default?" Polly asked innocently.

Julian sighed and rubbed his goatee. "You implied third-party candidates weren't eligible."

"The short answer is: only if they're polling in the top two," she replied. "To vote for marginal candidates would be mathematically the same as not voting. Wasting votes is passive, not active."

"And there's a logical solution?" Polly nodded again, grinning at his annoyance. Julian tried one more time to puzzle it out. "Okay, we're committed to voting as a bloc for one of the top-two candidates. If neither has endorsed the union's demands..." He paused. "We could always flip a coin."

His mentor's grin expanded, and she began to clap. "Yes; once you accept the responsibility for being the deciders, that's the only fair way to choose," Polly said.

Julian accepted the audible praise but admitted, "I was mostly joking."

"That is the ultimate threat for a union of voters—a general strike inside the ballot box that elects candidates and awards control of Congress at random. There are principled and practical reasons to make endorsements like that if all else fails," Polly told him, "but let me outline the rest of the process. Qualified members—did Idabee explain that?"

"Members who opt-in with the fast for peace can vote directly on policy?"

"Right. So every member who fasts on Muster Day, personally pledging to vote with the bloc, is qualified to vote on October 16 on the tie-breaking procedures for any remaining endorsements. They can vote yes, no, or abstain on three options.

"The first is to give incumbents a second bite at the apple if they supported the legislation's passage, but it didn't actually hit the president's desk. If there were more yes votes than no votes, the American Union would go ahead and endorse them anyway. Remember, that's only if their challenger refused to support the demand for immediate passage of the legislation."

Polly pressed on. "The second option is to endorse all remaining challengers and throw out as many incumbents of both parties as possible. You were correct to suggest this, Julian; the answer to 'What's the challenger's incentive to get on board?' is that challengers don't know what members will decide until they're committed. Even if this only flips a roughly equal number of seats from both parties and doesn't change the balance of power much, the quantity of defeats sends a strong message.

"Third is the so-called nuclear option; award all remaining endorsements to one party randomly. Think for a moment how demoralizing it would be to be in power knowing you're there on a vote of no confidence. Unsurprisingly, it's not an enjoyable vibe. One advantage of this option is that it crystallizes the choice for the majority party in the next election: meet the American Union's terms or willingly give up power.

"If that gets voted down, then two lists of the remaining candidates are published, roughly divided between the parties, and then a week before the election, one list is randomly endorsed. They've used different things in different years—could be based on the high temperature on a certain day, lottery numbers, the number of passengers on a certain route—but things outside of human control."

"The first couple options make sense," Julian said, "but I'm not quite sure how I feel about the random endorsements. What if a terrible politician gets elected and makes things worse?"

"That might be scary," she said understandingly. "What's MLK's first principle of nonviolence?"

"It's a way of life for courageous people. But Polly, there were real nuts who ran for, and won, public office." Carlton had asked, *Was the status quo worth violating the principle that every human is worthy of redemption?* He admitted to Polly, "I guess I can see the principled angle. What's the practical one?"

"For the American Union to be taken seriously as the deciders, the votes have to be on the table. Trying to weaken the winner's legitimacy by boycotting an election is ineffective, but picking a random winner works. It's like a big asterisk in the history books."

"This is game theory?" he asked.

She looked him over. "Did you play any sports, Julian? Any tournaments?"

"High school basketball. We came in fourth in a citywide contest one year."

"Okay, imagine you're in the quarterfinals, and they announce they're going to randomly award fifty extra points to one team at halftime. Your team wins, and in the finals, the same thing happens: you randomly get fifty points and win the championship. Would you feel proud?"

He shrugged. "Maybe if we scored more points than the other teams."

"Do you think both teams would play their hardest?"

Julian considered, then shook his head. "It would feel pretty meaningless; both playing and winning. It wouldn't be much to brag about."

"That's what the random endorsement does, Julian. This sort of leverage couldn't be wielded by any individual; only a union of voters could actually pick a winner in a way that undercut their legitimacy. When the American Union polled high enough to be the deciders, any candidate turning down the offer was indicating a willingness to lose or appear illegitimate. Taking a positive position always benefited them, just like the Oregon method of electing US Senators and the Anti-Saloon League's support for prohibition candidates."

Julian pondered. "I guess I can't see a candidate, given the opportunity to win, preferring to take their chances with a coin flip. But couldn't supporting the legislative package also hurt a candidate?"

Polly grinned. "Because of partisan polarization, it generally couldn't. Think about it: if a Republican candidate came out in support of the legislation and members of their base objected, what other option did those voters have? Thanks to Duverger's law, if they didn't help the Republican win, the Democrat would, so party loyalty saves them. Of course, building the American Union on principled nonviolence helped hold the moral high ground, making it harder to object.

"This is the power of a union, Julian, the willingness to go on strike and disrupt the status quo. Without the credible threat to elect people from both parties, a group of voters couldn't do anything but make polite

CHAPTER TWENTY-NINE

requests and hope their representatives listened. I think you saw how ineffective that was. A national bloc of swing voters had the power to gain leverage over the entire system and persuade Congress to act before the election."

Julian nodded. "Third parties usually only got a few percent of the vote—I think about six percent in the 2016 presidential election. But I can see how that could be decisive in close races."

"In an individual race, a third-party candidate needed about 35% of the vote to win," Polly explained. "The American Union was able to secure control over the balance of power in Washington with much less. The focus on swing states and swing districts let them influence as many races as possible. They received national press coverage because they were offering the same set of legislative solutions coast-to-coast, and then people wanted to know where their own candidates stood."

"And, let me guess," Julian grinned. "As that small percentage got bigger, politicians were more likely to come out in support?"

"Do you know the definition of a politician, Julian?" Polly asked. "It's a person who thinks the worst thing that can happen to the country is for someone else to win the office they want. Like Nixon, they persuade themselves to support the policies that will win their campaigns."

"Okay, but since political parties still existed, what role did they play in this system?"

"Officially, none. Remember, Duverger's law meant the system would tend toward two parties, but not because of specific policies. Instead, it's an efficient allocation of resources in a zero-sum game. There's a party in power, and a party trying to get into power."

"But, unofficially?"

Polly smiled. "Yes, that was the principled answer, but as a practical matter, national parties do exist. And so they create a sense of peer pressure and teamwork among candidates—incumbents and challengers alike. For example, say the Democrats had a majority in Congress. If they refused to enact the legislative package, that would open up an opportunity for Republican challengers to win the majority by supporting it. So the desire to keep power creates an incentive for parties to support the proposal—and all their candidates in those swing districts where the American Union controls the outcome—as long as it isn't too polarizing."

Julian laughed. "I've been picturing this backward, that the American Union is negotiating for passage of their legislation. But it's really the other way around; members of Congress are negotiating a contract extension for themselves."

"That's a pretty good analogy," she agreed.

"So, what happens if the House supports it and the Senate doesn't, or vice versa?"

"What do you think should happen?" Polly asked innocently.

Julian sighed. His brain was beginning to overheat, and there was still one very big question that he had on his mind. "It's been a long week, Polly. I give up."

"Okay," she agreed. "The American Union treats Congress like a unicameral chamber; if the legislation doesn't pass exactly as it was given to them on September 21, all the members are held responsible. As a practical matter, party loyalty is a big incentive for incumbents to work together across both chambers."

"And if they don't, you elect their challengers. Do they pass the legislation when they take office?"

"They've pledged to support immediate passage, and after the next Congress is sworn in, they're expected to make it happen. It hasn't come to that in a while, though; '56 was the last time Congress refused to act in an election year. Union members voted to keep the supportive incumbents, brought in as many challengers as they could, and the new Congress had the votes to put it on the president's desk in January. They let the incumbent sign it, even though he'd lost to his challenger for failing to get it through Congress."

Julian rubbed the back of his head, feeling the stubble under his fingers. "Are people really willing to elect a president at random?" he asked. "Would you vote with the American Union this November if it came to that?"

"Probably," Polly said. "The system mostly runs on inertia, but it's happened: President Tia Brando was endorsed based on the number of cars that crossed the Golden Gate Bridge on October 30, 2044. Four years later, she was spectacularly committed to working with the American Union and earning reelection legitimately."

They fell silent, and Julian looked at Polly. He took a deep breath, preparing to ask the question he'd contemplated ever since talking to Delroy. "Polly," he said, "I know it was in 2026 that the American Union first influenced Congress, but hypothetically, could you use your knowledge of political science and game theory to design an American Union campaign for 2024?"

"The Trump–Biden rematch?" Julian nodded. "Yes, I could. Why?"

He dodged the question. "Do you think it could work then? It was a terrible election."

Polly examined him closely and considered. "There's a psychology experiment involving game theory. One person is given one hundred dollars and told to offer a percentage to the other participant. If the offer is accepted, both parties keep their portion. But if the second person refuses, both parties get nothing.

"Game theory says the second person should accept any non-zero amount because they'll be better off than refusing; it's win-win. But human psychology doesn't work that way. A fair, or reasonably fair, offer is almost always accepted, but a blatantly unfair offer, like an 80/20 split, is refused half the time. No one gets anything: lose-lose.

"People have an innate sense of fairness, Julian. At some point, most people are willing to sacrifice—give up free money—rather than allow injustice to go unchecked. The American Union's threat of a general strike in the ballot box would give voters a chance to reject an unjust system.

"The real question is," she concluded, "would Republicans and Democrats be able to convince voters to accept an offer to maintain the status quo?"

Chapter Thirty

"I still can't believe Aunt Charlotte invented time travel," Ray said, scratching the back of his neck. He and Julian sat comfortably in the parlor, waiting for Reverend Shaver to appear. "Our families spent a lot of time together growing up; their girls were a little bit older than me. I knew she was smart, but time travel?" He shook his head in wonder.

"The way they explained it to me," Julian said, "was that it creates a parallel universe. So you don't have to worry about me doing something where you cease to exist."

Ray laughed out loud. "Of all the things I've ever worried about in my life, having a patient go back in time and stop my parents from meeting has never occurred to me."

Julian lifted a fist; Ray bumped it. "Still nothing to worry about," Julian said. "It's all good."

"Idabee agreed to come to dinner Friday," the doctor said. "I hope you can convince her this is for the best."

"Is it?" Julian wondered out loud. "Parallel worlds, Ray. I just told you that your existence isn't going to change if I go back and alter things. It works the other direction, too—nothing changes if I just live out my life in the tricentennial."

Ray rubbed his chin. "But isn't that why you asked to talk with Reverend Shaver, so you could change things?"

"True," he conceded without conviction. "We'll see what he has for me. Anyway, I'm going to see Idabee tonight in Professor Carlton's group. I'll have the whole month of April to go through the organizer training and

CHAPTER THIRTY

learn as much as I can."

The doctor shook his head. "I hope my daughter recognizes how much of an influence she's had. Embarking on a month of sobriety after pushing me into day drinking with you."

"I didn't push," Julian protested playfully. "It was a friendly invitation in the spirit of the holiday." The previous evening, the men had had a last drink together before Julian ceremoniously dumped the remainder of the alcohol down the drain.

"All I'm saying," Ray continued, "is if your self-purification kick helps you smooth things out with Idabee, I wish you the best of luck."

Julian shrugged. "Maybe it's worth doing on its own," he suggested. "Idabee said there are millions of American Union organizers. And she certainly thinks highly of Professor Carlton."

A quiet tone sounded, and Reverend Alvin Shaver appeared on the couch across from them. After they greeted each other, but before Julian could explain why he had asked for the meeting, the nonagenarian spoke. "Julian, we were interrupted in the restaurant," he said. "I didn't get a chance to fully apologize and explain why my fast directed atonement toward you. It was for my failure to listen when you showed up at my door all those years ago and tried to explain the American Union."

Julian nodded acceptance, his suspicions confirmed. "Can you tell me when that was?"

"In the fall of 2023," Shaver said, his expression slightly wounded, possibly by the implication Julian didn't remember the conversation. "You asked me to lead a national day of fasting on January 15, Dr. King's birthday, and the day of the Iowa caucuses. The fast was supposed to establish the American Union as a constructive alternative in the 2024 election. Needless to say, I was skeptical about how giving up food for a day could do that.

"Then you tried to explain that a people's assembly could seize the means of legislative production, the banking system could be restructured to provide everyone money and end poverty, and that natural rights were a bluff; duties came first. Julian, I didn't take you seriously, and the material you gave me so earnestly was thrown away, unread."

"I can understand your skepticism," Julian said. "Did you hear from me again?"

"Two more times—maybe three. About six months later, you returned to ask me to speak at a rally for the American Union on July 4, which I turned down because the 2024 election was too important to encourage distractions. A year or so later was the last time." The preacher turned to Ray. "Julian told me I was going to speak at a rally for reparations on March 18 and gave me an envelope, not to be opened until after I accepted the invitation."

"A blue envelope?" Julian asked, and Shaver nodded. "What did it say?"

"Don't you remember?" Shaver asked, shifting his attention back to the younger man. "I don't know how you predicted the date that far in advance, so when I read the letter, you'd earned some credibility. You asked me to do three things: keep the contents of the letter absolutely secret, wear a bulletproof vest at the rally, and look for a woman with a sign reading *Power concedes nothing without a demand*."

Shaver folded his hands together and studied Julian closely. "From the stage, I couldn't be sure that was you with the woman, since you'd shaved your head. But when I woke up in the hospital, I praised the Lord that I'd listened about the bulletproof vest." He touched the scar on his face purposefully. "It almost didn't matter."

"You got another letter in the hospital, didn't you?" Julian asked.

"A neat trick, I admit," Reverend Shaver said, "since you were supposed to be in a coma at the time. But your letter explained how a national day of fasting, combined with a specific set of demands, could help us create a critical mass of moral pressure behind reparations."

"And that time, you believed me."

The room fell silent for a moment. "The dozens of victims at the rally weighed on my conscience, Julian, almost as much as the violence that had flared up nationwide in the days after," Shaver continued. "The United States was on edge, balanced on a precipice. The fast functioned as a call to action; it was active and not passive, as well as a mechanism for thoughtful deliberation. Like your previous letter, you asked me to keep its existence secret and, if I used the concept, to take sole credit because it stemmed from my ideas."

The nonagenarian leaned forward. "Julian, I never quite believed that. I was not a man inclined toward fasting; I had never called for one before. How could it have been based on my work?"

Julian ignored the question for the simple reason that he had no answer. "The first time we met, what could I have said so you'd listen? How could I persuade you to lead the January 15 fast for peace?"

Reverend Shaver shook his head regretfully. "I don't think you could. It was too much to swallow in one bite."

Ray gave a deliberate nod, and Julian knew what it meant: tell him. Julian did, serving up the perfectly reasonable–unreasonable explanation, detailing how he hadn't yet done the things Shaver remembered but, armed with his knowledge from 2076, would do them in their past.

At first, Shaver laughed off the idea of time travel as though it were a prank. But when he accepted that he was being offered a second chance, tears came to his eyes. "I've never even considered that it would be possible to fix my mistake," he admitted. "The Lord heard my prayers over the decades, and He created this opportunity for redemption."

When Julian explained Edith Leete had given him a story from her past that would let him establish immediate credibility with her at their first meeting, Shaver nodded understanding and then fell silent. The other men waited patiently as he cast his thoughts back across the decades, searching for a memory that would carry significance to his younger self.

Finally, he lifted his head and focused a tight gaze on Julian. "You can ask me about the backgammon set I received as a child—if I still have it and if I ever learned how to play," Shaver directed. "One evening, during Christmastime, my parents introduced some friends of theirs to me, my brother, and our sisters. It was a family we'd never met before. They had a daughter, and I was at the age when I was starting to notice how girls were different; she was a few years older than me, starting to fill out, with long straight hair." The corners of his mouth twitched upward.

"They had gifts for us, which our parents said we could open even though it wasn't Christmas yet. I unwrapped the present she gave me to find a fake leather case. Inside were little black-and-white tokens, oval-shaped cups, and a strange die with an eclectic set of numbers. I'd never heard of backgammon, but before she left, the girl promised to come back and teach me this exotic game.

"Years later, I came across that set, and my perspective changed. We'd never seen that family again; the girl had never returned. I realized I'd been the beneficiary of a welfare Christmas, distracted from the poverty I was living in by the false promises of a light-skinned girl with a pretty smile."

He pressed Julian with an intense look. "I swore to fight the evil of poverty, but I ignored you when you knocked on my door and asked for help striking a killing blow." Shaver stroked his scar absentmindedly. "I've regretted it for a long time, Julian, and I hope you'll help me do better. Please, persuade me to listen and to throw my substantial weight behind the fast for peace so we can avoid the unnecessary bloodshed."

"Did you ever learn how to play?" Julian asked.

Reverend Shaver released a booming laugh, which echoed around the room and left the other men grinning. "If you want to find out, you're going to have to do your time travel trick," he said.

"Fair enough," Julian replied.

"But you haven't actually accepted my apology," Shaver reminded him. "Can you forgive me for not listening to you?"

Julian rubbed his ear. "There were two different Julians moving around at that point. Ray's daughter is angry with me for something the other one did, which seems a little unfair. Likewise, how can I forgive you for something that didn't happen to me?"

"Wasn't that like reparations?" Ray wondered. "Even if slavery didn't happen to you directly, you still had to deal with the effects."

The men fell silent for a moment. "Yes," Julian said. "I can forgive you, Alvin." The reverend's given name was awkward in his mouth, but it felt essential to the sincerity he was trying to communicate, one person to

CHAPTER THIRTY

another.

"Thank you, Julian. Forgiveness is a weapon of the strong," Reverend Shaver said. "I knew you had the strength to put your life on the line at the rally all those years ago. I'm pleased to find you have other strengths as well."

After a moment, Shaver continued, "I hope you'll carry my intention with you, so if you do end up in that situation, you won't feel angry or disappointed for failing to communicate a political paradigm that was outside of my experience. You'll know the error was on my end, and I ultimately accepted responsibility for it."

Julian nodded sincerely. This concept of carrying an intention seemed relevant to something else he was dealing with, but he couldn't yet make the connection. "You've obviously given thought to how things might have been different if you'd helped start the American Union two years earlier. How do you think it would have impacted reparations? Would an apology, a dollar, and an accounting have shown up in their legislation?"

The nonagenarian tented his fingers and leaned back. The change in his demeanor made it obvious that he had, in fact, considered how things might have gone differently and was hesitant to voice his opinion. Julian took a cue from Professor Carlton and waited silently, allowing thoughts to be gathered and organized for delivery.

"I think we were fortunate in the order that things came about for three reasons," Shaver finally said. "First, the fast for peace after the attack on the rally brought about a national catharsis that was divorced from electoral politics. Trying to connect it to elections before the efficacy was demonstrated would have been an additional barrier to adoption.

"Second, it demonstrated that the public could direct legislative language. Lobbyists had been doing it for centuries, but we pulled the curtain back and demonstrated there wasn't anything mystical about it.

"Third, it would have run into trouble because universality is one of the core principles of the American Union. It was once observed that 'The law, in its majesty equality, forbids rich and poor alike to sleep under bridges.' That's technically a universal policy."

Julian laughed, then sobered. "Like the policies that you talked about in your speech that were technically race-neutral, but targeted people of color?"

Shaver nodded. "The American Union avoided identity politics and used that strategy in reverse—universal practices that disproportionately benefited the marginalized. For example, the bridge policy could be flipped around to say everyone is welcome under bridges, then provide a safe place to sleep, sanitary facilities, internet access, and so on. As a practical matter, the rich would be unlikely to take advantage of universal services under a bridge, but as a matter of principle, they could.

"Julian, I believe that when unconditional basic income shifted the American people from a mindset of scarcity to a mindset of abundance, when we prioritized establishing justice, and when revamping our foreign policy sparked a reckoning of the exploitative practices the United States had utilized in the past, I believe that reparations for slavery would have followed as naturally as spring follows winter. But I can't be sure."

"Let's see if I've got this," Julian said. "If I use your story and advance the American Union, you think we might override getting reparations?"

Shaver shrugged. "There's a non-zero chance of that, but it's more likely the United States would have done the right thing before long. Forgiveness is a weapon of the strong, and we strengthened ourselves as a nation: socially, culturally, and politically.

"Julian, I expect that you recognize that if we succeed in 2024, you're more likely to override the attack on the reparations rally. Those misguided men eventually saw the error of their ways; shifting America's mindset might prevent them from making the errors in the first place."

"Crime did fall after everyone had an American Union Job," Ray reminded him.

Julian shook his head. "I don't buy it. They were white supremacists, and you expect me to believe that if someone threw a few dollars their way, they'd be down for singing kumbaya?"

"I've forgiven them," Shaver said. "I even sent a statement of support when their sentences were being reviewed; we've fasted for peace together."

CHAPTER THIRTY

"Connor Sullivan," Julian interjected. "He approached me two weeks ago in an assembly hearing, claiming we had unfinished business. Obviously, he's angry I stopped him from killing you and disappointed he didn't have better luck with me. Or do you want to put a positive spin on that?"

The reverend plucked a tablet from the couch next to him and tapped on it several times. Julian waited expectantly for some sort of information to appear in the air, but after a moment, the device was set aside. "One of the attributes of the fast, Julian, is that it can be a rebirth. You're under no obligation to be the same person afterward. I don't believe that Connor is the same person he was fifty years ago. Consider the possibility that he's looking to apologize."

"He tried to kill us," Julian said. "You really forgave him for that?"

"I have," Shaver said gravely. "We're all worthy of redemption; we're all capable of self-improvement."

"He tried to kill us," Julian said again. "What does self-improvement mean—he'll do better next time?"

A familiar tone sounded, and a new form began to appear next to Reverend Shaver. Julian watched in horror as the oscillation sped up, revealing the aged and clean shaven face of Connor Sullivan, who touched his hands together in greeting. "Why don't you ask him yourself?" Shaver suggested.

"Because I'm not interested in what a mass murderer has to say," Julian shot back. The look in the assassin's blue eyes, intense and committed, was still recognizable across the decades. "Count me out." Rising in fury, he stormed from the room.

Chapter Thirty-One

The knot in Julian's stomach was still there hours later, pulsing anxiety through his body as he returned to the parlor for Professor Carlton's thirty-day-challenge group. The room was empty, and he selected a chair that he'd never occupied before, giving him a slightly different perspective on the room.

His seat also allowed him to avoid looking directly at where Connor Sullivan had breached the space. He and Ray had ceremoniously disposed of the condo's alcohol yesterday to kick off the challenge, and large chunks of Julian's afternoon were spent trying not to think about how it might have calmed his roiling emotions. Instead, he distracted himself with his journal, recording impressions of the tricentennial and spreading his thoughts across the page.

Among those thoughts was Idabee—what would she say when she saw him? When she appeared a minute later in the seat farthest away from him, the only sign of familiarity was a curt nod. It was a little uncomfortable, but he was looking forward to hearing the discussion.

"Good evening," Professor Carlton announced to the room from the chair on Julian's left. "We'll give the others another minute or two to arrive, and then get started." He gave Julian an encouraging look, seeming pleased to have him there.

A flickering on his opposite side turned out to be Adon, who greeted him with a wide grin and a brief touching together of his hands. He shot a quick finger toward Idabee. "What's going on with you two?" he asked.

"It doesn't look like it's going to work out," Julian acknowledged, spotting

CHAPTER THIRTY-ONE

Faith arriving next to Idabee. "But it's good to see you again."

The last seat filled up, and Carlton called the group to order. "Let's get started; Adon, would you lead us in the Preamble to remind us of our duties?"

Adon gave a sharp nod that shook his locs. "We the people," he began, and the room joined in, "of the United States, in order to form a more perfect union, establish justice, insure domestic tranquility, provide for the common defence, promote the general welfare, and secure the blessings of liberty to ourselves and our posterity, do ordain and establish this Constitution for the United States of America."

Carlton thanked him and briefly introduced Julian before launching into a story. "One of Gandhi's students would have turned one hundred forty-nine yesterday. Cesar Chavez, for those who don't know, was a co-founder of the United Farm Workers in California during the 1960s. Agricultural workers, an occupation predominantly held by people of color, had been specifically excluded from many New Deal labor protections. Chavez dedicated himself to unionizing the workers in order to improve working conditions and the quality of their lives.

"Gandhi was his role model; his personality and organizing techniques intrigued Chavez. Besides the commitment to nonviolence, there was the voluntary poverty and the fasting. In February 1968, Chavez called a meeting to announce he had begun an indefinite fast to center the UFW on the principles of nonviolence. For more than an hour, he explained why violence was unacceptable as a means to an end. The United States was involved in a war in Vietnam, and if the senseless violence there was wrong, it was just as wrong in America.

"Finally, after telling the gathering that he loved them all, Chavez walked five kilometers to Forty Acres, the future site of the union's headquarters in Delano, California. Over the following weeks, thousands of people visited to show support, and a local priest held mass each night. Martin Luther King Jr. sent words of support, writing, 'You stand today as a living example of the Gandhian tradition with its great force for social progress and its healing spiritual powers.' Chavez kept himself busy with meetings, but after three weeks, he wasn't doing well. On the advice of his doctors, he added nutrients to his water and began planning for the end of the fast.

"Robert F. Kennedy was invited to be the guest of honor for the literal breaking of the fast. RFK was the brother of the former president and about to announce his own campaign for the Oval Office. He flew into Delano on March 10, 1968, and the two men broke bread together, ending the fast after twenty-four days.

"Although he was too weak to speak to the crowd, Chavez's written statement reiterated his commitment. I've often thought that it applies to the American Union as well, and I'd like to read a few passages. He wrote, 'We are gathered here today not so much to observe the end of the fast, but because we are a family bound together in a common struggle for justice. We are a Union family celebrating our unity and the nonviolent nature of our movement.

"'The fast was first for me and then for all of us in this Union. It was a fast for nonviolence and a call to sacrifice. I am convinced that the truest act of courage, the strongest act of manliness is to sacrifice ourselves for others in a totally nonviolent struggle for justice. To be a man is to struggle for others. God help us to be men!'" Julian recognized Reverend Shaver had quoted part of the statement in reference to his own twenty-four-day fast before the first Muster Day.

Carlton cleared his throat. "Julian, even if Chavez used the word man to refer to a specific gender instead of in the inclusive sense, we accept his statement as an ideal for all to strive for." Julian nodded. "But to struggle for others—that's an excellent description of duty if I ever heard one. Who wants to talk about the challenges they're taking on this month? Any stoic challenges?"

"I'm doing cold showers in April," a middle-aged man said.

Carlton beamed. "That's the spirit, Diego," he said. "Have you done this before?"

"No," Diego said, "and I haven't yet, either. I figure I can put them off for at least a day or two before my wife notices. Some of the challenges I look forward to, but not this one."

CHAPTER THIRTY-ONE

"Anyone have any advice?"

A young man spoke up. "Just accept it; don't fight it. It was uncomfortable at first, then tolerable, and then after two weeks, no big deal." He grinned. "They'd give me a nice stoic buzz."

"Good suggestion, Christopher," Carlton said. "Want to tell us what you're striving for this month?"

"I took on the celibacy challenge," Christopher said. "I'm not in a relationship at the moment, so my sex life was pornography and masturbation." Julian blinked, not expecting such frank conversation. "I'm looking to develop some new habits to replace it; see what I can do to recalibrate my normal by abstaining for thirty days. I don't want to be celibate forever, but I can see the value in taking a break on occasion."

"You can do it," Faith told him. "Adon and I tried that. I learned it's hard to keep my hands off my sexy man!" Everyone laughed. "Some nights we slept apart or went to bed at different times to help resist the temptation. I never reached any sense of acceptance, no place of recalibrated normal like Christopher is shooting for. But now I know I'm capable of this level of self-control, even if it's a sacrifice I don't want to repeat."

Carlton nodded encouragingly. "Thank you, Faith, for sharing. Did you feel like swearing off sex for a month helped you focus on other things that you wanted to accomplish?"

"Nope," Faith replied promptly. "It was like an itch that I couldn't scratch; thinking about sex was definitely a distraction. Although, I did stay up late writing sometimes, just so I'd crawl into bed absolutely exhausted. You could say that was more productive."

"Adon," Carlton prompted, "want to tell us if you had the same experience?"

Adon shifted and took a deep breath. "It was a real challenge," he admitted, casting an admiring glance at his wife before continuing. "What I learned is that Faith is more capable than I am in some ways. Like she said, it was a distraction. By the third week, sex was all I could think about, and I took matters into my own hand, you know?"

"Only once," Faith said quickly.

Adon nodded. "But after that, the last week was fairly easy. The tension was gone, and I did feel more productive and focused. I'm not sure it was a net benefit, though. I love Faith and our time together; purposely diminishing that was a sacrifice."

Carlton nodded. "Now I think you see the crux of the matter. To Gandhi, your desire for your wife and your relationship means that you're using energy that could be—should be—directed for the benefit of the larger community. He would say that valuing one relationship over the rest of humanity is a misplacement of priorities."

"But we don't live in Gandhi's time," Adon countered. "His country was overrun by poverty; we've eliminated it. He needed men and women to turn all their energy toward uplifting the community; we don't. Many hands make light work; we can have healthy sexual relationships and still generate sufficient energy to maintain a good quality of life in our country."

Carlton grinned. "That's a very practical argument—and I'm not going to disagree with you. But as a matter of principle, the mindset we bring to the work is important. As Chavez said, 'the strongest act of manliness is to sacrifice ourselves for others, to struggle for others.' Putting your own desires over other people's means you're not bringing 100% to the effort."

"As long as he's thinking about my desires, I'm happy," Faith declared.

When the laughter subsided, Carlton surveyed the room. "Leilani, what do you have for us?"

Leilani was a young woman who said, "I'm going to eat vegan and prepare all my own food this month; no community meals or restaurants. It'll be extra work, but I think it'll make me appreciate what others usually do for me and better my cooking skills."

"I have a question," Julian said. "With Adon and Faith, it sounded like the real goal was to have more time to spend on"—he gestured in a futile search for the right word—"productive things? But Leilani is spending time cooking when she doesn't actually have to, leaving less time for others. Isn't there a contradiction there?"

"Is there?" Carlton asked the group in general.

After a moment, Idabee spoke. "There could be, if that's the only metric

CHAPTER THIRTY-ONE

you use. But there's more to it than that, Julian. Another aspect is mindfulness—improving our awareness of what we're doing. Leilani might also be cooking meals for others and serving them."

"Good points," Carlton acknowledged. "Any others?"

"Cooking is being productive," Adon said. "Doing it for yourself may not be as efficient, but it's definitely work. Bread labor—the physical work Gandhi suggested everyone do each day to earn their keep."

Carlton nodded in approval. "Julian, anything you want to share?"

"I'm a newbie, so I'm starting off gentle," he said. "Thirty days of sobriety. In the last twenty years, I'm not sure I've ever done that voluntarily. I feel pretty good stating that intention, along with the two fasting days. Who knows what else I'll try in the future?"

"You can do it," Carlton encouraged him. "Idabee," he asked, "anything to add?"

Idabee scrutinized him before speaking. "Julian, if you bring the same intention to this challenge as others you've faced, you'll sail through," she said. Feeling like she was really seeing him again, Julian replied with an appreciative smile.

"I tried a perspective experiment last month," she said to Carlton. "I wore simple clothes. Kind of like Diego, it was one I'd avoided. It took an effort—no jewelry and the plainest outfits I could find. No one said anything about it, and I'm not sure how I would have responded if they had. In public, I felt a little self-conscious, which gave me a new perspective on myself. I never thought of myself as a vain person, but clearly I have a non-zero amount of vanity running through my veins."

"Gandhi was pretty vain in his younger days," Carlton explained. "One time, he challenged himself to wear only a loincloth for a month because he was asking the Indian people to use homespun cloth and wanted to lead by example. After discovering he liked the simplicity, he kept it up for the last quarter-century of his life. Even when he met King George, it was all he wore, joking to reporters that the king had on enough for both of them." Carlton looked back to Idabee. "How would you feel in that situation?"

A ripple of laughter passed through the room as she fumbled for words.

"No," she said, "I don't think I could do that." The silence grew for a moment before she continued, "It was hard to acknowledge part of my self-worth comes from how others see me. I don't think it's entirely a bad thing—being perceived as a person of competence can help me accomplish more. But if I were meeting the president, dressing up would feel like a sign of respect."

Carlton considered. "Would not dressing up be a sign of disrespect?"

"Maybe? Wearing ripped or stained clothes would be. But purposeful simplicity? I don't know."

"Anyone else want to add anything?" Carlton asked the room. "Brook?"

"I like the simple-clothing experiment," Brook said. "April is my third time. The first one, I stopped dressing up so much for work and found I liked the simplicity. The second time, I combined it with a minimalism challenge and downsized my wardrobe, getting rid of items with text, logos, or patterns." Julian observed Brook's clothes; they were plain, flat, and unisex.

"This time, I'm making an extra effort to underdress for the occasion," Brook continued. "Not in a disrespectful way, but someone has to come in last on a best-dressed list. If I intentionally move down, then the people around me move up. It's still uncomfortable, but I'm trying to bring a perspective of service to it, and I think that'll help."

"Service," Carlton said thoughtfully. "I like that. Perspective experiments are less binary—did you have an orgasm?—and more open to individual interpretation. We know people whose clothes demand respect, like a judge. To build on what Brook said, this can be a conscientious decision to do the opposite."

"But this isn't a zero-sum game," Faith said. "The amount of respect circulating isn't a fixed amount; that's an appeal to scarcity."

The group debated it for a few minutes longer, and then Carlton brought the meeting to a close. As goodbyes were said, Julian caught the professor's eye and indicated that he'd like to talk for a few more minutes. The other man nodded agreement.

"You should come out for another visit," Adon offered. "The kids liked

CHAPTER THIRTY-ONE

meeting you."

"I might do that," Julian said. He looked up to see Idabee watching them. Their eyes held for a minute.

Then, with a sad smile and a small wave, she disappeared.

Chapter Thirty-Two

"It's good to see you again, Julian," Carlton said. The rest of the group had vanished from the parlor, leaving the two men alone. "Did you have more questions about nonviolence?"

Julian shook his head. "No, about the American Union. You were there at the beginning." Carlton's eyes flashed enthusiastically. "Can you tell me more about how militarism was addressed?"

The septuagenarian folded his hands and relaxed in his chair. "The principled reason for reducing the military-industrial complex was straightforward—seeing the humanity in others makes violence a less appealing problem-solving technique. But the American Union also had to address the practical reason the military-industrial complex continued to grow. Do you know what was driving the economic demand?"

Teara Harper had mentioned two reasons that he'd jotted in his journal. "Since a growing economy needs money added to it, Congress used military spending as a justification for running up the national debt. And after the industrial revolution opened a structural gap in the economy, imperialism helped generate new markets for American goods."

Carlton's jaw fell open, and his eyes bugged out. "That wasn't what I was thinking of—not at all! But I suppose you're right." He stroked his beard as Julian grinned in pride. "No, Julian, there was another economic function that the military-industrial complex served—it pushed money out into every congressional district across the nation. The American Union Jobs Program established another mechanism for doing that.

"I like to think of unconditional basic income as a layer of snow falling

CHAPTER THIRTY-TWO

across the country; the same amount comes down on every person," Carlton continued. "As that snow melts, the water runs downhill and flows into streams, rivers, and lakes. Money collects in the cities with big commercial interests. Then, like the water cycle, it gets recycled and redistributed across the nation again as UBI.

"Before the American Union Jobs Program, many parts of the country were economically parched. The military-industrial complex was like a big water truck, and many of those dry areas depended on it for fiscal irrigation. The economic impact in their home districts kept many members of Congress supporting unnecessary and wasteful programs.

"Once everyone had an American Union Job, those programs weren't so essential. The first legislative package required four years of 10% cuts to the military budget, forcing an evaluation of how those dollars were spent. Waste was rampant since most of the money went to defense contractors, who raked in exorbitant profits.

"While military service continues to be a proud tradition, it turned out economic coercion was driving many young people to join. They didn't have better options, so they signed up." Julian thought he noticed a hint of bitterness in the man's voice. "American Union Jobs gave them the freedom to make other choices.

"The United States had a huge global military footprint, with ten times the foreign military bases as all other countries combined. The legislation triggered an initial round of closures by applying the duty of nonviolence to affirm meaningful consent. It mandated that referenda be held around foreign bases, asking the local population if they wanted the US military to remain. If they didn't, we left within a year. That was the low-hanging fruit."

"That sounds pretty reasonable," Julian said. "It seems like it would be hard to argue that we should have military bases where we'd been told we weren't welcome."

Carlton paused and looked meaningfully up at the indicator lights in the corner of the room. Their two green lights had a red companion. The professor turned away from Julian and toward the door. "Idabee, dear, you're welcome to join us," he announced nonchalantly.

Julian's heart skipped a beat. Maybe she did want to see him. He produced a smile. "Please."

The men waited. Idabee appeared on the loveseat, shoes off, feet folded under her. "I just want to listen," she said. "You always have fascinating stories."

Carlton nodded. "As I was saying, America's reputation on the world stage had some blemishes, including the indefinite detention of men without charges at Guantanamo Bay Military Prison."

"Wait," Idabee said, presumably forgetting that she only wanted to listen. "Doesn't the Constitution say habeas corpus can't be suspended?"

Carlton turned and waggled a finger at her. "It does, but since the prison was in Cuba, not on US soil, the Supreme Court allowed Congress and the president to set a different policy. Many detainees had been tortured, and some sat for decades without ever being charged with a crime.

"Nations like Russia, Pakistan, Iran, and Libya criticized us for our hypocrisy. Congress had prevented President Obama from closing the prison; the first legislative package reversed that policy and directed the handful of convicted men to be moved to a military prison in the United States. The remainder had to be charged with something or released." Idabee nodded understanding.

"Did the locals vote to close the military base?" Julian wondered.

"In Cuba? Yes; they'd repeatedly asked the US to leave, but we ignored them," Carlton said. "Another way we improved our moral standing was by supporting a reevaluation of the weapons of war. Similar to the international agreement banning chemical weapons after World War One, the development of lethal autonomous weapons, which took life-and-death decisions out of the hands of human beings, was restricted. This included landmines; we destroyed our stockpile and joined the international community in eliminating their production and use.

"These actions contributed to worldwide demilitarization, Julian. Russia, China, India, and other nations no longer felt an urgency to expand their own armed forces in an attempt to keep up with us."

CHAPTER THIRTY-TWO

"You said economic coercion pushed people into the military," Julian observed. "I never thought about it so bluntly before, until Idabee introduced me to Adon and Faith, and we had a whole conversation about it."

"Economic coercion usually flows down the socioeconomic pyramid," Carlton said, "and the United States had climbed to the top during World War Two. Unfortunately, we used that position to put sanctions on dozens of weaker countries, restricting their access to global trade. The first legislative package restricted sanctions on civilian populations, although it left a loophole for declared wars and international coalitions."

"Why?" Idabee asked. "Why did the United States use them?"

Julian repeated what Faith had told them. "Thomas Jefferson called it peaceful coercion."

"Of course sanctions appeared peaceful, compared to bombs," Carlton replied, before swiveling toward Idabee with exaggerated stiffness. "In theory, they had the same aims as criminal law: to punish, deter, and rehabilitate."

Julian scoffed. "Rehabilitate."

As Carlton turned back to him, Idabee rose and disappeared, then quickly solidified on the couch next to Julian's chair. Carlton touched his hands together in gratitude, then addressed the both of them. "Like the criminal justice system, it devolved into a tool for punishment. Cuba was still under sanctions because of a revolution that took place in the 1950s—five out of six Cubans weren't even alive when it happened, yet they were all suffering for it. The impact is like a reverse UBI; it primarily hurts the poorest and most vulnerable. Our sanctions caused hundreds of thousands of civilian deaths around the world."

The trio fell silent, reflecting. "As Dr. King said of the Vietnamese peasants," Carlton paraphrased, "'We must speak for them and raise the questions they cannot raise. These, too, are our brothers.'"

"Tell him about the Congress of Humanity," Idabee prompted.

Carlton nodded. "The fast for peace unlocked a route toward global cooperation. It started here, with the American Union using it as an opt-in for concerned citizens wanting to cooperate. There was no reason individual asynchronous action couldn't work on a larger scale; two billion Muslims observe the month of Ramadan each year, abstaining from food and water from first light until sunset. The fast for peace was a secular event, but it also had a moral code of sorts: the seven duties of nonviolence.

"Three hundred years ago, Julian, the Declaration of Independence and the Constitution established democracy as a constructive alternative to monarchy and the divine right of kings. The American Union model offered a software update that the citizenry could install with nonviolent action, upgrading an adversarial system to a collaborative one.

"People's legislative assemblies formed around the globe and drafted packages they wanted to help their representatives succeed at enacting. It worked better in some places than others; multiparty democracies were trickier to influence compared to America's two-party system, but within a decade, unions of voters were implementing policy in most industrialized nations.

"Once the assemblies were functioning around the world, multilateral cooperation—bottom up, not top down—was the next step. The first gathering of the Congress of Humanity took place in 2031 with delegates from forty-nine countries where voters' unions had been successful in getting crowdsourced legislation adopted. The American Union called for it specifically so its proposals could be brought forward in the 2032 presidential election. The delegates produced agreements on a handful of issues of global concern: environmental justice, military demobilization, and the abolition of nuclear weapons in a coordinated manner."

"People had been talking about that last one since Oppenheimer created them," Julian said. "How did we get rid of them?"

"Besides adopting a no-first strike policy, nuclear powers agreed not to be the nation with the most warheads," Carlton explained. "This produced a steady reduction down to zero, with dismantlement certified and celebrated."

"What about China?" Julian asked. "They were a nuclear power and not a democracy."

CHAPTER THIRTY-TWO

"China was susceptible to moral pressure, too. Their people's assembly drafted proposals, and publicized them through the fast for peace. They helped to shape the national debate, and eventually the Chinese government decided to accept a few reforms. But they fell into the same trap the two-party system did here."

"What was that?"

Carlton grinned. "Do you know the story of Gandhi and the Salt March?"

"He marched to the sea to make salt?" Julian guessed, sensing Carlton was about to launch into another story.

"True, but there's a bigger picture," Carlton said, settling in. "In 1930, the Indian National Congress—their people's assembly—was demanding independence. Gandhi decided on salt as the campaign's central issue; the British had a monopoly on its production and sale and taxed it heavily.

"But before beginning civil disobedience, Gandhi was honor bound to offer good-faith terms for avoiding it. He sent the British viceroy eleven demands, many of which were similar to the first legislative package the American Union demanded of Congress. They included reducing the military budget, monetary reform, civilian oversight of the police, the release of political prisoners, and licensing of firearms. The British turned him down.

"Gandhi set off with seventy-eight men, arriving at the ocean twenty-four days later. They stopped in towns and villages along the way, where Gandhi encouraged people to live a sober life, to use homespun cloth, and to end discrimination against so-called untouchables. News stories appeared around the globe, building pressure in the public consciousness. What would happen when Gandhi broke the salt laws?

"After announcing his goal of 'world sympathy in this battle of right against might,' Gandhi illegally gathered a clump of salt from the beach on April 6. The date commemorated the first national day of fasting eleven years earlier, which united Hindus and Muslims against the British." Julian recalled the quote about satyagraha Carlton shared from that occasion: *No nation has ever been made without sacrifice.* Idabee was listening intently; a tightness in Julian's throat reminded him of the sacrifice he was making.

"It was the signal for civil disobedience to begin around the country," Carlton continued. "People began collecting salt or producing it from sea water, then selling it illicitly. It was all done openly; one hundred thousand arrests were made during the campaign. Gandhi remained free until he announced he would lead a nonviolent raid on the Dharasana salt depot and liberate the mounds of white crystals. Then he was taken into custody and held without charges; the British refused to give him a public trial.

"The raid went ahead the following week, led by Sarojini Naidu. She was a famous poet who had also succeeded Gandhi as Congress president a few years earlier. More than two thousand volunteers—satyagrahis sworn to nonviolence—went forward in waves in an attempt to collect salt and were savagely beaten down by the police.

"An American reporter witnessed the brutality against the unresisting men and vividly described to the world 'the sickening whacks of the clubs on unprotected heads' which led to several deaths. The British had surrendered the moral high ground. It was too much; they released Gandhi and negotiated an end to civil disobedience.

"Gandhi was criticized for all the things he didn't get in the settlement. The tax on salt wasn't repealed, not all prisoners were released, and there was no substantial progress toward independence." Julian chuckled. Like the fast for peace origin story where Gandhi wasn't the hero, he was curious to hear what lesson the professor gleaned from this campaign.

"But Gandhi received one critical concession," Carlton said. "It wasn't written down, it wasn't a physical thing you could point to, but it was very, very real. The British had to acknowledge they needed India's consent in order to rule. Once Gandhi established the Indian people as a bargaining unit, it was only a matter of time until they achieved self-rule. That was the real success of the Salt March.

"That's what happened in China, when the government made concessions, and why the American Union worked. Julian, when candidates for federal office participated in the fast for peace, they were recognizing the American Union as a bargaining unit. Once it was established that a union of voters could negotiate directly for specific legislative policy, the monopoly political parties had was broken. It didn't make them irrelevant—political parties still have influence to this day—but it ensured citizens another option for representation."

Julian was quiet for a moment. The general strike in the ballot box that Polly Sigh had described—the threat of electing candidates all the way up to president at random—seemed to qualify as civil disobedience. It would withhold consent from an unjust system and demonstrate to the duopoly that they needed the American Union's cooperation in order to rule, but in a way where no one had to get arrested or whacked on the head.

Carlton allowed the silence to stretch, then patted his lap in a gesture of closure. "I hope that helps to answer your questions, Julian; I'd be happy to talk again whenever you like. Now, if you'll excuse me, Mother Nature is calling. But you two should stay and chat. Have a good night." Carlton rose with surprising agility and disappeared.

The pair sat frozen for a moment, then Julian spoke: "It's good to see you again, Idabee."

"I'm sorry I left you in Philadelphia," she blurted out.

"It's cool," he said lightly. "It worked out; Delroy and I had a lot of catching up to do." Julian verified their two green lights were unaccompanied. "Edith says you talked. I guess I've got one month left here."

"That's what Nana said." She laughed. "I spent ten years imagining what it would be like when you woke up. Only it turns out not to matter." Idabee looked at him wistfully, her countenance reminiscent of Edith's gaze a few days earlier. "Good luck, I guess."

Julian opened his hands. "Does this mean you're not mad at me anymore?"

Idabee's head fell, and the room was silent. Julian waited, and finally she spoke. "I'm not mad, exactly." When Idabee looked up, she had that same inscrutable expression he'd seen before. "Big heaping portions of disappointment, sure. But also some pride."

"Pride?" he echoed.

"We were a few hours away from checking into the hotel, Julian. I don't usually jump into bed with guys I've only known for a week, but I really thought we had something special."

"I thought so, too," he confessed. The lump in his throat was back.

"So, when you did your time travel thing, you wrote me that letter and told your friend to deliver it in the afternoon. As I see it, there are two possibilities. One is that I'm so horribly bad in bed that you needed to protect yourself from the trauma I was about to inflict on you."

They both laughed out loud. "Seems unlikely," Julian said.

"I think so too," she continued. "The other possibility was that you were actually listening when we talked about consent. You decided it wasn't appropriate to sleep with me under false pretenses, even if we didn't know better at the time. So you went out of your way to tell me. That's the pride, Julian. You were a good student."

"You were a good teacher," he replied. The moment stretched out, eyes locked, small smiles, basking in mutual respect. "Damn, Idabee. I wish you weren't a hologram right now."

Her smile faded fast. "No hard feelings, Julian. I hope you'll be happy with my grandmother before she's my grandmother, and that you stop the attack on the reparations rally."

"Is that what you think this is about?" Julian explained what Delroy had told him about their efforts to start the American Union and Reverend Shaver's story that would get his help during the 2024 election. "I don't know what'll happen with the reparations rally. If we pull this off and get the American Union rolling two years early, it might not come to that. But I already tried, Idabee. It didn't work."

"We're always capable of doing better," Idabee reminded him. "You're learning more this time around."

"I'm still worried it won't be enough," Julian admitted, "and I might fail." The last word echoed. Carlton had said something similar when he'd sought approval for his violence at the rally. *You failed. You allowed circumstances to develop where using physical force was necessary.*

Was it a coincidence? Or did Carlton know something about his mission in the past?

Chapter Thirty-Three

Julian looked away from his journal and at the Washington Monument outside his bedroom window. The icon's perpetual prominence could have been a comfort, but the events that had taken place beneath it continued to cast a shadow on his soul. Connor Sullivan's intrusion into the safe space of the parlor two days earlier still bothered him—those piercing blue eyes that had glared so malevolently at him before firing the shots that knocked five decades out of his life.

Reverend Shaver had shed tears when he learned there was a chance the past could be changed. It wasn't the shooting that was his biggest concern, but his failure to listen and advance the American Union. He claimed to have forgiven Connor, despite nearly being executed by the white supremacist. Julian wasn't quite persuaded, but the preacher's sincerity kindled regret for the forceful exit he'd staged.

Julian looked back to the holographic words hanging in front of him. *What if I didn't have to kill those men?* Questions gnawed at him. *Professor Carlton said I failed; would I have prevented the attack by nudging the nation into the new paradigm of nonviolence? Or is it my destiny to end up dead again, bleeding to death on that street corner hours before the rally?*

A knock at the bedroom door broke his reverie. "Hello, Julian," Edith said when he opened it, interpreting the action as an invitation to enter. She was sharply dressed and carried a small, colorful bag. "I wanted to talk with you before everyone else gets here for dinner. How are you?"

"Struggling." He looked pointedly at the monument before explaining his negative reaction to Shaver's guest. He assumed Edith could relate.

"Have you forgiven Connor Sullivan?"

"I don't know," she answered. "I haven't thought about him for years."

"He shot me," Julian blurted out. Anger surged in him; he tried to tamp it back. "He and his buddies tried to murder as many black people as possible." Julian exhaled deeply and ran a hand over his stubbled scalp. "I don't want to forgive him, but I think I want to want to forgive him. You feel me?"

"I feel you," Edith repeated, closing the bedroom door and moving close to him. "When it was fresh and raw for me, I wanted vengeance. Did you know I was going to testify at his trial? There was a plea deal, but I was ready to tell everyone what happened. Seeing you frozen all those years, the wound stayed open a long time before it scabbed over." She set her bag down and asked, "Julian, do you remember how screwed up the judicial system used to be?"

"I have the prison record to show for it," he agreed.

"But a commitment to ending mass incarceration helped turn it around. When everyone had an American Union Job, people were less angry." Ray had raised a similar point: that crime fell after the program began. "The desire to punish started to fade, replaced with a goal of rehabilitation. Even back then, 97% of incarcerated people were going to be released, hundreds of thousands every year; it was win-win to make their reacclimation into society as smooth and successful as possible.

"After serving ten years, Connor was able to request a sentence review. I was notified, as one of the victims, and given the opportunity to make a statement."

"What did you say?" Julian asked.

"I didn't say anything," Edith replied. "I wasn't the same person I'd been a decade earlier; I was willing to defer to the court's evaluation of whether Connor was, the same way they did for everyone who had their sentence reviewed. The judge found he was no longer a danger to others, demonstrated readiness for reentry, and that further punishment was not in the interest of justice."

Julian touched the scars underneath his shirt as he absorbed the idea.

CHAPTER THIRTY-THREE

"He killed people."

"He did," Edith agreed. "But you know the old saying: the worst thing a person's ever done is a statistical outlier. It's a terrible data point to define someone by, and to the best of my knowledge, it never happened again. Isn't that what you want rehabilitation to accomplish?" Julian agreed. "Since you asked if I forgave him, the answer is: I have now. It wasn't a conscious thought before, but yes."

Julian's slow nod signaled acknowledgment, but understanding still eluded him. Edith gave a sympathetic smile, then offered the colorful bag to him. "This may or may not help your mood," she warned.

Really noticing it for the first time, Julian realized it was a gift bag, which brought a rush of pleasure. The blue crepe paper on top was lighter than a robin's egg, and when he removed it, a wooden frame was revealed. Edith's eyes were bright with anticipation as he slipped it out for examination.

"Wow," he said. The picture frame showed his last moments in 2026, standing with Edith in front of the Washington Monument. They looked like a happy couple, smiling and displaying their signs, blissfully ignorant of the forthcoming chaos. "Edith, this is great." It was the only physical piece of memorabilia he had to show for the first thirty-four years of his life—the pages on his archived website didn't count. "Thank you."

Edith put a hand on his shoulder, relieved at his enthusiasm. "I did promise to get you a copy," she reminded him. Staring at the image of Edith in the picture, five decades younger, Julian recalled the urgency he'd felt to find her upon waking up in this room three weeks earlier. Now, they were together.

Her arm dropped to slip around his waist. "Have you given more thought to my birthday?"

"Yes," Julian admitted. He could see the young Edith through the lines of her face: the vibrant woman whose touch had awakened hope in him, the intelligent doctor who'd shepherded him on a path he never thought possible—into death and back.

She pulled him forward so their lips converged. In their first kiss, he felt the echoes of a million others never shared. There was a deep familiarity in the way Edith pressed her thin frame against him, soft and warm. Their breath spilled together as Julian planted his hand in the small of her back. Without Connor Sullivan's interruption, how might the future have unfolded?

When she broke away, Julian opened his eyes to see her smiling. "There'll be plenty more where that came from," Edith promised, still tight against him.

"I believe it," Julian replied, remembering the unspoken assertion of her hip pressed against him. Her granddaughter took pride in her ability to delay gratification. During one intense encounter, Idabee replied to his question: *If I can wait a week to eat, I can certainly wait a week for sex.* Neither expected a blue envelope to interrupt the highly anticipated night.

"We'll get it right this time," Edith said. "I couldn't claim your body after the rally. I couldn't recover the wedding ring. But maybe we can pick one out together before you leave."

Julian released her gently. "Edith, that's not the reason I would let Charlotte push me back fifty-odd years."

Her face crumpled in confusion. "What?"

"Delroy and I are going to start the American Union," he confided. "We're going to turn minorities into majorities."

Edith laughed. "Reverend Shaver did that."

"We're going to do it sooner," he insisted.

The lines returned to her face as Edith struggled with the paradigm shift, the copernican revolution pushing her out of her place at the center of the universe and into the orbit of an even more powerful force. "You came back for me," she said, but her confidence had crumbled.

"I'll still pass along the warning on August 15," Julian said, raising another concern. "I need to ask Charlotte: could I land in a universe where that other Julian West is planning the same thing?"

Edith seized on something she did know. "Charlotte won't be here tonight; she said she wasn't feeling well." Julian's spirits fell. He'd specifically asked Ray to invite the physicist to help explain how this process would work.

CHAPTER THIRTY-THREE

Before Julian could say anything else, they heard someone enter the condo. Idabee called out a greeting to her father, who belted his reply from the kitchen. "Want to join them?" he suggested.

Edith's eyes were distant, but she managed to meet his gaze. "Julian, when you meet me—when I meet you for the first time—if you're not sure what to make of me, just remember that I have potential."

He recognized her phrasing. "Like you did with me." There was something not right about the contortions that time travel put them through—would put them through—to rob them of the sweet innocence of a true first meeting.

The octogenarian still looked troubled. Awkwardly, she gathered the crepe paper and stuffed it into the gift bag. Julian placed their picture on his end table. "Thank you, again," he said. Edith nodded acceptance, and he followed her to the kitchen.

Idabee was watching as they emerged from behind the closed bedroom door, and Julian thought he could decipher her enigmatic expression. It was suspicion. His lips still tingling from Edith's embrace, Julian decided there were generational differences in the courtship rituals of the tricentennial.

What would he have said if Edith had asked for consent?

Chapter Thirty-Four

Delroy Jackson arrived for dinner a few minutes later, and Julian greeted his old friend warmly before introducing him to the rest of the Leete family. Ray welcomed him from behind the stove, where he wrangled pots and pans. Idabee apologized for the way she'd abruptly left Philadelphia and thanked him for helping get Julian back safely.

Edith possessed a vague recollection of Delroy delivering the robin's-egg-blue envelope to her at the hospital the day of the reparations rally and wondered if he'd also sent another years later. The mention of the mysterious letter he remembered from his childhood drew Ray's attention, and Delroy tipped an imaginary hat in acknowledgment. "My goodness!" Edith exclaimed. "You two must have been good friends to take on such a project."

"One time," Delroy began, launching into a story involving a BB gun and a can of shaving cream that Julian hadn't thought about in years. As both Edith and Idabee listened to the yarn unravel, Ray gestured to a stack of plates, bowls, and silverware. Julian reflected on his brief time in the tricentennial with gratitude as he arranged five place settings around the circular table and his good fortune to have made new friends and reunited with old ones.

"To this day, Miss Idabee," Delroy concluded with utmost sincerity, "when the weather is warm and the air just right, you can still smell the menthol in that tree." Idabee wrinkled her nose, not quite believing the tale.

Edith began questioning Delroy about the early days of the American Union, perhaps still adjusting to the idea she was not the main focus of

CHAPTER THIRTY-FOUR

Julian's temporal adventures. Delroy described their failed first attempt to bring together political malcontents and minor parties into a unified force that could reshape the electoral system.

"We struggled because they were all so used to fighting for scraps from the old system," Delroy explained, "that they couldn't imagine a different way of doing things, especially one that didn't revolve around them getting elected." Julian was pleased to be able to share the good news: Reverend Shaver wanted to help.

Ray finished cooking just as the familiar whoosh announced the arrival of side dishes from the community kitchen. Opening the compartment door added another layer of eclectic aromas to the room. Dishes were shuttled to the table, and the five settled into seats, with Idabee across from Julian and flanked by the other two men.

"Before we eat, I just want to say a few words," Ray said. "I'm thankful to have Delroy, Julian, and my family here this evening. Delroy, it's a pleasure to meet you. Julian, you've been a part of our lives for decades. In a real sense, you've been in our care all that time. We accepted responsibility for your welfare. I'm glad to have you breaking bread with us, and wherever and whenever you go next, I wish you the best of luck."

Julian was touched. "Thank you, Ray. It's an honor to know three generations of your family. I'm grateful for all the work that has gone into helping me and the welcome you've shown me in the tricentennial. I hope all your patients are just as well cared for."

"Julian," Edith said, "when we first met, I knew that you'd lead me on a unique journey—although I didn't know you had Delroy doing behind-the-scenes work. I'm happy to be with you again, all these decades later. Thank you for everything you've done." She looked to Idabee expectantly.

"I'm grateful I finally met Julian," Idabee said, the words hesitant at first, then tumbling out, "and that I was able to introduce him to the American Union and the fast for peace, and I'm glad he and Delroy were able to reconnect and that he's becoming an organizer before he leaves." The final three words were almost a mumble.

Delroy allowed the silence to build for a moment before speaking to each of them in turn. "Dr. Leete, I appreciate your fine work in freezing my friend for all these years, and Dr. Leete, I appreciate your fine work in thawing him back out. Miss Idabee, thank you for reuniting me with Julian last week. And last but not least, Julian, I'm grateful you helped me get sober all those years ago. Thank you, brother."

"I haven't done it yet, but you're welcome," Julian replied.

Serving dishes began to circulate around the table. "Delroy, how long has it been since you had a drink?" Ray asked curiously.

"I quit drinking on July 14, 2023," the octogenarian said proudly.

"Bastille Day?" Idabee asked.

Momentarily stunned, Delroy exploded into laughter. Julian choked on a mouthful of peanut soup as he joined in. "Yes," Delroy managed. "It was Bastille Day." He explained the paradox he and Julian had discussed earlier, trying to determine which of them had taught the other about the French holiday. "I guess we just discovered the source of your knowledge, Julian."

There was a lump in Julian's throat when he replied. "Idabee has been an incredible source of knowledge." Her brown eyes directed gratitude to him, overwhelming him with the realization that in four weeks, she would irrevocably be out of his life. Julian tried to communicate grief in his stare, searching impassionedly for acknowledgment in her face as Idabee gazed back at him. Only gradually did he become aware that the room had fallen silent.

The others were watching the pair's trance with mixed reactions. Ray's small smile persisted as he went back to eating, while Delroy seemed content, as though a mystery had been solved. The emotions radiating from Edith, seated on Julian's left, were so intense that Idabee could only glance at her grandmother briefly before flicking her eyes away.

Julian turned to the woman who'd kissed him so passionately earlier and felt the full force of her jealousy. Something in him rebelled at her unvoiced accusation of betrayal. His conscience reminded him that Edith didn't ask permission, even as he understood her feelings.

"That's not the whole answer to your question," Delroy said to Ray, getting the table's attention. "Julian changed my mind about alcohol: the

CHAPTER THIRTY-FOUR

truth was in the root word of intoxicated. I was poisoning myself with every drink." Julian caught Ray's eye, nodding affirmation that the doctor was his source of knowledge.

"But I did have a few drinks when Minnie—my wife—passed a few years back," Delroy continued, dropping his head in contemplation. The table waited in respectful silence for a moment. "She was an incredible woman, and when I lost her—well, I was lost. A little self-harm suddenly sounded appealing. That's the real answer; September 14, 2068, was the last time."

Edith offered him sympathy. "My husband also passed that summer; I know what that's like. But I was never quite as committed to sobriety as you, Delroy. When I was a delegate, the end of each month's session was an excuse for celebration."

"Idabee is serving as a seated delegate in the legislative assembly," Ray informed their guest.

"Del, any other tricks for how I convinced you to take up a sober life?" Julian asked. "Idabee and I are going through thirty days now—I get the demonstration of self-control and addressing the Boaty McBoatface problem, but I think I'm in Edith's camp."

A gleaming grin spread across Delroy's face. "Three words: Donald J. Trump."

Edith squinted her eyes in disbelief. "This is your high school friend who was a huge Trump supporter?"

"He had a sign in his yard for years," Julian confirmed. "How many times did it get stolen or destroyed?"

"Too many to count," Delroy replied cheerfully. "You reminded me that Trump lived a sober life and that it contributed to his success. And you encouraged me to follow his example." Edith could only shake her head as Delroy cackled. "You said his name was an acronym: Temperance really unlocks magnificent power."

Idabee grinned at the phrase. "Especially when it's voluntary," she added.

The conversation quickly drifted to time travel. Edith explained how her college roommate had unlocked the possibility of pushing Julian back to 2023 and that the next opportunity was coming up on May 1. With

Charlotte absent, Edith was the resident expert, leaving Ray looking awestruck as his mother delivered a brief lecture on the mechanics of time travel.

Delroy was relieved to learn that the past was malleable since the process created parallel worlds. "Let me get this straight," Delroy asked. "The Julian I met who caused all of this was from another universe?" Heads nodded. "Causal Julian: CJ," he cackled. "Julian, you got this. You're going to be twice as prepared as CJ was." As a naming convention, CJ was immediately adopted. It struck Julian as silly, but the discrete name for the person Edith and Delroy had met carried a certain clarity that he appreciated.

"But do we know if CJ was the original?" Ray asked. "Seems possible that Julian's gone through this more than once."

"Always trying to be better," Idabee suggested.

Delroy was realizing the ramifications. "But whatever you do, it won't change our past?"

"No," Edith answered, looking at her son and granddaughter. "The multiverse means if Julian lets me get killed at the reparations rally, no one here is going to disappear."

"And if Julian stayed, it wouldn't undo anything?" Delroy asked.

After Edith confirmed it, Ray said, "Are you suggesting Julian doesn't need to go back in time?"

"Well," Delroy said, "what happens if Julian lands in 2023 and gets flattened by a bus? Then he's created a new world where the American Union doesn't come about. CJ worked hard to shape things this way; he even sacrificed his life. Julian ought to consider staying to enjoy the inheritance." He dropped a wink to his old friend. "Maybe get hitched and settle down."

Idabee suddenly became very interested in her plate. "No," Edith protested.

"We'll always have our memories of CJ," Delroy said comfortingly, unaware of her real concerns. "But you and I had the blessings of decades of marriage and raising a family, and we've secured the same opportunity for our posterity. They should have the liberty to make their own path."

CHAPTER THIRTY-FOUR

The appeal to constitutional duty came across as plausible. "Sounds logical to me," Ray said. "Honestly, the idea of time travel and a multiverse makes my head hurt. You're getting pretty well acclimated to life in the tricentennial, Julian. I think you'd be ready to move out pretty soon." His glance at his daughter indicated he had no objections to their pairing.

"It's the parallel worlds," Delroy explained. "If you jaunted back, I'd never know how your adventure turned out. It'd feel like it didn't matter. Stick around, brother, and keep in touch."

"You have free will," Idabee reminded him. "Just because CJ went back doesn't mean you have to. There's still plenty of work to be done—someone has to figure out how buffalo meat should be labeled."

The next voice surprised him. "She's right, Julian," Edith conceded. "Charlotte didn't actually have to send that orange back for us to receive it. If you stay here, there's still a non-zero chance you'll arrive just like we'd planned." Idabee smiled gratefully at her, and Edith added, "I wouldn't mind some great-grandchildren in this universe."

Surrounded at the table by people who genuinely cared for him, Julian recognized the emotion forming in him as, one by one, each offered their support for his continued life in the tricentennial. Several times now, he'd felt like he'd succeeded in defeating this particular feeling, but like the graffiti in his old neighborhood, it often reappeared without warning. Julian spoke slowly and addressed them collectively. "You all don't get it, do you?"

"Get what?" Ray asked. "There's no good reason for you to go back there."

"And I hope there's a good reason for you to stay," Idabee said.

Sometimes graffiti bled through the efforts to cover it up. "Of course there is," he replied, his tone revealing pity and contempt at the young woman's naivete.

"It's okay, Julian," Edith said. "I had a good life."

Her self-centeredness pressed the red button of rage inside him. "Oh, alright," he said sarcastically, the words hissing out like flecks of paint escaping an aerosol can. "Edith Bartlett had a good life, so no need to take advantage of this time machine you and your college roommate whipped up. Where did you and Charlotte meet?"

"Georgetown," Edith answered, not understanding.

"Georgetown," he echoed. "I knew your family had money the moment I saw you. I knew it. You don't know what it was like for all the people who couldn't afford to go to college. You won the genetic lottery." A nasty suspicion came to him, and the poison sprayed out. "Would you have even been at the reparations rally if I hadn't given you the date?"

Edith was still staring when Ray spoke. "Julian, relax."

"Ray, man, I appreciate your hospitality, for real," Julian said. "It's great that your job at the hospital lets you take time off to help people like me get used to our brave new world. That's quite the job. Do you ever wonder what the odds were that, out of all the doctors in the country, you would get the exact same job your mother had? That's some crazy luck."

The anger was bright slashes of color as he turned to Idabee. "You won the temporal lottery. That's not a bad thing, really. Edith told me you didn't know anything about real life, doing your little play challenges for the America Union. 'I wore simple clothes,'" he said in a high falsetto voice. "What would you wear to high school in December? Last year's pants that are three inches too short and are going to get you mocked all day long, or shorts so you can freeze instead? It's all academic to you.

"But you, Delroy," Julian continued. The rage was beginning to slow, and he shook the emotion vigorously, spurring a few more blasts for his old friend. "You know. You know how poverty was where we grew up; you know it stayed that way because when people got out, they left everyone else behind. And I can't figure why you're trying to convince me to do the same thing. I can go back to fix it. I'm glad for you that some guy you used to play basketball with showed up at your door with a bag of cash. Love and respect, brother; you seem like you really did right by it. But you got lucky.

"You all got lucky," Julian proclaimed to stunned faces. "You're the foxes who got away, or never got chased, and just lived warm and happy lives. I escaped and woke up in the tricentennial, and, yeah, it seems great. People here keep telling me we have duties to others, except when I have a chance to end the fox hunt of an economic system, suddenly you all tell me not to worry about it—maybe some other Julian will do it. What's wrong with you people?"

Julian gestured at Delroy. "When you asked me who my people were, you helped me realize they were the marginalized millions, not based on the color of our skin but by the fact we were struggling. Delroy, didn't you see the cars in the parking lot of the plasma center every evening—people who worked all day and then came to stand in line, white and black, side by side, waiting for the opportunity to have blood drawn from their veins for an hour so they could cross the parking lot to buy food at ShopRite? Those are my people, and it doesn't have to be that way. I can fix that.

"Edith, don't you remember the hate that the political parties cultivated? Hate the other team, fight them, defeat them, again and again, election after election? That was the endless war that needed to end; don't you remember how toxic things were in 2024? People wanted a better way; I wanted a better way. You all show me that unionizing as voters sidesteps that hate, but then tell me 'don't worry about it' because you had a good life?

"I can fix all that," he announced, "and if you don't think it needs fixing, well, you don't know, or never knew, or just forgot. I'm going; that's all there is to it—I'm for real going."

Surrounded by friends stunned into silence, his anger burned to a blackened ember, Julian stood up. "Excuse me," he said, starting toward the hall to his room.

"Julian!" Delroy called. "Get back here so I can apologize to you!"

Scowling, Julian turned. "What?"

"You're right," the octogenarian said. "It's been fifty years; I forgot what the old wounds were like because they've healed. Scars fade. But you know what I haven't forgot?"

"What?" he repeated. Ray watched him, a coiled spring ready to jump if Julian began behaving erratically.

"Learning someone I knew was shot dead on a street corner," Delroy said.

The imagery brought him fully back to reality. "That's what happened to CJ; that's what might happen to you. I see the way you and Miss Idabee look at each other; well, I apologize for suggesting you enjoy living instead of rushing toward dying. I promise, you'll end up there eventually. If you want to risk taking a shortcut, maybe you have the fire to pull this whole thing off. But answer me one thing: Who was CJ married to?"

"How would I know?" Julian answered. "I never met the guy."

The pair stared at each other for a moment, Delroy growing more confused with each second. "Julian, did I forget to tell you about your journal?" he asked, scratching his head. When a bewildered look answered his question, the octogenarian continued, "My bad, I thought I did. It's in the suitcase."

"My journal?" Julian echoed.

"You left a notebook and asked me to return it next time I saw you. I tucked it away with the cash so it wouldn't slip my mind." He cackled. "Then I clean forgot."

"What's in it?" Julian asked, curiosity flooding over him and washing away any remnants of rage.

Delroy gave the room a broad grin. "Your past."

Part V

Why am I here?
April 14–17, 2076

This was not merely the desire to stop work. It was a strike on a wide basis against the conditions of work. It was a general strike that involved directly in the end perhaps a half million people. They wanted to stop the economy of the plantation system, and to do that, they left the plantations.

- W.E.B. Du Bois, *Black Reconstruction in America*

A general strike against the government is a revolution.

- Edward Bellamy, *Looking Backward: 2000–1887*

Chapter Thirty-Five

"Let me get this straight," Stella Freedom said to Julian. The historian's hologram was perched on the edge of a chair in the parlor, cheeks glowing and eyes bright. "You have evidence of three alternate timelines? How the United States could have turned out differently in the tricentennial?" Ray sat next to her, enjoying her enthusiasm.

Julian had spent a week poring over the journal. While the physical notebook contained handwritten entries from CJ's last few years and a brief summary of what had come before, it also directed him to look for their archived website. There, camouflaged but in plain sight, decades of entries spanning the lives of three predecessors were published. It was surreal to read his own words describing things he hadn't done and lives he hadn't lived, especially since they raised as many questions as answers.

"Stella, you taught me about the Phoenix Cycle, a radical reshaping of America every four generations," Julian reminded her. "Change was inevitable, but there was nothing inevitable about the United States lasting three hundred years. Civil war broke up the country in two of those worlds."

Her expression froze, then flattened. "I don't want to believe it, but I can. I've sometimes described the Phoenix Cycle as a dam," Stella said. "All the stresses and problems of the previous cycle build up tremendous pressure in a reservoir. There's no question of whether big, transformative changes will rush downstream every eighty years or so, only what form they'll take."

Julian nodded. "The American Union managed to channel all that energy into a peaceful and productive process, but otherwise the 2028 election

CHAPTER THIRTY-FIVE

would have breached the dam, washing the United States out of existence. When an orderly transfer of power looked impossible, Reverend Shaver organized a national fast for peace on the centenary of MLK's birth, and calmer heads prevailed. The times Connor Sullivan succeeded in assassinating him, the United States died too.

"That first Julian—I call him AJ—met Edith Bartlett at the rally, and they ran when the gunmen attacked. The slaughter didn't trigger a total race war, but a three-week skirmish known as The Terror—thousands and thousands of racially motivated killings across the country. Edith sheltered AJ during the chaos, and they fell in love." Ray was nodding his head. Julian, after apologizing for his outburst at dinner, had told him about his half-brother and -sisters in that timeline, even showing him family pictures tucked away in the National Archive.

"They survived the civil war, and eventually, AJ was able to go back in time and disrupt the attack on the reparations rally," Julian continued, deliberately vague about the details. "The Julian in that universe—I call him BJ—was still injured while saving Shaver's life. He woke up in the tricentennial; the American Union had formed from that first fast for peace. It's from his notes that our world learned about it, from my predecessor—CJ—trying to duplicate it." Julian smiled. "I have better notes and firsthand knowledge; next time, I'm going to get it right." Using Reverend Shaver's story would generate the needed momentum.

"But what happened in the civil wars?" Stella asked. "How did they come about? Who fought who? Who won?"

"They both started the same," he said. "After the election, red states and blue states each recognized a different President of the United States and started fighting for control. The one AJ lived through lasted five years, leaving eight million dead and sixty million displaced. Then nine regional alliances of states agreed to disagree, and that was the end of the US.

"The second one, fighting only lasted eighteen months. Eleven major corporations restored order by dividing the nation between themselves and refusing to supply the conflict. Millions of lives were saved, but those lives were subject to nonnegotiable terms of service. CJ woke up in the

Xinghurst sector and learned that if he didn't 'voluntarily' accept them, he'd be cut off from the economy."

Stella continued to pepper him with questions, trying to dislodge details like a pack of hound dogs trying to unearth a fox from its burrow. Julian answered as best he could, but stopped short of revealing the location of the journal entries. It was amazing the knowledge the Archive had preserved, but he wasn't ready to publicize the personal information within its digital pages.

"This is fascinating," Stella said. "To me, the 2028 presidential election was the most peaceful since James Monroe won reelection unopposed in 1820. The American Union had both major parties wanting to support their second legislative package with immigration reform, an employment guarantee, and strong antitrust actions. I know history is full of pivot points, but I never seriously considered that I'd learn how things could have been different."

"CJ spent almost four years in that corporate dystopia before the timepad was recreated," Julian said. "Xinghurst controlled everything: all the consumer products sold were licensed, not actually owned, and any violation of the terms of service let them revoke the licenses. He wrote that it reminded him of prison." The last word was delivered as a prompt.

Stella recognized the hint and asked with some regret, "You wanted to talk about how the American Union dismantled the prison-industrial complex, right?" Julian nodded.

"I'm almost afraid to ask for a definition of that," Ray said to the historian. CJ's journal entries contained a single offhand mention of Idabee's stepmother, Stella. Had Ray's on-again, off-again relationship stayed on elsewhere in the multiverse?

"Corporations used to be allowed to run private prisons," Stella explained. "They were never a large percentage of the total, but there was an inherent conflict of interest with the duty to promote the general welfare, since their goal was to profit from keeping human beings in cages.

"In prisons of any sort, privatization of services was another component. Many states outsourced things like healthcare, food provision, and

CHAPTER THIRTY-FIVE

communication services to private companies, generally with reduced quality. Since there wasn't really any competition—they literally had a captive audience—the corporations could charge outrageous prices for basic services like phone calls."

"Teara Harper would call that profit-pull inflation," Ray noted to Julian.

"Prisoners were also put to work," Stella continued. "The Thirteenth Amendment had a giant loophole. It prevented slavery or involuntary servitude except as punishment for a crime. Southern states began creating criminal codes designed to make it easy to arrest formerly enslaved people and put them to work; the 1870s saw the number of black prisoners in the deep South triple.

"Those convicts could then be leased out to for-profit companies to work in mines, sawmills, cotton farms, and other industries. For the states that used it, convict leasing was extremely profitable, generating revenues triple the cost of running prisons."

Julian sat forward in his chair, anger sparking in his eyes. "Basically continuing the same exploitation that had existed under slavery."

Stella nodded. "In many ways, it was worse than chattel slavery, Julian. Convict leasing allowed the same exploitation, but on a per diem basis with zero long-term investment in the prisoner's health. They couldn't negotiate for better working conditions or go on strike; they were disposable. Thousands upon thousands died, about 20% annually across the South, leading one newspaper editor to suggest it would be more humane to simply execute anyone with a sentence over six years."

"Twenty percent?" Ray said, frowning. "That's insane."

Stella nodded. "Convict leasing diminished as states realized they could use that labor directly. Men could be sentenced to chain gangs—groups of prisoners forced to do hard labor—for misdemeanors like loitering and drunkenness. Georgia used them to create thousands of kilometers of roads at half the price of what it would have paid free men."

"More cheap labor," Julian observed. "I did time with this guy, James. He told me during the Iraq War, they'd ship shot up Humvees to Gilmer, West Virginia, where he was in the federal prison, and make the inmates clean the blood out of them. Vehicles with warnings of radioactivity stuck on them; they'd get maybe three dollars an hour to scrub them out."

"You were incarcerated?" Stella said with enthusiasm. Apparently, Ray had filed that information under doctor-patient privilege. Even if it wasn't a secret, Julian approved of his discretion. "Can you tell me why?"

Julian was in the mood to talk. "Do you know what a pretext stop is?" he asked.

Ray shook his head, but Stella answered. "Before there were self-driving cars, it was a traffic stop based on racial profiling."

"Exactly like the slave patrols the police came from," Julian said bitterly. "White guys on power trips."

Stella hesitated before interjecting. "No, professional police forces were a response to the industrial revolution and people flooding into cities. London started theirs in 1829; Boston and New York followed a few years later." Julian stared at her; she stared back. "Egypt had a police force more than five thousand years ago," she insisted.

"Anyway," Julian continued, "I was pulled over on my way home from the grocery store, even though I wasn't going any faster than the rest of the traffic. It was three years after George Floyd was murdered, Stella, and despite all the protests about racial bias in policing, it continued to happen. The officer was a white woman, and I wasn't very polite or respectful about giving her my license and information. She asked me to step out of the vehicle and open the trunk."

"Didn't you have to consent to a search?" Stella asked.

"I didn't consent; I told her no. What I had in the trunk was two pints of melting ice cream among a week's worth of groceries, but it was none of her business. She told me refusing made her suspicious, and two more police cars pulled up, lights flashing, while she pressured me to reveal whatever I was hiding.

"I absolutely refused, and I guess I took a step toward her. Then another cop was pointing his gun at me, telling me to put my hands on the trunk; I'm under arrest." He shook his head ruefully.

"They pulled a gun on you?" Ray asked skeptically.

CHAPTER THIRTY-FIVE

"The police shot and killed a thousand people a year back then," Stella told him.

Julian let out a bitter laugh. "I was terrified of being the next one; I quit arguing and cooperated. They charged me with aggravated assault for—and I made my public defender give me the law—*attempting by physical menace to put an officer, while in the performance of duty, in fear of imminent serious bodily injury.* Second degree felony, not to mention the other charges of resisting arrest and anything else they could throw at me."

Julian stared straight ahead as he continued narrating his story. "They wanted twenty-five thousand cash bail. When they told me that, I thought I was going to lose my mind. I didn't have that kind of money, and I couldn't imagine how I was going to get out of there. They offered to drop the other charges and recommend a two-year sentence if I pled guilty. I didn't want to risk waiting for a trial just to get ten years, so I took the deal."

Ray furrowed his brow. "But you didn't actually assault the officer, did you?"

"You think the prosecutor would have a hard time convincing a jury that a little white policewoman was afraid of an uncooperative black man?" Julian scoffed. "Ten years, Ray; ten years if that happened. I took the deal. What was supposed to be a simple trip to the store took fifteen months and turned my life upside down."

"I'm sorry that happened, Julian," Stella said, although she was smiling. "Your story is a fascinating collection of unjust anachronisms like cash bail, which mainly functioned as a way to pressure plea deals from those who couldn't afford to pay. It's exceedingly unlikely that a similar thing could happen now.

"An arrest today spurs the intervention of a restoration advisor. They listen to both parties and try to mediate a satisfactory resolution. More often than not, that's the end of any criminal case, although a prosecutor has to sign off on the deal. If they want to press ahead, a plea bargain that includes incarceration is capped at four years. For someone to receive a sentence longer than that, a jury has to convict them."

Julian was working out the ramifications. "Four years? Reverend Shaver compared your modern prisons to a college campus."

Stella nodded. "Julian, what was your experience? You said fifteen months; did you feel like there was an effort to rehabilitate you?"

He snorted. "Ta-Nehisi Coates once wrote, 'There are all kinds of ways one can respond to a crime surge. Mass incarceration is appropriate only if you already believe that certain people weren't really fit for freedom in the first place.' Two-thirds of the men I was locked up with were black, and I felt like we were being warehoused." Julian explained he'd read *The New Jim Crow* several times inside. "I got my felony conviction, my scarlet letter, and then it was up to me to put my life back in order." He sighed and fell silent.

"What's a public defender?" Ray asked.

Julian echoed the question, reserving judgment on whether it was envy or anger he felt at his host's ignorance. "Criminal defendants were entitled to court-appointed lawyers," Julian replied. "Those were public defenders. But the poorest communities were the most likely to need them and the least likely to be able to afford them, so free representation usually turned out to be worth as much as you paid for it. Bryan Stevenson, who founded the Equal Justice Institute to review wrongful convictions, said it was better to be rich and guilty than poor and innocent. What do you have now?"

Stella began to explain. "When someone is arrested today, they immediately get a voucher for legal services to hire their own lawyer. Members of the legal profession are trustees of the judicial system. As guardians of legal knowledge, they have a duty to be stewards of justice."

"Stewards of justice, huh? That doesn't sound like the lawyers in my time."

"It was a nonviolent revolution, Julian," Stella said with a grin, "so Shakespeare's proposal to kill all the lawyers was voted down. Instead, the American Union's first legislative package established an excise tax on the practice of law. Establishing justice is a national duty, not a local one. A fee-and-dividend model ensured tax money was distributed into those impoverished communities as legal service vouchers."

CHAPTER THIRTY-FIVE

"Like American Union Jobs," Julian said, recalling Professor Carlton had described UBI as addressing the economically parched parts of the country.

"Very similar," the historian agreed. "Lawyers' fees had been increasing at twice the rate of inflation for decades, which exacerbated a two-tiered justice system. Vouchers created a business model for lawyers who actually wanted to be stewards of justice."

"A special tax on lawyers!" Julian laughed. "I can't tell you how many hours of my life were wasted by legal disclaimers and other nonsense. It's great the US billed them for the time they cost everyone, but I bet they put up a fight."

Stella shrugged. "Since the legal profession was highly disrupted by the development of artificial intelligence, many lawyers supported creating new markets for their services rather than risk being pushed out of the profession. As the kinks in the criminal justice system began to work out, the vouchers were expanded to other parts of the court system, like family court and civil matters. They were also transferable, so people could donate them to causes like that Equal Justice Initiative."

"Now they're one of the benefits of your American Union Job," Ray added. "Up to twenty-four hours a year."

"The judicial system isn't perfect; no dispute resolution system ever will be," Stella concluded. "But ensuring everyone a basic level of legal access eliminated the worst disparities under the old system."

Julian snapped his fingers. "Like abolishing absolute poverty with UBI did, even if relative poverty still existed." Stella nodded approval to the connection her student had made, and a broad grin spread across his face. "Sounds like a great reform."

"You know who was really helpful in building the moral pressure to deliver these reforms?" Stella asked. "Incarcerated people. The fast for peace spread throughout jails and prisons. When thousands and thousands of people behind bars were fasting each month in solidarity with those on the outside, it drew attention to their humanity and forged a common bond."

"Around a shared goal of dismantling up the prison-industrial complex?"

"Yes, but because the American Union was formed as a national bloc of voters, there were limits on what they could do with a single legislative package in Congress," Stella said. "Each state ran their own prison system, so although the Federal Bureau of Prisons incarcerated more people than any of them, it was only about 15% of the total.

"But by reforming the prison system at the top, changes trickled down to the states. In addition, the system of federal grants also gave Congress some leverage; for example, solitary confinement reform was a requirement from the very beginning. States that wanted to continue receiving grants had to make policy changes."

"What kind of changes?" Julian asked with an eagerness that he could feel Stella noting.

"The United Nations had set standards for the care and treatment of incarcerated people, commonly called the Mandela Rules for Nelson Mandela. They defined anything in excess of fifteen days as a form of torture. Although the Supreme Court had taken note of the many harms caused by solitary confinement as far back as 1890, there were still tens of thousands of Americans being isolated for months or even years. In Louisiana's Angola Prison, a man named Albert Woodfox was sequestered for more than four decades before his wrongful conviction was overturned.

"The first legislative package started by banning the involuntary use of solitary confinement for more than fifteen consecutive days—or thirty out of sixty—for those in federal custody. States were given two years to make the same changes or lose federal funds for law enforcement. Within an additional year, they also had to ensure people were given due process before they could be sent to the prison within the prison."

Stella appraised Julian before continuing. "Can I ask you about solitary confinement? If you don't mind telling me." He was quiet until she added, "Never mind."

"You have to try to escape," Julian began. "Not physically, of course. It's a room about a third of the size of this parlor; I could touch the opposite walls with my fingertips. You have to escape in your mind. Something to keep you thinking. Something that you can have control over. You can

CHAPTER THIRTY-FIVE

exercise, you can count the bricks in the wall, but mostly you're just alone, pummeled by a constant barrage of nothing happening.

"It was cold; they gave me a one-piece coverall that was impossible to tear." He continued in a monotone. "Because if you could tear it, you might be able to hurt yourself. Because that at least would be something. It's just dull; the waiting grinds you down. The food itself is torture, a block of tasteless nutrients. No utensils required."

The fast for peace spread throughout jails and prisons, the historian had said. *It drew attention to their humanity.* "I wonder, Stella, what the fast for peace would have meant for me? To feel hungry for a day and know that there were people, free people outside, living their lives, sharing the experience? To know that I wasn't alone in there?"

Julian recalled prison protests that had incorporated hunger strikes and knew officials sometimes resorted to force-feeding. But the fast for peace was a single day; there was no basis for claiming anyone's health was at risk. He imagined fasting in prison and knowing others on the outside were sacrificing as well to try to change the dehumanizing system. The imagery of feeling seen brought a smile to his face.

"Stella," he asked, "what's your connection with the American Union? Do you fast every month?" A warm glow was spreading inside him.

The historian's eyes flicked to Ray before she answered. "I did, when I was younger. But now it's just once or twice a year: Muster Day, and if there's something important in the people's legislative assembly that needs my direct support. Why?"

"I'm still trying to understand how everything fits together. I was going to start mine after dinner tonight, but I'm feeling it now." Julian's grin was insufficient to express the joy bubbling up in him, a sense of belonging like nothing he'd ever experienced. What was going on? "Are incarcerated people still a major component?"

"Not really," she replied.

"Oh." Even her answer wasn't enough to dampen the indescribable connection he was feeling.

"Julian, the American Union ended mass incarceration," Stella continued.

"The US has about one hundred ten thousand incarcerated people on any given day, less than a tenth of what it was in your time. There are four times as many American Union delegates and ten times again other members who fast. So, no, they're not a big fraction. But they're still there."

"They're there," Julian echoed. "I can feel them." It was true. The walls of the parlor were permeable, and he saw the single thread of his life was a tiny part of a brilliant tapestry of shared humanity. They were all connected, souls interwoven, and he found himself enveloped in a feeling that surpassed mere empathy.

Ray gave him a quizzical look. "Are you feeling okay?"

"I am," he said, so overwhelmed with gratitude for the doctor's concern that it nearly brought tears to his eyes.

Was this agape love?

Chapter Thirty-Six

When Julian entered the parlor the next evening for Professor Carlton's group meeting, he carried a single round cracker. Carlton had invited him to stay after the session again and break fast together. Julian hadn't eaten since that feeling of inescapable joy; it had faded, but even thinking of it brought a smile to his face.

There were only two people visible in the room so far, and neither one was Idabee. This would be their first time seeing each other since he'd cruelly mocked her across the dinner table, and that recollection brought the opposite of joy. Trying to anticipate where she might sit, his heart beat faster. There were two red indicator lights in the corner of the room besides his own; was she lurking, waiting to see his decision first, so she could avoid him?

Julian had learned so much about Idabee—or an alternate version of her—thanks to the journal. *Who was CJ married to?* An enamored Idabee offered explanations to a CJ who woke up as a subject of their corporate overlords. She'd purchased the necessary travel permits for their trip to Philadelphia, where they found Delroy and received the journal. Idabee held CJ as he wept for the terrible world his predecessor had inadvertently created. CJ fell for her even before she tracked down her great-aunt Charlotte and helped him persuade the civil war widow that time travel was possible.

Who was CJ married to? Idabee was radiant in the wedding photos the National Archive scraped from his long-expired website. Soon, that was all he'd have left of her, and he didn't want to spend those weeks avoiding her.

After setting his cracker on an end table, Julian plunked himself in the middle of the couch, across from the middle-aged man who'd announced he was taking cold showers. The man introduced himself as Diego and laughed when Julian asked how his experiment was going. "By the third day, I couldn't put it off any more. It was freezing, but I got through it, plus a few more since then."

"I'd never seriously thought about taking one voluntarily until you mentioned it a few weeks ago," Julian confessed. They'd been an occasional necessity growing up—practically a rite of spring—when unpaid gas bills culminated in a shutoff of hot water.

"My survival technique is pretty simple: avoid the water to the fullest extent possible," Diego explained.

Idabee oscillated into substance by Julian's side, and relief flooded over him. She offered up a brief smile before addressing Diego. "You're still fighting, as if it were something to be endured," Idabee told the man. "Open yourself up to the experience; let yourself be uncomfortable. I promise, it won't kill you." Diego agreed to try.

Julian welcomed Idabee, and she turned on him with a mischievous expression. "Hey, Julian," she said, "it's good to see you. Can we talk afterward?"

It would give him the opportunity to apologize in private. "Of course," he agreed. Something was on her mind; her look reminded him of the honeymoon pictures. The white sands of Playa Pilar in Cuba looked beautiful. Had she learned of the marriage independently?

Adon and Faith were the last to arrive; Julian's quick wave got a thumbs-up reply from Adon, who appeared enthused at the prospect he'd worked things out with Idabee.

With the parlor filled up, Professor Carlton called things to order. The septuagenarian stroked his beard and scanned the room before settling his gaze on Julian. "Julian, would you lead us in reciting the Preamble?"

Even though Idabee had cautioned him to expect this, Julian's pulse quickened as all eyes in the room swiveled toward him. Taking a deep breath, he began: "We the people of the United States, in order to form a

CHAPTER THIRTY-SIX

more perfect union, establish justice, insure domestic tranquility, provide for the common defence, promote the general welfare, and secure the blessings of liberty to ourselves and our posterity, do ordain and establish this Constitution for the United States of America." Idabee was beaming as he finished the last few words.

"As you all know," Carlton began, "it was fifty years ago today that the United States observed the fast for peace called for by Reverend Shaver in the aftermath of the attack on the reparations rally." An open hand acknowledged Julian. "Things might have turned out differently if someone hadn't acted."

"That was the beginning of the American Union," Idabee said. "How did you get Congress to join the fast for peace?" Julian had been wrestling with this question for two weeks. Idabee glanced sideways at him with a tight, impish smile, and he realized she'd steered the conversation in this direction for his benefit. Once again, he found himself marveling at her talents.

Professor Carlton hesitated; perhaps he had another story in mind. "I was a freshman in college at the time," he began. "After Reverend Shaver made his speech—*An Apology, a Dollar, and an Accounting*—a group formed on campus to try and organize for the fast. We went around talking to students; lots got on board. For anyone who'd heard his speech from the reparations rally, it was hard to argue that the United States had nothing to apologize for. Objecting to the dollar itself—or forty million of them—was also tricky, since the military was spending two million every single minute. The accounting involved haggling over the price. We listened to concerns it could turn out to be a big, scary number and acknowledged the fear. Listening is an important part of nonviolence because the best solution is one that's win-win, where both sides emerge with dignity.

"To persuade members of Congress, local affinity groups formed. They were teams of volunteers who cooperated to engage their quarry with the invitation to join the fast. There were also national affinity groups targeting celebrities, influencers, and the candidates for president in 2028." Julian recalled Stella Freedom describing what a peaceful election it had turned out to be, with the candidates on both sides supporting the American Union's second legislative package.

The septuagenarian grinned in recollection. "We'd coordinate posts on social media, working together to get their attention, pressuring them to publicly commit. The fast was a great equalizer. It didn't matter how much money or influence a person had, because they couldn't just write a check or issue a statement of support. Fasting required a sacrifice on a personal level, one that every human could relate to, one that all were capable of—if they were willing to bring the intention.

"One of the other things I helped do was persuade restaurants and grocery stores to close on April 15. We asked employees to request the day off and to refuse to participate in serving food during the fast. When a few were on board, we'd talk to the owner or manager, explain the fast, and list other restaurants in the area that were closing."

"So this was like the hartal—the one-day general strike—that takes place on Muster Day?" Julian asked.

"It was the model, yes—noncooperation with the economy. There have been some years, Julian, where the general strike lasted more than one day, if additional pressure is needed to inspire Congress to act," Carlton answered.

He returned to his story. "At the same time, online petitions were started to ask national restaurant chains to close for the fifteenth. Those who had previously offered support for Black Lives Matter were subjected to public pressure on social media. Reverend Shaver's call was effective in producing a binary choice for them: support a peaceful resolution or, by default, publicly oppose it. I don't know if the chains talked among themselves, but they were pretty much all on board by early April."

"What happened on the fifteenth?" Julian wondered. "Did you go out and picket those businesses that stayed open?" The heads shaking in the room made him regret asking.

"Julian, no one should ever be pressured to join on the day of the fast," the professor said gently. "We tried to persuade holdouts until then, but the fifteenth is a day for peace and unity, not highlighting differences. Respect

CHAPTER THIRTY-SIX

people's decisions. Nationwide, about a fifth of the labor force participated. In Congress, around three-quarters of members jumped in front of the parade, and they put the bill on the president's desk within the week."

Idabee thanked Carlton for his detailed answer, and he asked for updates on people's challenges. The professor turned to the young woman sitting next to him. "Leilani, how's your cooking?"

"Improving," she replied, summarizing the vegan meals she'd made. "Everything has been edible so far. When it works, I feel pride; I created this." Leilani beamed.

Adon volunteered that he'd been meditating for fifteen minutes every morning. "I'd like to make it a more regular habit. We'll see if it sticks." The group offered suggestions and encouragement.

Carlton looked to Christopher. "Want to tell us how you're doing with your celibacy experiment?"

"Still in hands-free mode," the man joked. "I've been going for some walks, getting out of my house, and just being aware that if I'm bored, there are other things I'd rather do with my time."

One by one, the rest of the group shared their challenges. Julian talked about how a stressful experience—he didn't mention Connor Sullivan—had made him think about drinking. "Alcohol wouldn't have changed anything about the situation; it was just a way to distract myself. Recognizing that, it made it easier to proactively look for something else. Drinking used to be a regular part of my routine, but being in a new place with new people has made it easier to not fall into the same pattern."

"How about you, Idabee?" Carlton asked. Her head jerked at the sound of her name, caught with her thoughts somewhere else.

"I chose a stoic challenge this month," she said. "I traded my bed for the floor. I was expecting to be more uncomfortable, but after a week, I actually feel like I'm sleeping better."

Julian shook his head, remembering the man he'd seen sleeping on the sidewalk grate the morning of the reparations rally. "Who categorizes these?" he wondered. "Walking through Washington fifty years ago, there were homeless people sleeping on benches, in the park, and on the sidewalk." Blank young faces stared back at him; Carlton nodded for him to continue. "Couldn't this be a perspective experiment?"

"Of course," Carlton agreed. "Or an abstinence one: willingly giving up a bed for a period of time. The intention a person brings to the experiment helps determine the results."

What was Idabee's intention? CJ's wife had never done anything like this, and Julian looked at Idabee, trying to decipher a motivation from her blank expression. It was impossible that she'd planned on avoiding beds for the month of April, when their relationship had been on the cusp of blossoming. His heart twisted as an explanation crystalized: if a robin's-egg-blue envelope forced her to give up having him in her bed, she would give it up too. Idabee had described this as a stoic experiment with a willingness to be uncomfortable.

"Professor Carlton," Julian asked, when there was a lull in the conversation, "that first fast fifty years ago? You quoted Gandhi as saying the national day of fasting was an experiment of building ourselves up without violence. What category would it fall into?"

The gray-haired man spread his hands, inviting the room to offer observations. Diego was the first to speak. "I'd say betterment—America did get into the habit with the monthly fast for peace."

"But not right away," Faith countered. "That first time, the United States had to do something uncomfortable and acknowledge the racist things the government had done in the past. So it was more of a stoic challenge." Heads nodded agreement.

"I watched Reverend Shaver's speech recently," Idabee admitted. "There's also an aspect of perspective to it. He acknowledged that many millions of Americans had no idea if it was a fair proposal, which is why he allowed three weeks for people to learn about that historical perspective before deciding if they were willing to share in the sacrifice."

There was some back-and-forth on this last point, then Carlton addressed the group again. "Does anyone want to argue it was an abstinence experiment?" The room fell silent.

"I will," Julian said cautiously. He looked around at the interested faces watching him. "I'm not sure anyone else here—besides Professor Carlton—appreciates how polarized politics were back then, especially for Congress. I see now how elections were treated as a pure zero-sum game; neither party could gain a seat unless they took it from the other side. So they refused to cooperate, thinking anything that helped their adversary would hurt them.

"The aspect of abstinence I see is that people gave up fighting, at least for a few weeks, at least for one thing. Even if it was just political posturing for some, getting in front of a parade, the fact that 75% of Congress participated in the fast to support reparations amazes me."

Carlton waved an encouraging finger in Julian's direction. "This speaks to the moral pressure generated by the fast for peace. After Reverend Shaver announced it would continue monthly and the American Union would collectively bargain as a bloc of swing voters in the November election, the abstentious act became a specific ask for voters: give up hatred for politicians and political parties.

"This was a hard thing for many to accept, especially if their identity was built, in part, on being superior to members of the other political party. Similarly, members of third parties carried a visceral dislike for the major parties—and not without good reason—and were now being asked to help create a path to success for those politicians.

"Martin Luther King spoke about building the beloved community through the power of agape love—selfless love." Julian listened to the professor of nonviolence studies intently, believing that was what he had experienced the previous evening. "American culture wasn't yet ready to embrace a profound and deep love for all humanity, but what was possible was to lay a foundation with a message of inclusion. The fast for peace offered a middle ground—welcome those who share in the self-sacrifice. For political adversaries, it was like signing a truce for the duration of the election cycle to advance common policy goals.

"Those goals were drawn from a challenge thrown down by Dr. King, and it's one that organizers are still asked to accept more than a century after his death. He said, 'Our only hope today lies in our ability to recapture the revolutionary spirit, to go out into a sometimes hostile world, declaring eternal opposition to poverty, racism, and militarism. With this powerful commitment, we shall boldly challenge the status quo.'

"When the American Union published their legislative solutions, it pulled back the curtain on Congress, revealing the technical ability to end poverty, mass incarceration, and the endless wars. With that ability came a moral duty to act. People respond to injustice, and to allow the status quo to continue would have been unjust. There were plenty of other problems in America, but things like green infrastructure, intellectual property reform, and a land value tax had to come later. The moral crusade was essential to establishing the American Union as a bargaining unit."

"Like Gandhi and the Salt March," Julian said, almost to himself.

The septuagenarian's sharp ears picked it up. "Like Gandhi and the Salt March," he repeated. "If the candidates and the political parties wanted to win, it was necessary to negotiate with a union of swing voters. It was the same dilemma the British faced; when the jails were full, they had to negotiate with Gandhi. In swing districts, candidates had a huge incentive to compete for the American Union endorsement. From there, things trickled up; the parties had to decide whether to support their candidates or willingly yield the seats. Plus, neither party wanted to come out in favor of keeping poverty, mass incarceration, and the endless wars just before the election, so while they grumbled about some provisions, going along was easier than sticking their necks out."

"Polly Sigh said that when the marginal cost of doing nothing was zero, Congress was able to get away with not taking action," Julian offered.

"Good point," Carlton agreed. "By making sure there would be high political costs for failing to act, the American Union changed the dynamic. Sometimes people focus on nonviolence as resistance, like civil disobedience, or noncooperation, as Gandhi often described it. But nonviolence is also about helping others succeed—helping them gain dignity. That's what differentiated the American Union from political parties: the willingness to help all candidates instead of predefining victory as someone else's defeat."

CHAPTER THIRTY-SIX

The rest of the room was quiet, and Juilan spoke again, feeling a little guilty about monopolizing the conversation. "Those people who were beaten up after the Salt March—what did you call them? Sachyuhgreease?" he asked.

"Satyagrahis," Carlton answered, enunciating the four syllables. "Those trained in nonviolence for the purposes of satyagraha."

"And that's why you train this group to practice making sacrifices? To be organizers and delegates—to be satyagrahis?" Carlton's expression delivered the acknowledgment. "And satyagraha means taking action; active resistance to evil, not passive."

"To establish justice is our first duty," Adon reminded him. Around the room, heads nodded, and Julian grinned. The cracker he'd brought into the room sat silently near him, a reminder he was still fasting. It was a simple experiment, and he was grateful it resulted in a sense of community and purpose.

Chapter Thirty-Seven

When Carlton closed out the meeting, Julian turned to Idabee. "Thank you for your help," he said. "That was exactly the kind of inside information I'm trying to learn." He hoped that his digital simulacrum in Idabee's parlor projected the sincerity he felt. "I'm sorry for what I said to you at dinner the other night."

"It's okay," Idabee replied, and the sweetness of her smile persuaded him all was forgiven. "And I'm happy to help." Her holographic projection leaned in close. "It's a trick I learned in the assembly; plant a friendly question to guide the discussion." Idabee straightened and folded her hands across her lap, seeming pleased with herself.

"You're amazing, you know that?" Julian said with a grin. Idabee impressed him. His cheerful expression faded, thinking of how cruel his typical follow-up question would have been.

"Of course," Idabee replied matter-of-factly. "And it's win-win—I'm learning too. I've never heard Carlton call this a training program for satyagrahis before. Usually, he says he does it because he finds value in self-improvement."

Julian nodded, recalling the explanation's phrasing from their first meeting. "And has since he went through the program more than five decades ago." He tilted his head. "Am I remembering that right?"

The parlor had emptied out, and Professor Carlton addressed them. "Remembering what?" he asked.

"You got involved with the American Union at the beginning, right?" Idabee said. "Organizing your campus after Reverend Shaver's speech?"

CHAPTER THIRTY-SEVEN

The septuagenarian stroked his beard. "Was that the beginning?" he asked Julian innocently.

"Carlton," Julian said slowly, "have we met before?"

A broad smile smoothed the wrinkles of his face. "When I first saw the video of the attack on the reparations rally, I wasn't sure it was you. You'd shaved your head, and I had a hard time believing that the man who lectured us on nonviolence brought a lead pipe to what should have been a peaceful event. Then Reverend Shaver made his hospital speech, calling for the fast for peace, and I was almost positive you had something to do with all of it."

Julian rubbed his temples. "Who was I lecturing?"

"You were training American Union organizers for the 2024 election."

"Wait," Idabee said. "You knew Julian back then? Is that why you invited me to your group, hoping I'd bring him with me?"

Carlton nodded. "Or that you'd be willing to arrange an introduction when he was revived. We met while I was stationed at Fort Liberty, serving in the military so I could afford college—this was back before all education was a free public good. Julian was trying to recruit peace activists to influence the election, and I found him on social media while searching for ways to end war."

CJ had recorded those efforts in his journal, but there had been no mention of Carlton. Did the septuagenarian know about his time traveling? Julian was unsure of how to interpret the reticence in identifying their earlier meeting and the way he'd explained the foundational basics of nonviolence as though Julian were hearing them for the first time.

"Our global military adventures weren't helping the mental health of service members," Carlton continued. "In the quarter century after 9/11, more than fifty thousand committed suicide—seven times more than combat deaths. I'd just lost a friend that way and wanted to see what I could do to help the United States become a force for peace and justice in the world—do things we could really be proud of. The American Union had a better plan than anyone else was offering."

He produced a clementine and began to peel the fruit. "I was cocky in those days, if you can believe it, and Julian caught me bragging to a new organizer that I'd completed the fast for peace six times already. 'Real peace takes a long-term commitment,' he said. 'Look me up when you hit six hundred.'" Carlton lifted an orange segment. "And here I am."

"Six hundred months!" Idabee exclaimed. "Why didn't you tell everyone else that?"

Julian retrieved his cracker from the end table and held it up. "That is an impressive long-term commitment—you should be proud," he said. "To the nonviolent nature of our movement." It was the only sliver of the Cesar Chavez quote he could recall. Idabee looked disappointed to be left out, and Julian broke his cracker in half, instinctively intending to share with her. Just in time, he remembered that handing it to her would be impossible, and smoothly—he hoped—put it into his mouth instead.

As they broke their fast together, Julian felt a wave of optimism as his connection with Professor Carlton strengthened. The man had been an active participant in the early days of the American Union, just like Delroy, and might be able to offer greater insight. First, there was another question on his mind: "Professor Carlton, you said I failed by allowing circumstances to develop where the gunmen thought killing was essential to their dignity. Do you also blame the people who preached hate and division? The companies who made their guns?"

Carlton fell silent for a moment. "Julian, it's interesting that you hear failure as blame instead of as an objective analysis. But I'll accept your premise for a moment; if I did, do you think they'd accept responsibility?"

"No," Julian spat with a vehemence that surprised him. "No one wanted to be responsible."

"And what about the people you've met in the tricentennial?"

Julian couldn't help but laugh, dissipating his anger. "I watched Idabee and Faith debate whether standards for labeling buffalo meat should be part of the American Union's demands this year." He sobered. "I guess that's them wanting to take responsibility. Is that what satyagrahis do?"

"That's exactly right."

"If you were an American Union organizer back then, did you accept

CHAPTER THIRTY-SEVEN

responsibility for the circumstances as well?" He held up a hand to interrupt himself. "That's not really my question; I'm not trying to blame you. What I really want to know is: how could we have done better?"

The gray-haired man smiled thoughtfully. "I've wondered about that over the decades. Reverend Shaver throwing his weight behind it really made a difference. If only we could do it over again." Carlton looked meaningfully at Julian's head. "Are you growing your hair out?"

Julian exhaled with relief. "I am," he confirmed, "but I don't think I'll have time for a set of locs before I meet you." Carlton's eyes glowed with enthusiasm at the implications. "On the plus side, Reverend Shaver agrees with your analysis, and he shared a personal story that will persuade him to help us in 2024. So I'm cautiously optimistic."

"Time travel; I've wondered," Carlton admitted. "You looked younger in the news footage. And—no offense—you occasionally offered very clear details of how things would work but didn't always seem to grasp the fundamentals. Your absolute certainty in the American Union model was convincing, even if your presentation wasn't very polished."

Julian laughed out loud. "So, the student has become the teacher? Okay, Professor, teach me—give me the pitch for the American Union's 2024 legislative package."

"End poverty, end mass incarceration, end the endless wars," Idabee said. "Wasn't that the pitch?"

"Julian knows the soundbite version," Carlton agreed, "but I think he's asking for details." After a confirming glance at Julian, he settled back in his chair, tented his fingers, and began to explain.

"The American Union structured its goals around the duties laid out in the Preamble. Since the Constitution is our foundation for government and a common political ancestor for the parties, it was a natural fit. 'We the people of the United States, in order to form a more perfect union,'" Carlton quoted.

"You know, Julian, when the colonies declared independence in 1776, they were walking out on strike. They refused to labor under King George any longer; they quit. When they formed the United States under the

Articles of Confederation, it was just 'a firm league of friendship.' They weren't really a union—working together for mutual benefit—until the Constitution was adopted. The Preamble was their mission statement.

"The first goal was to establish justice. Most people recognized that the criminal justice system in America was in need of a serious overhaul, especially after the murder of George Floyd and the extra attention that racial bias was getting. So major police, prison, and prosecutorial reforms were included." Carlton rattled off policies that Julian had discussed with Ray and Stella Freedom.

"Ending the federal war on drugs wasn't without controversy," he recalled. "There were some who supported it as a states' rights issue since the federal legislation repealed laws on the national level but let states continue to set their own policies.

"The second duty is insuring domestic tranquility, and partisan politics was one of the biggest instigators of division in the country. The American Union offered a way to sidestep the drama with a policy-driven approach to address the wedge issues of guns and abortion."

"I heard about that," Julian said, motioning for Carlton to continue.

"Next was providing for the common defense; America's trillion dollar 'defense budget' far exceeded the Framers' mandate. They had been so concerned about standing armies that Article 1, Section 8, prohibits Congress from funding the army for more than two years at a time. After World War Two, however, the military-industrial complex developed into the standing army the Framers feared. The package reduced the size of our global military footprint—we talked about the details two weeks ago—and worked to restore America's reputation on the world stage."

"What happened with military suicides?" Julian asked.

"They dropped, of course—all suicides did." Carlton paused before continuing. "It proved we were doing better at meeting our fourth duty— promote the general welfare. Do you know what the word welfare means?"

Julian supplied Teara's definition from the previous month. "Health, happiness, prosperity: well-being," he recited.

"Very good," Carlton said, suitably impressed. "The duty to promote

CHAPTER THIRTY-SEVEN

those things was largely met through the American Union Jobs Program. You've learned about UBI; what about Treasury Dollar Bills and monetary reform?"

Julian's answer took the form of a question. "The debt was all made up?"

"Truth as a guiding principle put an end to that," Carlton agreed.

"I'm talking with an economist tomorrow about the details; you can skip those."

The professor continued, "Besides unconditional basic income to abolish poverty, there was a public option for health insurance, based on Joe Biden's campaign promise, and eighteen weeks of paid family leave. Shifting to a trickle-up economy improved the general well-being of everyone in the United States."

"What about noncitizens?" Julian asked. "They didn't get American Union Jobs, right?"

"Good question," Carlton said. "They do not, so you're correct they didn't benefit as much as citizens did; in fact, since there was a one-time bump in prices as a result of new taxes, some people said immigrants were hurt by the program. But that was counteracted by all of the other social benefits. Eliminating poverty disproportionately benefited the communities they lived in, reducing problems like crime and creating new business opportunities—immigrants are frequently entrepreneurs. They also benefited as wages increased, and for those who needed help from the safety net, the net worked a lot better after tens of millions of Americans stepped onto a safety floor.

"In addition, the legislation also included some small updates to immigration policy—a truce of sorts. It created a path to citizenship for those children who were under sixteen when they were brought to the US—commonly called Dreamers—and updated access to the century-old registry program that allowed long-time residents to apply for legal status. In addition, utilizing a national employment verification system was mandated for large employers."

After Julian nodded understanding, Carlton continued. "The Preamble's fifth clause really has two parts: first, securing the blessings of liberty.

This is a duty to maximize personal freedom and minimize coercion, and the way that we secure these blessings in a democracy is by voting. We enshrined the principle of one citizen, one vote, with no exceptions.

"Of course, securing those blessings also requires functional government, so the package reined in two obstructionist tactics. First, the debt ceiling was abolished—it was about to become irrelevant anyway, with Treasury Dollar Bills replacing the national debt. Second, if Congress failed to pass a budget, the government no longer shut down; funding was maintained at the rate Congress had most recently established."

Julian laughed out loud. "But those constant crises were Congress' best excuses for why nothing got done!"

"That was the point," Carlton said, a hard edge creeping into his tone. "No more excuses. The United States needed to get its act together before things fell apart." Julian wondered how Carlton had fared in the worlds where civil war had broken out. Had he fought on one side or the other, or managed to position himself as a conscientious objector?

After a moment, Carlton continued. "The other half of the fifth clause—to ourselves and our posterity—is a duty to act sustainably, so that future generations will not suffer from a reduced quality of life. We are the trustees of their future. This included protecting the environment with new taxes on greenhouse gases and plastic, and since the US military was the largest single consumer of fossil fuels on the planet, military downsizing served this duty as well."

Julian took in all the information and thanked Carlton for condensing it. "There's a lot there; I'm having a hard time imagining all of this agreed to at once. Change is supposed to take time, right? Baby steps? It just seems like too much to ask for."

Carlton nodded sagely. "I heard that a lot, Julian. And you're right, the traditional model was incremental reform. But this is what the Phoenix Cycle delivers, Julian: the opportunity to make big, sweeping changes. The colonies could have asked to send representatives to Parliament instead of declaring independence. Slavery could have been phased out gradually. FDR could have insisted the New Deal stay small so the budget was

CHAPTER THIRTY-SEVEN

balanced. Thanks to the Phoenix Cycle, America had the ability to fix our problems—not as a one-off adjustment, but as part of an upgrade to the social contract, a new commitment to each other that we weren't going to allow these injustices to continue.

"It was wrong that the people of the United States were allowing twelve million children to go to sleep in poverty every night, it was wrong that we had two million people waking up in cages every morning, and it was wrong that we were spending a trillion dollars on the military-industrial complex while so many other needs went unmet.

"Advocates for incremental reform were stuck in a mindset of scarcity. They were asking for permission to make minor changes to a very broken system—could we please only have seven million children living in poverty?—instead of acknowledging that we had the ability to end poverty outright. Worse, we'd had that ability for decades and decades and hadn't used it. We'd known since the 1970s that our criminal justice system was moving in the wrong direction, and we hadn't changed course. We'd known about the dangers of the military-industrial complex for generations, and we allowed it to grow.

"The American Union was founded on a mindset of abundance. We didn't need permission to cooperate and deliver change, Julian; we needed forgiveness for allowing an unjust status quo to persist," Carlton concluded.

"That's an aspect of the fast for peace: atonement," Julian observed quietly.

"Especially on Muster Day, especially in those early years," Carlton agreed.

Grateful for all the knowledge he'd received that evening, Julian summarized the mechanics of time travel and invited Carlton and Idabee to a meeting in two days, when Polly Sigh would present her strategy for the 2024 election. "I'd appreciate your input," he told the gray-haired man.

Carlton agreed and suggested he come to Washington on May 1 to certify Julian as an organizer. "It would be nice to meet in person after all this time."

Julian was touched. This man had carried the faith for five decades and paid forward whatever investment CJ had made in him many times over. "Come early," Julian said. "If everything goes according to plan, I'm going to be blasted fifty-three years backward at noon." Carlton agreed, then excused himself, leaving Julian alone with the patiently waiting Idabee.

Idabee turned to him, and he marveled at the clarity of her bright smile. She began innocently enough with an invitation to the General Welfare committee meeting the next day. When he accepted, she opened up. "I know how much you like it when I talk about parliamentary procedure," Idabee said. "So what if we applied nonary logic to our problem?"

Julian accepted her premise that the blue envelope's truth was their mutual problem. "Okay," he replied, intrigued by the mischievous look she was giving him.

"First, we identify our variable. That's Julian–Idabee time, and it's going to drop to zero in a few weeks. Do we have consensus on the direction we'd like it to go?"

He played along. "Up?"

"More time, yes. Next, we decide whether to try and influence the supply or the demand for Julian–Idabee time. This seems like a supply-side problem; do you agree?" He did. "The supply of Julian in 2076 is going to disappear, but there will be an increase in 2023. Now, the supply of Idabee in 2023 is currently zero." She stared expectantly at him.

Julian laughed as her solution became clear. "Increase the Idabee supply in 2023? That's the answer? You want to travel back in time with me?"

"Of all the places I thought you might take me away to," she said solemnly, "I admit that was one I never considered."

"Idabee," he murmured.

"I already informed the Assembly Clerk this would be my last month," she continued earnestly. Her eyes brimmed with sincerity and hope. "On May 1, I'll be available to start a new adventure."

Truth had many facets, and Julian tried to show her the softest one. "It won't work," he said, and described the two oranges Charlotte had brought for her lunch, and how only one had arrived in their world. "They're parallel worlds; we probably wouldn't arrive in the same place."

CHAPTER THIRTY-SEVEN

She was a persistent woman. "What if there was a way?"

"Idabee," Julian said. A harder aspect of the truth was needed. "No. This isn't a vacation." A ripple of anger moved within him, frustration at his inability to communicate, but the placidity from their fast pulled it flat. "Edith seems to think I'm going to spend two years lounging around, then rush in at the last minute and stop Connor Sullivan's team so we can live happily after. No. Delroy and I, and"—he gestured to where Carlton had been—"everyone else we can get, are going to build a national political movement from scratch."

"I know, Julian," Idabee replied. "I can help."

"Are you good with social media?" Julian asked. "Do you know any influencers? Any contacts with the press—or political advocacy groups? Idabee, can you drive a car?"

"I can learn," she insisted, but her voice exposed the cracks in her certainty.

He reached out a hand, palm up, across the space between them on the couch. Idabee mimicked his movement; the warm, tingling sensation when she rested her holographic hand on his, palm down, was no substitute for physical contact. "I know you could. But you're asking me to commit to being responsible for you. Remember what Carlton said? Something about how that energy should be directed to the whole community instead of valuing one relationship over the rest of humanity."

"Yes, Julian," she shot back. "I've heard his celibacy-experiment talk several times. But I've never had it applied to me before."

"It's another solution to your nonary logic," he said softly. "If the demand for Idabee drops to zero, there's no problem." Julian held her gaze as he said it, and saw her heart sink.

She floundered for an explanation. "Your letter said we had no future in the tricentennial. How can you be so sure we don't have a future back then? Because you're planning one with my grandmother?"

He refused to take the bait. "I'm sorry it didn't work out, Idabee." The Archive had images from CJ's wedding; she had been radiant, just like Edith was with AJ. They were each a beautiful rose in a dung heap of an alternate history, and he was willing to take responsibility for building a better one. Another sliver of Chavez's speech came to mind: *the strongest act of manliness is to sacrifice ourselves for others.* "I'll see you tomorrow."

Chapter Thirty-Eight

The following evening, while waiting in the parlor for Teara Harper to arrive, Julian watched Ray fidget anxiously. At dinner, he'd made a halfhearted suggestion that he might skip Julian's discussion with the economist. Julian reminded him of their first conversation about the US Treasury and Ray's admission that he didn't know all the details. Tonight, those would be cleared up.

Julian had spent the afternoon with Idabee as she participated in a full committee work session. They met in person, so they could converse without disturbing anyone else's holographic viewing. River Place Towers' virtual conference room was heavily attended; digital avatars stacked a dozen deep in each chair produced multiheaded human hybrids with far too many arms. Julian kept an eye out in case Connor Sulivan appeared among the holographic forms moving about. Reverend Shaver had requested Julian *consider the possibility that he's looking to apologize.* Julian had.

Like the assembly session, explainer videos prefaced each policy proposal, but here the delegates debated—sometimes fiercely—the merits. Idabee demonstrated how members could submit questions through the committee sage, who, assisted by artificial intelligence, frequently uncovered answers to individual queries without taking up the full committee's time. The discretion made people more willing to ask about things they didn't know. Remaining questions and comments were managed by the committee moderator, Delegate Denton, which he often directed to the head of the subcommittee or investigative panel who'd done the groundwork.

Julian lost interest as the afternoon dragged by. Idabee's conversation kept it bearable, but he saw that his refusal to consider accepting her help in the past still bothered her. Did she regret her decision to resign her assembly seat at the end of the month? When the committee session was over, Idabee left promptly, leaving Julian to return to Ray's condo alone.

Relaxing back into the parlor couch, Julian ran a hand over his scalp for the dozenth time that day, enjoying more texture than he'd felt in years. His doctor noticed the motion. "How's the hair?" Ray asked.

"For real, that cream smelled foul! But it's working."

"It wouldn't be much of a cure if it didn't," the doctor grinned. The expression faded quickly; there was something on his friend's mind, Julian decided.

A cold front arrived in the room along with Teara Harper. Her robe-clad casualness from their breakfast table discussion was gone; the lines of her suit, crisp and sharp, accentuated her bearing. Having chosen a place on the loveseat across from Julian, the economist angled slightly away from Ray when he touched his palms together in greeting. "Hi, Julian. Nice to see you again," she said.

He reciprocated, thanked her for meeting with him, and summarized what he'd learned so far. "I understand everyone gets a Treasury account, and unconditional basic income is paid into it with Treasury Dollars—debt-free money. But I'm still not clear on all the details of how it came about."

Teara began with questions. "Are you familiar with the Phoenix Cycle?" Julian's confident nod ended abruptly when the economist continued, "and the way our banking and monetary systems were upgraded at each stage?" He quickly shook his head. "Have you heard the phrase 'not worth a continental'?"

Julian hadn't, but Ray answered. "It was the money they printed during the Revolutionary War, and it became almost worthless—there was some quote about a wagon load of money scarcely buying a wagon load of provisions."

CHAPTER THIRTY-EIGHT

"That's correct," Teara said neutrally, not looking at the doctor, and launched into her explanation.

"The first iteration of the Phoenix Cycle found thirteen of the British colonies forming the United States under the Articles of Confederation. The Continental Congress was authorized to create money—continentals—but prohibited from creating taxes that would have pulled them back out of circulation! That fundamental flaw led directly to widespread inflation and indirectly to Shays' Rebellion a few years later, after Massachusetts farmers couldn't pay their taxes with the currency they'd earned soldiering during the war.

"In 1787, the Framers produced the Constitution, giving the new Congress the responsibility to create money plus the power to tax it back. Alexander Hamilton, Secretary of the Treasury, asked Congress to charter a national bank as part of a multifaceted solution, which it did. He consolidated debt from the Revolutionary War and increased revenue from tariffs and excise taxes. The bank money it issued wasn't a national currency, but the notes circulated widely, and the government would accept them for payment of taxes. America quickly found its financial feet, although Hamilton was limited in how he could manage the national economy since mailing letters was the fastest form of communication."

There was a brief moment of silence, and Julian wondered why Teara had added extra stress to her final word. When Ray shifted awkwardly on the couch, he considered she intended it as a public/private denunciation of the doctor's faults.

"In the next iteration," the economist continued, "the telegraph had been invented, enabling the Panic of 1857. When banks started to fail because of the speculative loans they'd been making, the rapid spread of the news caused the first national, then international, financial crisis.

"After Abraham Lincoln won the presidency in 1860, demand for government bonds dropped. Bidders demanded interest rates as high as 36%, so Congress passed legislation directing the Treasury to issue legal tender—paper money not generally redeemable for gold or silver but required by law to be accepted for payments. Greenbacks were base money and our first national currency. Lincoln also signed the National Banking Acts, regulating the banking system from coast to coast as well as could be done with the telegraph.

"Greenbacks, full employment, massive government spending, and supply shortages created inflationary pressures. The United States established the first income tax on the top 3% of earners, imposed excise taxes on many goods and services, and encouraged people to put their money into government bonds instead of making purchases."

"Promoting delayed gratification?" Julian asked.

"You can think of it like that," Teara agreed. "It's one way to address demand-pull inflation—don't pull so hard."

She took a breath before continuing, still not looking at Ray. "Four generations later, Franklin Delano Roosevelt was elected during the Great Depression. The problem then was deflation; the circulation of money in the economy had slowed dramatically. Prices fell in a desperate attempt to entice purchases, crushing many farmers who were unable to recover their production costs. Factories didn't need to produce as much as before, so workers were laid off, which meant they didn't have as much to spend, so factories didn't need to produce as much as before, and so on. The deflationary death spiral drove the unemployment rate in cities like Chicago and Detroit as high as 50%. FDR addressed this problem by taking the US off the gold standard and putting more money into circulation through government spending."

"Wasn't this similar to one of the People's Party's demands?" Julian asked. "To grow the money supply by including silver?" Ray lifted an eyebrow at the obscure knowledge he'd received from Polly Sigh.

"It was," Teara said. "They had made a big deal in 1896 about how deflation was hurting the farmers. However, wheat prices rose just before the election, thanks to poor harvests in India, Australia, and Russia. It negated their most powerful argument, even though the underlying structural problem hadn't been addressed. Then the Klondike gold rush increased the money supply and really took the wind out of the sails of the silver movement.

CHAPTER THIRTY-EIGHT

"America needed a more permanent solution by the time the Phoenix Cycle rolled around. Taking us off the gold standard enabled the economic growth that was so desperately needed, but FDR created powerful enemies when he did so. The administration was also able to enact two Banking Acts, boosting regulations now that the telephone was the fastest form of communication. Unfortunately, borrowing bank money into existence remained the primary method of growing the money supply, which of course led to tens of trillions in unpayable debt by your time."

Julian nodded soberly but inwardly chuckled in anticipation of the next part of the story. The internet was a huge advance from what he thought of as snail mail.

"In the fourth iteration of the Phoenix Cycle, the first American Union legislative package upgraded our money by paying unconditional basic income in base money—sovereign currency," Teara reminded him. "Instantaneous global communication let us upgrade banking as well. Every citizen received a US Treasury account with the ability to transfer funds to any other account, completely separate from the for-profit banking system."

Julian stroked his goatee before speaking. "The history lesson was cool—I had no idea how it all tied together—but this is the part I was hoping you could explain."

"Cash has always been free to use," Teara said. "You could take a ten dollar bill to the store, and when you physically handed over the money, the storekeeper received all ten dollars. But by the twenty-first century, most transactions were electronic, and banks extracted a percentage. Their payment system was like a toll road that people had to use to conduct business; bank fees added about 2% to the cost of all goods and services sold in the United States.

"Treasury accounts created a free public payment infrastructure, which translated into lower prices for consumers and more economic opportunities. Micropayments changed the way the internet functioned, allowing sites to collect tiny amounts instead of depending on subscriptions or ad revenue.

"Other countries had already done this. India, for example, had a nonprofit overseeing their public payment infrastructure, and by 2022, they were processing four times more digital payments than the US, Britain, Germany, and France combined. They were also leading the way in connecting with the platforms of other nations, like Singapore. The US was at risk of falling behind in global financial relevance.

"The Phoenix Cycle helped us become a leader in innovation again because we overhauled the monetary system along with the banking system. As we've talked about, Julian, the moral way to add to the money supply is by distributing it universally and unconditionally to every citizen, and a digital currency is the most practical way. Once citizen accounts were in place, the Treasury made accounts available to businesses and other residents. And of course, all government offices accepted Treasury Dollars for taxes and fees. Creating a public payment infrastructure was the real purpose of the American Union Jobs Program."

Julian laughed. "You've given me three different real reasons!"

Teara laughed too. "Some aspects really jump out, depending on what I'm talking about. But establishing a public payment infrastructure really was an essential part."

"But weren't digital dollars inevitable, even without the Phoenix Cycle? Cash was becoming less common."

"Maybe," Teara conceded, "but Treasury Dollar Bills were different because they were interest-free base money. Without the American Union, there would have been a very different policy choice made. In March 2022, President Biden issued an executive order related to cryptocurrencies and digital dollars. He defined the terms very carefully. Cryptocurrencies, created by individuals, were defined as digital assets. Digital dollars, on the other hand, were defined as digital liabilities, which would have ensured the US borrowed money into existence for a long time to come."

Julian nodded. "So Treasury Dollar Bills were a cryptocurrency, like bitcoin?"

"No," Teara corrected. "They were both digital assets, but very different in how they were made. Treasury Dollar Bills were created by the US

CHAPTER THIRTY-EIGHT

Treasury, our central bank, while bitcoin was generated by a set-it-and-forget-it algorithm. The thing about money, Julian, is that for it to hold a stable value, it has to be managed as economic conditions change. This is why every nation in the world gave up the gold standard. It was inherently unstable because no one could manage the amount of gold."

Without breaking her gaze from Julian, Teara waved a dismissive hand toward Ray. "Remember how he said it would have been malpractice to prescribe a fixed amount of blood in the body? It's blood pressure that serves as a measurement of health—how well the body is managing the supply. Money is like that; a stable value is a sign of good health.

"Bitcoin could never hold a stable value because it was designed to generate artificial scarcity. While you were sleeping, Julian, the quantity of bitcoins expanded from 19.3 million to 20.8 million—an 8% increase. The world's population, however, rose more than 30%."

"But it's still around?" Julian asked. "I saw billboards in my neighborhood encouraging people to buy it, promising their kids would thank them."

Teara smiled. "Ponzi schemes depend on new investors. Bitcoin declared that a collection of digital ones and zeros was an asset. By 2030, conventional wisdom recognized it could never serve as a functional currency, and that asset became a collection of mostly zeros."

Julian nodded. "Debt-free money and a public payment infrastructure sound better than what the banks had going on: charging interest to borrow money into existence plus fees for people to spend it—what a scam! But I'll bet some people objected, worried about privacy and big government."

"Treasury accounts were an essential part of ending poverty, mass incarceration, and the endless wars," Teara said. "So, yes, spreading fear around them was one tactic used by those who profited from the status quo.

"If you think about it, a primary reason people had lost faith in government in the decades leading up to the fourth Phoenix Cycle was that they recognized it wasn't serving their needs. The American Union helped restore that faith by giving citizens agency to influence national policy. When it came to crafting the details around Treasury accounts, delegates were able to ensure legitimate concerns were addressed through the people's legislative assembly.

"Since the Treasury was required to establish an account for every citizen, additional privacy protections were included. Their transactions could be anonymized, so no details were recorded except the amount. People could always withdraw their money as cash; the Treasury used post offices for access to ATMs and in-person banking services. And actually using the US Treasury account was—and still is—optional. Private banks offer pass-through accounts, where American Union Job wages are directly deposited."

"What were people afraid of?" Ray asked.

Teara ignored him and gestured to Julian, who answered, "Well, the idea was that if the government controlled digital dollars, they could cut people off from access to the system, manipulate their behavior, or spy on them."

The economist laughed. "As if private banks weren't doing all of those things already! One analogy I've heard, Julian, compared Treasury accounts and the public payment system to the development of the interstate highway system in the 1950s. This public infrastructure for transportation had many positive benefits for America's economy—goods could be moved around faster and cheaper; the network of roads encouraged tourism, which spurred more business development; and it helped unify America, connecting rural and urban areas and opening up more job opportunities.

"But giving the federal government greater control over the nation's roads raised concerns. What if they threatened to withhold highway funds from states? Similarly, driver's licenses might be taken from individuals to cut off their access to the system. In a non-zero number of cases, these came true. Millions of people lost their licenses for reasons unrelated to driving, like unpaid court debts. States were coerced into raising the drinking age to twenty-one and enacting mandatory seat belt laws.

"Even if they'd seen this future, would it have been reason enough to not build the interstate system? I don't think you could find anyone willing to claim that the United States would be better off without it.

"As it turns out, Julian, since the protections for Treasury accounts were

CHAPTER THIRTY-EIGHT

baked into the original legislation, there haven't been any systemic abuses or even any serious attempts. Because universality is one of the core principles of the American Union, members of Congress know if they violate it, the next legislative package will force them to either reverse course or commit electoral suicide. As a universal program, it's incredibly popular: everyone gets an American Union Job. Social Security was the same way in your time; it had been around for ninety years without ever being used to manipulate seniors' behavior, only to improve their lives.

"A public payment system enabled other efficiencies as well. Americans used to spend billions of hours and dollars filing taxes each year. Once there were enough Treasury Dollar Bills circulating, the Treasury was able to offer free payroll services, like the Faroe Islands had done for decades, simplifying the process immensely.

"Julian, once the citizenry had control over the government, its economies of scale could offer all sorts of services better than the private sector."

Julian thanked Teara for her explanations. "Ray asked me a few weeks ago if I knew all the details of how my cell phone worked, and of course I didn't. But now I feel like I have something of a handle on how the American Union Jobs Program works.

"Idabee gave me this quote by FDR, 'The American people should control their money; their money should not control them.' It sounds like we really pulled it off," he concluded with a grin.

"You did," Teara agreed. "Did you smooth things out with Idabee? You seemed pretty down about it."

"No," he replied, "it's not going to work out."

"That's too bad," she said. "What happened between you?" She settled back, folded her arms lightly, and gave him her full attention.

Julian hesitated. Teara had been extraordinarily helpful in understanding how the United States had addressed the economic injustice he had known all his life. But explaining the troubles that time travel had caused—and even that there was such a thing—seemed like more than he wanted to disclose. It was a thoughtful offer, but he said, "It's really too complicated to get into."

"That's okay," Teara said, her tone suggesting the exact opposite. She invited Julian to reach out with any other questions and said goodbye to him—and only him—before disappearing.

Ray sat quietly as Teara's indicator light turned red before disappearing a moment later. "Wow," he said. "Sorry about that."

Julian leaned back and turned to face his friend. "She is not happy with you," he agreed.

"We had a good time the other night, but it's not going anywhere," Ray said. He rolled his neck and took a deep breath. "Look, she wanted to know the same thing from me; details about what happened with you and Idabee. I wouldn't tell her—your whole time travel thing isn't really my story to share."

Once again, Julian was touched by his host's discretion. "I appreciate that, but you didn't have to let it break up your relationship." Ray's integrity, like his daughter's, impressed him. "That was why Teara said something about communication?"

"Well, not just that," Ray admitted. "It was probably something else I told her; I've been meaning to give you a heads up, too." Julian waited as Ray scratched the back of his neck. "Stella and I got to talking—we're going to give things another try. She's coming out from Seattle for the weekend."

Julian laughed uproariously. "You're getting back together with your ex? That's probably the reason, for real." Ray's bashful expression only made him laugh harder. Finally, he sobered. "I guess I can appreciate your dilemma."

"Of course you can!" Ray agreed heartily. "Teara and Stella are both fine-looking women. Now, on the other hand," he said, rising from the couch to exit the parlor, "I can not relate to your dilemma, trying to choose between my daughter and my mother."

It was true, Julian realized. Elsewhere in the multiverse, on this very day, in countries that had been torn apart by civil war, there was a Julian West involved with each of them. For all of Ray's positive qualities, for all of the social benefits he generated as a doctor, he couldn't relate to a choice to willingly abstain from both of them. For Ray, Muster Day's fast for peace was something to be endured rather than an experience to be opened up to.

Julian saw all this without judgment and began to smile. He was a flawed human being too, just like Ray and every other person on the planet, each with the ability to evolve. Hadn't Gandhi said racist things? The faculty for self-improvement was a strand that bound all of humanity together; a braid of possibility for individuals, cultures, and countries. It was beautiful, the potential for greatness within everyone, and joy began to flow through him, naked awe at the interconnectedness of life.

Connor Sullivan's capabilities were part of this tapestry, Julian recognized, and he realized he'd made another decision Ray wouldn't understand.

He wanted to listen to the man who'd tried to kill him.

Chapter Thirty-Nine

"Ray won't tell me what the journal said about our past," Edith complained to Julian. She stood in the open doorway to his bedroom, arms crossed in front of her slender frame, demanding answers. "What was it? We had a life together, didn't we?"

It was nearly noon on Friday, a few hours before Polly Sigh was going to present her proposal for a 2024 election strategy to Julian and those helping him prepare. Before that, he planned to talk with Reverend Shaver and ask him to facilitate a conversation with Connor Sullivan. The wrongness of how he'd left their previous encounter bothered him, and he hoped to clear his conscience.

Ray had been in an especially good mood all morning, cleaning up the condo in preparation for Stella Freedom's arrival. She was bringing a parting gift for Julian: a flash drive, backward compatible with Windows 10, containing an archive of election results and the American Union legislative packages for ten years, plus a general world history for the last five decades. Ray promised to help him download the journal entries from AJ, BJ, and CJ from the National Archive; he would bring those back and install them on his website.

Edith was waiting for an answer; from his seat at the desk, Julian felt compelled to tell her the truth. "I was wrong to suggest that you were only at the reparations rally because I gave you the date," he admitted. "Once upon a time, we met there spontaneously. Remember when Reverend Shaver was shot, and you pulled my arm and suggested we run?" She nodded. "On that occasion, the Julian West with you—I call him AJ—agreed

CHAPTER THIRTY-NINE

to flee from the six gunmen. You two escaped the slaughter unharmed, and you kept him safe as the city began to burn. During the weeks of race riots that followed, he fell hard for you, and it seems like it was mutual, because Julian and Edith West were married for five decades." The wedding had seemed ridiculously extravagant to AJ, but the honeymoon offered a deep draught of relaxation that soon proved impossible to replicate.

"I knew it," Edith said triumphantly. "I knew it." She crossed the room, opening her arms for him, and Julian rose from his seat. Their embrace reverberated with the echoes of those decades, but when she kissed him, he released her.

"No," he said simply.

"No?"

"No," Julian continued from an arm's length away. "AJ is an alternate Julian, Edith; I'm not him." That reality had been blurry when he first began to read from the Archive, its entries coupled with pictures of himself decades older, but separate names for each of his iterations had helped clarify the distinction. "Ray will share the journal when I'm gone and you'll see how much it cost the country. The assassination moved us to the edge of the precipice, and we fell into civil war a few years later. AJ wrote about the struggles of fleeing south with a baby and a pregnant wife. You settled in what became the Republic of Carolina after the United States fell apart and raised a family there."

The photographs AJ preserved constructed a story almost as vivid as his written words. The deep desire for Edith was framed by his love for their family, but within the foundation was an obsession with the civil war. Their route out of Washington had taken them through the blackened husk of Richmond, firebombed early on, and his pictures recorded the death and destruction. His camera's lens often captured other atrocities during the years of fighting.

"AJ loved you all very much, but he always felt guilty for not standing to fight at the rally," Julian continued. "You and Charlotte kept in touch—her husband was among the eight million who died in the war—and eventually started searching for ways to try and change the past. Then she found one."

Edith stood enraptured by the story. He'd once suspected her of being the puppeteer pulling his strings across the decades, and there was some truth to that.

"That's how much you loved AJ, Edith. You were willing to sacrifice your remaining years together to help him assuage his guilt, and it worked. When Charlotte pushed him back in time, he stopped the assassination and the civil war; the American Union came about instead of a marital union."

"I don't understand," she said. "You—CJ—had a wedding ring."

"His marriage happened during the three years of waiting for the next time orbit to open," Julian explained. "He sacrificed that relationship in order to steer the world we live in." BJ's misguided motivations had desperately needed unraveling.

"That relationship?" Edith repeated, her eyes searching his face for clues about who it was—or confirmation of her suspicion. Soon enough, she'd see the pictures of CJ and Idabee enjoying their honeymoon in Cuba. Would her granddaughter criticize her for disrupting the life that might have been?

Edith's worldview was crumbling before his eyes. "I could have woken you up decades ago," she said bitterly. "After the first successful revivals took place, I planned on it. Ray was ten; he would have had two good men as father figures. Then a blue envelope arrived, telling me that time travel hadn't been invented yet, but in thirty years it would be. You asked me to have you revived on February 15, 2076, and I changed your medical records so that would happen."

Julian, who already knew what CJ had done, replied, "Thank you."

"Why?" she asked. "Why did you want to wait, unless you were going to go back to meet me while you were still young?"

From the hallway, the soft tone announcing a visitor in the parlor could be heard. It was certainly Shaver arriving, but Julian answered Edith's question anyway. "That was the date CJ's predecessor—I call him BJ—was revived. The expectation was that certain things would work out the same." The duplicated connection to Idabee had led to Philadelphia on the exact

CHAPTER THIRTY-NINE

same Sunday. "CJ feared he'd failed to start the American Union and hoped to position me to try again. And here I am."

"Here you are," she repeated. "And I missed out on the life we would have had."

Julian sighed. "It's not the only thing you missed out on," he said.

Edith looked unconvinced as Ray appeared in the doorway, rapping on the jamb. "Reverend Shaver is in the parlor. Are you ready?"

Without breaking eye contact with Edith, Julian answered, "Ray, can you give me a few minutes? I'll meet you in there. We're almost done." His host's retreat was followed by the parlor door opening and closing.

"Can I read you something AJ wrote?" Julian asked. Switching off the holographic display from his tablet so that Edith wouldn't recognize the green and blue border as being from the National Archive, Julian pulled up one of AJ's journal entries. He read aloud the single sentence that encapsulated his ancestor's motives, taking breaths when he could and varying his tone between clauses, Edith listening with growing emotion.

> (October 26, 2072) When Charlotte told us the time window to prevent Reverend Shaver's assassination will put me back a month before Edith's rape—that tiger which stalked our bedroom for years, mauling our intimacy without warning, leaping out after some movement, some touch, ignited a memory; pouncing on her happiness, leaving her wounded, crying, curled in a fetal position on the far edge of the bed with the beast warning me away, the no-man's-land between us still warm from our interrupted exchange of friction, its feline lips twisted into a taunting smile at my impotence to appeal the sentence of inconsolability, knowing the predator who unleashed this predator was forever outside of my reach, a stranger whose blurred face had perhaps been glimpsed a single time across a crowded room when her dancing, the frenetic release of the week's accumulated tensions, ground to a halt even as the band played on, making the words "that was him" audible only to

a husband sharply attuned to his wife's frequency; the sharp tug of her hand announced our departure, the flight delayed by the entering couple who reeked of weed, permitting my quick survey of the sea of faces, scanning for a spark of recognition, of conquest, of triumph, of contempt at our retreat, even knowing the attempt to fish significance from the ocean of indifference was grasping at smoke; thick, oily smoke as if we'd doused the club in gasoline and lit a match, burning it to ashes, scorching the earth, abolishing in perpetuity the possibility of return to what had been until forty-nine seconds earlier one of our favorite Friday night pleasures, destroying it to give physical form to the unspoken commitment made as we passed united over the threshold—I knew it wasn't coincidence, but destiny.

Edith's eyes were misty when he concluded. "Thank you," she said softly.

"Whatever Charlotte's machine does, I'm not creating a world where that happens," Julian said. "August 15, Fifth Edition; I'll be there that night. I promise, Edith."

"All night?" she asked, her hopeful plea like a flower yearning for the warm rays of the sun.

Julian sighed. "No."

"One night, Julian," Edith wheedled. For her, the relationship was a fantasy constructed over the decades. AJ's journal was a window into what had been reality elsewhere in the multiverse.

Julian waved the tablet, drawing attention to the knowledge it held, and set it down. "Looking backward at those decades together, knowing everything I know–" He clutched her hands, staring deep into eyes so open and wide that Julian imagined he could see Edith's very soul. "What makes you so confident I could stop after a single night with you?" Julian exhaled. "Zero is safer; I'll have work to do." He allowed a moment for her to respond before continuing, "Like I do now." Edith released his hands, stepping aside, and he left the bedroom.

In the parlor, Ray looked up anxiously as he entered. "He just walked in,"

CHAPTER THIRTY-NINE

Ray said reassuringly to Shaver. The nonagenarian was slumped back on the loveseat, thin arms folded against his chest, as if attempting to hold onto whatever energy he had left.

Julian scrutinized him as he made his way to the couch. "He doesn't look well," he said privately to Ray before taking a seat; the doctor nodded. Shaver's face brightened when the third indicator light turned green, and Julian appeared in his view.

"Julian," he said, "you wanted to see me?" Shaver leaned forward, his hands resting on his knees as he awaited Julian's response.

"I came into some new information," Julian began, summarizing the existence of the journal and the history of the alternate worlds. "You'd asked me before how the fast for peace could have been based on your work, and I didn't have an answer for you. Now I do."

After explaining how the disputed 2028 election had left the nation divided, triggering a civil war in two parallel worlds, Julian described the preacher's call for a national day of fasting on January 15, 2029. Shaver smiled as he recognized the date. "The centenary of Dr. King's birth."

"Congress deadlocked for three days in selecting a president and vice president," Julian continued, "no thanks to the Speaker of the House, who realized they would claim the Oval Office if no decision was reached. You suggested a trade to resolve the impasse: enactment of a handful of progressive policies in exchange for the Republican's inauguration."

"Sounds like the election of 1876," Shaver said, "and the deal to end Reconstruction."

"Except instead of being a backroom deal, it was front-page news. You asked the American people to give their consent through the fast. It was a fast for peace, you said, and it worked. Civil war was averted, and you established that fasts of moral pressure could direct policy. Different groups tried to repeat it, eventually combining to form the American Union."

Shaver thanked him for the explanation. "Julian, I hoped you wanted to talk about Connor Sullivan," he said, then fell silent.

Julian nodded agreement, acutely aware of Ray's eyes on him. "Something happened the other night," he began, describing the conversation with Stella Freedom about prison reform. "We talked about solitary confinement, and I imagined participating in the fast for peace from inside a cell, cut off from the world but connected to a web of people through our shared experience.

"And then I felt it—what I'd only glimpsed the month before. The thread of my life was part of a greater tapestry, not just of those who were fasting but of everyone. There was such joy in that connection, Alvin, like a warm and nurturing ocean of understanding." This time, the man's given name felt natural.

Reverend Shaver seemed to gain additional strength from Julian's words. "Agape love is the foundation of the beloved community," he said. "A powerful love for all of humanity, unconditionally."

"It was the afternoon of the fourteenth," Julian continued. "I planned on starting my fast for peace after dinner, but that feeling made me realize I already had. To eat dinner would have been to willfully break it and sever that connection I was experiencing."

"When the Apostle Paul was transformed on the road to Damascus," the reverend said, "he fasted for three days."

"I didn't go that far," Julian said, "and it's faded now, but I felt the humanity in Connor. You said you've fasted for peace with him, and however many millions of others. Can you invite him to join us again? I want to apologize for refusing to listen last week."

"Wait," Ray interjected. "You want to apologize to the man who tried to kill you?"

"Maybe we're not the same men anymore," Julian said.

Shaver retrieved a tablet from the end table. His thin hands wavered as they tapped on the digital surface. "Compassion and understanding can traverse many barriers," he said to Julian, "including prison walls. Connor spent many years incarcerated in voluntary isolation, away from the less compassionate souls who would have harmed him."

Julian nodded. "I would have expected him to get shivved pretty quick." Ray gave him a quizzical look, and he explained the archaic verb, "Stabbed with a makeshift weapon."

The air grew thick with tension as the three men waited in silence. Julian tried to summon the deep empathy he'd recently experienced, but instead found his heart was beating faster. A few weeks ago, Edith had asked why he'd smuggled a lead pipe into a peaceful rally. It was hard to imagine that a Julian West with an American Union Job would have felt that way, but he could remember the frustration and lack of options that had driven him to an action that felt so foreign in hindsight. Would he be able to apply that same understanding to Connor?

A fourth indicator light appeared, bright red.

He was about to find out.

Chapter Forty

Julian inhaled deeply as Connor Sullivan began to take form on the loveseat next to Reverend Shaver, and what had been theoretical became reality. The piercing blue eyes targeted him with the first flicker, and Julian exhaled, expanding his view as each new flash came. Connor's wispy gray hair only extended a hand's width above his ears but was neatly combed back. He wore a button-up white shirt over tan khakis, and the expression on his clean-shaven face was friendly but guarded as it solidified.

They sized each other up for a moment. Julian was very aware that he was face-to-face with the man who'd tried to kill him, recognizing intellectually that Connor was face-to-face with the man who'd killed his friends and would have tried to kill him if he had ammunition. There was a non-zero amount of similarity between their actions.

"Mr. West," Connor said, pressing his palms together in greeting. "I appreciate you hearing me out." With his hands lifted, Julian saw a yellow stain about the size of a silver dollar on Connor's otherwise clean shirt. The septuagenarian promptly placed his arm over the discoloration, hiding it, and Julian felt a stirring of empathy.

"First, I want to thank you for what you did," Connor continued. "If you hadn't stopped Clive and Vincent, who knows how many other people might have been hurt? I don't know if you have any guilt, or regrets about killing them, but you shouldn't. You did the right thing—they would have done the same to you." His steel blue eyes were intense, laser-focused on Julian, and projected sincerity.

Julian nodded to the gray-haired man, indicating he should go on. "I

CHAPTER FORTY

also want to apologize and ask for your forgiveness. Not just as the man who shot you, but as the man who orchestrated the whole assault. The evil things I did back then, Mr. West, the harm I caused, I can never undo. It's a burden I still carry to this day.

"I'm not asking you to ignore what I've done. If I can quote Dr. King, forgiveness means 'the evil act no longer remains as a barrier to the relationship.' Can you forgive me—see me as a man who has made mistakes and tried to do better?"

The feeling of agape love and empathy no longer overwhelmed him, but Julian knew it was still within him. "Yes," Julian replied. "And I'm sorry for refusing to listen to you last week."

Connor released a wry chuckle. "There was a counselor that worked with me," he said. "One of his favorite phrases was, 'Your actions may not have been justifiable, but that doesn't preclude them from being understandable.' It was very understandable, Mr. West."

That understanding furthered his belief he was doing the right thing. "Call me Julian," he said. Ray watched him skeptically. "Can you help me understand how you ended up like that?"

Connor began his story. "I was raised by a single mom, me and my two younger sisters. After my dad left, she moved us back to Kentucky—I was eight—to be closer to her family, so they could help us. We were poor, but so was everyone else. There was just never enough money." Julian found himself nodding in recognition.

"I knew things were broken in America, and when I was in high school, I found some websites with a nice, neat explanation—it was the fault of the blacks and the jews." Connor scratched at his chin. "My grandfather had a slew of racist jokes, so white supremacy wasn't much of a stretch, but what was compelling was the sense of identity it offered. That community had an atmosphere of purpose that I wasn't seeing anywhere else. They were going to fix things.

"Alvin brought me a book in prison, *Breaking Hate*. The author was a former skinhead from a white-power band, and he'd founded an organization to help others emerge from the dark world of hate. His theory was that humans seek ICP—identity, community, and purpose—and that young people who'd been radicalized hadn't been finding it elsewhere. That resonated with me because it was my experience.

"Shooting you haunted me for a long time, Mr. West—Julian. When it came out that you'd been frozen at the moment of death, I didn't know if I'd actually killed you or if you'd survive." Connor offered a small smile. "I'm glad you recovered."

"So am I," Julian admitted. Hearing Connor's story was a bit unnerving, remembering that he'd been an angry young man not long ago. He was fortunate his family and neighborhood had provided him with a sense of identity and community. "What snapped you out of it?"

"Alvin helped," Connor admitted. "The first weeks in jail were pretty sobering. We hadn't started a race war, my friends were dead, and I was going to be locked up for a long, long time. I skimmed his hospital speech in the paper, looking to see if he'd said anything about us. He had. With the invitation to fast for peace, he called us out and said there was no obligation to be the same person afterward, that we were worthy of redemption.

"I ignored it, but after I saw some of the footage of the April 15 march, I wondered if I'd missed out. When he announced that the fast for peace would continue as a way to lobby Congress in the midterms, I actually felt some hope. Maybe there was another way to fix America."

Connor gave a thankful look to Reverend Shaver before turning his full focus back to Julian. "That was the real purpose of the American Union," he said emphatically. "To offer a new political identity that avoided demonizing anyone, a community built around the principles of nonviolence, and to give people a clear sense of purpose, a call to action based on our constitutional duties."

Julian laughed. "Everyone gives me a different reason for the American Union Jobs Program." His face fell still. "But you didn't say that. You said the American Union."

"The American Union was modeled on a Gandhian constructive program," Reverend Shaver reminded him. "It wasn't just our political structure that was in need of healing."

CHAPTER FORTY

The room fell silent for a moment. Julian briefly debated revealing the possibility of time travel to Connor Sullivan, but any possibility of cooperation with him in the past seemed terribly unlikely.

"Do you know how Gandhi died?" Reverend Shaver asked suddenly, his previously slumped shoulders now held upright with a sense of purpose. It was as if a fire had been lit within him, perhaps ignited by the reconciliation he'd facilitated. Without waiting for a response, he launched into an answer. "He was tested. His decades of work toward a free and independent India had produced bitter fruit. As the British left, they carved the subcontinent into pieces—Gandhi called it vivisection—and put millions of families on the wrong side of the new borders."

"I heard about the August 15 fast for peace," Julian said.

Shaver nodded and continued. "In January 1948, Gandhi was in New Delhi. The capital of India was in crisis. Trainloads of Hindu and Sikh refugees poured in daily from Pakistan. Mosques were gutted to house the new arrivals. Nationwide, violence between the different religions had claimed hundreds of thousands of lives. Could calmer heads still prevail?

"Gandhi was willing to gamble his life—again—on his belief that all humans possessed an inherent ability for self-improvement. The seventy-eight-year-old announced he would begin an indefinite fast to try to restore peace, admitting 'Death for me would be a glorious deliverance rather than that I should be a helpless witness to the destruction of India.' The fast pushed his aged body to its limits; his kidneys started shutting down after just a few days. After decades of sacrifice, his internal organs were all he had left to offer."

Julian's mouth fell open, and Shaver caught his eye. "I've never fasted beyond twenty-four days, but I had quite a bit of fat to burn back then. They say there's a wall you hit—true hunger—where your body lets you know it has nothing left to spare. I admire the fortitude it must have taken to continue."

"How long did he live?" Julian asked solemnly.

"On the sixth day, more than one hundred community leaders brought him an agreement that they, themselves, with no help from the government or police, would guarantee the peace. They would lead by example, even at the cost of their own lives, and Gandhi broke his fast with a glass of juice.

"Two days later," Shaver continued with a grim smile accentuating the deep lines of wisdom etched into his face, "Gandhi was lamenting at his nightly prayer meeting how many white Americans didn't care that blacks were being lynched in the South. Would-be assassins detonated a bomb nearby, planning to attack during the confusion. They were Hindu extremists, offended by what they saw as support for Pakistan, but they lost their nerve when Gandhi encouraged those around him to keep calm. After the assassination attempt, the police asked Gandhi to restrict access to his prayer meetings; they wanted to search attendees."

"This was his test?"

Shaver nodded. "Gandhi immediately refused. His life was his message, a core belief in the fundamental goodness of all human beings. Distrusting people, even for self-preservation, would have corrupted that message. On January 30, a fellow Hindu ended his life with three bullets at point-blank range. Like Jesus, he was murdered on a Friday.

"Gandhi's final sacrifice worked. India and Pakistan united in shock. The wave of death and destruction the partition had sent crashing down on the subcontinent began to recede. It forced people out of apathy—abstaining was no longer an option. They had to accept responsibility for the binary choice that every community faces: trend toward peace and justice, or away from it. Nonviolence or nonexistence, as Dr. King phrased it." With that, Shaver fell silent.

Julian sat in quiet contemplation, trying to understand the purpose of Reverend Shaver's story. Then Connor spoke. "Alvin?" The nonagenarian was clutching his chest. "Are you okay?"

Reverend Shaver offered a beatific smile to the room, communicating a soul at peace, and then collapsed, his body slumping forward, passing frictionlessly through the hands that Connor stretched out instinctively, slipping from the loveseat, falling toward the floor mutely as his holographic form snapped into nothingness.

Chapter Forty-One

"That's so sad about Reverend Shaver," Idabee said, standing in Julian's bedroom door. He turned to see her mournful look, hands clutched right over left against her denim skirt, elbows tight against her muted green blouse. She met his eyes and admitted, "I was really looking forward to meeting him today."

"I'm sure he would have liked that," Julian said, rising to greet her. Ray had swung into action as soon as the nonagenarian had fallen, alerting paramedics to his physical location. When they reached him, the reverend was beyond revival.

The pair embraced; unlike her grandmother hours earlier, Idabee made no attempt to kiss him. Instead, Julian felt her arms weighing him, gauging the amount of comfort he might need, and he exhaled the accumulated tensions of the morning. He held her, grateful for everything she'd taught him, shared with him, explained to him. Their breathing slowed until they only existed in each other's arms.

When they separated, Idabee's gaze evaluated him. "How are you feeling?"

"Better, thank you," Julian said. "I'm glad I had a chance to meet him, and glad that he's going to help me in the past when I remind him of his childhood backgammon set." From the hall, the parlor emitted a single musical note, summoning their attention. The first guest had arrived. "I hope Polly has a good plan to take advantage of it."

"Well, let's find out," she said, and led the way.

Delroy was waiting on the couch, and chuckled as he saw six red indicator lights appear in quick succession—Edith, Ray, and Stella followed them into the parlor. "Lot of fuss over something we'll never know if it worked," he announced to the room. "But I have faith in Julian."

Julian took the other end of the couch, with Idabee snagging the chair beside him. Edith, not to be outdone, made herself comfortable in between the two men. Ray and Stella sat across from them on the loveseat, knees touching unobtrusively.

The sixth light turned out to be Professor Carlton, appearing next to Idabee with his hands pressed together in greeting. Idabee offered up a general introduction, then looked puzzled by Delroy's gleaming grin. "Sid's an old-school organizer," Delroy said, using the professor's given name. "He was one of the First Hundred back in the 2024 campaign."

Stella leaned forward to speak. "Until last week, I had no idea the American Union started that far back," she said. "Some historian, huh?"

"We filed the paperwork September 11, 2023," Delroy explained.

Idabee gasped. "That's my birthday!" She cast an adoring look at Julian.

Carlton cleared his throat. "It's the birthday of satyagraha, in 1906."

Delroy cackled. "I'm sure that's the real reason," he offered graciously.

Another tone sounded. Heads shifted to watch Charlotte Grayson flicker into the chair next to Delroy. She was dressed casually, silver hair cascading to her shoulders, and promptly waved to all the faces staring at her.

"You created those alternate histories?" Stella asked her with awe.

"Julian does most of the work," Charlotte replied. "All I'm going to do is kick him backward in time." She made a flicking motion with her fingers. "Again."

"It's so exciting," Stella said, placing her hand over Ray's. "Not that I'm trying to get rid of you, Julian, but I can't wait to read the journal after you leave. I've already started outlining the book I'll write. What do you think of this title: *Whispers Across Worlds*?" She smiled enthusiastically.

"What about *Warnings Across Worlds*?" Charlotte suggested. "Julian says my husband, Anton, was killed in the civil war."

"When did I say that?" Julian wondered. Charlotte produced an envelope, robin's-egg blue. "Okay," he announced to the room, "if anyone else has

CHAPTER FORTY-ONE

one of those that they haven't told me about, now's the time." Julian cast a suspicious look at Professor Carlton, who held up his hands innocently as everyone laughed.

"What did I miss?" said a new voice. Polly Sigh had slipped in during their laughter, filling the last empty seat at the far end of the room. The pink-haired woman grinned at the friendly faces and introduced herself.

"This is your show, Polly," Julian said as the group came to attention. "We've talked about pitting incumbents against challengers in Congress to create the leverage needed to pass the American Union legislative package. But how would you deal with the Trump–Biden rematch? It was a train wreck."

Polly sat up straighter in her chair, digital tablet clutched in her left hand while her right entered information. "Okay, participant screen sharing is enabled," she muttered to herself as Ray flashed a thumbs-up. "Here we go." Above her head, a large screen materialized with the candidates' faces. "Can you all see that?" Polly twisted to verify it was working.

"When Julian asked me to design this campaign, he said it was hypothetical." Polly tsked and continued. "As far as our history was concerned, 2024 was the culmination of decades of dysfunction. Moving up the American Union paradigm by two years could prevent millions of needless deaths worldwide, which makes this an exciting opportunity. Although the only candidates with a mathematical chance of winning in 2024 were Donald Trump and Joe Biden, there was a huge demand for other options.

"The American Union will have to present itself as a constructive alternative to partisan politics right up front. To frame the debate and ensure that both candidates emerge with dignity, the legislative package to upgrade the United States to America 4.0 has been renamed for them: the Trump–Biden Peace Plan."[7]

Julian laughed, drawing heads. "Polly, there's no way they're going to work together. They hate each other."

"The Trump–Biden Peace Plan," Stella echoed. "Julian, this is the *big truth*

---

[7] A legislative summary of the Trump–Biden Peace Plan is included in Appendix II.

propaganda technique. Keep repeating the name until people believe the truth—there are zero technical obstacles in the way of cooperation."

"Power concedes nothing without a demand," Edith added, reminding Julian of the sign she'd so earnestly carried fifty years earlier.

"You're still holding on to a mindset of scarcity," Carlton added, "and looking for reasons why things can't be accomplished. Our task was to shift people into a mindset of abundance, recognizing that when we seized the means of legislative production, every problem was capable of being addressed."

"The Trump–Biden Peace Plan," Delroy said, tasting the name and liking the flavor. "I like it. You're going to need Donald Trump's negotiating skills to get this through Congress."

Edith managed to look offended. "You'll need Joe Biden's decades of institutional knowledge to get this through Congress."

"Cooperative democracy means America needs both of them," Polly agreed. The next slide showed a two-by-two grid with the candidates' names appearing along the axes. "Because the United States was stuck with a two-party system, led by their presidential candidates, a national union of swing voters offers a huge incentive for cooperation. If only one candidate gets on board, the American Union awards their party the trifecta—the House, Senate, and Oval Office—and the other loses everything. If they both do, then everyone wins: the Trump–Biden Peace Plan ushers in decades of prosperity."

Julian scratched his chin thoughtfully. "This is the prisoner's dilemma, isn't it?" he asked.

Polly nodded, pleased at his recognition. "Almost," she said. "Yes, there's the same grid of options, and the best outcome arises from the two parties cooperating. But there's one feature here that's very different." The room fell silent. Julian could see Stella biting back the answer, her eyes gleeful as she watched him. "They're treating the election as a zero-sum game, and you're going to help them do something that doesn't seem rational," Polly hinted.

What was the setup for the prisoner's dilemma? The men were held in solitary confinement, the way he had been in that cell years ago, unable to communicate. But now he saw the fast for peace had the ability to unite, to connect, to breach even the thickest walls. That's what Polly had said before: *The fast for peace overlays a non-zero-sum game, so there's an advantage—the bloc of swing votes—to communication.*

"They can communicate," Julian answered.

"They will communicate," Polly emphasized. "Either they publicly lead the United States in the fast for peace on Muster Day, demanding Washington cooperate and immediately enact the Trump–Biden Peace Plan, or they will publicly oppose it by default. The other important ingredient in a non-zero-sum game is trust. That's one of the aspects of the fast for peace; candidates can't just make a statement. They have to put skin in the game—share in the self-sacrifice." Julian nodded understanding.

"What if they both refuse?" Ray asked. He scratched his head. "I'm not sure I remember that happening."

"Not since 2044," she agreed. "Then everybody loses. Julian, if both parties have the opportunity to end poverty, end mass incarceration, and end the endless wars, and both are willing to throw the American people under the bus?" Polly shook her head solemnly. "Then a general strike against the political system: a random endorsement that sweeps away any vestige of credibility the duopoly has left.[8] Julian, the traditional deadline is October 30."

Delroy began to cackle. "Mischief Night," he said. "Julian, remember that year we egged–" The look from his high school chum ended the interrogatory.

"We have one hundred million Americans coming forward on Muster Day today," Idabee pointed out. "How many will Julian need? To no longer submit quietly to the status quo?"

"Do you want the principled answer or the practical one?" Polly asked.

---

[8] Although Polly's plan is summarized here, Appendix III includes additional specifics on how it works in the 2024 election, including the details of a general strike in the ballot box.

"Principled," Idabee said firmly. "It's 3.5%, isn't it?"

"That's right," Polly confirmed. "Research into nonviolent movements found it took 3.5% participation to secure serious political change, or about five million voters nationwide." Seeing Julian's eyes widen, she added, "That may sound intimidating, but 2016 had more than seven million third-party votes."

"But most races weren't that close, thanks to gerrymandering," Julian observed.

"That's true," Polly admitted, "but 10%–20% of House and Senate races were the competitive ones that parties fought over, the last kilometer of seats needed for a congressional majority. A union of swing voters gains control of those districts first."

Polly flashed the next slide up on the screen. It was a map of the United States: Pennsylvania and Michigan were in red, Arizona and Georgia were in blue, and Wisconsin had stripes of both colors. "Now, as a practical matter, presidential elections were always close. Since Electoral College votes were a zero-sum game, it was literally tens of thousands of voters in the swingiest of swing states that controlled the outcome."[9]

Julian was shocked. "That wouldn't even fill up the Linc! You're saying a sports stadium worth of voters has the ability to stage a nonviolent revolution?"

"This was the new political paradigm that brought us through the Phoenix Cycle," Polly replied. "We were due to radically change the way government worked and how it served the people. Because of the accumulated polarization and gridlock in the system, the American Union was uniquely positioned to make it happen." She advanced the slide to display a list of bullet points.

"Unionizing as voters didn't require changing the method for counting votes.

---

[9] In 2020, had 21,561 swing voters across AZ, GA, and WI gone for Trump instead of Biden, the outcome would have been reversed. In 2016, 38,875 swing voters changing from Trump to Clinton across MI, PA, and WI would have flipped the election.

CHAPTER FORTY-ONE

"Unionizing as voters didn't require petitioning for ballot access.

"Unionizing as voters didn't require fielding long-shot candidates.

"Unionizing made voters deciders, not spoilers.

"Unionizing as voters put people and policy over partisan politics."

Polly flipped to the next slide. "No one could stop a people's legislative assembly from writing their own legislation; by the people, for the people."

"Although," Idabee interjected, "it does take a good amount of work for the delegates."

Polly nodded and continued, "No one could prevent a union of voters from offering one set of demands to all the candidates nationwide and putting real solutions before the American people.

"No one could prohibit a union of voters from agreeing to vote as a nonpartisan bloc nationwide.

"No one could stop a union of voters from staging a general strike in the ballot box if their demands were rejected.

"Unionizing as voters, Julian, didn't require one iota of government permission, and there was absolutely nothing the entrenched interests could do about it. They tried sowing fear and distrust, of course, hoping to keep people divided so they could continue to rule." She advanced the slide before continuing. "The American Union was able to overcome it with five tactics.

"By building on constitutional duty, it appealed to everyone.

"By adopting the principles of nonviolence and recognizing the human dignity in each of us, it resisted division.

"By using an open-source legislative process, it directed sunshine on a shady system.

"By recruiting conscientious objectors to partisan politics, it inoculated voters against the lesser-of-two-evils mindset.

"By using the fast as a low-but-real barrier to participation, it brought people together through shared self-sacrifice and created the moral authority to act.

"And that, Julian, is how the people of the United States can form a more perfect union in 2024." Polly Sigh tossed her pink hair as she sat back, pleased.

"Turning minorities into majorities," Julian said. "You make it sound easy."

"I have a question," Charlotte said to Polly. "You said if the Trump–Biden Peace Plan is enacted, everyone wins. But it's impossible for both to win the presidency."

"That's true," Polly agreed. "But what better stopping point for their political careers could there be than ushering in America 4.0 and a new age of prosperity? Enactment of the Trump–Biden Peace Plan is the signal for both men to retire." A discussion ensued with Stella about the historical precedents and the logistics of the Presidential Succession Act, then Polly returned to the slide showing the two-by-two matrix representing the prisoner's dilemma.

"Since billions will be spent on the election cycle, it's hard to imagine Trump and Biden wanting to risk giving total control of Washington to the other party or betting everything on a random event, knowing that if they 'win,' the entire planet will see them as illegitimate. There's far greater dignity in cooperating and becoming a globally recognized force for peace."

Julian recalled that Professor Carlton had recently said, *The best solution is one that's win-win, where both sides emerge with dignity*, and the gray-haired man spoke as if prompted. "The real threat of a general strike in the ballot box is the American Union withdrawing consent from the legitimacy of the process. It withholds dignity from the winner."

"Let's hope it doesn't come to that," Julian said, but at the moment, seeing a clear path in front of him, failure was hard to imagine. Optimism shone brightly on everyone's face; supporting, encouraging looks lifted Julian up on a wave of joy.

One face was missing this afternoon—a gap in an otherwise perfect smile. "Can we have a moment of silence for Reverend Shaver?" Julian asked. Faces somebered and heads bowed, and in the stillness, Julian reflected on what it would be like to see the preacher again in a few months, restored to his former bulk with jet black hair.

CHAPTER FORTY-ONE

"Thank you," Julian said. "He's going to unlock something better for us this time." Smiles returned, although Polly Sigh's expression revealed she didn't understand. "When I ask Reverend Shaver about a backgammon set he received as a boy," he explained, "it'll establish my credibility, and he'll promote the January 15 fast for peace with us."

"That is a great story," Stella agreed. "Realizing he'd been the beneficiary of a welfare Christmas."

Julian reeled as if punched. As soon as he remembered to breathe, he demanded, "How do you know that?"

Stella shrugged. "It's in one of his biographies."

The room seemed to grow dim as he moaned, "Stella, it's supposed to be a story from his childhood no one else knows." His body felt numb, shoulders melting into the couch. "If it's public knowledge in 2023, all it will prove is that I have a library card. It would be useless."

The historian shook her head. "Sorry. I can try to look it up. Want me to?" Stella rose and strode from the room.

Idabee put a supportive hand on his shoulder. "It'll be okay," she said. "You're still from the future; you'll figure out some way to convince him."

"CJ was from the future, too," Julian said. "Idabee, you take the American Union for granted, but things were very different back then. It took years of effort and a near-death experience before Reverend Shaver came around to a different way of looking at things." His gut cramped. Shaver had given him a key for unlocking peace in 2024. Would it fit the lock?

"Maybe there's some other evidence you could give him?" Charlotte suggested. "Recordings of his speeches from the last fifty years?"

Delroy cackled. "The internet had a series of deep fake videos with him promoting his favorite brand of condoms." Julian smiled, his mood temporarily lightened, recalling the fictional reverend extolling the prophylactic's virtues with great sincerity and describing a multitude of partners in various scenarios. "He's not going to believe anything like that."

"Can't you go back to last month and ask him again?" Polly wondered. Charlotte explained there were only certain points in time, forty-two months apart, where that was possible.

"I know!" Edith exclaimed. "On May 1, send me back three years—I'll talk with Alvin, get a better story for Julian, and then show up today with it. I should walk in right about now!"

There was a noise at the door; eight heads swiveled to look.

It was Stella Freedom. "What?" the historian asked.

"Well, it was worth a try," Edith admitted.

Stella's movements were somber as she returned to Ray's side on the loveseat. "*Alvin Shaver: Prophet of Peace* was written fifteen years ago," she began. "The citation for the backgammon story was from a 2029 biography, which quoted an interview in *The Boston Globe* from November 2021. Sorry."

Julian closed his eyes as defeat washed over him. Shaver's story of Gandhi's final test, told in this room hours earlier, now made a horrific kind of sense. If the nonagenarian suspected his anecdote would be worthless, he had been encouraging Julian to risk death in service of a just cause.

The exuberance for Polly Sigh's plan was gone now, swept out of the parlor. After a moment, the room's silent mourning was broken by a slightly hysterical laugh from Julian. "Well, I'm screwed," he proclaimed.

The lack of argument was deafening.

Chapter Forty-Two

Charlotte was the first to speak. "So you need to get back before then," she said. "I can put you back forty-two months earlier."

"Start the American Union during the pandemic?" Julian said. He took deep breaths, as though he could reinflate his hopes and dreams.

"You might have to count me out, brother," Delroy said. "Juggling things with Alba when they shut the schools down, I don't think I'd be able to take on this kind of project."

"I was still in high school," Carlton said. "I couldn't even vote."

"That would be right as the Phoenix Cycle is triggered," Stella pointed out. "It would be hard to build a people's legislative assembly before video conferencing becomes widespread."

Edith reached over and wrapped her smaller fingers over Julian's hand. The physical touch calmed him momentarily, then summoned a realization. If anything untimely happened to him in the intervening years, he wouldn't be there for her on her birthday.

Julian shook his head. "I didn't ask for this responsibility," he said.

"Okay," Carlton said calmly, leaning forward to gaze at Julian.

"You told me I failed," Julian accused the professor. A glance to his left encompassed Edith, Delroy, and Charlotte. "You all know I'm supposed to end up dead the night before the reparations rally." His odds of success seemed more fragile with each passing moment. "What if I just stayed in the tricentennial?"

"You can," Carlton agreed, summoning Julian's attention. "You have free will. Julian, if you decide this responsibility isn't for you, you don't have to convince me. Likewise, if you decide you are responsible, you wouldn't have to convince me of that either. It's what you believe that counts; what you believe is what's true. That's what duties are—a decision to accept responsibility. But duties can be limited by capabilities; if the agency to act doesn't exist, the duty is meaningless.

"We've talked about the five duties in the Preamble and how they're a mission statement for the United States. At the beginning, though, there's a sort of prime directive. Do you know what it is?"

Julian couldn't help but laugh at how the professor had steered the conversation. "To form a more perfect union?" By his side, Idabee nodded.

"Cooperation," Carlton agreed. "If social problems need collective action, there's an individual duty to work together to better the status quo. The American Union and the satyagrahis who organized it accepted responsibility for making America capable of addressing our problems. No one forced them; they believed they could cooperate to make it true. That was one of the most important aspects of the fast for peace, Julian."

"What was?"

"The tacit acknowledgment that we are incapable of individually accomplishing the desired results. We've talked about some of the stoic aspects of the challenges; practicing desirelessness. But that indifference can only be a facade; we must desire the help of others—a higher power, if you will—to achieve our goals.

"You can't accomplish peace on your own, Julian. No one can. But your friends are here today to offer you our strength."

"Thank you," he replied sincerely, looking to each of them in turn, "Stella, Ray, Polly, Charlotte, Delroy, Edith, Idabee, and"—he pressed forward and used Professor Carlton's given name for the first time—"Sid. But I'm not sure it'll be enough." Their faces were overwhelming, pressing in, surrounding, smothering, offering concern but no hope. "Excuse me," he said. "I need some fresh air."

Julian rose, his legs still numb from the shock, and made his way to the door, voices rising behind him. From the hallway, he glanced at the kitchen table where he'd pontificated two weeks earlier. *I can fix all that,*

CHAPTER FORTY-TWO

he'd proclaimed, *and if you don't think it needs fixing, well, you don't know, or never knew, or just forgot. I'm going; that's all there is to it—I'm for real going.*

Going to die was more like it.

Retrieving his jacket, he headed to the elevator and punched for the thirtieth floor. This was the same elevator he'd taken with Idabee when they left for Philadelphia. As soon as the doors closed, their lips had merged with frantic desire, warm breaths coming short and fast, hands roaming and clutching, bodies pressing tight as a down payment on their impending night together, breaking apart only when the compartment slowed to a halt, joy radiating even as they stepped out into the garage holding hands. It was a day with such promise.

Then a robin's-egg-blue envelope spoiled everything. What if it hadn't?

The community garden was at the south end of the hallway, with an orange glow from the setting sun visible through floor-to-ceiling glass. A cool breeze tugged at the door when Julian pushed it open. In the distance, the Washington Monument stood unchanging; he turned away and found a bench facing the sunset instead.

Schemes and strategies played out in his head, searching for a tactic that would let him overcome the forces of history. A sense of doom overwhelmed him as he stared into the distance. The presidential candidates were going to raise billions of dollars; what could a suitcase worth of cash accomplish against that?

Far more enjoyable were the thoughts of Idabee that danced through his head: the pleased look she'd given him as he served little Maggie, the gentle firmness when she'd pushed him away after his misguided kiss, her curiosity to learn more about Ota Benga. She'd comforted CJ's despondency as well, when he realized his own predecessor had triggered a civil war and a corporate takeover of the country. Idabee was luminous in their wedding pictures, their few glorious years before time made its claim on CJ.

Julian sat thinking while the sun dropped and brushed the horizon. Whatever his predecessor had written in those blue envelopes decades ago didn't bind him to anything. Everyone said he had free will—this was a burden he could put down.

A familiar voice punctured the serenity. "I always liked the view from here," Idabee said.

Julian's spirits soared, tugging at his mouth, feeling her appearance validate the decision he'd reached. "You're welcome to join me."

Idabee did, leaving an arm's length of space between them on the bench, and together they watched an elevated train slice across the landscape. "How's the fresh air?" she asked.

He was in no mood for small talk. "Idabee," he said, his heart beginning to pound. "May I hold your hand?"

Surprise melted into anticipation. "You may proceed," Idabee answered softly, and the fingers she stretched toward him were warm as they intertwined with his.

"I've been so lucky to have met you," he said, his voice a symphony of sincerity, "and I'm so grateful for everything you've shared with me. I want to change history with you."

"What did you have in mind?" Her face was a canvas splattered with joy and curiosity.

"I want to prove CJ wrong when he said we have no future in the tricentennial," Julian said, gazing into her brown eyes. "Idabee, will you marry me?" With the gordian knot of time thus unraveled, the remnants of their lives could be bound together into a new pattern.

Idabee's eyes widened as her mouth opened slightly. "Really, Julian?" The tone was all wrong, streaked with skepticism, and she jerked her hand free. "You coward."

"What?!" Was there some sort of ritual that he didn't know about?

"What what?" Idabee shot back. "What are you afraid of?"

"Dying?" Julian asked defensively.

"That's not the Julian West I met," said another voice. He twisted to see Edith standing behind them, her arms crossed. "Did I call it, Beebee?"

"You did, Nana," she admitted.

"Call what?" Julian demanded, as though he were a mouse being toyed with by a pair of cats.

CHAPTER FORTY-TWO

Edith gently set a hand on his stubbled scalp, fingers drumming in rhythm as though trying to massage his brain into motion. "You're a twentieth-century man, Julian, with all the baggage that comes with."

"But he's a good student," Idabee defended him. "I thought for sure Professor Carlton explaining it would be enough." A slight smile exposed her amusement at his situation.

"What, that people have to work together for change?" Julian demanded. "I already knew that, and now I know Reverend Shaver won't be helping." He couldn't shift the United States alone; the odds were insurmountable. But change was possible—it was the only constant—and 2024 was full of people looking for a constructive alternative to the worst election he could remember. He tried to think of other resources he might be able to draw on in the past. Idabee's look reminded him that she'd offered assistance a few weeks ago, and he turned her down.

Suddenly, he knew.

Asking for help.

That was what he was afraid of.

American history was full of stories of self-made men and rugged individualism: the lone foxes who overcame the odds and outran their pursuers. More power to them, but Delroy had said, *We struggled because they were all so used to fighting for scraps from the old system that they couldn't imagine a different way of doing things.* Was he like that, stuck with a worldview that couldn't be upgraded?

CJ asking Delroy for help was acceptable within their bonds of brotherhood, and he was willing to ask Reverend Shaver and coordinate plans with Professor Carlton. Idabee was a young woman. Admitting that he needed her help—someone he felt a primal instinct to protect—would feel like a weakness.

He sensed the threads of the thirty-day challenge woven through his struggle. Putting his pride aside, even temporarily, to ask for help would make him uncomfortable, but it might also be the start of a better habit. Was he willing to take the challenge?

The two women watched him, waiting silently for his next words.

"Idabee," Julian said softly, "will you help me?" Edith's fingers beat a happy rhythm on his skull. Carefully scrutinizing Idabee's expression, he waited to see how it would pass judgment on him.

The verdict was in his favor. "Of course," Idabee answered, pride flowing into her voice. Relief flooded over him. She was a wild card, but maybe it would be enough.

Edith gave the top of his head a congratulatory squeeze before clearing her throat. Julian turned; she was waiting, her eyebrows quirked. In for a penny, he thought. "Edith, will you help me?"

"I expect you'll also be willing to ask my younger self that question," the octogenarian said, "but I might be able to facilitate her assistance." Edith handed him a business card.

He read its face with surprise. "Delroy Jackson, American Union organizer. You want me to put you—her—in touch with Delroy?" The reverse side held a few lines written in a tight cursive script, but he couldn't translate them at a glance.

"Well, he'll be the treasurer for the American Union, right? I was recently accused of coming from a family with money." Edith's smile signaled all was forgiven. "Supporting a plan to make Donald Trump look good will be a tough sell, but Delroy has a certain charm."

Julian motioned for Edith to sit with them. "Thank you, Edith," he said.

"Well, we may or may not be family," Edith replied, sliding close to him on the bench and patting his knee affectionately. "Since you just proposed to my granddaughter."

"Julian was trying to take control of the situation to avoid asking for help—just like you predicted," Idabee said defensively. She moved nearer. "Julian, CJ was right when he said we have no future in the tricentennial."

"Okay," he agreed. The trio fell silent, watching the western horizon as the sun continued its nightly retreat, withdrawing both light and warmth. Idabee shivered, and Julian slung an arm around her, which she nestled into. Edith gave him an impish smirk until he reached his other arm out, and she drew herself against him with a sigh.

Once again, their contact imbued Julian with hope, as though their linked

CHAPTER FORTY-TWO

arms and energy formed a powerful chain that could tug the destiny of the United States toward a glorious tricentennial. "Idabee? Do you have a plan?" he asked.

"I can make sure Reverend Shaver believes you," she answered simply. "Julian, if Charlotte sends me back to December 2019, I can use the backgammon story and tell him to expect you on a certain date in the future."

Julian shook his head. "But there's still the same problem; the odds are that we won't end up in the same universe."

"Charlotte has a theory," Edith said. "Assuming you didn't actually end up in our past and immediately get hit by a bus, you're going to create a parallel world. Charlotte thinks she can calculate Idabee's time orbit so it intersects yours at precisely the same moment that your new universe splits from ours. She'd be pulled into the same one and arrive forty-two months earlier than you."

Julian felt greater sympathy for Ray's frequent complaints that time travel and the multiverse made his head hurt. "And you believe this?" he asked Idabee. He struggled to imagine her adapting to life back then. Her capabilities here were impressive, and practical knowledge of the American Union and the workings of the people's legislative assembly could be helpful to his mission, but her naivete would bring complications.

"As much as I believe any of this," she answered. "But you asked for my help, Julian, and I'm willing to try."

"What if Reverend Shaver has already told the story, like in a sermon?" Julian wondered. "He might not listen."

Edith spoke up. "He doesn't have to believe her on the spot, just by the time you show up. Predicting a global pandemic will make her credible in hindsight."

The imagery drove home the years that would separate them. "But, Idabee," he protested, a lump forming in his throat. "How are you going to manage by yourself?"

She prodded his ribs with her elbow. "Think of it as a real-world challenge," Idabee said mischievously. "Besides, you already gave me homework assignments." She ticked them off with her fingers. "Learn to drive a car, get good with social media, connect with influencers, make contacts with the press, and with advocacy groups. That should keep me busy for a few years."

"Beebee, remember me telling you about the Peace Vigil that used to be across from the White House?" Edith asked. "It's been in the same place since 1981; get to know Philipos, and when Julian arrives, maybe he can help you two reconnect."

The last of Julian's despair and doubt burned away, leaving a smoldering pile of ashes. He inhaled sharply, igniting a new feeling. Optimism rose up like a phoenix, warmth unfurling, its lightness permeating his being and lifting his spirit. Perhaps sensing this, Idabee and then Edith pressed against him, anchoring him to the reality of their plan. Together, they would change the past for the better.

The apricot sky had taken on the muted tones of evening, and the illumination's insubstantiality awakened a bank of lights above the garden. "I think that's my cue," Edith said, rising with a slight stiffness. "I'm headed back inside."

"Agreed," Julian said. He stood, reborn, saturated with gratitude and appreciation for each woman. Idabee remained firmly planted on the bench. "Are you coming?"

"Not yet," she replied, her eyes locked on the remaining sliver of sun. "I'll be back in in a little while."

"Aren't you cold?" he asked.

"Julian," she said, not deigning to look at him, "what do you think it's going to be like in December 2019?" The question sparked an alternate motive for her recent stoic challenge, and he shook his head in gentle admiration for her fortitude.

Edith touched his elbow, and they walked away, leaving Idabee staring at the rays of light released by the sun eight and a half minutes earlier, looking backward in time and contemplating the future.

Part VI

Where do we go from here?
May 1, 2076

One of the best proofs that reality hinges on moral foundations is the fact that when men and governments work devotedly for the good of others, they achieve their own enrichment in the process.

-Martin Luther King Jr.,
Where Do We Go from Here: Chaos or Community?

When a man gives up his arrogance and becomes humble like dust, only then is the power of nonviolence awakened in him and the divine strength becomes his.

- M.K. Gandhi

Chapter Forty-Three

On his last day in the tricentennial, Julian woke to the sound of Idabee in the shower. He came alert quickly, thinking of what needed to be done that morning before people arrived at Doctor Leete's condo to say goodbye. As promised, Professor Carlton was on his way from Maine to meet him in person, along with Faith, Adon, and their kids. He would officially be an American Union organizer.

The previous night had been one of intentional relaxation, the calm before the storm. Idabee had introduced him to modern cinema with *A New Hope Rises*, the Star Wars remake. The holographic power of the parlor had been on full display. Gratuitous 3-D effects aside, Julian appreciated the foreshadowing of the story arc: the hints at Darth Vader's eventual redemption through his son's satyagraha campaign, conscience reawakened by the power of unconditional love.

For Julian, it might only be a few hours or days before he saw Idabee again, but on her end, it would be more than three years, if at all. Aware that much could go wrong, Idabee was still confident that when she arrived on Christmas Day, she would be able to find her way to Reverend Shaver and deliver her message. Everything after that would be a bonus.

Idabee had never asked him about the contents of the journal or repeated Delroy's question about who CJ was married to, and Julian had never volunteered that specific information. They had free will and had made different choices than their predecessors. Julian's spontaneous marriage proposal had never been mentioned again, firmly shelved by a better understanding of his duties and reinforced by a single passing comment

CHAPTER FORTY-THREE

Idabee made about celibacy. Without any sexual tension between them, their friendship found new depths.

The pair talked for hours, trading stories of their pasts and scrupulously avoiding speculation about their own forthcoming campaigns. They also divided the cash Delroy had given him, ensuring Idabee only had Federal Reserve Notes from 2019 and earlier. Finding that Julian's share came to $45,480 injected more unease into the whole situation—it was what CJ had carried. Was he trapped within a maze of destiny, doomed to duplicate disappointment?

The spray of the shower slowed to a halt. Idabee padded around the bathroom for a few minutes, then her footsteps exited into the hallway. As she meandered past his door to Ray's study, where she'd slept, Idabee delivered a trio of firm knocks.

It was time for action.

Julian propelled himself into the bathroom, a twist in his smile hinting excitement. Catching a glance of his reflection in the mirror, he took a moment to appreciate the full head of hair growing in. Had he lost a little weight? The series of scars revealed when he stripped merited no special attention; forgiveness of Connor had included acceptance of them.

Once cleansed and reinvigorated by the strong shower spray, eyes bright with anticipation, Julian dressed quickly, ready to embrace his final hours in the tricentennial.

The kitchen was unusually silent as he walked down the short hallway, and he halted when he saw Ray and Idabee holding each other tightly. Julian reversed course, retreating to his room to double-check his traveling bag, giving father and daughter the space and time to say a final goodbye.

Ray's eyes appeared moist when he reentered a few minutes later, and Julian peered into the study, where Idabee fiddled with her own travel bag. Boxes she'd brought over the previous day were stacked in a corner, and there was a quilt laid out on the floor, folded into a rectangle about her size. A flock of flying triangles ran along it. "Is that the quilt you told me about?" he asked. "I hope you slept alright."

"It was very comfortable," Idabee said sadly, "but I can't bring it with me." She knelt, flipped it into a compact bundle, and held it tight to her chest. "I'm going to give it to Maggie. And yes—I did." She stepped close to him and confided, "Your snoring was barely noticeable through the wall." Before he could respond, she walked past him.

"Well, it's official," Idabee announced. "The Assembly Clerk published May's calendar. I am no longer a seated delegate."

"You had a good run," Ray said. "Time for new challenges. Julian, that's what I'm going to tell people about your revival; in less than two months, you were off to bigger and better things. I wish you both success."

"Thanks, Ray," Julian said. "I appreciate all your hospitality." In another history, his host had generously paid Xinghurst Corporation for his daughter's marriage license, purchasing full upgrades of the optional legal benefits. CJ had liked Ray as a father-in-law.

"My pleasure," Ray replied. "The parlor is going to be pretty quiet after you leave. I hope you've had all your questions answered."

"I have one more; for you, actually," Julian admitted. "We've shared all these conversations about the beginning of the American Union, but I haven't heard your opinion. What do you think the real purpose of the American Union Jobs Program was?"

Ray shrugged. "I don't know, Julian." Idabee directed an amused look at the men from where she was swiping through the kitchen menu,

"Okay," Julian said, "but what's your analysis? Any ideas seem more compelling than the others?"

"It's just a government program," the doctor replied. "Don't overthink it."

Before Julian could try another angle, they heard someone at the front door. "I'll get it," he volunteered. As he made his way down the hall, he decided Ray's indifference didn't matter.

Adon's grin greeted him. "Big day, brother," he said as he shepherded the children, Maggie and Alvin, into the condo. "How are you feeling? Ready to break your fast?"

"Idabee's ordering up some fruit in the kitchen," he explained. "We're still waiting for Professor Carlton."

CHAPTER FORTY-THREE

"Fruit!" Maggie repeated excitedly. Julian gestured down the hallway, and the girl scampered away. Alvin followed his sister sedately.

Faith wrapped him up with a hug. "I can't believe we're never going to see you two again." He and Idabee had visited the family for a session day the previous week and outlined their plan. Faith had been the first to believe the outlandish story.

"You sure you wouldn't rather babysit for us next week instead of jaunting off through time?" Adon asked.

"Tempting," Julian agreed, "especially if you threw in some of your cooking, but we're pretty committed at this point."

When Carlton arrived wearing an infectious grin, Julian returned it. "You shaved your beard," he observed as they shook hands firmly.

"I thought I'd make it easier for you to recognize my younger self," the gray-haired man replied, stroking his naked chin. "It's a pleasure to finally meet you in person after all these decades."

Julian led him to the kitchen, where the rest of the group sat at the round kitchen table. They claimed the two remaining seats next to Idabee; Adon's family took up the other three, with little Maggie squirming on her father's lap, eyeing the two trays of fruit, possibly calculating the optimal order to sample the selections. "I appreciate you all being here this morning," Julian said after greetings were exchanged.

"Since you won't be able to attend tonight's meeting," Carlton said, "it's the least we could do." He eyed the young man sitting across from him. "Alvin, can you lead us in reciting the Preamble?"

Looking thrilled at the grown-up responsibility, Alvin did, his voice balanced on the edge of adulthood. "We the people of the United States, in order to form a more perfect union, establish justice, insure domestic tranquility, provide for the common defense, promote the general welfare, and secure the blessings of liberty to ourselves and our posterity, do ordain and establish this Constitution for the United States of America." His father clapped a proud hand on his shoulder.

Carlton thanked him before adopting a more formal tone and launching into a semi-serious interrogation. "Julian West," he began, "did you observe the fast for peace on the fifteenth, giving up food for twenty-four hours and only drinking water?"

"Yes," Julian replied. Idabee had reviewed the series of questions with him in advance, explaining that new organizers had to have participated in the fast for peace at least twice—his spontaneous decision in March served to qualify him.

"Did you keep your pledge to abstain from recreational intoxicants for thirty days?"

"Yes," he said, proud of setting the intention and achieving it.

"Did you conclude the thirty days by completing another twenty-four-hour fast?"

Glancing at the wall clock, Julian admitted, "It's closer to thirty-six hours now."

Carlton's eyes twinkled as he continued, "Are you a member of the American Union, and wish to become an organizer?"

"Yes."

"Do you accept Martin Luther King's challenge to 'declare eternal opposition to poverty, racism, and militarism?'"

"Yes," Julian answered firmly. Idabee's eyes glowed with pride.

"As an organizer, will you participate monthly in the fast for peace, and actively invite others to join as well?" Carlton pressed him.

"Yes." Adon had explained previously that no one was expected to be perfect; missing an occasional fast was okay, but skipping two consecutive months would be disqualifying.

"As an organizer, do you understand the seven duties of nonviolence on which the American Union is based?"

"Yes." Even without the in-depth conversations, the last month had given him a basic grounding in the principles.

"As an organizer, will you accept responsibility for ensuring any American Union events you arrange are sober ones?"

"Yes," Julian replied, the relevant duty being to lead by example.

"As an organizer, will you promote the solutions generated by the people's legislative assembly in a scrupulously nonpartisan way?"

CHAPTER FORTY-THREE

"Yes."

Professor Carlton broke into a wide grin. "All right, Julian; it's great to have you on board!" His friends offered up overlapping congratulations, and Julian basked in the warmth for a moment before Carlton's voice became serious. "Now, go organize the 2024 election."

The weight of the task dampened the mood for a moment, then Maggie chirped, "Can I have strawberries now?" Idabee lifted a tray and held it out to the girl, who happily plucked a red berry. Faith placed a gentle hand over her daughter's to caution her to wait.

One by one, the table selected pieces of fruit. Julian held a slice of apple in front of him, remembering the words Cesar Chavez had offered after his twenty-four-day fast: *We are gathered here today not so much to observe the end of the fast, but because we are a family bound together in a common struggle for justice. We are a Union family celebrating our unity and the nonviolent nature of our movement.*

"Who'd like to offer a tribute?" Carlton asked.

"To Julian and Idabee?" Faith suggested; her son nodded approval.

"To the American Union?" Idabee countered. At the kitchen island behind her, Ray watched with a guarded expression. Did he feel left out, or was he amused by the ceremony? Either would be understandable, but whatever his friend's opinion, Julian was secure in knowing they were binding themselves together in a common struggle for justice.

The thought prompted a phrase he'd mindlessly parroted in school countless times. The words had never rung true, but thinking of them now, he experienced a swelling of emotion. What had always sounded like a pithy sentiment might actually be possible.

Julian hefted the apple in his hand and proposed: "To liberty and justice for all." Affirmations surrounded him, and with the shared vision, the group broke their fasts.

As the tart flavor burst across his tongue, Julian realized he'd found his own answer to the question he'd raised with Ray. What was the real purpose of the American Union Jobs Program? He'd lost track of exactly how many responses—all of them different—people had offered. Idabee suggested it was to give people freedom to pursue their passions; others said it was to reduce needless deaths by building a safety floor under everyone, alongside a public payment infrastructure, which let them resist economic coercion and fully participate in democracy.

Those were all good, tangible reasons, but Professor Carlton and Reverend Shaver's had been more philosophical. Carlton stressed the principle of bringing people together universally and unconditionally, while Shaver asserted the real purpose was to flip the broken structure of the United States and remind people that duties came before rights. Julian had just recited the five duties of Americans along with his friends, the five goals that made up the mission statement for the people of the United States, and there was a reason the first held the top spot.

The real purpose of the American Union Jobs Program, Julian decided, was to bring substance to those often echoed and formerly hollow words—liberty and justice for all.

Fasts broken, the adults mingled around the kitchen. They had a little time before leaving for the warehouse, where Edith and Charlotte were waiting with the timepad. Faith gave Julian another hug. "Are you nervous?" she asked.

"He should be," her husband affirmed with a chuckle. "'Go organize the 2024 election.' No pressure, or anything."

"I'll have help," Julian said, watching Idabee introduce Professor Carlton to her father. The tricentennial had been wonderful, but the 2020s still felt like home. He imagined Ota Benga might have had a similar feeling. "Am I allowed to worry about Idabee, though?"

"No more than the rest of humanity," Adon said. "At least that's the theory. Think she'll still be into you after forty-two months?" Faith poked her husband.

"We're just friends," Julian affirmed. If they succeeded in the past, it was possible their romance could be taken from the shelf and reopened—with mutual consent. "There's too much to be done, too much at stake."

"Go organize the 2024 election," Adon said again with a laugh. "Go bring peace to the United States."

CHAPTER FORTY-THREE

"Peace," Julian echoed. "You just don't know what it was like back then, brother. We were told to think that Russia and China were the big threats, but they weren't killing two hundred thousand Americans each year—poverty was." He raised his voice and spoke across the room. "You told us why you joined the military, Carlton. Even things like job training programs ignored the fact there was a whole ecosystem of employment that could only exist because people were trapped in poverty."

"Martin Luther King said 'an edifice which produces beggars is in need of restructuring,'" Carlton offered as he approached.

Julian seized on the word. "Yes, we needed a restructuring, but the marginalized millions didn't have any leverage to make it happen. The American Union can fix it—with liberty and justice for all."

"The American Union can fix it," Idabee repeated as she joined them. "Julian, didn't people want to end poverty, end mass incarceration, and end the endless wars? Who wanted to keep those things?"

"You're going to find out," he promised. "The entrenched interests were quite happy the way things were, and they won't like our message. Fold, spindle, and mutilate—that's what's going to happen to it. We'll have our work cut out for us, even if you get Reverend Shaver on board."

"If?" Idabee repeated, playfully stabbing Julian's stomach with a finger. Faith and Adon chuckled. "When. You can count on me, Julian."

"Not to mention the problem of persuading people that voting can actually deliver change," Julian added. "Elections were a big reality show, not a serious mechanism for setting policy."

"There's an aspect of truth to that," Carlton interjected. "Back then, elections were yet another pointless war; big flashy battles for ratings and attention, and innocent civilians were the primary casualties when nothing fundamentally changed. One of the things I learned in the military was that wars are won on their supply lines. The way to bring an end to the fighting was to control the supply of swing voters that determined the balance of power in Washington every election.

"I remember you were skeptical about the fasting when we talked a few weeks ago," he said to Julian. "The duopoly will be, too. They won't know how to handle it. January 15, February 15, March 15, month after month, giving the people of 2024 the courage to stop fighting. Courage is contagious."

"Courage is contagious," Julian echoed. "You're saying a national day of fasting was the idea America needed?"

"Maybe as a symbol," Faith agreed. "But the idea was the real lesson of the Constitution."

Julian nodded. "Reverend Shaver told me: the Constitution is a framework for government. It's about duty, not about rights."

Carlton waved a hand dismissively. "Of course duties come before rights, but that wasn't the lesson."

"Cooperation?" Idabee suggested, perhaps remembering Carlton's speech about the Preamble's prime directive.

Faith shook her head and began to explain. "In 1787, after Shays' Rebellion, there was widespread agreement that the Articles of Confederation weren't working, so delegates from a dozen states convened in Philadelphia.

"Over four months in Independence Hall, they debated the duties of a national government. And when they were done, not a single person liked everything in the Constitution. George Washington concluded the document was 'the best that could be obtained at this time.'

"That was the true spirit of the Constitution, Julian: compromise. By the time of the pandemic, that quality had been long lost. America had a culture of greed, of self-centeredness, of hyperpartisanship. That culture was failing us, and the American Union produced a broad legislative package where not a single person liked everything in it."

"Fasting and compromise are two sides of the same coin," Idabee added. "Willingly giving something up."

"The Framers compromised," Faith concluded, "because America was worth saving."

"America was worth saving," Julian echoed. The group fell silent, and he looked at each of his friends in turn, drawing strength from their hopeful expressions about the possibilities. Even Ray's face revealed optimism.

CHAPTER FORTY-THREE

A warmth began to spread through him, starting in his torso and radiating to the bottom of his feet and the tips of his fingers. It was an even stronger sensation than he'd previously experienced. Julian was helpless as he smiled wildly at Idabee; she returned it immediately. "I love you," he proclaimed.

It was time, he knew, to go to Charlotte's warehouse and embrace the destiny of duty. The certainty that they had the power to change history overwhelmed him. Mere words were inadequate to describe the emotion—the feeling of what could be accomplished through cooperation—but to refuse to speak would have felt unjust. The four words he declared were not addressed simply to those in the room but to the totality of humankind across time and space.

"I love you all."

Chapter Forty-Four

The bus dropped the eight of them off three blocks from Charlotte's warehouse. Alvin set the pace, leading them with long strides, and they made their way through the city streets. Julian was struck by how clean everything looked. He fell to the back of the pack with Carlton, content to follow as he absorbed a few more memories of the tricentennial. "How are you feeling?" the gray-haired man asked.

Still riding high on agape love, Julian could only smile uncontrollably. "Sid,"—the professor's given name was not a familiarity, but a necessity in his blissful state—"I have an incredible sense of well-being."

Carlton clapped him on the back. "Promoting your general welfare, eh?"

A joyous laugh escaped Julian, prompting Ray and Idabee, walking close together, to peer back at him. Words followed: "I love you, Sid."

Carlton looked upward, letting the warmth of the sun fall squarely on his face. When he was sufficiently energized, he said, "Thank you, Julian; I can see that. Now I can share why you—CJ—failed before and why Reverend Shaver succeeded."

"Why?" If the professor had been holding out on him, Julian wanted to understand the man's motivation.

"CJ had all the mechanical details for the American Union—the game theory, the legislative package, the election returns, the principles of nonviolence, and so on. It was enough to convince me and many others, even if it didn't succeed. It took many years for me to realize he was missing a key component—love."

"Love?"

CHAPTER FORTY-FOUR

"That was the essential ingredient that Reverend Shaver brought. You know he offered to forgive his assassins in his speech from the hospital?" Julian nodded. "It was that example of boundless love that was the real spark. Dr. King described it as disinterested love, where 'the individual seeks not his own good, but the good of his neighbor.' You're feeling that now, and you're going to carry that with you. I hope you can rekindle that selfless love of all humanity in the past to build the beloved community."

"I can," Julian affirmed, smiling so hard that his cheeks hurt. "It's like no drug I've ever tried; it's better than any high I've ever felt."

"The best way to test if your love was disinterested, King said, was to give it even if hostility and persecution were all you could expect in return." Carlton eyed him before delivering the query. "Can you love Donald Trump?"

Such a question would have flattened him a month earlier, but now it was barely a hiccup. "I can," he pledged.

"And Joe Biden?"

"I can," Julian said again. The beauty of the world stung his eyes. "How can we not, Sid? We're all flawed, but we're all—each and every one of us—capable of so much more, especially together. To deny someone love is to deny their humanity."

The professor nodded encouragingly. "You won't be able to persuade everyone—selling hate was big business—but do try to cultivate that quality in your organizers," Carlton advised. "As a nonpartisan voting bloc, the American Union offered an island of calm consensus in a stormy sea of polarization; a safe harbor where all were welcome, if not loved." *Like signing a truce for the duration of the election cycle*, he'd said.

The smell of electricity was strong in the air as the group reached the door to Charlotte's warehouse and came to a stop. Idabee tapped an unlock code into a keypad as Carlton concluded, "As your organizers try to persuade 3.5% of the electorate to land on that island, consider one more question: Is it better for the right thing to happen for unprincipled reasons, or for the wrong thing to happen by adhering to principled ones?"

Julian pondered as everyone began to file inside, then shook his head as he held the door for the septuagenarian, not sure what answer was expected. Carlton's response was cryptic: "When you see the solution, explain it to my younger self."

As their eyes adjusted to the dimness of the warehouse, three elderly figures came into view. Delroy raised a hand in greeting from where he and Edith were conversing by the workbench, and Charlotte knelt by the timepad, its lights flashing a kaleidoscope of colors on her white lab coat.

Julian approached the physicist first. The circular disc he would stand on was missing from the timepad, exposing the rod it balanced on at the bottom of a spherical divot. "Everything looks good," Charlotte announced, standing to greet him. "How are you feeling?"

The truth was the best approach. "Skeptical," he admitted. "Do you really think you can stack the deck so time travel deals me and Idabee into the same universe?"

"From a math perspective, it's gorgeous, but the theory is technically untested. Getting your time orbits to converge at precisely the right moment—I think that's straightforward. Space probes have been intersecting asteroids and comets since the turn of the century." Charlotte gestured to a device the size and shape of an old refrigerator. "Idabee needs to leave exactly four minutes, sixteen seconds after you. As long as the capacitor is recharged, everything should work out." She read his face. "Your trip will be fine; don't worry. The capacitor is primed and ready. We're just waiting for the orbital window to open."

At the workbench, Idabee was setting out stacks of cash next to the two identical discs that would carry them back in time. She'd recruited the children's help to pack Federal Reserve Notes into the discs' open compartments. "I'm more worried about Idabee making it," Julian said.

Charlotte put a hand on his arm. "You'll still be able to prevent a civil war, right? You told me Anton died, but you didn't give details."

Julian exhaled, suddenly less confident in the physicist's assurances, but nodded. "The same way CJ did: allow a national tragedy to focus attention on Reverend Shaver and feed him a formula for peace."

"Good," she said, seeming to forget such a plan of action resulted in CJ's

CHAPTER FORTY-FOUR

death. Even Charlotte's reminder of what he was committing himself to wasn't enough to extinguish his feeling of joy at the opportunity to serve humanity.

Edith approached them with slow, somber steps and asked Julian if she could speak to him. He followed her over to a rack of electronic components sitting idle. "This might be the last time I ever see you," Edith said softly. "It's not how I pictured it. But, however things turn out for you, I hope you have a long and happy life."

Julian could sense emotions rising off of her like multicolored balloons, strings of frustration, hope, and jealousy twisted and tangled. The deep gratitude for everything she'd done for him spilled out as an aspect of truth she desired. "I love you, Edith," Julian said.

The wrinkles of her face lightened. "I love you too." Edith held out her hands, and he took hold of them. "You were the first person I ever told about Izzy Robynham; I saved that story for you all these years because I believed I'd see you again. Now I want to tell you something else I've never done. There's a cryonics facility out west," Edith said, naming the venture, "and they do good work. I refused to ever visit, Julian, to ensure I couldn't learn if you were a patient there. If you ever find yourself missing me, you can use their services to sleep your way back to the future. I'll be here."

Julian crinkled his forehead in a vain attempt to make sense of Edith's latest. If it were possible that another version of himself had been stored in cryonic suspension, he didn't need to understand it now. "Thanks," he replied, "that's good to know."

Edith hesitated before delivering one more data point. "I was in my 40s when revivals began—plenty young enough to make your head spin," she confided with a mischievous grin, her eyes daring him to test her.

He laughed and opened his arms; she stepped into them. Julian held her tightly, offering the Leete matriarch what comfort he could, then whispered, "Goodbye, Edith."

Professor Carlton and Delroy were talking animatedly when he approached, and Julian felt another wave of joy wash over him as he stepped into their presence. He'd watched their first physical meeting moments earlier; an offered handshake had quickly escalated to a hug of brotherly love, black and white limbs interwoven as bonds formed in the virtual world took corporeal form.

"Jules," Delroy began, "we're working on ideas you can take back with you. How about this: A general strike in the ballot box will reboot the system—turn it off and turn it back on to try and get it working properly."

Julian scratched his chin. "Not bad. I voted for Cornel West; it didn't help at all. But do you think people would follow through with a threat to elect Trump or Biden at random?"

"Every election cycle, it happens with some offices," Delroy said.

"It may not matter, Julian," Carlton offered. "When I was in high school, there was this viral event to storm Area 51 out in Nevada. It was completely stupid; the idea was that if enough people charged the base at one time, they couldn't stop everyone. When over two million people—and I was one of them—said they were going to do it, the government had to prepare, just in case we all showed up."

"Boaty McBoatface would be proud," Julian grinned.

"Once the American Union is polling at 3.5%, they'll have to respond," Carlton continued. "Politicians and parties who want to win won't be able to take the chance that millions of people are all bluffing."

Delroy cackled. "To trigger an avalanche, you just need to get enough snowflakes together. Get it?" He slapped his thigh. "Jules, you should be writing these down."

"For real," Julian agreed. He threw an arm around his old friend. "I love you, Del. See you soon."

Faith and Adon stood close together, and moved apart to welcome Julian when he drew near. They were watching Idabee demonstrate the timepad to their children. She held the circular disc up, showing how the supporting rod fit into its convex base, then balanced it in place. It swiveled slightly when Alvin stepped onto it. Idabee picked up a circular tube the size of a hula hoop and passed it over his head. The boy crouched down, and Idabee held the hoop nearly vertical, the bottom edge slipping inside the gap between the disc and the corresponding concavity of the timepad's base.

"What worries me is the moment of launch," Julian ruminated, watching Idabee trace a sphere around Alvin's body, ensuring none of it touched the hoop. "That platform will be weightless for a moment, and I'm afraid I'll fling my arms out trying to catch my balance."

Adon began to chuckle. "It'd be pretty hard to hold a tablet fifty years ago without your hands."

"I wish there was a handle for me to grip," he said as Alvin stepped down and Maggie climbed up onto the timepad.

"Got any duct tape? We could make one," Adon suggested, clapping his friend on the back.

Faith poked her husband. "Julian, it was a pleasure to meet you; best of luck to you and Idabee. We're rooting for you, even if we won't know how it turns out."

"Thanks for introducing me to your family—and good luck with your book," Julian replied. "Idabee suggested I write something about my adventures. Maybe I will." Faith hugged him warmly and waved the children over to say goodbye. Little Maggie threw her arms around his waist, and Alvin delivered a firm handshake. Julian considered the kids: would they have a better life in the parallel universe he created, a worse one, or never exist at all?

Ray had been hovering around Idabee, absorbing his last moments with his daughter. Julian removed the doall from his wrist as he approached and held it out to his host. "I won't need this anymore," he said.

"Don't you want to bring some fancy future tech back with you?" Ray asked.

"Ideas," Julian said. "That's the fancy future tech I want people to have—how to change the rules of the fox hunt. Thanks for all your help, Ray."

"Just–" The man's voice was thick with emotion. "Just look out for Idabee."

"Father," Idabee protested. "That's backward; I'm going to be looking out for Julian." She grinned. "How surprised will you be if I'm there waiting to pick you up in a sports car?"

"What, you couldn't get a limousine?" Julian replied.

Ray threw his arms around both of them. "Be careful," he pleaded.

"Things will work out the way that they're supposed to," Idabee assured him.

"They have so far," Julian agreed. "Ray, can you give us a minute?" Ray's arm lingered on his daughter for a moment before he retreated.

Idabee's eyes were soft as they faced each other. "Thank you for helping me," Julian said.

"I'm glad you asked—I knew you had it in you," she said. "But even if something goes wrong on my end, Julian, I still think you can make this work."

He glanced at Edith. She'd just said he was the first person she'd told about Izzy Robynham. Her granddaughter could have been the second. "Will you be able to get help from Edith if you need it?"

Idabee's face lit up. "I'm under very strict instructions not to tell anyone else about her mysterious patient," she said. "And if I do need help, I'm to explicitly explain that I'm the second person that she told." She bit her lip and scrutinized Julian. "Nana won't say when you first met."

Julian considered telling her; it would be an extra line of defense in case anything happened to him in the six weeks after his arrival. Ray was watching them, and Julian remembered how much he appreciated the doctor's discretion. "That's her decision," he said to Idabee. "Pick me up in a limo, and maybe I'll bring you along."

She laughed and threw her arms around him. There was an incredible lightness to Idabee's spirit, and he inhaled deeply, as if he could capture it. After a moment, her embrace became heavier, and she clung to him. Julian matched her pressure and, as he had with Edith, tried to offer her what comfort he could.

Charlotte signaled for his attention from a respectful distance away. "Two minutes, Julian." Time had run out.

The years that would soon separate them crystallized, and she whispered in his ear, "You're not like Ota Benga. You're going home."

Her observation penetrated his heart, and his smile, which had never

CHAPTER FORTY-FOUR

really gone away, widened painfully. Awash in elation at having met Idabee, he said, "I love you."

Idabee released him and patted his cheek gently. "I know," she replied. "You said it back at the condo." She sighed, her brown eyes holding his gaze. There was something else she wanted to tell him, and he waited, watching her assemble courage.

Suddenly, there was a muffled knock from the warehouse entrance. Heads turned in that direction. Adon spoke first. "Should I see who it is?"

"No," Charlotte replied. "We're not expecting anyone else. They'll go away." She gestured toward Julian. "Ready?"

"Goodbye, Idabee," Julian said. He couldn't understand how he could feel such bliss and still have a lump in his throat, but there it was.

"I don't like goodbyes," she replied. "See you later, Julian."

With a wave to his watching friends, Julian grabbed his nearly empty backpack and clutched it to his chest. When he approached the timepad, Charlotte had opened the top of one compartment and was holding up a small mylar pouch. "The flash drive is in the faraday bag, along with your identification documents." She dropped it on top of the Federal Reserve Notes and let the lid fall shut. "Your chariot awaits."

Julian stepped on the disc and crouched down, feeling the grit underneath his shoes. "Hold still, so I can get an accurate weight," Charlotte warned him. The muted metallic clangs of her magnets attaching themselves to the circular base reached his ears simultaneously with the vibrations of their forceful leaps traveling up through his feet. Closer and closer, Charlotte moved him to the required one hundred thirteen kilograms. Finally, she stopped. "Almost there. Any last words?"

Julian raised his head and looked around at his friends one last time, clustered around the workbench with expressions ranging from wonder and excitement to sadness and loss. "Be excellent to each other," he advised, quoting a time travel movie he'd seen as a boy. Maggie gave a bashful wave goodbye.

He turned his gaze to Idabee, who stood at a panel dancing with lights. Her finger was poised to push him backward in time, starting the countdown for her own trip, and she wore the same inscrutable expression he'd seen not long after waking up in the tricentennial. Unable to interpret her feelings, he gave her a final nod, and she mouthed something—cube block is beautiful?—that might have been a reference to the aesthetics of American Union housing.

The knocking on the warehouse door came again: harder, faster, louder. Whoever or whatever was outside wanted attention. A muffled shout could be heard, but the words were unintelligible through the building's walls.

Charlotte spoke as soon as the banging stopped. "Ready?" Julian tucked his head down. "I'd keep your eyes closed; it might be disorienting," she warned him. "Idabee, are you ready?" The answer must have been affirmative, because she continued, "Good luck, Julian."

"Good luck, Julian," came a burst of overlapping voices.

Julian felt small grains fall on his head and neck as Charlotte sprinkled the last few milligrams of weight. "Now, Idabee," she directed.

The crisp closing of the switch, a moment of weightlessness, and then he was gone. Against Charlotte's advice, he kept his eyes open for the journey.

Infinity was black.

It was truth.

It was God.

It was good.

And it bent toward justice.

Epilogue

Julian West's anxiety rose even as the August sun set. Up the street, a steady trickle of people flowed through the door under the hand-painted wooden sign for Fifth Edition, a bar popular with doctors and nurses at the nearby Washington General Hospital. He'd staked it out for ninety minutes, watching for Edith Bartlett's appearance, but hadn't recognized her. Was he early, or had he missed her arrival, perhaps failing to recognize the woman decades away from being an elderly grandmother? Was she celebrating her birthday somewhere else tonight? And if so, was she safe from the rapist who'd caught her in AJ's universe; that distant cousin of the one he stood in now?

The six weeks since his arrival in 2023 had been a mix of setbacks and successes. While Julian hadn't really expected Idabee to meet him with a limousine, it was concerning when he'd visited the Peace Vigil and found that no one knew anything about her. He'd loitered in the city, checking back in Lafayette Square at all times, scrutinizing the rough sleepers on the park benches across from the White House in case she was among them.

His heart ached at seeing the nation's capital glowing with inequality, knowing that Congress had the power to address it at any time but would only pass twenty-seven bills in all of 2023. Did the people living in the parks sleep better knowing there would be a limited-edition US Marine Corps commemorative coin in a few years? Finally, after leaving a generous donation and a message with Philipos at the vigil, he headed north to Philadelphia and Delroy Jackson.

The trip, made by bus to minimize scrutiny of his fake ID, took only a few hours. Julian managed to fill the time with worried wonderings. Who had been banging on the warehouse door in the moments before his departure? Had Idabee's trip been interrupted? Or had she been misguided into a parallel world where he would never see her again?

Fortunately, Philadelphia had been better. Delroy's simmering anger at the world was mollified through hours of hopeful conversation, and after breaking the fast for peace with him and Minnie, Julian had given Delroy a bag of cash to begin setting up the American Union PAC. It was something totally outside their experiences, and Julian wondered what ideas Ota Benga might have brought home to Africa, given the opportunity.

A lean white woman exited Fifth Edition and pushed a cigarette into her mouth. When she tilted her head back to exhale a stream of smoke, Julian recognized Charlotte Grayson. The physicist's hair was auburn, not silver, and pulled back in a simple ponytail. Relief washed over him; Edith was certainly inside.

Julian started back toward the car Delroy had procured for him, ready to jettison the campaign materials he'd been distributing. A young couple approached, walking casually, and he pointed the back of his clipboard at them. "Excuse me," he said, smiling without showing teeth, "could I ask you a question about Congress?"

The man looked uninterested, but the woman stopped. "Sure."

He recited the text printed on the clipboard: "What would you like to see Congress actually do? End poverty, end mass incarceration, end the endless wars, or all of the above?"

"Um, all of the above?" she said.

"That's the best answer," Julian agreed, introducing himself by his alias and holding out campaign literature. The woman took it willingly, the man grudgingly. "I'm an organizer with the American Union. We're a union of swing voters backing a crowdsourced legislative package that will do these three things"—he tapped at the clipboard—"and demanding Congress pass it before the 2024 election. If they do, they can earn our votes. If they refuse, we can push them out of office and out of power by voting for their challengers. Republican or Democrat, it doesn't matter;

EPILOGUE

we just want to see them get something done. Can I send you some more information?" He offered her the clipboard.

"Absolutely; we need a third party," the woman said, scribbling her email address.

Julian smiled politely. "The American Union isn't a political party—third parties don't work," he said. "Republicans and Democrats win 99% of the time, so the most powerful voters in the electorate are the swing voters who decide which ones."

The woman finished writing and looked at him carefully. "I don't want them to win."

"It's not my preference either," he replied empathetically. "But since they're going to, we might as well get something for it. A union lets us look out for each other, since the Republicans and Democrats aren't."

"Hell, I'll sign that," the man said, reaching for the clipboard. "The union's always looked out for me at work. Why can't we have a union of voters?"

"We do—if you want to end poverty, end mass incarceration, and end the endless wars," Julian replied. "We're going to collectively bargain for a better social contract." He hoped it would be in 2024; his life might depend on it.

When they continued on their way, Julian found his spirits buoyed by the man's enthusiasm. It was enough to give him a quick taste of agape love, but not enough to trigger a self-sustaining reaction—not tonight, not while he carried the burden of what might happen to Edith.

He tossed the clipboard inside the car and took a moment to check his appearance, including his hair, appreciating the box fade he'd had touched up at the barber shop the previous day. It was a nice souvenir of the tricentennial.

There were more smokers standing outside Fifth Edition; he dodged the tendrils of toxins and descended the few steps to the entrance. As he pulled open the door of the bar, Julian took in the lively scene. People were dancing, the smell of alcohol and perfume mixed in the air, and the music was blaring loud enough to make conversation difficult.

Julian scanned the room, looking for familiar faces, and spotted Charlotte's auburn ponytail at a high-top near the dance floor. She was facing away from him, and as he began to circle toward the table, Charlotte turned, revealing the woman across from her.

It was Idabee!

She was safe: she'd survived the pandemic, she was here with him in 2023, here with Edith, here with Charlotte, and all the accumulated tension of the last six weeks whipped away like a bullet train across an open field. Idabee was the missing piece; he couldn't wait to hear everything she'd accomplished in the last three years. Her gaze flicked around the room, and when their eyes touched, it summoned the last phrase she'd spoken. *I don't like goodbyes; see you later, Julian.*

She looked absolutely stunning tonight: no simple clothes for her, but a sleek black dress that begged for attention, inviting appreciation of all the lovely curves of her body. He'd never seen her with makeup before, her hair perfectly coiffed, tasteful pearls dangling from her ears. Still working his way toward her, Julian was grinning with joy when her survey of the room came back to him. She returned the smile, checking him out as he approached, her eyes guiding his path like a set of landing lights.

But something was wrong. Her probing look contained no flicker of recognition, her skin was lighter, and as Julian realized she was slightly shorter, reality crashed in on him: this young woman was Edith Bartlett.

He shifted mental gears as quickly as he could, raising a hand in greeting as he reached the table. "Happy birthday, Edith," he said, his voice barely audible above the music. "Can I talk to you?"

Sizing him up, Charlotte asked, "Hey hey, who's this handsome stranger?" She leaned in, trying to catch Julian's attention. "I'm Charlotte."

"Nice to meet you," Julian said casually. "I just need to talk to Edith."

"Ask her to dance," Charlotte suggested coyly. "Got to get this girl out on the floor."

"Want to dance?" he asked.

"Have a drink with us first," Edith countered, a hint of slurring to her words as her eyes scanned his left hand. Unlike CJ, his ring finger was bare. It was just one of many changes he hoped to accumulate in this world.

EPILOGUE

She lifted a glass of white wine. "You're Phil's friend, right? What's your name?"

Julian shook his head. "I don't drink, thanks. And I don't know Phil, but I do know"—he leaned forward, speaking distinctly into her ear—"Izzy Robynham."

The name caught her attention. "For real?!" She downed the rest of her wine. "Let's see how you move." Charlotte hooted as Edith grabbed him by the arm and half-dragged him to where couples were dancing.

The music guided their movements, and Julian tried to keep his focus on Edith as she swayed gracefully, completely present in the moment. But his mind was racing, and when one song ended and the next began, he finally spoke, "Who else have you told about Izzy Robynham?"

"What about him?" she said loudly.

"Izzy Robynham wasn't a time traveler," Julian told her.

She nodded in understanding, blending it into her movements. "No one at all—yet," Edith replied, her eyes dark with desire. She began to dance closer, grazing her curves against him. "And yet, here you are. Mmmh! I must have been a good girl this year, because you look like the best birthday present ever." With her hands gliding over his body, she proclaimed, "I can not wait to unwrap you."

He dislodged her hands with gentle firmness. "That's not why I'm here," Julian said, trying to home in on her eyes and look past the intoxicatingly sexy pout she was giving him. "I'm trying to protect you from getting raped tonight. Don't go home with anyone."

Edith's movements ground to a halt, beats ricocheting off her as her expression twisted into a search for understanding. She stepped closer to Julian, grabbing his arm. "What are you talking about? Who's going to rape me?"

Julian hesitated, trying to project the right words with urgency and sincerity. "I don't have all the details, Edith. But you told me it happened tonight, from someone you left with. Please, listen to me."

"Oh my God," she whispered, eyes wide, "I need another drink." Tugging on his arm, Edith steered him to a quieter corner of the bar and signaled the woman wrangling alcohol. "When did I tell you all this?"

"Years from now," Julian answered before delivering his own question. "You haven't heard about Izzy Robynham from anyone else? A woman about your age?"[10] Edith shook her head, and Julian's shoulders sagged as the weight of worry returned.

"Is this a joke?" she asked, and looked disturbed when he shook his head. "And who are you?"

"It's not important."

Her laugh covered a broad spectrum of emotions. "'It's not important,' he says." Edith glanced toward the bartender again. "How does this work? We're going to see each other again?"

He'd given thought to the precise words to use. "The first time I met you," Julian said, "we were looking up at the Washington Monument on March 18, 2026."

She digested the information as casually as possible. "Two and a half years?"

"Well," he hedged. "I won't know you. Izzy Robynham, remember?" He flashed her a winning smile. "But you should take that day off work."

"March 18, 2026," Edith repeated, her tone serious and calculating, before falling silent.

A TV behind the bar was tuned to the news, and polling numbers flashed onto the screen. Trump and Biden were tied with 43% each. "Can I ask you something?" Edith looked back at him hopefully. "Who are you voting for for president next year?"

Edith spat air through her teeth. "They both suck," she said. "Why, who wins?"

"I can't say," he answered, knowing it was literally true. There is no fate but what we make.

"Hmmph," she replied. "There's a lot you can't say." The bartender appeared, and Edith said, "Susi, give me my usual." Then she jerked her head toward Julian. "I don't think he's twenty-one."

---

[10] Determining which woman is older is left as an exercise for the reader.

EPILOGUE

"ID," demanded Susi, a wisp of a woman with a face kind and firm, holding out her hand to Julian, practically daring him to object. Edith emanated amusement as he fished out the driver's license Charlotte had given him, totally fake but produced to the exact standards of the present day.

It passed muster with the bartender. "Okay, Dante Julian Unitas, what can I get for you?"

He shook his head. "Nothing; I'm fasting today." Susi handed the thin plastic rectangle back without comment, giving Edith a nod in solidarity before disappearing. "You were always clever." Edith's impish grin acknowledged she knew it.

Their eyes held for a moment, then she wondered, "People call you DJ?"

"You are the very first," he admitted as Susi planted a white wine in front of Edith.

"And you won't drink with me on my birthday," Edith pouted, lifting the glass by its stem and taking a swig. "Are you an alcoholic or something?"

He shook his head and began to explain. "There's a stereotype of the alcoholic who hits bottom and turns his life around because there's nowhere to go but up. It's a stereotype because it happens. The thing is, hitting bottom is optional. People can turn their lives around at any time. It just takes a strong enough intention.

"The United States is like that. Yeah, if we hit bottom in a couple years, we'll have to turn things around because there'll be nowhere to go except up. But we don't have to hit bottom, Edith. There's no one person alone who can change America's direction. But as a nation of individuals, we have the power to turn things around, together, through a shared intention."

Edith sipped from her glass, watching him. "You think America's going to change?" she scoffed.

"There's no question about that," Julian answered sincerely, knowing the Phoenix Cycle guaranteed it. "The real question is when and how." There was so much to be done, so much to be accomplished in order to create that better future he'd witnessed in the tricentennial, and he knew without question that he couldn't do it alone. "Edith, will you help me?"

"Help you? Help you what?"

He produced Delroy's business card. "You asked me to give you this."

"American Union," Edith read, then flipped the card over. He saw recognition jolt her, and she held the white rectangle closer to her eyes, her vision tight on the inscrutable cursive script that doctors surely practiced in medical school. "Where did you get this?"

Julian laughed, remembering his own reaction when Delroy handed the robin's-egg-blue envelope to Idabee. "It's freaky, isn't it? Seeing your handwriting on something without knowing how it got there." Too late, he realized how shaken she was. Julian stretched a comraderily arm across her shoulders.

Edith seemed to gather strength from the grounding. After a moment, she turned toward him. Her face was close, too close, as she reached down the front of her dress and tucked the card safely away. When her hand emerged, it found his knee. "You could help me," she suggested. "Walk me home and keep me safe?" Fingers slid up his thigh.

It was the same proposition she'd made in 2076, and if they succeeded in influencing the election, he would be free to take her up on it. Until then, her breath was warm and wet with wine. The Julian West she was going to meet would leap at such an invitation, but her granddaughter, her posterity, was an excellent teacher.

Julian removed his arm and sat back. "I can't," he told Edith, firmly but with obvious regret that he hoped would give her some comfort. "I've got to get back to work." The sands of time were spilling past them as the pivot point of history grew closer. For all he knew, the future would unfold in nine hundred forty-six days just as it had before, leaving him dead on a street corner.

Edith nodded and stared back toward her friends as she drained her glass. The disappointment radiating from her rekindled worry. "Be safe tonight, Edith. Listen to your own warning."

"Thanks, DJ," she replied, delivering his name with incredulity. "Who are you really?"

Julian took her hand and held her gaze as he denied her for the third time. "I'm just a man who wants to see you live in the best possible world," he said simply.

Edith accepted the answer with a small, sad smile. "I believe you," she said.

They walked together across the bar before going their separate ways. As they parted, Edith leaned up and kissed his cheek, perhaps intending it as a down payment on their next encounter. She strolled away without looking back, leaving his orbit and returning to her friends. At the door, Julian allowed himself one last glimpse at the woman he knew as Mrs. Leete.

In a different timeline, they had had decades of love; in this one, all but brief conversations and a quick peck might be sacrificed. Another voice came to mind, long dead but still inspiring. *Declare eternal opposition,* Dr. King had challenged America, *to poverty, racism, and militarism.* He turned away and pushed the door open, the respite of air conditioning retreating before the sultry night breeze.

Julian stepped firmly into a sometimes hostile world, answering the call of duty.

Afterword

> You never change things by fighting the existing reality. To change something, build a new model that makes the existing system obsolete.
>
> - Buckminster Fuller

Julian West is a fictional character created in 1887, but his mission to organize an American Union of swing voters and deescalate the 2024 election is very real. Will 3.5% of Americans come forward on Muster Day—Tuesday, October 15, 2024—and demand immediate enactment of the Trump–Biden Peace Plan? You can read a summary of the legislative package in Appendix II. The timeline for the 2024 campaign is in Appendix III, including the mechanics of a general strike in the ballot box, should Congress refuse to upgrade our social contract and end poverty, end mass incarceration, and end the endless wars.

If this mission fails, Julian West is on track to end up dead just like his predecessor did. If it succeeds, he will not only survive, but be free to end up with either Idabee or Edith. This is a "choose your own adventure" for the United States; the outcome of the 2024 election will guide the plot of *Looking Forward to the Tricentennial*, planned for release in January 2026.

The people of the United States will have to demonstrate their power in order to save Julian West. Here are eight ways to build the American Union:

AFTERWORD

1. **Polling power:** When asked about any federal election (US House, US Senate, President), insist you are a true swing voter who will vote with the American Union. Candidate endorsements are made at the end of October, just before the election. When the American Union polls at 3.5% nationwide, politicians and parties will get in front of the parade rather than willingly give up power to the other-color team.

2. **Financial power:** Become a dues-paying member of the American Union by contributing twenty-five cents a day ($7/month) or more at bit.ly/LBFTTjoinAU (Link is case sensitive.) The American Union represents individual citizens of the United States; contributions from corporations or other organizations are not accepted. As a super PAC, all funds are used to grow the power of the voting bloc, and not one dime will ever go to any candidate or candidate's committee.

3. **Moral power:** We'll all have to give something up to produce a peaceful election. The fast for peace each month on the 15th—no food, just water for twenty-four hours—demonstrates our ability to compromise and helps ground the American Union in nonviolence. Invite others and find or form an affinity group to persuade high-profile Americans to join this fast of moral pressure. It is shared on social media with #fastforpeace—lowercase by intention.

4. **Creative power:** *Looking Backward from the Tricentennial* is published under a Creative Commons license, empowering everyone to freely distribute, adapt, and build on it in any format for noncommercial purposes. Besides the obvious copying and giving away any or all of the text, this could include creating memes and other social media objects; AI images for important ideas; recording an audio drama with different people playing each character; or writing fan fiction speculating on who Julian might end up with—if he survives.

5. **Labor power:** Plan to take Muster Day (October 15) off work and to avoid spending money that day. Halting the national economy with a one-day general strike will demonstrate the power of the people, incentivizing Congress to enact the Trump–Biden Peace Plan within one week.

6. **Consumer power:** How would UBI and the American Union Jobs Program benefit your local businesses? Encourage them to show support by publicly announcing they will close on Muster Day, and look for (or start) online petitions to pressure national chains.
7. **People power:** Help grow the American Union as an organizer! After completing the thirty-day training, get access to additional resources for spreading the message, including PowerPoint presentations, referral links, private discussion forums, campaign literature, and more!
8. **Crowdsource Congress:** Organizers can become delegates in the people's legislative assembly, fine-tuning the Trump–Biden Peace Plan and writing the 2026 legislative package.

We the people of the United States have the power to make our existing political structure obsolete. Now that you know, the choice is yours: challenge the status quo or perpetuate it.

Learn more at AnAmericanUnion.com, and vote with the American Union in 2024—Julian West's life may depend on it!

Appendix I

Text of Reverend Alvin Shaver's speech, *An Apology, a Dollar, and an Accounting*, delivered at Washington General Hospital on March 24, 2026:

Americans have debated the equality between Whites and Blacks going back to the framing of the Constitution and the choice to count enslaved Blacks as three-fifths of a person. We enshrined racial inequality and racial injustice into that sacred text, and it took eighty years and the violence of the Civil War to overwrite it. Our proclivity for fighting makes us unique in the world—we were the only nation that chose to wage war over the institution of slavery. All others managed to excise it peacefully.

The result of our choices left a deep wound in our country; the Confederate flag continues to serve as a rallying call for white supremacy. It has affected countless lives for more than one hundred sixty years, and there are passionate people on both sides, as we saw last week in the shadow of the Washington Monument.

That choice was a costly one. The United States stayed united, but more than seven hundred thousand Americans gave their lives before the final battle was concluded. The last to fall was President Abraham Lincoln, when an angry assassin chose to shoot him in the back. That the Great Emancipator should have had his life sacrificed was an epic tragedy. All across the continent, men and women would always remember where they were when they heard news of his assassination, and his passing, on April 15, 1865.

How can we choose to move past a national trauma? After Lincoln's death, President Andrew Johnson called for the nation to observe a day of fasting. Today, I'd like to offer Americans, as individuals, a choice that builds on our national traditions. On April 15, I invite you to join me in a day of fasting—a fast for peace. We the people have the power to make peace, if we can agree on the terms, and this is my proposal.

Last week, I demanded reparations for the descendants of enslaved people, and I continue to believe it is necessary, not just for economic justice, but for an emotional catharsis. To help this nation heal from the psychic wounds of the Civil War, we must acknowledge the errors of our past and embrace our ability to learn from them. Congress has in its possession HR 40, a bill that would examine the issue of reparations. I propose that such legislation be amended to cover three points.

First, an apology for the United States' government's endorsement of slavery. There is no other way to put the issue behind us than to accept responsibility for the long years of racial injustice.

Second, to allocate one dollar in reparations for each qualified person, with a commission to determine if any additional compensation is justified.

Third, to aid them in their determination, the commission shall enumerate the policies undertaken by the federal government that harmed Blacks exclusively or disproportionately. In addition, the commission shall catalog the positive programs enacted by the federal government that benefited Blacks disproportionately, including the billions of dollars spent on the Civil War itself. The pros and cons: how do they balance out?

An apology, a dollar, and an accounting. A few moments ago, I received a message from the president, who assured me that if this proposal makes it to their desk, they will sign it into law. The president has also committed to participating in the fast, not as the chief executive of our nation or by issuing a proclamation, but as a private citizen, as an American who believes this is a fair proposal.

Some of my friends will ask, one dollar? That's less than a penny for every year our ancestors were in bondage. Surely twenty-five, fifty, one hundred thousand dollars is the amount we should start with. My friends, this is a complex and nuanced issue, without a doubt. But this proposal boils reparations down to a simple, binary choice. Zero, or not-zero?

On April 15, each citizen will have a binary choice to make as well—to fast, or not to fast. There are tens of millions of people who just don't have an instinct for that proposition, and so every American has three weeks to learn more and make an educated decision if they're willing to accept that offer. An apology, a dollar, and an accounting.

Half a world away and a half-century after Johnson issued his proclamation, Mohandas K. Gandhi issued his own call for the people of India to observe a day of fasting, for Hindus and Muslims to stop fighting each other and focus on their common goal of independence from King George. Gandhi said that when hundreds of thousands of countrymen fasted together, it ennobled individuals and nations.

What makes an individual or a nation noble? Nobility is not a title, something granted, but a quality, something earned. To act nobly is to follow your conscience; to be noble is for others to trust the choices of your conscience.

I have faith in our Holy Father above and his accounting, that on Judgment Day the pros and cons of our lives shall be added up.

I have faith that if a committee examines the pros and cons of America's life, an accounting will find the economic costs of justice are in excess of one dollar.

I have faith they will behave nobly and conscientiously.

An apology, a dollar, and an accounting. We, the people of the United States, have the power to choose our path forward. We can continue to fight and tear our country apart, or we can choose not to. Peace will take an intention. April 15 is a fast of moral pressure directed toward Congress to spur their consciences to act on our behalf and ennoble America. That moral pressure is also directed inward; the sacrifice of the fast can be a tempering process, both individually and collectively. For those who have acted out violently this past week, including the men who attacked me, you are under no obligation to be the same person; you are worthy of redemption. As Jesus said, "Go, and sin no more."

I understand there are those who want their outrage at this week's tragedy heard. I ask people to cancel large gatherings for the next three weeks and instead go out in ones and twos to ask their friends and neighbors to commit to joining the fast for peace. In addition, I encourage people to contact their members of Congress in support of HR 40 with this amendment.

We the people have the power, and we the people can establish justice—the choice is up to us. Thank you, and God bless America.

Appendix II

A summary of the Trump–Biden Peace Plan

The Framers wrestled with the question while writing the Constitution in 1787: What should a government do? At the beginning of the 4,400-word framework we still use today, they outlined five duties for the new nation to focus on. After 237 years, we've lost our way, but we can get back on track with the American Union.

It's easy to approach reforms from a mindset of scarcity: only little, minor changes are possible, to be taken in incremental steps. But, as the Phoenix Cycle (Chapter 4) demonstrates, America in 2024 is at a tipping point where big, sweeping changes are not just possible, but inevitable in the next few years. The Trump–Biden Peace Plan is a legislative proposal that comes from a mindset of abundance, offering dozens and dozens of reforms, largely grouped around addressing Dr. King's triple evils of poverty, racism, and militarism.

The Preamble and its five duties are the framework for the American Union's set of demands for the upcoming election: end poverty, end mass incarceration, and end the endless wars. This summary is based on the policies introduced January 15 in the first session of the people's legislative assembly; details may change through the year. Many of these policies are described within the novel, so chapter numbers are provided for reference. Think big!

We the people of the United States, in order to form a more perfect [American] Union,

Establish justice [by reforming the criminal justice system],

Ending mass incarceration includes police reforms, prosecutorial reforms, and prison reforms. This section is divided into three subtitles, each bearing the name of a victim of injustice.

The George Floyd Justice in Policing Act would reform law enforcement policies and procedures:

- In general, these reforms would immediately apply to federal law enforcement officers (LEOs), with federal Byrne grants or COPS grants reduced or withheld from states starting in October 2026, unless they enacted corresponding state laws.
- Federal LEOs would be required to take a training course establishing a clear duty to intervene when any LEO is using excessive force against a civilian, with states incentivized to mandate the same training.
- Federal LEOs would be prohibited from using deadly force, except as a last resort after de-escalation techniques and less lethal force had been attempted, and only if there was no substantial risk to third parties. States would be incentivized to enact the same policy. (Chapter 19)
- A public, searchable, national police misconduct registry would be established, making grants to states conditional on their submission of the relevant information as well as meeting national certification standards for employing LEOs.
- Chokeholds and carotid holds would become a civil rights violation, with states incentivized to do the same.
- LEOs' qualified immunity for civil rights violations would be removed; suits could now be brought against federal agents (Bivens claims); and the burden of proof for prosecuting violations would become acting

"knowingly" or "recklessly" instead of the current "willfully."
- Forced entry for federal warrants would be restricted to daytime hours (6am–10pm), and unless a judge authorized a no-knock warrant, repeated knocking and identification would be required first. States would be incentivized to enact a similar policy, including an end to the issuance of no-knock warrants in drug cases. (Chapters 11 and 19)

The Weldon Angelos Prosecutorial Reform Act would reform the prosecutorial system, end the federal war on drugs, and amend other statutes:

- Civil asset forfeiture would be eliminated at the federal level and restricted at the state level. (Chapter 11)
- Federal cash bail would be ended. States would be incentivized to meet decreasing annual targets for the percentage of cases where cash bail was used, from 75% down to no more than 10% by 2029. (Chapter 35)
- All mandatory minimums would be struck from the United States Code, and federal judges would be prohibited from using acquitted conduct for sentence enhancements.
- Funded by a tax on lawyers, a program providing transferable vouchers for legal services to anyone arrested would ensure universal and immediate access to basic legal knowledge. (Chapter 35)
- The Espionage Act of 1917 would be reformed to require specific intent to cause harm, protecting whistleblowers and journalists who are often charged under this law.

Ending the federal drug war can be summarized as follows:

- The United States would withdraw from UN treaties that bind us to the drug war.
- Legitimate businesses that engage in the sale of "recreational intoxicating products" would no longer be prohibited from utilizing the

banking system.
- The FDA would establish purity and labeling rules for the sale of "recreational intoxicating products," which states could opt into. A 12% retail sales tax would be imposed. (Chapter 11)
- A Drug War Restorative Justice Office, using funds from the sales tax, would provide grants for substance use treatment and other community services. (Chapter 11)
- Drugs would be essentially decriminalized federally upon passage, with the Controlled Substances Act repealed January 1, 2026. States would be able to enforce or repeal their own drug laws, but national drug prohibition would end. (Chapters 11 and 37)
- Completed sentences for federal drug crimes would be automatically expunged, and those currently incarcerated would qualify for a sentence review.

The Matthew Charles Prison Reform Act would humanize incarcerated people, recognizing our innate ability for self-improvement:

- Federal prisoners would be eligible for a sentence review after serving more than 10 years; for repealed drug offenses; or if sentenced to a mandatory minimum that had been eliminated. A sentence reduction would require a judicial finding that the person was not a danger to others, ready for reentry, and that such a finding would be in the interests of justice. Consideration of a victim's statement would be required. (Chapter 33)
- The use of solitary confinement as punishment would be restricted, in line with the UN's Nelson Mandela Rules, to 15 consecutive days, or 30 days in 60. States would be incentivized to enact the same policy in two phases, by October 2026 and 2027. (Chapter 35)
- To correct the recent *Shinn v. Ramirez* decision, 28 U.S.C. 2254(e) would be amended to permit evidentiary hearings after a finding of ineffective assistance of counsel.
- To correct the recent *Jones v. Hendrix* decision, 28 U.S.C. 2255 would

be amended to permit hearings after a court makes an error in reading the statutes.
- The use of for-profit prisons by the federal government would be phased out (Chapter 35) and the Bureau of Prisons would be required to help people leaving incarceration obtain identification documents.
- The Prison Litigation Reform Act, which created a higher bar for access to the legal system for the incarcerated, would be repealed, along with grant programs to the states that incentivize higher incarceration rates.
- Education being a proven way to reduce recidivism, eligibility for federal Pell grants would be fully restored for the incarcerated.

Insure domestic tranquility [with a truce on wedge issues],

Guns and abortion are used as wedges to drive the American people apart—we can bring down needless deaths by addressing root causes. This section offers a compromise on these issues, where each side gets concessions in exchange for not introducing any bans for 10 years. (Chapter 19)

- Federal law would block states from restricting access to abortion through viability (as under Roe v. Wade); when the life or health of the mother is at risk; when a lethal fetal abnormality makes it unlikely a newborn would survive; and in cases of criminal, non-consensual pregnancy. A repeal of the Comstock Act would secure pharmaceutical options by mail. The Hyde amendment, which prohibits using federal funds for abortion, would be codified into law.
- Universal background checks for gun sales would be required; transfers between family members, estates, and temporary loans are among the exceptions. A firearm registry would be explicitly not authorized.
- No federal bans on guns of any type, or any federal bans, further restrictions, or state prohibitions on abortions, could be introduced for a decade. It would be a criminal misdemeanor for members of Congress to break the truce, which would be repealed after 10 years.

Provide for the common defense [by reducing the military-industrial complex],

America has exceeded our constitutional mandate. Ending the endless wars has two major components: reducing our global military footprint and budget (which is greater than the world's next 10 largest defense budgets combined) and improving our moral standing on the world stage.

Reducing America's global military footprint includes:

- The 2001 Authorization for Use of Military Force (AUMF), which was passed after 9/11, would sunset in 240 days. Congress would be free to pass another one if needed.
- The 2002 AUMF, authorizing the Iraq war, would be repealed along with its 1991 predecessor.
- The military budget would be cut by 10% annually in fiscal years 2026–2029, reducing spending by one-third and about $1 trillion less than projections. Congress would need a two-thirds supermajority to override this provision. (Chapters 32 and 37)
- The Secretary of Defense would be directed to hold referenda around our 750 foreign military bases, asking the local population if they want the US military presence to remain. If not, the base would be closed within two years of enactment. (Chapter 32)
- The Secretary of State would be directed to present Congress with a plan to formally end the Korean War and to review current restrictions on travel to North Korea.
- The 1033 program, which transfers military surplus to local police departments, would be repealed. (Chapters 11 and 19)
- On January 3, 2022, the White House released a joint statement with other world leaders, seeking to "prevent an arms race" and make "progress on disarmament." This legislation would accept that challenge, scaling back planned ICBM upgrades and requiring a 50% reduction in the nuclear stockpile by 2029.

APPENDIX II

Improving our moral standing on the world stage includes:

- The United States would follow China's lead in adopting an unconditional "no first-use" policy for nuclear weapons—never as a preemptive attack or first strike, or in response to a non-nuclear attack of any kind. (Chapter 32)
- The use of unilateral economic sanctions as coercive measures against civilian populations would be prohibited, with exceptions during military hostilities or as part of a broader coalition. The US currently imposes sanctions on more than 30 countries; countries such as Cuba would see them lifted. (Chapter 32)
- Current policy prohibiting the acquisition of landmines would be codified, and the US would cease using them on the Korean peninsula by 2029. (Chapter 32)
- The US would be prohibited from developing, producing, or acquiring lethal autonomous weapons that engage targets without human intervention. (Chapter 32)
- After two decades of indefinitely detaining men, Guantánamo Bay Military Prison would be closed in 2025. Detainees who have been convicted or have pending charges would be transferred to Fort Leavenworth, Kansas. (Chapter 32)

Promote the general welfare [with the American Union Jobs Program],

Welfare has a specific definition: *the state of being or doing well; condition of health, happiness, and comfort; well-being; prosperity.* The constitutional duty to promote this can be best met with unconditional basic income (UBI). Under this legislation, over 300 million citizens would get an unconditional American Union Job, a no-strings-attached reminder of our constitutional duties, as compensation for the value that all of us create.

- The Secretary of the Treasury would be directed to create digital

Treasury accounts for each American, along the lines of the existing Treasury Direct program, and issue UBI of $1,400/month to every adult ($16,800 annually), with a cost of living adjustment beginning in 2026. (Chapters 5, 6, and 38)
- Digital accounts would establish a 21st century public payment infrastructure, enabling account holders to transfer money in real time without banking fees, which currently add about 2% to the price of all goods and services in the US. (Chapters 5, 7, and 38)
- American children would receive an apprentice's wage of $467/month ($5,600 annually), divided evenly between the parents unless altered by agreement or court order. Expectant mothers could enroll in the program (as sole beneficiaries) at any time in exchange for not seeking any medically unnecessary abortion. This would replace the current child tax credit. (Chapters 6 and 19)
- The Social Security Administration would oversee the management of the American Union Jobs Program, with administration costs projected at less than 0.5%. (Chapter 6)
- Wages from an American Union Job would not be considered substantial gainful activity for the purposes of SSDI, and the resource limit for individuals on SSI would be increased to the annual UBI amount.
- No cuts to the safety net are included in this legislation. However, it is expected that many programs will atrophy when there is a safety floor under every American; they can be reevaluated, consolidated, or eliminated in future legislation.
- American Union Jobs would be paid with Treasury Dollar Bills, debt-free digital legal tender issued by the US Treasury, valued at precisely one Federal Reserve Note and exchangeable for such. (Chapters 16, 25 and 38)
- If you like your bank, you can keep it! Financial institutions could link existing accounts to a Treasury account, so funds would be directly deposited. The US Postal Service would also be authorized to offer pass-through bank accounts and other basic banking services, just like post offices do in almost every other country. (Chapter 38)

- Issuance of Treasury Dollar Bills would be statutorily limited to UBI payments, approximately $4.5 trillion annually, so that dividends of the economy's growth are shared with all Americans. For Americans unwilling to use their digital Treasury accounts, the balance can be applied as a refundable tax payment.
- To maintain stability in the purchasing power of the dollar, express public policy in the distribution of wealth and income, and address economic costs to our shared natural resources, new taxes would "claw back" approximately half of the issuance of Treasury Dollar Bills. (Chapters 6 and 16)
- Starting in 2026, a 12% subtraction-method value-added tax (VAT) is projected to raise $7.76 trillion over the first four years. The Congressional Research Service has concluded, "The imposition of a VAT would cause a one-time increase in this country's price level." A 12% tax would apply to imports, but other than military weapons, exports would be exempt from the VAT. (Chapters 6 and 16)
- Companies may elect to pay a higher VAT rate through voluntary value sharing; the IRS would promote a public list of the top 200. The sums raised would be used to pay down the national debt and then be reissued in Treasury Dollar Bills as a year-end bonus to all Americans.

Healthcare-related provisions include:

- An American Union Job comes with benefits! A public option for health insurance, based on Joe Biden's campaign promise. Besides giving people an alternative to giant for-profit insurance companies, encouraging the de-linking of insurance and employment will give people more freedom to change jobs without losing access to healthcare. (Chapters 15 and 37)
- Eighteen weeks of paid family leave would be offered and paid for by a 0.25% payroll tax on employees and employers. (This is unrelated to American Union Jobs, which are unconditional; only those with additional employment income would be eligible.) Bringing America's

infant mortality rate down to the European average would prevent 7,700 needless newborn deaths each year. (Chapters 15, 19, and 37)
- The Affordable Care Act penalties on large employers not offering health insurance would be repealed, reducing the regulatory burden on employers.
- Drug prices would be addressed with a requirement to negotiate for all Medicare part D and part B drug prices. Restricting pharmacy benefit managers (PBMs) from using "spread pricing" is estimated to save $1 billion over 10 years.
- To increase the supply of doctors, six-year medical programs (conferring both a bachelor's and a medical degree) would be incentivized, both through grants to teaching schools and student access to Stafford loans. The Conrad-30 program, which incentivizes foreign doctors to work in underserved areas, would reallocate the hundreds of waivers that are currently wasted each year, and 3,400 additional residency positions would be funded annually through 2030.

Secure the blessings of liberty to ourselves and our posterity [by stabilizing government systems and stewarding the environment for our children].

- The blessings of liberty are secured by voting: universal suffrage would establish voting privileges in federal elections for all Americans, with states incentivized to inform people convicted of a criminal offense about this provision. In addition, prison gerrymandering would be addressed. (Chapters 5 and 37)
- To protect the freedom to travel, the provision of the REAL ID Act which relates to air travel would be clarified to apply only to those required by federal law to show ID as a condition of boarding a commercial aircraft.
- Social Security would be protected by raising the cap where people stop paying in from the current $168,600 (2024) to 25x the base wages from the American Union Jobs Program, or $420,000.

- No more government shutdowns; continuing resolutions would be automatic if Congress fails to pass a budget. (Chapter 37)
- Showdowns over the debt ceiling (currently planned for early 2025) would be ended by abolishing the debt ceiling limit. (Chapter 37)
- An overhaul of the immigration and asylum systems is needed, but not within the scope of the 2024 legislative package. However, some minor issues are addressed: A path to citizenship for those brought here illegally as children (Dreamers); restoration of the state option to determine eligibility for in-state tuition; access to the Registry program for those here for more than 10 years; and a requirement for large employers to participate in a national E-Verify program. (Chapter 37)
- An additional $19.2 billion for border security and immigration courts is appropriated. This includes purchasing autonomous surveillance tower systems, mobile video surveillance systems, and subterranean detection capabilities. It includes authority to hire additional border patrol personnel, judges and other court officials, asylum officers, and to provide legal counsel to unaccompanied children (under 14) and adults found to be incompetent.
- Two pollution fees serve as clawbacks for UBI. A carbon fee would be instituted, starting at $20/metric ton and rising at an inflation-adjusted $10 per year, and a carbon border tax would be put into place to make adjustments for products entering and leaving the United States. These are projected to raise $760 billion over the first four years. (Chapters 7, 16 and 37)
- A plastic fee would be instituted on sales of virgin plastic resin, starting at 20% and rising 3% per year, thus encouraging recycling. A flat $.05 fee on individual plastic products would discourage single-use plastics. They are expected to raise $448 billion over the first four years. (Chapters 16 and 37)

We can accomplish more together...

If a candidate for president were running on this platform, it would sound like meaningless campaign promises. No one would like all of the policies, but the candidate would attract support from many people who recognize the system needs big reforms. Ultimately, it wouldn't matter: even if they were elected, accomplishing even a tiny fraction of this in the swamp of Washington would be nearly impossible.

No one candidate can change the system. The American Union can inspire candidates across all 470 federal races to come together toward making our nation that more perfect union the Framers were striving for by taking up this one platform simultaneously. Like corporations that donate to candidates on both sides of the aisle, a union of swing voters (built on the principles of nonviolence) can focus on good policy instead of being distracted by party affiliation. The Trump–Biden Peace Plan is that good policy, addressing Dr. King's triple evils. To shepherd it through Congress prior to the general election will require both the negotiation skills of Donald Trump and the institutional knowledge of Joe Biden.

Will your candidates for Congress support the Trump–Biden Peace Plan? The game in 2024 is not Republican vs. Democrat, but incumbent vs. challenger. (Read more in Appendix III.) When 3.5% of voters join the American Union, we'll control the balance of power in Washington and have the leverage to win a better social contract.

What would you like to see Congress actually do?

- End poverty;
- End mass incarceration;
- End the endless wars; or
- All of the above?

Learn more at AnAmericanUnion.com and vote with the American Union in 2024!

Appendix III

In his *Letter from Birmingham Jail*, Martin Luther King Jr. laid out four steps for a nonviolent campaign: **collection of the facts to determine whether injustices exist**; **negotiation**; **self-purification**; and **direct action**. These correspond to the phases of an election-year campaign. In 2024, the legislative package is named for the presidential candidates: the Trump–Biden Peace Plan (summarized in Appendix II.)

The American Union undertakes the crowdsourcing of Congress through the people's legislative assembly, producing and refining the year's legislative package in three sessions. The direct action phase includes endorsements by the American Union across all federal races just before the November 5 election, with the threat of a general strike in the ballot box if candidates refuse to support the Trump–Biden Peace Plan.

Collection of facts to determine injustices [prior year]

The injustices that exist in the United States are widespread. Dr. King identified the triple evils of poverty, racism, and militarism; the legislative package is structured around addressing them through the three planks of ending poverty, ending mass incarceration, and ending the endless wars. Enactment of the Trump–Biden Peace Plan is a moral crusade.

During previous years, qualified members of the American Union were able to suggest policies for inclusion. Policy proposals needed to be relevant to the package's theme as well as our constitutional duties and apply universally. (No identity politics.)

Collection of facts + Negotiation (Internal) [January–April]

The assembly opens January 15, the birthday of Martin Luther King Jr. This first session introduces the package of policies. They are evaluated within the larger whole to ensure consistency and that nothing is working at cross purposes. Additional information is gathered, details sharpened, and a draft piece of legislation is compiled and published.

Once a satyagraha campaign is underway, no new demands can be added. (There is an exemption for brand-new injustices that arise, such as Supreme Court decisions.)

Negotiation (Internal+External) [April–July]

The second session of the legislative assembly provides for further review. It consists of public hearings on each policy proposal within the draft legislative package, live-streamed for all to see. This offers an opportunity for external input into the process.

By writing clean legislation outside the swamp of Washington, the corrupting influence of lobbyists is minimized. After all amendments are adopted, the components are assembled into the Trump–Biden Peace Plan. The complete legislative package representing the demands of the American Union of swing voters for the 2024 election is then submitted to the members for ratification.

Negotiation (External) [August–September]

On August 1, the Trump–Biden Peace Plan will be published and submitted to Congress. This is the third session and the external negotiation phase. The people's legislative assembly can be thought of as a third chamber of Congress, submitting one proposal to the other two. What the House and Senate do with it determines whether the majority party stays in the majority after the election. (Fortunately for this paradigm, Congressional leadership consistently demonstrates greed for power.)

Through Labor Day, individual members of Congress may propose amendments to the legislative package. These amendments may be needed to correct technical flaws, address unintended consequences, or build the required support in Congress. Policy committees in the legislative assembly will review them and make recommendations to the full assembly.

Distribution of facts [September–October]

After final amendments, the Trump–Biden Peace Plan will be published on September 21, giving everyone time to review the legislative proposal before making a decision. Unlike traditional political campaigns, which feature a candidate making nebulous promises of things they pledge to accomplish if elected, the Trump–Biden Peace Plan offers a concrete package of legislative solutions. Like ratifying the Constitution, this is a take-it-or-leave-it offer for the people of the United States.

For three weeks, information sessions will be live-streamed, breaking down exactly what each policy in the legislative package does. All of America can discuss and debate if they are willing to leverage their votes behind the American Union's demand for immediate (pre-election) passage of the Trump–Biden Peace Plan.

Self-purification [Monthly]

As a nonviolent campaign, self-purification is an important component. The American Union invites all who are able to take part in a 24-hour fast on the 15th of each month. It is a fast for peace, shared on social media with #fastforpeace, and helps the American Union seize the moral high ground to act. The fast creates a new community, separate from the divisive two-party system, identifying with the principles of nonviolence, and for the purpose of upgrading America's political structure.

No one is expected to like every single provision of the Trump–Biden Peace Plan, but as a whole, addressing poverty, racism, and militarism will improve everyone's quality of life. The fast demonstrates a willingness to give something up, an essential ingredient for compromise. In addition, American Union organizers and delegates to the people's legislative assembly give up recreational intoxicants one or two months a year.

For those able and willing to generate additional moral pressure, there are other, longer fasts which may be observed. During the third session, there are three 72-hour fasts: August 6–9 is the fast for nuclear disarmament, August 21–24 is the fast for prison reform, and September 1–4 is the fast for UBI. For those absolutely committed to nonviolent revolution, the 24-day fast of stewardship runs September 21–October 15.

Direct action [October–November]

The campaign culminates on Muster Day, three weeks before the election, on Tuesday, October 15, 2024. This combines a one-day general strike and a national fast for peace, offering all citizens a way to demand Washington immediately pass the Trump–Biden Peace Plan and pledging to vote with the American Union. On October 16, qualified members of the American Union will vote on tiebreaker procedures. (Chapter 29)

Having seen the depth of support nationwide, Congress gets one week to pass the legislative package exactly as written. (Leadership can replace the text of a committee of conference report with the Trump–Biden Peace Plan, which would then go to both chambers for a straight up-or-down vote.)

Once this is accomplished, the president will be expected to sign the legislation on October 30, one week before the general election, ushering in a new era of peace, justice, and prosperity. The United States' demonstration of competence will amaze the entire world, and Donald Trump and Joe Biden will go down in history as the most influential politicians in generations. Perhaps they will share the Nobel Peace Prize for their accomplishment!

How this plays out October 15–30 determines which 470 candidates are endorsed across all federal races. The final list of endorsements is published the evening of October 30, and on November 5, 2024, the American Union takes direct action, voting with power to determine the outcome of the election.

Recognizing the American Union as a bargaining unit

Everyone, but especially candidates for office, is invited to recognize the American Union as a bargaining unit through public participation in the monthly fast for peace on the 15th of each month. The shared self-sacrifice is a 24-hour period without food or recreational intoxicants; water can be taken in any quantity. (Accommodations are available if it would be unsafe for an individual to just drink water for a day; Gandhi recommended taking fruit or fruit juice.) The specific 24 hours are up to the individual, but they should include noon (local time) on the 15th. Going from dinner on the 14th to dinner on the 15th is a popular option, which avoids going to bed hungry.

Recognition of the American Union does not obligate anyone to vote in any certain way at the end of the campaign. Instead, it indicates support for a constructive alternative to adversarial politics, demonstrates an ability to compromise by willingly giving something up, and shows a readiness to consider backing the final version of the Trump–Biden Peace Plan after it is published September 21, the International Day of Peace.

Accordingly, no candidates will be endorsed until the end of October. However, candidates who share in the sacrifice of the fast for peace as a recognition of the American Union as a bargaining unit will have their public statements shared and/or promoted. (The American Union is a super PAC, and only public cooperation with candidates is permitted.) For challengers who want to disrupt the status quo, this is an excellent opportunity to gain attention, especially if they have a contested primary.

The congressional endorsement process

Candidates for federal office compete for the American Union endorsement and bloc of votes by participating in the October 15 fast for peace. Public participation, announced across social media with #fastforpeace, signals a candidate's commitment to the American Union's demand for immediate passage of the Trump–Biden Peace Plan. In legislative parlance, this is a roll call vote; nonparticipation is recorded as opposition.

In Congress, all incumbents (regardless of party) have the first chance to earn the American Union endorsement. There are two requirements: the fast for peace and voting to successfully advance the Trump–Biden Peace Plan through Congress by October 23. That's it—bipartisan cooperation means bipartisan reelection by a nation grateful for their service. This is the carrot.

However, if Congress refuses to act, the stick of electoral consequences must be wielded. Major-party challengers who participated in the fast for peace as their commitment to enacting the Trump–Biden Peace Plan will be endorsed to the fullest extent possible. (Even if Congress does act, these challengers will still receive endorsements in races where the incumbent declined to support the legislation.)

If both incumbent and challenger come together through the fast and agree that immediate passage of the Trump–Biden Peace Plan is in the best interests of the county, the non-endorsed candidate shall support the one endorsed by the process previously described.

In any remaining cases, tie-breaking procedures (described in Chapter 29) are chosen by qualified members and applied in the following order:

1. (Second bite) If the challenger refused to endorse the Trump–Biden Peace Plan through the fast for peace, and the incumbent did but failed to enact it, the incumbent can be endorsed anyway.
2. (Replace all) Endorse all challengers, regardless of party, as a commitment to throwing out as many members of Congress as possible.
3. (Nuclear option) All remaining ties can be resolved in favor of

one randomly selected party, giving them control on a vote of 'no confidence.'

If the qualified members vote down any or all of these options, and/or there are edge cases that still need resolution, two lists of candidates will be generated, and one will be selected at random on October 30.

As conscientious objectors to partisan politics, these processes scrupulously avoid the lesser-of-two-evils game. Peace is possible when 3.5% of the electorate refuses to fight but remains committed to deciding the outcome of the 2024 election.

The presidential endorsement process

The Trump–Biden Peace Plan is an opportunity to bring dignity to two of the oldest candidates that the United States has ever seen, allowing them to retire after accomplishing more together before the election than either could with four adversarial years in office. As a national union of swing voters (someone willing to vote for both Republicans and Democrats), control over the outcome of the Oval Office is fairly easy.

The five battleground states of Arizona, Georgia, Michigan, Pennsylvania, and Wisconsin have 71 electoral votes combined, and in the previous two presidential campaigns, no candidate received more than 51% of the vote in any of them. A 3.5% voting bloc is more than enough to dictate the outcome. As Samuel Johnson said, "When a man knows he is to be hanged in a fortnight, it concentrates his mind wonderfully." The metaphorical hanging, in this case, would be the political party of the man who refuses to cooperate with the American Union.

Cooperation includes a very specific set of conditions here, and the first is to demonstrate stewardship in ushering in a new era of collaborative democracy. Both candidates will be invited and encouraged throughout the year (via affinity groups) to join the monthly fast for peace and recognize the American Union as a bargaining unit. This culminates on October 15; their cooperation involves leading the United States, and their respective political parties, in the fast for peace to de-escalate the 2024 election.

Their skills will be needed to shepherd the Trump–Biden Peace Plan through Congress. In 2024, the House is 51% Republican, so it is Donald Trump's responsibility. The Senate is 51% Democrat, and Joe Biden is responsible for passing it through that chamber. These are thin margins; in the spirit of cooperation, each candidate must also deliver at least 20% of their party's caucus in the opposite chamber. That works out to 42 House members and 10 Senators.

Peace is possible; these leaders are capable of producing it. The Trump–Biden Peace Plan would be a great step forward for the United States and the world, and after accomplishing this, both men are expected to retire with dignity. Perhaps they will share the Nobel Peace Prize!

In 1972, Benjamin Spock ran for president with the People's Party and wrote a letter of resignation in advance, to take effect if he did not remove all American troops from Vietnam within 90 days. This same mechanism can be used again, effective immediately after the inauguration. Besides the obvious possibility of a vice president then taking office, there are numerous ways to put another individual into the Oval Office with the cooperation of Congress. For example, the Speaker does not have to be a member of the House, and with the resignation of the president and vice president, that individual is next in line according to the Presidential Succession Act. (That Act itself can also be amended.)

The very name of the Trump–Biden Peace Plan reminds us that peace is possible; there are no technical obstacles to cooperation, only a failure of imagination. The United States has always had the ability to address Dr. King's triple evils, but the marginalized millions needed a better way to organize for political power. That's the American Union.

To sum up, the conditions for each of the two presidential candidates to compete for the American Union bloc of votes are:

- lead the United States on Muster Day, October 15, in the fast for peace;
- commit to signing the Trump–Biden Peace Plan as presented on September 21;

APPENDIX III

- no later than October 23, shepherd passage of the Trump–Biden Peace through the chamber controlled by their own party;
- no later than October 23, deliver no less than 20% of their caucus' votes in the chamber controlled by the other party to assist passage;
- file a post-dated letter of resignation for January 20, 2025, contingent on the other candidate doing the same; and
- possibly, securing a post-dated letter of resignation from their vice president.

The carrot of cooperation allows both men to retire with dignity; like the prisoner's dilemma, this is the optimal outcome. To gently persuade those in power that this is in their best interest—not to mention the nation as a whole—a union of swing voters also carries the stick of electoral defeat. If one candidate cooperates and the other refuses, thus demonstrating they are the primary obstacle to America's rebirth, the American Union will award the Oval Office to the candidate who has pledged to sign the legislative package, as well as majority control of Congress to that candidate's party.

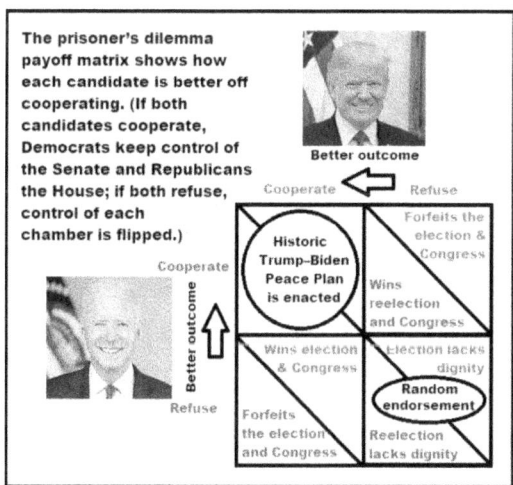

Like the prisoner's dilemma, the rational thing for the candidates to do is cooperate rather than risk seeing the other win the Washington trifecta. When both candidates cooperate, control of the House can remain with the Republicans and control of the Senate with the Democrats. (Like the presidency, control of these chambers is determined by small numbers of voters; in the 2022 midterms, 36,000 swing voters across five House districts and two states could have flipped the majority party in both chambers.) Those in power can stay in power—if they enact the Trump–Biden Peace Plan before the election. This is a win-win outcome!

A general strike in the ballot box

The power of a union stems from its ability to strike and disrupt the status quo. This is how a union of voters can do so: If both major-party candidates for president refuse to support the demands of the American Union, one will be endorsed at random, based on the close of the Dow Jones industrial average on October 30, 2024. If it is an even number, Joe Biden can remain the 46th president; an odd number translates into Donald Trump as the 47th president.

In many places around the world, political minorities have tried election boycotts with the intention of undercutting the winner's legitimacy. However, Brookings Institute research into three decades of election boycotts finds the effect "is generally disastrous for the boycotting party."[11] This is exactly what has happened to third parties for decades: by being spoilers instead of deciders, they are doomed to irrelevancy.

Since Duverger's law (Chapter 8) ensures that our system of elections will maintain a two-party system, threatening to elect the President of the United States at random guarantees the American Union relevancy in 2024. There is nothing that the entrenched interests can do to stop a November 5, 2024, general strike in the ballot box:

---

[11] https://www.brookings.edu/articles/election-boycotts-dont-work/

- In a close election, a tiny percentage of voters in key swing states can easily control the outcome.
- The Dow is a widely publicized number and can even be calculated directly from the 30 stock prices that make up the average.
- Shutting down the stock market one week before the election would carry severe political ramifications—a cure worse than the disease.
- It's impossible to test voters' motives for selecting a presidential candidate; striking voters cannot be prevented from casting their ballots.

The Dow has traditionally represented the interests of the powerful and connected; the leading digits in the stock market grow their fortunes constantly. By using the smallest digit—the ones' place—to determine the endorsement, members of the American Union pledge allegiance to looking out for the least of us: with liberty and justice for all.

How will the tricentennial remember the 2024 election?

The power to destroy a thing—in this case, the credibility of the highest office in the land—is the power to control it. That power can be used to guide the United States into a glorious future. When our children and our children's children are looking backward from 2076, will they recognize this as the beginning of a new age of peace, justice, and prosperity?

If 3.5% of voters refuse to fight or demonize Donald Trump and Joe Biden, and instead commit to helping these men succeed at enacting the Trump–Biden Peace Plan, peace will be possible. Join the American Union and the nonviolent revolution! Reread the novel's Afterword to help make this happen in 2024.

Notes/Bibliography

Although presented as fiction to allow readers to suspend disbelief in the delivery of a call to action, the facts and history underlying the political innovations in *Looking Backward from the Tricentennial* are the result of extensive research. A partial bibliography is included below. Citations and other notes on the text (primarily factual, but occasionally related to the plot) are available to read or download at: bit.ly/LBFTTnotes

Ages of American Capitalism: A History of the United States (Jonathan Levy, 2021)
American Prison: A Reporter's Undercover Journey Into the Business of Punishment (Shane Bauer, 2018)
Basic Income and Sovereign Money (Geoff Crocker, 2020)
The Cosmopolitan Tradition: A Nobel but Flawed Ideal (Martha Nussbaum, 2019)
Debt: The First 5,000 Years (David Graber, 2011)
Falling Behind: How Rising Inequality Hurts the Middle Class (Robert Frank, 2007)
Freezing People Is (Not) Easy: My Adventures in Cryonics (Bob Nelson, 2014)
Gandhi and Beyond: Nonviolence for a New Political Age (David Cortright, 2009)
Gandhi: Naked Ambition (Jad Adams, 2010)
Hell Is a Very Small Place: Voices from Solitary Confinement (Edited by Jean Casella, James Ridgeway, and Sarah Shourd, 2016)
Miracle at Philadelphia (Catherine Bowen, 1969)
Money from Nothing (Robert Hockett and Aaron James, 2020)
Nonzero: The Logic of Human Destiny (Robert Wright, 2000)
Not a Crime to Be Poor: The Criminalization of Poverty in America (Peter Edelman, 2019)
The People, No: A Brief History of Anti-Populism (Thomas Frank, 2020)
The People's Case for Quantitative Easing (Frances Coppola, 2020)
A People's History of the Supreme Court (Peter Irons, 1999)
A People's History of the United States (Howard Zinn, 2015)
The Skeptical Economist: Revealing the Ethics Inside Economics (Jonathan Aldred, 2009)
The Spirit Level: Why Greater Equality Makes Society Stronger (Richard Wilkinson and Kate Pickett, 2010)

Index

Page numbers **in bold** indicate portions of the book not presented as fiction.

abortion 166–167, 190, 330, **419, 422**
advertising 57–59, 159, 174–175, 227, 341
agape love 126, 191, 315–316, 323, 354, 389–391
alcohol, problems of 18, 57, 68–69, 95, 102, 159, 199, 221, 224, 321, 402–403
American Revolution 27, 153, 329–330, 332, 338
American Union 27, 30, 33, 35, 56, 60, 61, 64, 69, 70, 73, 75, 77, 84, 89, 104, 107, 127–128, 130, 133–134, 136, 138, 144, 152–156, 161, 168, 169, 173, 174–176, 179, 181, 190, 204, 207, 209–210, 225–232, 235, 241, 257–265, 267, 276, 282, 285–286, 294, 296, 297, 303, 306–307, 314–316, 319, 323–329, 343, 358, 362–368, 372, 376, 384–388, 390–391, 394, 400–401, 406, **408–410, 426–437**
    affinity groups 319, **409**
    basic member pledge 204, 210, **409**
    dues 89, 107, 183, 204, 210, 227, 228, **409**
    election strategy 89, 209–211, 258–265, 268, 289, 363–368, 394, 400–401, **430–437**
    endorsement process 89, 170, 257–265, 324, 364–365, **432–437**
    general strike in the ballot box 260, **436–437**
    organizer qualification 108, 266–267, 384–385, **410**
    see also thirty-day challenge
    political action committee 210, 226, 228, 230–231, 362, 400, **409, 431**
    principles of 34, 49, 70, 77, 83, 85, 89, 105, 148, 154, 161, 191, 208, 213, 260–261, 263, 271–272, 282, 331–332, 345, 358, 367, 386, **426–427**
    sobriety 159–160, 172–173, 192, 226–228, 267, 279, 298–299
    see also Muster Day; people's legislative assembly
American Union housing 174–178, 217
American Union Job 41–42, 96, 144, 188, 199, 228–230, 283, 292, 313, 344–345, 355
American Union Jobs Program 32–34, 42, 43–52, 126, 128, 129, 130, 136, 144, 147, 161–162, 166, 167, 172, 174, 176, 185–186, 190, 199, 230, 331, 342, 345, 358, 382
    real reason for 46, 129, 134, 147, 161, 167, 172, 176, 186, 190, 230, 342, 358, 382, 386
An Autobiography: The Story of My Experiments With Truth (M.K. Gandhi, 1927) 105
Anti-Saloon League *see* prohibition (alcohol)
antitrust 308
Area Fifty-One 394
Articles of Confederation 329, 339, 338
asynchronous voting 86, 172, 178–179, **430**
Bank of America's ridiculous fees 41
banking fees 41, 57, 341
bank money 142–146, 148, 231–232, 339, 341, 381, 392, 397, **123**
base money 144, 147–148, 231–232, 236, 331–332, 338–345, **422–423**
Bastille Day 225, 228, 298
Bell, Daniel 242
Bellamy, Edward *iii*, **305**
Benga, Ota 109, 119, 226, 235, 373, 386, 396, 400
Bhagavad Gita 77
Bible, the 77, 220, 354, 360, 413
Biden, Joe 28 (quoted), 265, 331, 342, 363–365, **366f**, 368, 391, 394, 404, **426, 433–437**
Birmingham bus boycott 154
bitcoin 342–343
Black Panther Party 78
blockchain voting 180
    see also bitcoin
Boaty McBoatface 106–108, 183, 299, 394
Breaking Hate: Confronting the New Culture of Extremism (Christian Picciolini, 2020) 357–358
Bryan, William Jennings 66–67, 144, 145, 147, 169
Cantillon effect 145–147, 191
cash bail 311, **417**
Chavez, Cesar 78, 275–276, 278, 328, 336, 385
civil asset forfeiture 98, **417**

civil disobedience 154, 190, 261–262, 288–289
  see also Gandhi, Salt March
Civil Rights movement 67–68, 133–134, 154, 208
Civil War 31, 125, 127, 144, 153, 155, 339–340, 411–412
Coates, Ta-Nehisi 312
Congress (legislative branch) 8, 10–12, 28–35, 44–47, 61, 63–71, 77, 84–85, 88–90, 94, 99, 126–128, 134, 137, 143, 153, 156, 166–168, 170, 173, 184, 209–210, 229, 240, 258–265, 282–284, 314, 319–21, 323–324, 330–332, 339, 345, 358, 364, 399–401, **408–410**, 412–414, **415**, **426**, **432–436**
Congress of Humanity 285–286
consent 192–194, 214–215, 245, 288, 290, 295, 351
  see also economic coercion
Constitution(al) 12, 29, 30,31, 63, 65, 69, 77, 107, 129, 168–169, 170, 284, 286, 329–332, 339, 388, **411**, **415–426**, **427**, **429**
  Amendments 11f, 31, 69, 131, 168, 169, 309
  duties 31, 33, 45, 50, 77, 130–131, 147, 186–187, 207, 275, 300–301, 308, 312–313, 325, 329–332, 358, 367, 372, 386, 388
  rights 129–131, 207, 388
  see also Congress (legislative branch); Framers; Preamble
constructive program 75–76, 174, 208, 241, 272, 287, 323, 358
continentals 338–339
convict leasing 309–310
COVID-19 (pandemic) 25, 97, 102, 199, 207, 217, 255
criminal justice reform 95, 96, 98–99, 101, 120–121, 166, 168, 190, 230, 272, 285, 287, 292, 308–316, 330–331, 333, **416–419**
cryonics 22–25, 117, 137, 139, 186, 297–298, 343, 393
cryptocurrency see bitcoin
Cuba 285, 318, 350, 398, **421**
Declaration of Independence 9, 31, 129, 286, 329
deficit spending 232, 240, 339–341
deflation 66–67, 145–147, 339–341, 343
Democrats see duopoly
direct democracy 107, 168
domestic violence 190
Douglass, Frederick 3, 10, 195
Dred Scott v Sandford 11, 11f, 31
drug policy 97–100, 159–160, 166, **417–418**
Du Bois, W.E.B. 305
duopoly 27–29, 31–32, 63–71, 153, 156, 164–166, 169, 209–213, 228, 232, 258–265, 289, 303, 319–324, 329, 363, 366–367, 400–401, **426**, **430–437**
duty 31, 33, 45, 50, 77, 106, 129–131, 159, 207, 267, 275–276, 286, 303, 311, 312–313, 324, 325, 329–332, 372, 380, 386, 389, 407
  see also Constitution, duties; nonviolence, duties of
Duverger's law 63, 65–66, 71, 156, 262–263, 364, **436**
economic coercion 74–75, 125–126, 188–191, 230, 283, 285, 303, 344, 387
Einstein, Albert **203**

Electoral College 63, 66–68, 107, 366
electricity 56, 178
employment (job) guarantee 308
environment 49–50, 51, 56, 149, 286, 324, 332, **425**
Fair Labor Standards Act 11, 32
fast for peace 60–61, 71, 73, 78–79, 86–87, 94, 105, 127, 154–158, 169–170, 172–173, 181–183, 208–210, 212, 221, 225, 227, 231, 258–259, 267, 269, 271, 285, 288, 297, 313, 315–316, 319–321, 325, 327–328, 353–354, 358–359, 365, 367, 369, 384, **409**, 412–414, **429–434**
  aspects of 61, 73, 86, 123, 154–156, 273, 285–286, 320–321, 323, 333, 358
fasting, extended 75, 78, 103–105, 209, 275–276, 359–360, **430**
fasting, health benefits of 94, 103
Federal Reserve 144, 148, 231
Federal Reserve Notes see bank money
First Gilded Age 66, 169
Floyd, George 310, 330, **416–417**
Ford, Henry 113
foreign military bases 283, **420**
fractional reserve banking 143, 148–149
  see also bank money
Framers 29, 31, 63, 107, 129–131, 168, 330, 339, 388
France, Anatole (quoted) 271
free silver see gold standard; monetary reform
Friedman, Milton 147
Fuller, Buckminster **408**
Gandhi, Mohandas Karamchand 29, 60–61, 74–79, 105, 152–159, 174, 190, 208, 211, 241, 275, 278–279, 287–288, 322, 324–325, 347, 358–360, 370, 413, **431**
  quoted **1**, **17**, 74, 76, **113**, 154–155, 159, **203**, 208, 211, 271, 279, 287, 359, **379**, 413
  Salt March 287–288, 324–325
  see also constructive program
game theory 156, 168–170, 188, 261–262, 265, 366, 390
  see also non-zero-sum game; zero-sum game
George III, King 12, 27, 129, 329
George V, King 279, 413
ghrelin (hunger hormone) 104, 243
gold standard see deflation
Grace, Annie 226
gratification (instant or delayed) see self-control
Great Depression 31, 153, 166, 340
greed see self-control
greenbacks 144, 339–340
gross domestic product (GDP) 52, 138, 142, 143
Guantanamo Bay Military Prison 284, **421**
gun control 165–167, 287, 330, **419**
Hamilton, Alexander 339
hartal 209, 287, 320
healthcare 24, 35, 51, 88–89, 96, 130, 133–135, 167, 190, 199, 206, 215, 331, **423–424**
  public option 134, 331, **423**
  universal 24, 35, 133–135, 167
  see also paid family leave

INDEX

Hockett, Robert 144
Hofsteader, Richard (quoted) 66
Homestead Act 11, **11f**
household debt 51, 142, 145, 189, 239–240, 242, 329, 331, 341, 344
Idiocracy (2006) 22
immigration 42, 308, 331, **425**
imperialism 282, 283
industrial revolution 239–241, 282, 310, 340
inflation 138, 145, 148–149, 239–240, 309, 313, 338–340
intellectual property 109–111, 131, 324
Jefferson, Thomas 12, 129, 155, 189, 285
Jesus *see* Bible, the
Johnson, Andrew 412
Johnson, Lyndon B. 67
Johnson, Samuel **433**
Kennedy, John F. 67, 208, 276
Kennedy, Robert F. 276
Keynes, John Maynard 240–241
King Jr., Martin Luther 8, 13, 34, 46, 75–77, 120, **126**, 128–129, 144, 149, 152–154, 157, 160, 183, 188, 208, 230, 255, 259, 261, 267, 275, 285, 307, 323–324, 353, 357, 360, 379, 384, 387, 391, 407, **415, 426–428, 434**
 quoted *epigraph*, **1**, 8, 12, 13, **17**, 34, 46, 128–129, 144, 154, 259, 275, 285, 324, 357, 360, **379**, 384, 387, 391, 407
 triple evils 13, 34, 74–75, 95, 120, 127, 149, 153–154, 160, 324, 384, 407, **415, 426, 427, 434**
 Letter from Birmingham Jail 77, **427**
Ku Klux Klan 107
landmines 284, **421**
law of marginal utility 238–239
legal vouchers 312–313, **417**
lethal autonomous weapons 284, **421**
Lincoln, Abraham 31, 68, 127, 155, 157, 194–195, 229, 339–340, 411–413
liquid democracy 172, 179–180, 184, 204
lynching 360
Mandela, Nelson (Mandela Rules) 314, **418**
Maslow's hierarchy of needs 51
McKinley, William 67
military downsizing 286, 287, 330, **420–421**
military-industrial complex 136, 166, 239, 282–285, 319, 327, 330, 332, 333
mindset of abundance 47, 51, 272, 333, 364
mindset of scarcity 47, 51, **51f**, 86, 161, 238, 272, 280, 333, 364
monetary reform 66, 67, 113, 142–149, 189, 191, 232, 267, 287, 331, 338–345
money in politics 28–29, 65, 88–89, 164, 209–210, 368
Monroe, James 308
Muster Day 71, 77–78, 84, 94, 169–170, 208–209, 230, 258–260, 276, 315, 320, 333, 347, 365, **408, 430, 434**
national debt 28, 52, 129, 142, 143, **143f**, 144, 148, 282, 331–332, 339, 341
natural rights 129–131, 141, 267
New Deal 11, 31, 85, 153, 275, 332

new Jim Crow 11, 96
New Jim Crow, The (Michelle Alexander, 2020) 96, **96f**, 312
Nixon, Richard 34, 67–68, 96, 263
nonary logic 58–59, 95, 165–167, 212, 334
nonviolence 34–34, 76–78, 89–90, 105–106, 148, 152–162, 173, 207–213, 259, 261, 275–276, 286, 291, 319, 324–325, 327–328, 358, 360, 367, 384
 principles of 49, 108, 148, 156, 159, 161–162, 207, 208, 211–213, 259–261, 271, 275, 279, 319, 324, 331, 367, 413
 duties of 106, 153, 159, 207, 209, 211, 283, 286, 319, 324, 384–385
non-zero-sum game 156, 212, 214, 226, 238–239, 259, 365
Norris, George 169
nuclear weapons 56, 136, 286, **421, 430**
Obama, Barack 106, 284
Oppenheimer, J. Robert 286
Oregon method 169, 262
paid family leave 134, 167, 331, **423–424**
Peace Vigil (Lafayette Square) 136, 378, 399
people's legislative assembly 32, 56, 69, 80, 82–91, 104, 133–134, 159, 163, 170–173, 174, 178–184, 197, 241, 267, 286, 287, 301, 316, 324, 334, 337–338, 343–344, 367, 382, 385, **410, 415**
 Assembly Clerk 172, 183–184, 334, 382
 Chief Moderator 170–173, 180, 241
 delegate qualification 156, 172–173, **410**
 investigative panel 56, 82, 86, 88, 171, 181, 184, 337
 policy committee 82, 86, 88, 171, 181, 337–338
 Qualifications Committee 182–183
 see also liquid democracy
People's Party 66–67, 145, 169, 340, **434**
Perot, Ross 232
Phoenix Cycle *iii*, 30–32, 35, 61, 63–64, 136, 149, 153–154, 166, 208, 227, 306, 332–333, 338–343, 366, 371, 405, **415**
Plessy v. Ferguson 11
police 19, 98–99, 310, 360
 shootings 166, 310–311
 reform 98–99, 166, 287, 330, **416–417**
 see also criminal justice reform
political polarization 30, 64, 153, 164, 166, 167–168, 173, 211, 212, 262, 303, 323, 330
Ponzi scheme 130, 343
postal banking 41, 344, **422**
poverty 10, 43, 44–45, 46–47, 190–191, 269–270, 285, 302, 333, 357
 leveling effects 47–48, 331
 Like a fox hunt 44, 146, 217, 237, 302–303, 375, 395
 see also unconditional basic income; wealth inequality
Preamble 31, 33, 50, 77, 130, 170, 275, 318–319, 329–332, 372, 383, 388, **415–425**
prison reform 121, 284, 308, 311–312, 314–315, 330, 333, 354, **418–419**

441

prisoner's dilemma 168–169, 364–365, 368, **435–436**
prison privatization 308, **419**
Prohibition Party 69
prohibition (alcohol) 68–69, 94–95, 262
prohibition (drug) 10, 11, 31–32, 68, 95–99, **96f** 159–160, 330, **417–418**
public payment infrastructure 57, 59, 341–345, **421–422**
Ramadan 84, 286
ranked choice voting 65, 70, 366
rat park experiment 97–98
Reagan, Ronald 255
Reconstruction 11, 31, 353
redlining 11
reparations, slavery 4, 6, 8–14, 126, 127, 140, 229, 268, 271, 319–321, 323
representative democracy 28, 31–32, 34–35, 63–71, 84, 89, 128, 156, 169, 173, 179, 184, 210, 229, 254, 258–259, 261, 263–265, 286, 303, 308, 323–324, 332, 353, 364, 366, 368, 375, 386–387, 394, **409, 427, 436**
Republicans *see* duopoly
Revolutionary War *see* American Revolution
Reynolds, Mack *iii*
Roosevelt, Franklin D. 34, 57, 153, 332, 340–341, 345
sanctions, economic 285, **421**
satyagraha 154–155, 173, 287–288, 325, 362, 380, **428**
satyagrahis 288, 325–326, 372
Schelling, Thomas 259
Second Gilded Age 27, 28, 43, 49
   see also wealth inequality
self-control 86, 108, 201, 208, 242, 277, 294, 340
sex 176, 215, 245, 277–278, 351–352, 383
Shays' Rebellion 339, 388
slavery 10, 12, 31, 68, 153, 189, 270, 309, 332, 411–413
Smith, Adam 237
Socialist Party 64
Social Security (Administration) 31, 46, 345, **422, 424**
solitary confinement 284, 314–316, 354, **418**
sovereign currency *see* base money
Spock, Benjamin **434**
Star Wars 107, 380
Stevenson, Bryan 312
Suhrawardy, Shaheed 157–158
suicide(s) 166, 190, 235, 327, 345
Supreme Court 10, 28, 166, 284, 314, **418–419, 428**
swing voter(s) 68, 70, 89, 164, 184, 209–211, 263, 323, 324, 367, 387, 391, 394, **430–437**
   defined 68, **433**
   needed to flip election outcome 366, **366f, 433, 436**
   see also American Union; election strategy
taxes 149, 287, 331–332, 339–340, 345, **423–425**
   advertisements 57–59
   income tax 69, 149, 239, 340, 345
   land value tax 324
   lawyer tax 312–313, **417**
   plastic tax 149, 332, **425**
   pollution (carbon) fees 49–50, 56, 149, 332, **425**

value-added tax 49–50, 149, **423**
Tennessee Valley Authority 85
third parties, nonviability of 64–70, 78, 169–170, 232, 260, 263, 340, 366, 401, 434
   see also Duverger's law; duopoly
thirty-day challenges 61, 104–108, 138, 160, 183, 204, 207, 227, 266–267, 274–280, 297, 318, 321–323, 325, 327, 410
Thurman, Reverend Howard 76
tipping 125–126
Tirado, Linda (quoted) 43
Treasury accounts 36, 45, 107, 204, 230, 341–345, **421–423**
   see also public payment infrastructure
Treasury Dollar Bills 41, 144, 148, 191, 231–232, 236, 242, 331–332, 338, 341–343, **422–423**
   see also base money
Trojan horse 32, 89
Truman, Harry 35, 127–128
Trump, Donald 34, 127, 265, 299, 363–365, **366f**, 368, 376, 391, 394, 404, **426, 433–437**
Trump–Biden Peace Plan 30, 68, 134, 165–168, 210, 283–285, 312, 314, 323–324, 330–332, 341, 363–368, **408–410, 415–437**
unconditional basic income (UBI) 33, 36, 45–52, 56, 144, 147–148, 160–162, 166–167, 175, 183, 185–186, 190–191, 230, 267, 272, 282–283, 285, 313, 331, 341–342, **422, 423**
   Alaskan oil dividend 50, 230
unions 34, 60–61, 74–75, 181, 190, 242, 262, 275–276, 329–330
universal suffrage 41–42, 192, 332, **425**
US Treasury 36, 41, 57, 137–138, 144, 147, 242, 339, 341–345, **422–423**
   see also Treasury accounts; Treasury Dollar Bills
Vietnam War 34, 275, **434**
voluntary temperance 99–100, 158–160, 299, 384
   see also American Union; sobriety
variable-one-zero (VOZ) metrics 58, 110, 165–167, 211, 212
war on drugs *see* prohibition (drug)
Wallace, George (American Independent Party) 67–68
Washington, George 10, 27, 64, 155, 388
wealth inequality 10, 28, 34, 43–51, 160–161, 166, 167, 175, 216–217, 228, 238–241, 302–303, 313, 322, 331, 333, 339–340, 357, 387, 399
Wealth of Nations, The (Adam Smith, 1776) 237
wedge issues 164, 367, **419**
West, Cornel 28
Widerquist, Karl 51
Wilson, Woodrow 11, 34
Winfrey, Oprah 189
Woodfox, Albert 314
World War One 34, 60, 157, 239, 284
World War Two 34, 75, 149, 239, 285, 330
yes-no-abstain voting 38, 59, 84, 86, 139, 180, 197, 260
zero-sum game 64–65, 147, 156, 211, 212, 239, 259, 263, 265, 279, 323, 364, 366

www.ingramcontent.com/pod-product-compliance
Lightning Source LLC
LaVergne TN
LVHW021754060526
838201LV00058B/3089